BLACK MONEY

BLACK MONEY

▼

MICHAEL M. THOMAS

CROWN PUBLISHERS, INC.   NEW YORK

The characters in this book are imaginary.

Published by Crown Publishers, Inc., 201 East 50th Street, New
York, New York 10022. Member of the Crown Publishing Group.
Random House, Inc.   New York, Toronto, London, Sydney,
Auckland
CROWN is a trademark of Crown Publishers, Inc.

Manufactured in the United States of America

Book design by June Bennett-Tantillo

Library of Congress Cataloging-in-Publication Data
Thomas, Michael M.
    Black money / Michael M. Thomas. — 1st ed.
            p.   cm.
    1. Government investigators—California—Fiction.   2. Money
        laundering—California—Fiction.   I. Title.
        PS3570.H574B58   1994
            813'.54—dc20   93-33813
                                                CIP

ISBN 0-517-59523-0

10 9 8 7 6 5 4 3 2 1

First Edition

Fic.

For H.J.W.
1935–1991
Never Forgotten

BLACK
MONEY

▼

O N E

▼

The young woman was close to tears.

The flat Indian planes of her face quivered. For the third time, she repeated the answer she had given her interrogator.

"No, señor, I am certain!" she declared. " 'Ees no Thun'erbol' here. Ees only thees store. I swear eet! Was never no Thun'erbol' in thees place!"

The señor must be mistaken, she added. This was the only video store in the North Coast Mall. For certain. She made as if to cross herself. She might have been a village peasant being ruthlessly interrogated about *bandidos* by a Central American captain of police.

Her interrogator was relentless. How long had she been working here, he asked again.

For over a year, señor.

And in all that time, this had been the only video outlet in this shopping center?

Yes, señor, yes. For sure. Yes.

Her questioner pursed his lips and regarded her with disbelief.

"I swear eet," she added in a low helpless voice.

The man sighed. He was in fact a government official, but this time, for a change, he wasn't after bandits, the people responsible for yet another instance of rape and plunder of the American body economic, but was trying to rent a video.

True, it had been bandits—of a sort—who had brought him

here. But it was not in connection with the pillaging of the surrounding countryside, a lush coastal landscape once thickly forested with
great trees, that Clarence Greaves was vexing the clerk of a flyblown
video shop at a low-grade shopping mall fifteen miles inland from the
scene of the crime: Bordrero Bay, California, a coastal town of sixteen
thousand people roughly two hundred miles north of San Francisco.

This does not make sense, he thought. The bank's records
showed that there was a Thunderbolt Video outlet in the North Coast
Mall, and if the bank computer said so, there must be.

He repeated his initial question.

"No, no, no, *no,* señor!" The girl's voice rose. It was clear to
Greaves she was about to crack.

He sighed, shook his large grizzled head, thanked her, and left
the shop.

Outside, he hesitated on the walkway and examined the lacklus-
ter display of dusty video boxes in the window.

This is weird, he thought. Something here doesn't compute.

According to the bank's records, there was a Thunderbolt Video
outlet here at the mall, but it seemed there wasn't. Not only that,
there never had been.

So how come the Thunderbolt Video account showed regular
deposit-and-withdrawal activity right through last week? Businesses
that didn't exist don't have bank accounts.

It was a puzzlement. A loose end.

Loose ends were not something that Clarence Greaves let go
unsnipped or unknotted.

In the various agencies of the federal government in which he
had worked for close to four decades, he was known as a man of rare
stubbornness and persistence, especially when it came to going by the
book. Admirable qualities, which many also found aggravating. In his
thirty-six years of federal service, his obsession with crossing every *t*
and dotting every *i* had rankled as many superiors and colleagues as
malefactors and their lawyers. He had spread vexation through the
FDIC, the Treasury Department, the Office of the Comptroller of the
Currency, and the Federal Home Loan Corporation. Currently he
was displaying his vexatious talents within the Resolution Trust Corporation, the federal agency created to dispose of the assets of failed
financial institutions. At the RTC, he held the position of assistant

field supervisor, Northern California Division, with line responsibility for bank and S&L cleanups and bailouts from the Marin County end of the Golden Gate Bridge north to the Oregon border.

He was presently part of a team working to sort out the rubble following the multibillion-dollar implosion of a California thrift, banking, and commercial finance conglomerate, GoldWest Financial Services. Greaves's team was dealing with GoldWest's "Golden Gate" division, a network of sixteen units dotting five counties in northern California, of which Bordrero Bay Bank and Savings functioned as the hub and clearing point.

That morning, Greaves, having checked out the television schedule in the local paper, had decided to rent a VCR and a couple of tapes, pick up some fast food, and make a high old evening of it in his motel room. What he had in mind was *Dirty Harry* (maybe even a double feature), a McDonald's pig-out, and a six-pack of Coors Light.

He recalled seeing "d/b/a Thunderbolt Video" as a line entry on the printout of the Bordrero Bay Bank's accounts. The account address was a local post office box, but a "d/b/a" notation indicated a place of business in the North Coast Mall.

It would have been more convenient to rent from the video store right down the street from the bank, but even if the place hadn't looked artsy-fartsy to Greaves, like so much else in Bordrero Bay, which was a real "wicks 'n wax" town, he would have headed for the Thunderbolt unit.

Out of sheer self-interest, because, as it happened, Greaves was a Thunderbolt Video stockholder.

A happy Thunderbolt stockholder, moreover, and therefore a dedicated Thunderbolt customer.

Thunderbolt Video—ticker symbol TVU—was one of the hottest stocks around. The company incarnated that singular entrepreneurial genius some people had for finding a way to make almost obscene rates of profit in a mundane, generic, highly competitive business. The chain had blown by its older rival, Blockbuster, like a jet passing a DC-3, growing from sixty to two thousand outlets in just five years, and from $38 million in revenues to over a billion and a half. What McDonald's was to hamburgers, or Home Depot to do-it-yourself, Thunderbolt was to video rentals and sales. The company logo—twin jagged lightning bolts—was as well-known a feature of the consumer landscape as McDonald's golden arches.

In the two years since Greaves's Silver Springs investment club purchased eight hundred shares of TVU at $26 a share, the stock price had risen to within a small fraction of $80. Greaves's share of that gain amounted to $4,483.32 before commissions—he ran the figure on his laptop every day based on the stock table in *The Wall Street Journal*. By his standards, $4,483.32 was real money.

When they closed up shop at the bank at the end of the day, Greaves had headed for the mall. When he got there, Greaves traversed the center fruitlessly twice, like most of his gender trusting that some higher power would guide him automatically to where he wanted to go. Finally, admitting defeat, he consulted the directory in the shabby atrium.

To his surprise, there was no *Thunderbolt* in the alphabetical listing.

The service categories index showed two entries under *Video:* a convenience store that anchored the north end of the complex, a unit of the Tip 'n Take chain, which Greaves knew to be a sort of downmarket Wal-Mart, and a Perez Video. The latter proved to be a cracked-linoleum mom-and-pop operation, heavy on Spanish-language and Bruce Lee tapes, hardly a high-tech, spick-and-span Thunderbolt.

On his way back to his motel, Greaves kicked himself mentally. He was an informed TVU stockholder; he knew perfectly well that Thunderbolt Video had stayed out of California, that there wasn't a single Thunderbolt store in the entire state!

That was the secret of the company's success. Thunderbolt protected its uniquely high profit margins by staying out of the overcompetitive, oversaturated markets like California.

Of course, he supposed it *was* possible that Thunderbolt had chosen to test the market, to dip a toe into the brackish California economy now that recession was knocking off its less-heeled competitors by the battalion.

But with a single store in a crummy shopping center twenty miles from nowhere?

No way!

It really doesn't compute, thought Greaves.

What didn't compute with Greaves didn't go away. The puzzle

gnawed at him through the night; it was as if the account records were projected brightly on the ceiling and woke him with their glare. Unable to sleep, or to come to grips with this new puzzle, he watched some television, tried to read, glared at the furniture.

His room was costing the American taxpayers forty-three dollars a night, which the government considered a fair sum to spend on field-level public servants handed the responsibility for cleaning up multibillion-dollar busts like GoldWest. A lousy deal; it was one of the reasons you heard the things you did in the agency cafeteria: gossip about kickbacks, secret accounts, GS-8s buying Porsches with their payoffs on sweetheart sell-offs. Not that Greaves was under any illusions about his own importance; in the GoldWest bust, he was responsible for one of the outmost ripples of default: the busted Goliath's Far Northern California division, a string of sixteen GoldWest banks and thrifts between Petaluma and Crescent City. The Bordrero Bay Bank, where he was headquartered, served as administrative and money transfer center for the division.

Greaves thought Bordrero Bay an odd choice for division hub; in these parts, GoldWest had units in bigger, more conveniently situated places like Eureka. On the other hand, Bordrero Bay had a kind of Victorian quality, and people tended to mistake nostalgia for probity when it came to banking, especially after the go-go 1980s.

Sixteen units out of the 147 subsidiaries and affiliates that made up the GoldWest system. Peanuts. The sixteen's footings on the day Uncle Sam moved in added up to approximately $980 million, or less than one percent of GoldWest's consolidated book assets. Chump change. Chicken feed.

Still, chicken feed or not, Greaves thought it was pretty chintzy of Uncle Sam to budget a lousy forty-three dollars to house the hardworking men and women it charged with cleaning up after a crowd that in its palmy days, according to the gossip at the bank, had courted Arab depositors with $500-a-bottle vintage champagne in $1,000-a-night Monte Carlo hotel suites, which came equipped with $2,000-a-night call girls.

Greaves knew it would be Days Inns for him for the rest of his career. That was where Uncle Same sent people who were vexing. Days Inns—and backwater assignments like Bordrero Bay.

Still, at least the place was pretty—and cool. Most of Greaves's assignments seemed to send him to dead, baking outposts on the far side of nowhere: banks and thrifts in Texas and Florida, Elmore Leonard country, where strip malls sprouted from ponds and lakes of concrete and asphalt, punctuated with dreary condominiums built on the cheap and cracked and falling down after less than a decade. Bordrero Bay was a real place, New England in character, with a sense of permanence: not just some prestressed concrete mock-up pasted on the landscape by a bunch of crooks or cockeyed optimists who'd got their hands on the suckers'—read "taxpayers' "—money.

Greaves was frankly glad not to be on the A Team at GoldWest headquarters down in Encino. That would have meant killer hours trying to unscramble a spaghetti of financial flows. Trying: That was about as far as it got. Thanks to modern computer software, money was like Merlin: It changed shape and being at will—or a few keystrokes. Greaves was too old for that game now, too worn, too out-of-date. The dreams of advancement were finished, the fires of ambition banked. His old idealism remained, but with every passing day it seemed less substantial, more abstract. Retirement and pension grew slowly larger on the horizon, like friendly sails, and Clarence Greaves waited quietly at the dock.

But puzzles were made to be solved, so it was six o'clock the following morning when Greaves let himself into the bank.

First he rechecked the account register. Sure enough, there it was: account no. G/X 657/65/2, in the name of North Coast Enterprises d/b/a Thunderbolt Video. Just as he'd remembered, the account was addressable at a box number in the North Coast Mall post office.

The prefix "G/X" struck him as odd. Why hadn't he noticed it the first time? Of course, then he'd only been skimming the roster; trying with half an eye and a quarter of a mind to develop a rough feel for the bank's local customer base.

"G/X" designated a GoldWest distribution account. An account assigned to the Bordrero Bay unit but in fact run out of the San Fernando Valley headquarters of the parent company. In a $16-billion financial conglomerate like GoldWest, there would be literally thousands of such accounts: pockets into which GoldWest shuttled deposits—many brought in by Wall Street money brokers representing offshore clients taking advantage of the high rates that federally insured outfits like GoldWest could offer.

It was a disgrace, Greaves thought, using the American taxpayers' dollars to pay off a bunch of Japanese, Arabs, and God knows what else. But that was what the law said. The only inconvenience to the scam artists was that federal deposit insurance was limited to $100,000 per account. Which meant someone with a million dollars to deposit would have to spread it around ten accounts or more. Hence GoldWest's distribution accounts, which were just a way of getting around the deposit limit.

G/X 657/65/2 currently held the grand sum of only $315, although over the last eight weeks its overnight balances had run as high as $57,000, and a total of close to $400,000 had passed through the account. As a lodging for money, G/X 657/65/2 was strictly a hot-sheet operation. Nothing ever checked in for more than a few hours.

Greaves found this odd. Although the big trick of modern finance was a technology that permitted money to be moved in milliseconds picking up infinitesimal quanta of incremental return on its high-velocity journey, most GoldWest G/X accounts were high-yield time deposits that sat still and collected interest for thirty, sixty, and ninety days.

He punched up the account's activity record, going back six months, and studied it. And then it hit him!

Distribution accounts did their business entirely in blips; they were paperless computer entries. But the "d/b/a Thunderbolt" deposits were recorded as "lockbox"! Lockbox meant cash! The folding green stuff, not an impulse pushed around in cyberspace by computers, but real, physical paper money deposited by merchants in point-of-sale safes called lockboxes; picked up and transported to the bank by Courier Services, the Brinks-type armored car outfit that serviced a lot of Bordrero Bay Bank's regional and area accounts. There was some kind of incestuous connection between Courier Services and GoldWest, or maybe it was one of GoldWest's big stockholders.

He studied the figures some more. Maybe, he reasoned, the G/X designation only applied to the account's outbound activity. That could be it, although he would want to run a comparison to see if Bordrero Bay or any of the other units under his purview had booked similar, one-way G/X business.

He inferred from the account data that there were standing instructions for an interbank wire transfer of $15,000 a month to a branch of Oystermen's Trust Company on Maryland's Eastern Shore, which Greaves knew to be a hoity-toity Baltimore outfit that catered to rich people—"high net-worth individuals" in the language of glossy bank brochures.

In addition to the transfers to Oystermen's, there had also been other regular wire debits, which looked to Greaves like "sweeps," regularly scheduled withdrawals sufficient to bring month-end balances down to a few hundred dollars. These were transmitted to the account of Payton TV Franchise Sales, Inc., at a savings bank in Bethesda, just outside Washington and not far from where Greaves lived. On the surface these would look like payments for inventories and support services, but anyone who knew anything about Thunderbolt Video would have smelled a red herring. A principal reason for the company's success was an undeviating commitment to strict financial and inventory controls centralized in a massive complex in Hannibal, Missouri.

Then Greaves spotted something else. These wire transfers were the *only* debits on the "d/b/a Thunderbolt" account. There were no payments to Pacific Gas or the telephone company, no payroll checks, no sales tax remittances.

Clearly "d/b/a Thunderbolt" wasn't doing business at all. So how had it generated close to $400,000 in cash deposits over the last eleven months?

By now, other people were starting to come into the bank. Greaves didn't want anyone made curious, so he unholstered his Sharp personal computer-organizer, hooked it up to the bank computer, and downloaded the "d/b/a Thunderbolt" data. This way he could feed it into his own laptop back at the motel and figure out where to go from here.

When lunchtime rolled around, he got in his car and drove ten minutes to a spot he had staked out shortly after arriving in Bordrero Bay, a scenic turnoff hard by the old coastal highway on the northern of two identically shaped spits of land that stuck out into the ocean like the horns of a young bull. These were known as Point Estelle and

Point Clara, after the twin daughters of Lemuel Browning, founder of Browning Timber and Pulp and progenitor of the family whose presence had once been as palpable in Bordrero Bay as the Medicis in Florence.

Point Clara was a fine place to sit and gaze at the ocean: to gobble a sandwich and a Snickers, knock back a Snapple, and ponder the few great mysteries of life that came Greaves's way. His preferred bench sat next to a pair of coin-operated viewing scopes that pointed out to sea like shore batteries. Some yards to his left, or south, the Pacific had worn a deep, fjordlike notch in the cliff line; this separated Clara from Estelle. The latter's northern face was topped by an ill-maintained low wire fence, which also demarcated the property of the fancy Cephalod Inn.

The inn maintained an exercise circuit for the exclusive use of its guests; it wound through a copse of weathered cypress and sea pine and along the cliff's edge. Some evenings, after knocking off, Greaves would don an exercise suit at the office, drive to Point Clara, sneak through the Cephalod fence, and take a couple of turns. If anyone noticed the trespasser huffing and puffing like a stout beetle with Day-Glo body and ebony head, nothing was said. Bordrero Bay was a pretty laid-back place: laid-back, or—in Greaves's opinion—still in shellshock after the pounding it had taken in the 1980s from the junk bond fusiliers and, more recently, the GoldWest gang.

According to the town's lady mayor, the Cephalod Inn symbolized the new and future Bordrero Bay: tourism, second homes, corporate "retreats," packaged romantic weekends. Especially the retreats. The inn now sported a conference center with enough telemetry to track a space shuttle, and its rooms were "smart" in every sense of the word: from chintz to compugraphic capability.

Greaves unwrapped his sandwich and devoured it in four quick bites. He unfolded *The Wall Street Journal* and scanned the financial news summary on the front page. The big news of the day was the foreign exchange crowd had been up to its new tricks again. This time the space cadets at the computer screens had ganged up on the Spanish peseta, knocking 10 percent off its value, and forcing the Bank of Spain to abandon any attempt to defend the currency in the face of financial firepower several times greater than its own.

It made no sense to Clarence Greaves. He'd grown up in a world where a nation's central bank controlled the value of his money; it was unimaginable to him that thirty-year-old hot shots could lay their hands on enough credit to overwhelm the Bank of Spain or the Bank of England. If things kept up this way, perhaps someday it would be the Federal Reserve's turn.

This stuff had nothing to do with the real world. According to the *Journal*, the Spanish economy was doing just fine, but the kids with their computers and long, long lines of credit had decided that the Bank of Spain lacked the foreign currency reserves sufficient to defend the peseta against the kind of selling power they could lay their electronic paws on, and so they hammered it.

It was an upside-down world. Even here at home, Uncle Sam was dipping into one pocket, the Fed, and lending to the financial markets at two whole percentage points lower than he was paying those same markets to replenish his other pocket, emptied by the deficit, by buying Treasury bonds. That giveaway amounted to billions.

Crazy, Greaves reflected.

Just like this Thunderbolt business.

He stared out to sea, broad, fleshy hands flat on his thick thighs, thinking. The light was changeable, and the Pacific was putting on a good show this noon, altering from lead gray to molten brass then back again as westerly moving clouds scudded across the face of the early afternoon sun.

You're crazy, Clarence, he told himself, to worry your curly head over a few hundred hundred, even a few hundred thousand dollars.

It wasn't what the taxpayers were paying him for. His mission was to sort out and get out. Clean up the mess, using the taxpayers' folding money like paper towels, and hit the road for the next disaster.

The last thing the agency wanted was any kind of complication, no matter how small. The word from on high had been emphatic: GoldWest was to be strictly a damage control operation. No questions asked, pay off the insured depositors up to the $100,000 limit, kick any "anomalous transactions" that turned up in the branches to the FDIC team down at Encino. Put the lid on.

Washington wanted the S&L scandal dead and buried, the cortege broken up, the mourners dispersed, the gravediggers' spades back in the shed: no evidence on the ground except the odd bunch of withered flowers. The out-of-pocket cost of GoldWest's collapse to the American taxpayers wasn't likely to run more than $3 billion. Compared to what had already been spent on the S&L-bank bailout, that was peanuts.

So what was he doing spinning his wheels over an account with a lousy $315 current balance?

Anyone who knew him would have said he was just being Clarence Greaves.

He rose, stretched his arms straight up, tried a tentative deep kneebend, halted creakily halfway down, and sank back on the bench. The days when Clarence Greaves had been a star in the pickup half-court games at the "Y" around the corner from the FDIC were long, long gone, he thought ruefully. He figured he was forty pounds over-weight.

The last five years in particular had taken their toll: the S&L cleanup and bank bailout had meant too many Days Inns, Burger Kings, Mr. Pizzas. Too many french fries at the desk, too many beers after work, too much appetite-sharpening, thirst-building frustration. He patted his gut, and without thinking, the pat became a stroke, as if he were rubbing himself for luck.

Damn, it was hot! The hottest June in living memory, folks in Bordrero Bay said. Hotter than any place this far north had a right to be. Eureka was only another fifty miles up the coast, and Eureka was practically Canada!

He scanned the lifeless surface of the ocean. Under certain con-ditions, Greaves had been told, southerly migrating whales moved close enough inshore to be observed with the naked eye. The whale migrations were the region's big tourist draw now. Whale watching boats operated out of Bordrero Bay and a half-dozen other snug har-bors up and down the Mendocino coast. People came from around the world to see the show; in the ten days he'd been up here, Greaves reckoned he'd heard a dozen different languages in the course of his lunchtime strolls along Browning Street.

He plucked a handkerchief from the breast pocket of the suit jacket he had draped over the back of the bench and wiped his fore-head, then his close-cropped whitish-gray pate, then under each arm, where spreading circles of perspiration darkened his white shirt. The breeze off the ocean barely dented the thick, still air, which sat on the coast like a blanket.

Why the hell had he felt the need to rent a damn video?

Now he had a problem that either he couldn't let go of, or that wouldn't let go of him.

The agency book was clear on such matters. So-called anomalous transactions in affected institutions involving more than $25,000 were to be reported to district headquarters. No exceptions. Anomalous transactions was agencyspeak for "smells funny." As in: smells dirty, or smells *too* clean—fresh from the laundry.

So what did "d/b/a Thunderbolt" smell like?

A small-time wholesaler, or perhaps a pot dealer servicing the Versace-shirt, hot tub, big-ticket weekend crowd at the Cephalod Inn, washing money using a name picked out of the air and a convenient address. A name picked out with a certain sly caution, however: with the knowledge that the real Thunderbolt didn't operate in California.

However you looked at it, it was still chicken feed, thought Greaves.

But an "anomalous transaction" for all that.

And yet . . .

Suppose it was something more.

Suppose "d/b/a Thunderbolt" was part of a larger picture, suppose it was the rough underside of the carpet, a loose end that someone had carelessly forgotten to snip off? If so, what might the other side of the fabric look like?

Theoretically, he should file an anomalous transaction report. If he did, his AT would be batched with hundreds of other ATs, and the lot computer-scanned for connection and pattern in the hope that the scattered dots might arrange themselves into a readable, meaningful pattern with fixable target coordinates.

That was the way it was supposed to work, especially now that the people upstairs had the JEDI system up and running flat out. But Greaves and every field-grade operative knew differently. Once field-generated ATs got into the bureaucratic mainstream, they seemed to disappear. Greaves had heard stories; he had a couple of his own; everyone with over a few months of field experience did. Out in the trenches, what you heard was that back at headquarters, the fix was in.

In other words, *if* his suspicions were well founded, and *if* he went by the book and kicked them up to District in San Francisco, it was likely that not only would Clarence Greaves never hear another word about "d/b/a Thunderbolt," but also no one else would either.

Was he being paranoid? Greaves didn't think so. One heard too many stories. Like most people involved in the S&L-bank bailout operation *below* a certain civil service grade, Greaves believed that *above* a certain civil service grade, the bailout program was a sewer of conflicts of interest, self-dealing, and payoffs.

The more he thought about it, the more the "d/b/a Thunderbolt" coincidence seemed to coalesce with one of Greaves's pet theories: that the U.S. financial system was, thanks to mindless deregulation, literally riddled with big-time drug money.

The party line on the S&L crisis was that it was about bad loans and bum investments made by overeager, inexperienced thrift types, with now and then a bigtime financial crook like Charles Keating taking a hand if the pot was big enough.

But big drug money? No way! Organized crime? No way!

That was the official view, the message engraved on the tablets.

And yet, a guy had to wonder.

Domestic U.S. narcotics profits were generally estimated to run around $100 billion annually. It didn't take a whole bunch of financial common sense to figure that dirty money *that* big *had* needed a washing machine equal to the job: a laundry big enough to handle ten-digit sums.

Why shouldn't that Money Maytag be the "legitimate" U.S. financial system? A multitrillion-dollar unsupervised electronic galaxy that for a dozen years had run unregulated, off its head and blind with greed?

What else but Wall Street, considered globally, both in the United States and offshore, could handle that size action? Wall Street in all its powers and dominions: banks, securities exchanges, investment institutions, mutual funds, hedge funds, the junk bond market, brokerages.

According to a guy from DEA—the Drug Enforcement Agency—whom Greaves lunched with regularly, the worldwide drug business was worth $300 billion a year. That meant $200 million in offshore money that didn't need washing but wanted a safe place to go. Offshore, people held to higher standards of investment safety: What could be safer than the United States, where you got paid market rates of interest at a level of risk no greater than owning Treasury bonds, thanks to federal deposit insurance. It was the greatest disparity of risk to reward ever concocted; people smart enough to build a $300-billion-a-year global business subject to immense difficulties of transportation and distribution, and immense legal pressure, would surely be intelligent enough to perceive that simple fact.

Greaves's DEA source said the market was growing again. After a couple of flat years, crack cocaine had recaptured its old unit volume, while heroin was regaining U.S. market share. There were big new players, what with the Russians coming in as low-cost opium producers. If the markets were growing, so would the need for industrial-size money laundries. The U.S. financial system was measured in trillions, a galaxy of a size sufficient to render even very large financial constellations inconspicuous to the untrained or naked eye.

Where else could money that size go? Panama was screwed down; the other traditional offshore havens lacked capacity; the new JEDI system was said to be patroling the international electronic highways like an unmarked police cruiser. Sheer logistical problems militated against moving more than a few million cash offshore at a time; "money mules" flying into Grand Cayman, or Curaçao, or Macau had to damn near fight their way through plainclothes narcs from a dozen countries to get to airport customs.

Interpol projected worldwide drug profits as being in the hundred billions! You couldn't hump that kind of money in backpacks or even 747s. So how was it being laundered? To Greaves, there could only be one answer: The big money was going directly into the financial mainstream, possibly without ever leaving the United States, although the best way was to move it offshore, give it the electronic equivalent of plastic surgery, and bring it back with a wholly new face and passport.

Where could "d/b/a Thunderbolt" fit in? As part of a big overall scheme? Hardly likely; you'd have to blow this size money up by a factor of about 100,000 to approach the kind of volume Greaves had in mind, and even a blind man would have noticed that!

Still, mightn't it be possible that this slender thread he'd picked up might be attached to a string attached to a cord and so on? A series of increasingly larger diameters of connection until there would be Clarence Greaves with the dirty-money equivalent of the suspension cables of the Golden Gate Bridge in his pudgy hand!

He was enjoying this fantasy when the dire thought hit him that "d/b/a Thunderbolt" might not be a scam but a sting. A DEA or IRS trap.

Was that a risk he ought to run? The agencies were full of tales about the dire fate of X or Y who'd stumbled onto and compromised a sting set up patiently over months, even years. The stories weren't pretty. Blunders like that had cost people their pensions.

The allure of the problem pushed Greaves's misgivings out of the way. This itch needed to be scratched, no matter what. He reached into his jacket and pulled out a scuffed leather scabbard marked with his initials. He'd had it made the year before when he and his niece went to Club Med in Mexico. From it he slid the Sharp "Wizard" OZ8200 electronic pocket organizer, which was his pride and joy, his Excalibur.

His flat, broad fingers worked the small keys clumsily, and the alphanumerics out on the small screen were difficult to make out in the hazy sunlight. He studied them intently. No way, he thought; what I need is more firepower.

Yes, he thought, JEDI is not only the ideal solution, it's the only solution.

Not that he really understood JEDI. To people at Greaves's level, the crime-fighting software—the acronym stood for Joint Expedited Data Interface—was mostly hearsay, its parameters a matter for heated speculation in government cafeterias and messes, its real-time capabilities known only in corner offices furbished with signed photographs of the President. The law enforcement data base was hush-hush, highest clearance, top secret: accessible only at the level of Deputy Director, Assistant Secretary, or higher (and then "eyes-only") and under the personal supervision of the Vice President of the United States, the federal government's ranking technocrat.

Greaves had never actually used JEDI, his civil service grade wasn't within a mile of JEDI user privilege, but he had heard enough about it to have an idea of how the system worked and what it could do. With JEDI, an agent could connect up the dots in nanoseconds.

This capability would be indispensable, especially if the trail should lead offshore—into a thicket of Lichtenstein nominee trusts and Bahamas asset protection schemes—which, if "d/b/a Thunderbolt" was drug derived, it most likely would. These days, a data packet representing a billion dollars might touch down in twenty or more offshore destinations in less than a minute and change its appearance at every port of entry.

If he could access JEDI, Greaves was certain he could make it dance for him. The system's operating protocols were said to be pretty straightforward; they would have to be, since the higher you moved in government, the greater the degree of computer illiteracy you were likely to find. Typically butt backwards, as with most things in government. The people who could really make JEDI deliver the goods, front-line people like Greaves who understood the possibilities of cyberintellect and needed all the weaponry they could get, were denied ready access, while the big shots in the corner offices with the JEDI terminals up and glowing within arm's reach could barely type their own names and spent most of their time thinking about lunch.

He slipped the Sharp back into its scabbard. You crazy, Clarence, he thought. The odds against this being anything but trouble for you are terrible. Stick to your knitting, boy.

But he knew he couldn't. Speculation had given him a taste of something larger than the problem itself. The fact was, like most Americans living in a celebrity-besotted age, Clarence Greaves secretly craved his quarter hour in the spotlight. Now he allowed himself a flickering moment of fantasy, projected himself talking to Bryant Gumbel, getting paid a ton of hard cash for going exclusive with "Hard Copy" or some show like that, maybe even "60 Minutes," growing rich and famous, retiring to Sarasota on the royalties from the book he'd coauthor with Bob Woodward of *The Washington Post* or that guy on *The Wall Street Journal* who wrote the best-seller about Milken.

Whoa, boy! he told himself sternly. One step at a time.

Still, it would be a good idea to work with someone outside government, someone in the media, with the resources to follow up any lead Greaves might throw their way, someone to whom he could function as a Deep Throat, leaving himself room to bail out until the cat was in the bag and fame and fortune sure at hand.

But who? The trouble was, he didn't know many such people. You didn't just walk into the *Post* offices over on Seventeenth Street with a paper bag full of wild surmises about money laundering and get Bob Woodward's attention.

Then there was the plain fact that on financial matters, the press wasn't worth a damn. Hell, the damn press had sat there right during Noriega's indictment, with the federal prosecutor waving a chart in their faces on which every other box was labeled "BCCI," and not one single reporter had asked what the hell "BCCI" was!

Hey, he told himself, slow down! You're way ahead of yourself, boy! Before any big-time media is going to be interested, you're going to have to flesh this out, give it names and faces and at least the possibility of a fat nine-zero profile. Right now, what you have isn't hard enough to interest anyone!

If I could only get on JEDI . . .

But how am I going to do that!

Greaves kicked at the ground in frustration. A hundred yards out to sea, a school of seabirds swooped low in pursuit of a school of baitfish being driven to the surface by some terror closing in from the depths.

Greaves watched idly. Then, suddenly, he knew exactly how to get what he wanted.

He rose, tingling with excitement, and turned toward his car.

They say that blood is thicker than water, he thought. Clarence Greaves was pretty certain it would also prove thicker than security clearances.

T W O

▼

The final item on the agenda was the state of current trade and tariff negotiations. When the Secretary of Commerce, a blunt-featured, no-nonsense woman, concluded her doleful summary, the President looked around the glum room and wished a happy Independence Day weekend to his Cabinet and the aides ranged against the walls.

As was customary at the end of the weekly Cabinet meetings, the President and his Cabinet now dispersed about the room into conversational clusters of two or three, and made heavyweight small talk while the staff people hovered on the fringes like uncertain electrons orbiting high-voltage nuclei. This would last for ten minutes or so, long enough for the President to circumambulate the room, here nudging a Secretarial rib, there lightly clasping a Secretarial elbow, working hard to rekindle the sense of mission that, minute by minute, he saw ebbing out of his administration.

Beneath the confident chatter, the general edginess was unmistakable. If anyone in the room had dared to speak about it openly, he or she would have identified the proximate cause as an apparent—if not yet publicly enunciated—sharp turn in the President's ideological orientation. Washington ran on inference, the vapor of fact. By some in the room, the current inferences were regarded as profoundly disturbing; by others, as unsettling but premature—to be waited and seen about; to still others: as a hopeful portent of change and opportunity.

The Vice President was in the middle category. From across the room, he studied his chief. He still didn't know what to make of the man.

Unlike his Number Two, the President was neither by training nor bent of mind a market-economy technocrat, but up to now he had governed like one: as if he genuinely believed that the great issues of society and political economy were most effectively dealt with by "process," by turning them over to MBAs or Ph.D.s from first-rate graduate schools working in harness with Congress and heeding the inexorable (and thus irreproachable) dictates of the market.

But the process wasn't working the way it was supposed to. All the king's statistics and all the king's charts and all the king's subcommittees and consultants and councils of the great and good seemed to have availed precious little in putting the nation back on the track to economic and societal renewal. As one cabinet secretary, a personage of wider reading and remembrance than his colleagues, remarked to his personal assistant: "If they ever write one of those multiple-personality books about America in the 1990s, they ought to call it *The Twenty Faces of Humpty-Dumpty.*"

There was no doubt that three years in office had aged the President. He seemed slacker, grayer; there seemed limits now to his energy, good humor, and patience, although on this particular morning, he seemed refreshed and had conducted the meeting with his old confident, joky exuberance. "This is the problem, these are the reasons why it occurred, and here is our sixty-point plan for fixing it."

It was good to hear him this way again, the Vice President thought. Hard edged and practical; no bleeding-heart crap. In recent weeks, the President had now and then displayed a disquieting tendency toward the philosophical and abstract, along with a drift back to his former populism in matters of political economy that alarmed the Vice President. He had thought that sort of garbage long dead in the President's philosophy—and good riddance, too!

Backstairs White House gossip reported that Number One was undergoing some sort of spiritual crisis. Ideological backbone stiffening is definitely in order, the Vice President thought. It had occurred to him that the First Lady, an articulate, sure-footed, impeccably credentialed student of process, was the person for the job. Perhaps Oltington, the Vice President's special assistant for appointments and protocol, a man who had the ear of the President's wife and kept his own ear to the red carpet, should pass along some of the things that had been said last weekend at the meeting of the Productivity Council. These were people to whom it was painful to criticize someone in whom they had invested so much blind faith and cold cash. They had backed the campaign handsomely; within the bounds of propriety, they were entitled to a fair return on their investment. So far, they were barely getting it.

No one minimized the fact that these were difficult times. But then, since the mid-1980s, nothing had turned out to be as easy as expected. This was a different world from the one in which the Vice President and his chief had taken their first political steps. The God whose favor had carried these men and women to triumph, whose angels had borne them to this elegant, awe-provoking room where history hung as heavy as the thick brocade curtains and the heavily varnished portraits of Millard Fillmore and Chester A. Arthur behind the Vice President's chair, was proving a stubborn old cuss on matters economic, social, racial.

Still, it could be worse. World financial markets were booming. Wall Street was making more money than ever, and doing it with a hundred thousand fewer people, which showed what you could accomplish if you really focused on productivity and got tough. *Productivity* and *process:* those were the watchwords. Human resources should be cost effectivized no differently than machine tools or computers.

Yes, things could surely be a lot worse. Inflation was down; corporate profits were up. Iraq was, if not quiet, manageable. It looked as if the country was ready to buy into the notion that free trade was the horse for the future, the splendid golden steed that would carry the nation to eternal glory and prosperity.

People liked to dwell on the problems, however. Not the Vice President. He was a realist. You played the cards you were dealt—at least until you could change the deck. There was a slogan Russell Oltington, the VP's appointments secretary, was fond of quoting, words Oltington had picked up during his time at the CIA: You had to work within the logic of the situation.

"The logic of the situation." The Vice President liked the

phrase's ring. Deft government was simply a question of adapting the process to present realities.

Of course, men and women who understood process knew that present realities were exactly the same as past realities. Nothing really changed in Washington—except faces, and in a single generation, not even those. The great chanceries of government might be redecorated for their new occupants, hung with bright, spanking new curtains, but behind those pristine drapes moved the same old shadowy figures, pulling the same invisible, unbreakable strings. The same inside deals were being cut—and boasted about—by the same people who'd cut them back in LBJ's day.

The conversational knots unraveled, the Cabinet officers and their aides left the room. As the Vice President made ready to leave, the President came up and gently touched his elbow.

"A moment of your time in my office, please, Ken."

The line, taken from the television show "L.A. Law," was a private joke between the two men, who had both begun their working lives as lawyers.

The Vice President found the little joke reassuring. In recent weeks, the President had often seemed ill-humored and distant. The Vice President and his people had pondered hard whether to take this personally. Not yet, they concluded. It was just the strain of office, of so little working out the way it was supposed to. Still, the old closeness didn't seem to be there, and the Vice President knew what Washington was saying (and he supposed the President did as well): that the carefully forged symbiosis between the two men was fraying, at least at the edges.

To many Washington insiders, it was only to be expected that a bond so obviously artificial should start to come apart when the going got tough. As George Will had pointed out on television the previous Sunday, the two men came from different, "ultimately irreconcilable" quadrants of the political and intellectual compass: the President a small-town boy whose native political cunning had been "marinated in a post-La Follette rural populism that the degraded political estate of the nation had accepted *faute de mieux*," a skilled pol who'd climbed the ladder from state legislature to Congress to state house to White House without putting a foot wrong. So far.

The Vice President was the insiders' kind of man. He had come to Washington twenty-odd years earlier, leaving a lucrative New York law partnership to take a minor position in the first Nixon administration. In the capital, he developed a taste for power of the Washington kind; he survived Watergate and contrived to stay in government through successive changes of party. Republicans and Democrats alike recognized that his manipulative skills were too valuable to let go, as were his ties to the money power in the country, itself perfectly bipartisan so long as its wish list was properly attended to. As a career in unelected government it was hard to top, with a resume to drool over. Which is exactly what every big Washington-New York-Los Angeles law, lobbying, or investment banking firm was doing.

His nomination for the Vice Presidential slot had come as almost as great a surprise as his acceptance. This was a man who stood to have his pick of any number of multimillion-dollar offers, including the managing partnership of a major law firm, the chairmanship of a prestigious New York bank, and the biggest corner office in a top investment bank. It was clear he had been invited on the ticket as a concession to the money power by a party not normally allied with Wall Street; his nomination was clearly intended "to reassure the financial markets"—a political rubric that meant keeping the dollar sound and the Dow-Jones up.

Prior to the convention, the President and his Number Two-designate had barely been acquainted, but they seemed to take to each other immediately with a liking that had ripened since into genuine mutual trust and reliance. Since the election, the President had delegated "operational responsibility" for many of the administration's notionally cutting-edge initiatives to his Number Two, including the Productivity Council, Operation Interdict, and JEDI.

The Vice President's mind was racing as he followed his chief down the corridor. The President's tone implied that he was about to spring a surprise. What the hell could it be? The Vice President found himself wishing that his top staff people were there to help him react. But Di Maglio, who handled domestic issues, was sitting in on a Capitol Hill hearing in which certain friends of the Vice President had a special interest, and Craxton, who oversaw matters touching on foreign policy and national security, was in Walter Reed with a slipped disc.

Rusty Oltington, trotting eagerly along in his master's wake, was hardly an adequate substitute. It had just happened that, on the point of leaving the Executive Office Building that morning for the Cabinet meeting, the Vice President's eye lit on Oltington—he was always there in the background, tail wagging, doing the little things in the reflexively smooth, unobtrusive way of a natural courtier—and without really thinking, he'd waved to the aide to come along on the reflexive theory that to show up for a Cabinet meeting without at least one staffperson would have been an unthinkable breach of appearances.

Just outside the anteroom to the Oval Office, the President halted, turned, and took the Vice President aside.

"Ken," he said in a low voice, "I'm going to have to renege on the Grove, I'm afraid."

Now wait just a damn minute, the Vice President thought, trying to keep the flush of exasperation from his face.

The Grove was the summer encampment of San Francisco's Bohemian Club, an annual conclave of the nation's movers and shakers. It was not a commitment anyone—including heads of state—reneged on lightly. To be invited to give a lakeside address to the distinguished audience pausing in its gambols amid the club's private stand of soaring redwoods was an honor eagerly sought. No sitting President had ever addressed the Grove. To arrange this break with precedent had been a delicate business, a feather in the Vice Presidential cap.

"I'm afraid I don't understand, sir."

"You will shortly," said the President, eyes twinkling. "I think the best course will be to hold off saying anything until the last minute, make it look like a crisis has kept me here. It'll go down better that way. Naturally, I hope you'll be willing to stand in for me. Those are your people, Ken. You can do a better job than I of putting across to them what we're trying to do."

"Of course, sir."

The Vice President followed the President into the outer office, his feelings changing from pique to anger.

Get hold of yourself, man, he muttered inwardly. At the door to the Oval Office, he cleared his throat to catch the President's eye and cocked a dismissive eyebrow at Oltington, as if asking whether to shoo a dog off a sofa.

"It's okay, Ken," the President said, gesturing Oltington to come in. "Rusty can stick around. You'll want to have a second pair of ears on this one. Just for the record. Besides, I want to talk about global finance, as I think you Street types call it, and if memory serves, that's a line of country Rusty's familiar with."

True. Seventeen years before, when the Vice President and Oltington first came in contact during the future Number Two's shift as CIA general counsel, the latter was a spear carrier in the agency's Covert Operations-Finance section under the legendary Henry St. Albans Carew. It was strictly a grace and favor job, company gossip said, obtained through a relative's connections after Oltington had bombed as a trust officer at a series of New York and Philadelphia banks.

Oltington made it immediately clear that he thought the new Agency general counsel was a comer. He'd made himself useful, both as a dogsbody of all work and as a source of first-rate, accurate gossip on Langley doings, gotten a firm grip on the future Vice President's coattails, and ridden them all the way up.

The President threw Oltington one of his patented you-and-me-buddy grins. He had grown fond of Oltington, as had his wife. The little guy was dog loyal, and the First Couple gave highest marks for loyalty. The President was secretly relieved that neither Di Maglio nor Craxton was there. They were the sort that gave Washington a bad name, men who spent their entire lives poised on the balls of their feet, intriguers, leakers. If there was anything the President loathed, it was a leaker.

Oltington, despite his reputation as a capital gossip, knew when to pull up. Unlike most Beltway types, he wasn't in helpless thrall to his own ambition.

He played the First Lady like a violin, but the President wasn't jealous. She had grown dependent on Oltington, not merely as purveyor by Presidential warrant of the choicest gossip, but for the little touches.

Also, try as hard as she might to disguise the fact, the First Lady was a woman, and it was to this side of her that Oltington appealed. The President's wife was a formidable person, an economics prodigy with an MIT doctorate in monetary theory, a fellowship at the Hoover Institute at the age of twenty-five; she regularly sat in on the deliberations of the Council of Economic Advisers. She was much more at ease with a computer spread sheet than a seating chart and was famous for her utter lack of small talk.

These were gaps Oltington filled. She would have shanghaied him to be chief of protocol or White House social secretary, but there the President had intervened: Oltington was virtually indentured to the Vice President, and the best way to raise a ruckus in Washington was to start poaching someone else's staff. Besides, Oltington had made it clear that he was happy where he was.

In the Oval Office, the Vice President settled into an armchair one away from the copy of JFK's old rocker the President had taken to using, and waved his aide to a chair against the wall. He noted a Presidential assistant hovering expectantly by the door leading to the west corridor. Someone was obviously waiting on the other side. They're giving this the full Vegas treatment, he thought. Why?

The President entered and nodded to his assistant; the door was opened and a tired-looking man in his middle sixties, rumpled, bull-dog-featured with shiny small eyes, came in.

"You all know the Chairman of the Federal Reserve Board," said the President. Hands were shaken around the room, then the President waved the newcomer to the chair next to his.

The Vice President and Oltington looked at each other. This was not good. The Fed Chairman was not on the team; he was one of the bad guys, an interventionist and regulator, a closet Keynesianist whose concern for sound money was tempered by a socioeconomic conscience appropriate in, say, a Secretary of Social Services but not in a Chairman of the Federal Reserve. He lacked the fanatical anti-inflationist bias the Vice President's "people" liked to see in the head of the Fed.

The Vice President had discreetly, indirectly intrigued against the Chairman's confirmation on Capitol Hill. The First Lady had also put the knife in on the First Pillow. But the President had hung tough on this one, and had prevailed.

The President looked around the small circle of men. He had what Oltington called his "game face" on: an expression that said, underestimate the seriousness and confidentiality of what is about to be under discussion at your own total professional and political peril.

"Before we get to the substance of this meeting," he said, "I want to make plain that what we're going to discuss is deep graveyard. You don't tell anyone, including your wife, your mother, your significant other. Is that clear? I have not told mine."

The President's unsmiling gaze traveled from face to face. Instinctively, the Vice President nodded, but inwardly he was determined to keep his counsel until he heard what was about to be put on the table. Obviously it was big, obviously it was related to the President's decision to bail out on the Grove, which meant it was something that wasn't likely to make the Grove crowd happy.

"Now," said the President, "there comes a time in human affairs when enough is enough. I read somewhere once that a nation that cannot control its own currency is not likely to be able to control much else about itself. I think we are in that position, and I can tell you that my view is shared by my opposite numbers on the other sides of both oceans and in the Persian Gulf. To make myself clear, I believe the speculative elements in the foreign exchange market are out of control and need to be reined in."

The men in the room knew what he was talking about. A year earlier, foreign exchange speculators had crashed the British pound. Two weeks earlier, they had rounded on the peseta. Operating in utterly unregulated markets, with seemingly unlimited resources to call upon for backing, they seemed unstoppable.

The Vice President had heard all this before. It was true, even he would concede, that the private currency speculators exerted a destabilizing influence on currency parities, and this contributed to the inability of governments to govern and of industries to plan. There was no doubt that the currency traders, when they ran as a pack, had demonstrated the ability to tear a given currency limb from limb. The private money arrayed against the reserves the Fed and the other central banks could mobilize was tremendous. In the great bear run on the pound sterling, they had defeated the Chancellor of the Exchequer in hand-to-hand combat and driven Britain out of the European currency scheme; one speculator was said to have walked away from the duel with over a billion dollars in profit.

But that was life, the VP thought: you might deplore that "kids" playing "computer Monopoly" with real money had more influence on the economic destiny of great democracies than anything decided on Pennsylvania Avenue or Downing Street, that they could topple governments more readily than an armed mob. So what? Since 1980, the world had come to accept the market's decisions as not merely efficient but also just, regardless of how much misery or discomfort these decisions caused. The up side was that free markets disciplined the natural tendency of governments to inflate, free markets kept the bureaucrats in line. Not to mention that enormous wealth had been created.

The President was speaking again. His voice was as angry as anyone in the room could remember. It jolted the Vice President out of his reflections.

"These sonsofbitches are out of control and we have got to do something about it! Since the only thing they understand is money, and since it is the judgment of the wise that fire is best fought with fire, the only solution is to bankrupt the bastards!"

He turned to the Fed Chairman.

"All yours, Fred."

The Chairman spoke for fifteen minutes. Much of what he said was highly technical, involving currency and exchange controls, unified transaction taxes, adjustments in central bank lending rates and policies, flexible reserve and margin requirements. It was obvious he had consulted with his counterparts in Tokyo, Bonn, Paris, London, and Riyadh in evolving a coordinated strategy to trap the foreign exchange speculators, using the French franc as the bait, the goat tethered in the clearing to draw the tiger to the gun.

The Vice President, listening, let no hint of his agitation show on his fine square features. Inside he was steaming. This was arrant interference with the working of free markets! This was a repudiation of everything he and the President had stood for, everything he had worked for as head of the Productivity Council!

And the worst part of all was that it would work. It was ingenious. The Fed and other central banks had contrived the biggest ambush in the history of currency and securities markets. The traders—the *markets*—didn't stand a chance. Not against the central banks deploying all their resources in a combined, coordinated effort. The trick to foreign exchange speculation was divide and conquer, a strategy that only worked as long as the central banks were thinking every-man-for-himself.

Worse still, there wasn't a single goddamn thing he could do to head it off! This was obviously going to be a Fed operation, and the Fed was its own master. If it had come out of Treasury, he could arrange to have it perish stillborn in Congressional subcommittee, strangled by the umbilical of "process."

The Chairman was winding up: "When we pull the plug, we'll be coordinating with our opposite numbers at the money desks in Tokyo and elsewhere. Our best estimate is that if all goes as planned, the bastards will be crying 'uncle' within forty-eight hours, and then we'll be able to return to our main business of trying to build a financially rational world."

The Vice President felt he should say something. He looked squarely at the Fed Chairman.

"Assuming you succeed in—as you say 'bankrupting' the ForEx crowd, Fred, we are talking a lot of damage. Billions upon billions is my guess. Damage means bailout. I assume you've worked out what this is going to cost the taxpayers?"

The Chairman's reply was couched in an equally contemptuous tone.

"We have. This time any bailout program will represent a fair deal. A piece of future action backed by ironclad financial commitments. And of course a promise, subject to extreme penalties if not kept, that the whiz kids will be very, very good boys for a very long time to come."

Sunlight poured into the room. The Fed Chairman examined his hands. The Vice President stared at the ceiling, thinking: no wonder Number One's ducking the Grove. Pull something like this and he'll never get out of the redwoods alive. He knows it as well as I do, which is why I'm the boy who gets to carry his water.

After a long beat, the President broke the silence.

"Ken, you're my point man on both the financial markets and

JEDI, so I'll want you to be on top of this all the way."

"JEDI, Mr. President? What's JEDI got to do with this."

And what the hell *did* JEDI, the highly classified interagency data network, have to do with stampeding the ForEx boys? JEDI had been established to fight crime, not meddle with markets! To deal with tax evasion, narcotics trafficking, money laundering, terrorism: not foreign exchange trading!

The President looked at the Chairman of the Federal Reserve.

"I can answer that, Mr. Vice President," the Chairman replied. Was there an edge to the way he pronounced Number Two's title? The Chairman reached into his briefcase and took out a thick, bound sheaf of printouts, then placed the stack on the table before him and patted it.

He summarized the contents quickly. These JEDI data bases— along with similar intelligence furnished by the Bundesbank, Bank of England, Bank of Japan, SAMA, and so on—made up a sort of satellite map of the ForEx markets worldwide: a chart of the enemy's order of battle, as it were, except that instead of elements of topography, hills and streams, or copses where batteries of artillery might be concealed, JEDI showed interbank funds flows and account encryptions; instead of elements of military calculation, weaponry, or troop stagings, JEDI had identified lines of credit and other sources of currency-trading finance; it kept running track of long and short positions, of swaps and other derivatives footings, of buy and sell hedges, and intercurrency arbitrages.

"No question about it, Mr. Vice President," the Chairman said, "without JEDI, we wouldn't have gotten to first base in putting a strategy together. JEDI permits us to monitor funds flows in real time, in fact it gives us overall real-time response capability, especially when it comes to moving money to meet money at key points of application."

"Like bringing up troops from the rear," the President added helpfully, grinning at the Vice President. He obviously loved this.

The Vice President hardly heard them. He was burning with fury. In the last enlargement of JEDI's universe of information, banks around the world had been persuaded—strong-armed—into making the data base privy to their most secret encryptions, the account and transaction codes that identified individual money movements on

CHIPS (Clearing House Interbank Payment System), the global bank wire. The Vice President had played a key role in the strong-arming, arguing that only by opening up to JEDI was any realistic offensive against big-money laundering possible. Now the banks' cooperation was going to be turned against a perfectly legitimate banking function: the provision of funds to above-board speculative markets. This was a criminal breach of good faith!

The Vice President himself felt double-crossed. Twice over: since not only was this a perversion of JEDI, but it was also a gross incursion on his turf.

In his mind, the corruption of JEDI was the more pressing consideration. The foreign exchange crowd were grown-ups; they could take care of themselves. But JEDI was his baby. As the administration's highest-ranking computer mentality, the Vice President had naturally served as the White House's alter ego on Project Omniscience, which had been the cover name for the vast interactive, interagency data base whose final Star Wars designation was the brainchild of a hotshot acronym jockey at the Defense Department.

JEDI had been a hard sell politically and technically. Opponents of the concept had termed the system "Big Brother in a pin-striped suit." Government satrapies like Defense and the IRS were public repositories of highly confidential financial information on millions of institutions and individuals. The banks' encryptions were also dynamite, informationally speaking, as were the files of TRW and a half-dozen other private-sector credit Gestapos, which all had been persuaded that it was powerfully in the national interest for them to open up to JEDI. There had been a lot of heated talk to the effect that JEDI was Orwell's Big Brother digitalized and updated for the space age. The technological and software problems had been humongous; it had been necessary to bring in people from all over to work on this piece or that.

He knew he should put himself on the record, and was looking for the right words when the President spoke up.

"Let me just say that I believe this to be the most important—and essential—single initiative undertaken by any administration since the Cuba missile crisis. I think the security of the nation is at stake."

He paused and looked hard at the Vice President.

"I expect you to back me up on this with your crowd, Ken. I

know it won't go easy for you at the Grove. But if anyone can get the message across, it's you."

He grinned and punched the air in a victory gesture.

Don't count those chickens yet, thought the Vice President. He looked over at Oltington and saw at once that his aide was on his wavelength. They had been shut out of the loop on this one. You could put a number on that fact. Men known to be out of the loop had a private market value of zilch.

He was still searching for the right thing to say when the President rose, signaling an end to the meeting. The Fed Chairman departed. The look of clear triumph on his face was like a dagger in the Vice President's vitals.

The President sensed his Number Two's discomfiture. Taking the Vice President gently by the elbow, he guided him across the Oval Office to the French windows opening on the White House gardens. Washington was enjoying a gorgeous early summer; the air seemed perfumed by a crisp, unmistakable afterscent of spring. The President gazed out on the leafy scene, seeming to drink in the joy of the day.

"Ken . . . ," he began, then reconsidered, halted in midphrase. He looked over at Oltington and said, smiling, "I think this time I will ask Russell to wait outside, if you don't mind."

The Vice President told Oltington to take the car back to the Executive Office Building. He would foot it back through the White House grounds.

When they were alone, the President looked warmly at the Vice President and said, "I've been doing a lot of thinking about where we've been headed in this country. I'm sure you have, too. I think we've got to make some basic changes. For one thing, I think we've been running the country for Wall Street's benefit for too long."

The Vice President shrugged. Before he could say anything, the President continued. "I think things have gotten off the track. Priorities seem skewed. I think the termites are back in the woodwork. This foreign exchange business is merely a symptom."

"I'm not sure I follow you, sir."

The President paused and studied his Number Two. How was he going to put this? It occurred to him he didn't really know the Vice President all that well.

"The bottom line," said the President slowly, "is that I think your Productivity Council is also a dog whose day we have to regard as done."

"Are you suggesting, sir, that the Council no longer has a function, or that it—or I—have been co-opted?"

The President grinned. "Not at all. You're no Dan Quayle."

Seeing the Vice President fail to respond to the little joke, the President continued in a solicitous voice.

"I think we both recognize we've got to start rethinking a bunch of our initial premises. Take productivity, for example. Increasing output is one thing, but, damn it, Ken, these days, all the word seems to mean is firing people! There's a moral issue there. I'm sure you see that. As well as a very potent political one. A lot of educated people are losing their jobs. People like that get angry; it doesn't go down very well with someone who's been canned from Kodak in the interest of increasing stockholder profits to hear that Merrill Lynch is making more money than ever doing whatever the hell it is they do. Angry people vote. You know that."

That's crap, thought the Vice President. The old anti–Wall Street populist bullshit. He tried to keep his voice level.

"I can see that some people might see it that way, sir. On the other hand, corporate profits are up nicely, which clears the way for substantial incremental business investment at only a modest increase in disemployment."

The President's grin thinned. Don't talk to me like a damn business school professor, his expression said. He kept his tone genial.

"Maybe so, but it bothers me. I can't see that the evidence squares with the claims. The country's not going well."

"Well, sir, what would you like me to do? Break up the council? If you want that, I'd like some guidance as to how you want me to present the idea to the council members. These are pretty important people, you know. Not just to the party, but to the nation."

The President brushed away an invisible fly. "I take your point," he said. "Let us just say we shall for the time being put the council on the back burner, in a barely simmering mode. Just as long as the fat cats get the message that the lock on the Treasury vault has been changed."

The Vice President let the implied slur pass.

"Very good, sir. Is there anything else?" he said in a sarcastically servile manner, at the same time smiling in an attempt to take some of the edge off his tone of voice. We have crossed a threshold, he thought. Something definitive has gone out of our relationship.

"Just one more thing," the President said. His voice was chilly. "On this foreign exchange business: I'm counting on you to quote reassure the markets endquote."

He invested the words *reassure the markets* with his own palpable contempt.

The door opened; a Presidential aide advised the chief that the Prime Minister of Sri Lanka's limousine had just passed through the White House guardpost. The President nodded him off impatiently.

"As you wish," said the Vice President. He paused, and studied his chief in a lordly fashion. A stranger entering the room at that moment would have been hard pressed to tell which man considered himself Number One.

"There is one thing I feel in conscience bound to put on the record, sir," the Vice President said after a moment's silence. He heard his voice rising in ire, but couldn't help it. He saw the President's eyes warm in amusement. To provoke someone, colleague or opposition, into a momentary loss of control was the bureaucratic equivalent of a service ace. Well, the hell with it, the Vice President thought.

"I have to say, sir, that deploying JEDI to attack the legitimate financial markets strikes me as a gross perversion of the system's mission. This sort of thing was never contemplated as part of the JEDI universe. JEDI is basically a crime-fighting tool. To help affected agencies coordinate their efforts in the drug war, or against terrorism."

There was no geniality left in the President's expression or in his voice.

"Come off it," he said. "Cut the crap! What these foreign exchange hotshots have been up to strikes me as a prima facie form of grand larceny. Or—if you prefer—terrorism!"

He turned away and headed for his desk.

In the anteroom, Oltington was chattering merrily with the President's secretary. The sharp voices through the half-opened door caused him to pause. Like most people who lived off chatter, Oltington had developed a useful body language to supplement the oral.

Now he managed to shrug all over: eyebrows, lips, shoulders, palms—as if to say: Well, what's this now?

But behind the scrim of busy gossip, Oltington's mind was racing. This ForEx sting the Fed was planning would be gold, pure gold to Mona! The sort of inside information that justified everyone's commitment to the Project. She would wet her pants when she heard!

He did some rapid calculating. With this quality of information, Mona's people could turn a couple of hundred million profit easy.

The question was, should he ask for a bonus, an extra point or two on his override? An extra million or two never hurt.

THREE

▼

The encircling mountains muffled the engines of the incoming aircraft until it was almost overhead, sweeping up the sierra preparatory to turning back on final approach. The sun winked on its wings as it fled up the valley. As it roared by, the man standing beside the dark green Range Rover studied the jet and reflexively nodded approval, like a breeder watching a yearling make its first gallop.

It was a handsome plane, a brand-new British Aerospace commuter jet with special short takeoff-landing capability. Don Escobedo had bought it to bring guests in from outside the country when the activities of the Peruvian *guardia* or the American antidrug mercenaries made the usual routes unsafe.

He hoped the flight from São Paulo had been smooth. As always, Don Escobedo was looking forward to Mona's visit with an eagerness he reserved for no one else. Mona had an elegant spirit. He dealt with her as with few others; most of those with whom the Don had contact he regarded as mere raw material for his lifetime's research project: an effort to ascertain which was more effective in making people grovel—fear or money.

Mona seemed susceptible to neither. Don Escobedo pictured her as he pictured himself: a shark smoothly, dangerously cleaving the blue waters of human greed and gullibility in search of prey. Now and then he speculated as to what use Mona and he might have made of their complementary talents if they had not found their present calling. He had concluded that they would have made a splendid team to run a Hollywood talent agency.

He saw Mona and himself as being altogether superior, socially and culturally, to their clients. Don Escobedo had been baptized fifty-four years earlier by the Cardinal-Archbishop of Caracas as Bonifacio Jesus-Maria Obregon Escobedo y Lucientes. He was a child of prosperity and privilege. His father had been the ranking member of a Caracas law firm whose principal clients were international oil companies with extensive drilling and production interests at Lake Maracaibo. The Don had been educated in England, Paris, and at the Stanford Business School. He spent eleven years with the Banco Hidalgo in Madrid, specializing in worldwide import-export finance, and then had returned to head up the bank's correspondent office in Bogotá, which is where he had come to the attention of his present clients. These were three "agricultural" syndicates headquartered in and around Medellín and Cali notionally engaged in the cultivation of coffee and fruitwoods, but in fact industrial-scale producers-processors-distributors of cocaine and other narcotics.

For thirteen years, the Don had functioned as the syndicates' investment manager, with sole discretion over an investment pool—designated "the combined account"—which presently aggregated just under $12 billion spread across a score of capital markets from Brussels to Shanghai and allocated among a dozen major currencies. The bulk of the combined account's assets were dollar-denominated, the greenback being the reserve currency for the global narcotics trade, the medium in which—as was also the case with the oil cartels—accounts were settled at the producer level.

Don Escobedo felt comfortable with the sum under his supervision and had no need to seek additional clients. Twelve billion was a manageable sum. Large enough to give full play for the Don's commitment to investment diversification and his enthusiasm for inventive solutions to knotty problems of asset allocation, cash management, currency arbitrage, and portfolio strategy. Small enough to be mobile and flexible in a financial universe where over a trillion dollars flowed over the bank wires every day.

There were billions more out there that were his to manage if he chose, but these huge sums were controlled by people whose fundamental crudeness of outlook—no better than thugs, really!—repelled him. It never ceased to amaze the Don that people of such elemental, brutish coarseness should have managed to build enterprises whose annual takings matched those of General Motors and IBM and exceeded the gross national products of most of the nations on earth.

The jet was descending rapidly now, gliding down across the narrow barranca that separated the runway from the Andes foothills. With a puff of orange dust, the plane bumped down; as it rumbled past, the pilot touched his forehead in salute.

The jet taxied back and came to a halt, engines idling; the door sprang open and a male flight attendant handed down three enormous Vuitton duffels.

Don Escobedo smiled. All this luggage for a mere thirty-six-hour visit, he thought: how very Mona. Well, she was a woman who was always on the move. He doubted she slept twenty nights a year in her Avignon town house.

She followed her luggage down the ladder, posing just for an instant, like a movie star arriving at Cannes. She strode briskly over to Don Escobedo and embraced him collegially, bending to kiss each pitted cheek. The jet revved its engines and taxied off.

The Don and Mona Kurchinski watched it vanish into the late afternoon haze. In less than two hours, it would be back at its hangar in Aruba, where it was registered to an Ecuador-headquartered oil company incorporated in the Cayman Islands but controlled by a Lichtenstein nominee trust. Like so much else in the world according to Don Escobedo, the aircraft was a citizen of an order of being of which no self-respecting inhabitant traveled with less than a half-dozen passports, and where most went about their business mantled in cloaks of invisibility woven by lawyers and accountants from electronic thread.

When the aircraft was no more than a faint sound in the sky, the Don turned to his guest. Mona Kurchinski was a distractingly distinctive-looking woman, with strong features built around a magnificent Roman nose. You would not have called her pretty, but you might have called her beautiful. Her figure was a bit low slung and behind heavy—at least to her host's taste—and her bosom was nothing remarkable, but most men found her extremely sexy. The fact was that sexually Mona was an enigma. She electrified the air around her, but you would have been hard put to find anyone who could prove he had been to bed with her.

Her passports placed her age between thirty-four and forty-two; Don Escobedo knew her to be thirty-nine, an age when women were said to be at their hottest. She was much too old for the Don's taste, however. He was extremely finicky about the matter of age in the two great passions of his life: women and art. The latter he preferred to be between two and five centuries old, the former between thirteen and sixteen years.

From behind his mirror-lensed sunglasses, the Don studied his guest's profile. There was one part of Mona he truly craved. Her nose: fleshy and aquiline. He yearned to bite into it, to hold its splendid curving tip in his teeth. A nose like that deserved to be immortalized in marble on the Capitoline.

Mona has true star quality, he thought. Like Callas, the diva whom he had heard in *Traviata* years before in Paris. When Mona comes onstage, everyone else simply disappears into the scenery.

Mona tipped her sunglasses up onto her forehead. She had deep-set eyes, dark brown running to black, emphasizing the pallor of her skin.

She scrutinized her host with the frank, level gaze that was her characteristic expression. He was not a handsome man. His complexion, savagely pocked, was the sallow legacy of a life misspent mainly indoors. He had a cruel, junta colonel's mouth that twisted down at the left corner; his dark hair and moustache were slick and shiny as a seal's coat, threaded here and there with yellowing gray strands.

Poor lamb, she thought, he takes such pains—and to so little effect! His fading cream linen suit, rumpled just so, would have cost the best part of three million lira on the Via Fatebenefratelli in Milan, she knew; his Borsalino planter's hat was blocked to order at Gelot in Paris. There was something silly about him, something contrived, like that fake Colombian planter in the coffee commercials on American television.

"I must say you're looking extremely well, *mi Don*," she said, grinning. "The mountain air agrees with you."

"As do you, my dear Mona," he said, smiling back.

Indeed, he thought, she seems radiant, very upbeat. This could only mean she was immersed in some new scheme. Deals, not men, the Don knew, were what set Mona Kurchinski afire.

There had been times when Don Escobedo had seen Mona virtually besotted by her own brilliance, intoxicated by the complexity and inventiveness of a scheme. Such infatuations could be troublesome, they needed to be monitored. The Don sought to be balanced in his dealings with her. She was his most valued associate, if not his most trusted, but that was only because the Don ultimately trusted no one. With Mona, he thought, leading her to the car, it is a matter of giving her enough rope—but not enough to let her hang herself.

"I have something for you," she said and paused to fish in her battered shoulder bag. Don Escobedo was pleased to see she still carried it after all this time. He had bought it for her at a shop on the Via Condotti in Rome back in 1982 when they had first become associated. That was when she was still working out of Lausanne, just after quitting the CIA to represent a pool of Middle Eastern money looking for high-return action, and before her Arabs had put Credit Provençal in business.

She continued to root around in her bag. Amazing, the Don thought. Here was a woman who could keep a four-way currency arbitrage straight in her head to the third decimal place, and yet seemed consistently unable to locate a lipstick in her purse.

"Ah," she said at last, "here it is. It's William Safire's column from last Monday's *New York Times*. More BCCI, of course."

She handed him a newspaper clipping. One line was highlighted in bright orange: "Who in Washington tipped the drug lords to a crackdown," Don Escobedo read, "enabling them to withdraw their money first?"

The Don read it again, then looked questioningly at Mona.

"Not to worry," she said gaily. "This has nothing to do with 'Washington.' As I said, he's talking about BCCI, which is a diversion sent from heaven for us!"

The Don nodded. BCCI was a mug's game; any simpleton should have figured it out. "Washington"—on the other hand—was truly a work of genius.

Don Escobedo started the automobile and headed out the narrow track toward the villa.

"So," Mona asked, "how did your session with the Amigos go?"

The Don had met recently with his clients.

"Satisfactorily," he replied. "The U.S. volume is picking up again. They have some interesting negotiations under way in Uzbekistan concerning next year's poppy harvest. Speaking of which, how was your stay in Russia?"

"Interesting. I think we can do business there. Over half the old Soviet oil production is being siphoned off and sold in the black market at half the posted price. We should cut ourselves a piece of that action. Any news on the Palermo front?"

She had heard the Don's clients were negotiating with their Sicilian counterparts for an equitable partition of Eastern European drug markets.

Don Escobedo shook his head. So far, no progress had been made. "I sense that an agreement's still a long way off. These are difficult people. Stubborn and secretive like peasants. I've kept out of the negotiations."

Which was true. There was only so much he wished to know. He wasn't privy to his clients' production and marketing strategies, and he preferred it that way. These were also highly excitable, violent people—prone to overreact.

Mona had no such qualms. To her, information was power, the more the better. But she wasn't going to argue the point with her host. Next week she would meet in Naples with certain Taormina and Calabrian interests to discuss a financial services–cum–investment package modeled on the one she had developed for the Don.

It was not a meeting he needed to be told about. As Mona saw it, there was nothing disloyal in soliciting new accounts for the bank. As Credit Provençal's principal stockholder (although in twenty-seven different names), the combined account stood to benefit the most from the bank's growth. It would be silly simply to concede huge potential markets to others. Someone was going to get the Sicilian accounts, so why not Mona and CP? If she and Claude and Bruno, her partners in CP, were going to build it into a worthy competitor for the big Swiss private banks on these kinds of accounts, people had to know they were seriously in business, and the only way to do that was to go aggressively after new business. Just stay out of the Don's clients' backyard, that was all.

Besides, she had a tastier dish to set before Don Escobedo.

" 'Washington,' " she said in a voice filled with an approximation of maternal pride, "has come through with a major coup, his biggest yet!"

She took the Don through the Americans' plans to sting the foreign exchange speculators.

Amazing, the Don thought, simply amazing. This had explained why the franc was unaccountably weak. There had been rumors that the Germans were behind the selling, trying to draw the markets' attention away from their own wretched economic situation. Now he saw what was really going on: It was a setup.

"I've already started accumulating six-month calls on the franc in various Lichtenstein and Swiss segments of the combined account. Everyone's jumping on the bandwagon the other way and the premiums are next to nothing. I think we'll move into the spot markets next week. When the Federal Reserve pulls the trigger, it should be fun."

"How much fun?" asked Don Escobedo.

"I'm projecting two hundred million, give or take ten percent."

"Very satisfactory," he said. From the Don, there was no higher praise.

The villa came into view. They drove past a guard who raised the muzzle of his submachine pistol rifle in salute.

"One other thing," said Don Escobedo, "can you give me an estimate of our losses from Los Angeles? When can we expect that system to be operational again? My friends in Seoul are very upset. The alternatives are proving acceptably expensive."

Through Mona's bank, the combined account had gone into partnership with Korean interests in establishing a facility that provided small-business finance to émigrés setting up in U.S. ghetto markets, principally liquor and convenience stores. It was a good way to recycle the Korean balance-of-payments surplus, and the stores offered an excellent vehicle for laundering ghetto drug revenues close to the point of sale. But the Los Angeles riots in the wake of the first Rodney King verdict had destroyed 111 collecting points in South Central Los Angeles, a network that in its first full year of operation had laundered close to $300 million, and the promised federally funded reconstruction had as yet not come through. The Koreans were threatening to pull out of the arrangement. They preferred a less volatile investment climate and a government that kept its promises.

Mona filled him in. It didn't sound promising. Perhaps, instead of looking to rebuilding, consideration should be given to setting up an alternative in a less racially charged environment. What might be lost in proximity would be offset by gains in safety. Don Escobedo braked to a halt before the low, sprawling stucco villa.

"One last question," said Mona, "do you have any idea how much is going to be added to the combined account at the end of this fiscal year? I need to do some planning."

"I'm told we can count on a billion six hundred million in incremental capital."

She whistled softly. Business must really be coming back. Allowing for the drug lords' life-styles, including the cost of their private militias, a billion six free and clear on the bottom line probably worked out to twenty billion on the street.

A white-jacketed houseman hurried toward the car, followed by a uniformed lady's maid. Her flat Indian features made an odd contrast with her pert, puffy lace cap.

Mona looked at her watch. "If it's all right with you," she said, "I think I'll have a little lie-down. It's been a long day. What's your pleasure, *mi Don*? Drinks at eight as usual?"

Mona came down early. She had been too excited to nap. Her mind was racing with "Washington's" news and its implications. Obviously the central banks had finally had it with the foreign exchange crowd. They were pushing their luck, she'd advised her friends at CP, the way markets always did when they got on to what seemed a sure thing.

She checked herself in a gilt-framed mirror that had once hung in the Petit Trianon, one of four great Louis Seize pieces in the room, a suite stolen on commission from a famous Paris *antiquaire*. You look good, she thought. She had chosen an elegant, full-length gown by Givenchy. Most people would have thought it better suited to a ceremonial feast at the Élysée Palace than dinner for two in a drug mogul's mountain *estancia*.

A picture across the room caught her eye. She didn't remember it from her last visit. Always something new, she thought, moving over to examine it. The painting depicted two elegantly dressed women, one playing a harpsichord or virginal, the other singing while a cavalier wearing a plumed, broad-brimmed hat listened.

"Beautiful, is it not?" said Don Escobedo from behind her. She had not heard him approach.

"It's the Vermeer from the Gardner Museum in Boston, of course," he said in a voice full of the pride of the true collector. "It's practically a pendant to my other one."

He gestured at a picture hanging farther down the wall. Mona knew about that one: It had been stolen by the Irish Republican Army from the Beit Collection at Russborough House in County Wicklow.

"Exquisite, no?" said the Don. "I daresay no other private collection in the world boasts two Vermeers."

"You are fortunate in your art dealers, *mi Don,*" said Mona girlishly.

The Don made a mincing, knightly bow in acknowledgment.

Mona's point was well taken. Outfits like the IRA, perennially short of weapons, money, and self-respect, were important sources for avid collectors like Don Escobedo. The big Caravaggio at the end of the room had come from Calabria courtesy of the Naples Mafia; the Signorelli *Pan* in the dining room had been one of the treasures of the old Berlin museum; generally assumed to have been burned up in the Russian Sector of Berlin in 1945, it had come to the Don via Switzerland; the sellers were a group of senior KGB officials making certain of their post-Soviet life-style. In the Don's library was a Shakespeare quarto filched from the vault of the Elizabethan Club at Yale, and a fine example of the British Guiana "two-penny black," the world's rarest stamp, which a Stockholm museum had not yet noticed was missing. The market was growing broader day by day, the objects on offer choicer and more varied. In the drug trade, hot art was considered as acceptable and negotiable a medium of exchange as cold cash.

"It's much better that such works find peace here," said Don Escobedo. "Ireland is a troubled, violent place: unsafe for a tranquil master like Vermeer. Do you like Zoffany?"

"I don't think I know his work."

"An eighteenth-century Swiss-English painter of exquisite elegance. I've arranged to buy one of his masterpieces, recently removed from Houghton Hall in Norfolk. You shall see it the next time you come."

He offered Mona his arm and they went out onto the terrace.

It was a spectacular evening. The villa was set high above a lush valley. In the distance, the lights of peasant villages resembled a sparkling necklace dropped carelessly on a black velvet cloth. Jose materialized out of the shadows and made them drinks: rum and lime for the Don, whisky neat for Mona.

"Well now," said Don Escobedo, raising his glass in a toast, "what other news do you bring? I must say I'm very pleased with this intelligence from your friend 'Washington.' It more than justifies the expense to date."

"He'll be pleased to hear that. The penny may have dropped in the States. The next thing the government may try is to reflate its way out of the deficit so it can resume spending. There have been hints: schemes to index Treasury bonds, that sort of thing. America's running out of options, and when they do, we want to be ready, because gold's going to a thousand dollars an ounce and probably higher!"

"So why not add to our holdings? Merely as a hedge. These things can happen very quickly. You might be away from a phone."

Mona smiled. "*Mi Don,* you know I am *never* away from a phone! As a matter of fact, we bought seventy million dollars for the combined account yesterday. For Macau settlement. The trade'll be on your screens by now, I expect."

"Macau? That would be Russian gold, then. What did you have to pay?"

"Five hundred and fifty dollars an ounce."

The Don nodded appreciatively.

"An excellent price. Is there more where that came from?"

"Plenty! The word in Zurich is the old *nomenklatura* emptied the vaults. As much as ten billion dollars. In bullion!"

"Extraordinary. And speaking of collapses, while I think of it, how did we come out on GoldWest in the end?"

"Net net net: about three hundred and twenty million dollars ahead. When the regulators put it on the Watch List, it seemed prudent to leave a little—twenty million dollars—on the table. Strictly for appearances' sake. Most of that will be recouped through deposit insurance, of course."

"Washington's" JEDI watcher had flagged the addition of GoldWest to the top-secret regulatory Watch List, usually a precursor by about ninety days of eventual federal takeover. Mona had acted quickly. The combined account had about $200 million in brokered deposits scattered through the GoldWest system. She withdrew the maturing savings certificates and discounted the remainder in the secondary market.

She was pleased with the bottom line on GoldWest. Credit Provençal had unloaded its shares a year before the collapse, when it still seemed that GoldWest was going to be one of the few big 1980s financial conglomerates to survive. Through a series of classic "push-pull" operations, pushing cash in at one end as insured brokered deposits and pulling the equivalent cash out at the other in the form of high-interest "junk" loans to straw-man borrowers—loans that were never intended to be repaid—she'd cycled $180 million of combined account cash twice, taking out a total of $420 million. All tax- and risk-free.

The Don found it amazing. One of the wonders of postmodern finance was the willingness of the American government to put the American taxpayers' full faith and credit on the line to underwrite the risk-free doubling (or better) of literally billions in crack and heroin profits!

"There won't be another GoldWest, I'm afraid," Mona said. "The golden goose is finally dead of a thousand self-inflicted cuts. 'Too Big to Fail' is no more."

She bowed her head in mock bereavement.

The Don shared her regrets. Too Big to Fail might have been the most idiotic financial policy ever instituted by a market-oriented government. It was a purely political reflex that had been lobbied into public policy beginning with the 1982 crisis at the Continental Illinois Bank. Under Too Big to Fail, all investor and depositor losses in an insured institution, whether or not legally entitled to federal protection, were made good with the taxpayers' money provided the regulators deemed the afflicted institution to be a significant part of the financial system. Thus, when Continental Illinois collapsed, the policy had resulted in the expenditure of taxpayer dollars to pay off junk bonds held offshore by Arab speculators.

An outsider studying Mona's manipulations at GoldWest and elsewhere among U.S. thrift institutions and banks might have judged her prescient, possessed of supernatural powers, in league with djinns and geniis.

In fact, there *was* a genii involved, although instead of a magic lamp, his powers reposed in a bank of powerful work station computers in a small office near San Francisco. This genii of Mona's monitored the traffic on JEDI and passed his findings along through a complex system of scrambled and rescrambled telemetric "call forwarding."

Her penetration of JEDI made Mona an invisible kibitzer in a table-stakes game in which she was also a player: a kibitzer ceaselessly circling the table, checking her opponents' cards, reading her opponents' minds, then playing her hand accordingly.

The Don reflected for a moment, then frowned and asked the question Mona had been expecting—and to some extent dreading.

"I suppose I should ask you about Phoenix? I trust it is proceeding according to schedule?"

Phoenix Capital Associates was Mona's latest gambit, a "vulture fund" formed by CP to pick over the carcasses of ruined corporate capitalizations, principally by buying up defaulted junk bonds at a few cents on the dollar.

"It's going fine," she replied. She knew the Don didn't like the scheme.

"And Gorton? You still think he's reliable? My other sources tell me he's a blowhard who talks too much!"

Leo Gorton, whom Mona had chosen to front Phoenix, had been a second-tier star of the 1980s boom. A lesser Milken, but untainted by scandal. Right through the decade, Mona had used him to broker deposits and handle security offerings.

"Leo is what he is, *mi Don*. He does not overthink nor ask questions. Like everyone else on Wall Street, he's concerned with one thing and one thing only: whether the check clears."

Over the past ten years, another man might have wondered where all the offshore money came from that CP had given Gorton to broker into insured deposit accounts. Not Leo.

"I can control him, Don Escobedo. You should give Phoenix a chance. I think you're looking at it from the wrong angle. It's better you should consider it not so much as a profit opportunity as a vehicle for prudent damage control."

She explained what she meant. The Don nodded; he had heard it before, and in theory her point was well taken. When Phoenix bought up junk bonds issued by fraudulent borrowers to now-bankrupt institutions in the hands of federal agencies, there would be no need for evaluations of the underlying assets, investigations that might prove embarrassing. At, say, ten cents on the dollar, it was very cheap insurance. His only regret was that CP was publicly connected with Phoenix. Better if the investment had been made through a clever series of jurisdictional cutouts.

He smiled at Mona to reassure her, but she felt a chill. His smile seemed the equivalent of a Doberman's growl.

After coffee, Don Escobedo went off to bed. Mona wasn't sleepy. She had passed through the zone of fatigue; in Avignon, where she had begun her day, the sky would be pink fading to azure, the air warming, the sun's early rays would be dancing on the Rhone, the day's business would be starting.

She decided to go down to the computer room, do her housekeeping, and afterward take a sleeping pill.

The guard outside the computer room was armed with a Heckler & Koch .9mm submachine gun. He watched as she punched in an electronic key sequence on the steel door, and followed her into the room, standing beside her while she sat down, kicked off her bejeweled evening pumps, and booted up the three screens she was authorized to operate.

There were half a dozen other darkened screens in the room; had Mona attempted to light them up, the guard would have shot her on the spot. She could guess what those computer files contained: account names and breakdowns of fund sourcing and ownership, product routings, distribution centers, ladings, inventory, and the other raw data necessary to implement and track the transportation and distribution of an important world commodity.

If she wanted to, and if the guard hadn't been poised with silent menace at her back, Mona was pretty sure she could get into those other data bases. The entry keys would probably be based on Don

Escobedo's birthday, or his mother's name, or a numbergram of his initials. Men were such chumps. They all thought exactly the same way. You could pick their pockets with a golf club.

She dialed up her own computer in Avignon and checked her E-mail. Next she ran the portfolios. They were about clear of GoldWest, she noted. The net risk position was actually below what she had told Don Escobedo: It was down to $46 million in high-yield, insured savings certificates.

She checked the latest inputs from the JEDI Watch. Nothing much going on. All quiet on the intercept and interdiction front; no new operation codes had been entered. Operation Pickaxe—a San Diego sting—was being shut down and dismantled because of blown cover. Mona, smiling at that one because the feds had spent two years and a few million dollars setting it up, read on. Another coordinating session between DEA and the Italian *carabinieri* was being put together for Milan next month. The Secret Service was coordinating with the IRS in checking out certain accounts at a busted Fort Lauderdale thrift.

An afterthought nagged at her, and she went back into the GoldWest file. She was relieved that her memory was correct; nothing showed regarding the special accounts she had set up to take care of some petty "Washington" business. Leaning back in her chair, she rubbed her eyes, and keeping them closed, reflected whether she ought to shut these accounts down. Why should she? The chances of their being noted were nil. GoldWest's banks would continue to conduct business as usual, at least those that had some community standing and history. GoldWest itself was a multibillion-dollar disaster. These innocuous accounts, just the sort you'd expect to find on the books of full-service country banks, would show a mere few millions in deposit and withdrawal activity over the brief time they'd been open. There was nothing to worry about: When Uncle Sam played financial detective, he didn't even polish his magnifying glass for less than a hundred million.

Mona wandered purposefully through financial cyberspace for the next quarter hour. The succession of screens amounted to a virtual atlas of her world, demarcated in electronic blips and packets rather than longitude, latitude, and time zones. A world ceaselessly on the move, following a course from market to market with the same relentless regularity that the light of the sun moved from east to west across the face of the earth.

Finally, satisfied that everything was either where it should be, or en route to its newest destination, she shut down the screens. Very tired, she leaned back and blew out a long breath. She had a great deal of money to think about. The computer had reported the disposition of $11.925 billion in investments of all types. Mona idly picked up a scratch pad and ballpoint and wrote out that figure: $11,925,000,000.

A lot of money. Enough to rank its possessors at the top of *Forbes'* list of the world's 291 billionaires.

It seemed huge, but everything denominated mathematically existed in two dimensions, as it were: the absolute and the relative. Economics was the science of choosing whichever best bolstered the argument you wished to make.

For example, America's national debt aggregated close to $4 *trillion*.

Mona wrote that out: $4,000,000,000,000.

Somehow the three extra zeroes didn't seem to make a difference. Perhaps that explained everything. Perhaps when it came to numbers, an individual, an electorate, a nation, had a conceptual point of no return, a number of zeros beyond which sums ceased to mean anything to anyone except astrophysicists, beyond which every quantity might as well be infinity.

When you get to that many zeros, she thought to herself, what does it matter? The thrill, the fun, was all in the game—which only a very few could play. Buoyed by the thought that on the morrow all would be afoot again, and she at the heart of the action, Mona gathered up her shoes, nodded to the guard, and went off to bed.

FOUR
▼

The striking, stark naked woman in her early thirties glared at herself in the mirror above the cheap combination dressing table-desk, swung round, examined her rear view over her shoulder, and gave her reflection the finger.

"Screw you, Yvonne!" she declared.

"Yvonne" was a nickname that had been pinned on Lee Boynton as a teenager by her Uncle Henry, who claimed her dark looks were identical to those of Yvonne De Carlo, a sultry B-movie actress of the 1940s and 1950s. "Lee" was short for Leonore, as in Leonore Marie Carew Boynton; Carew was short for Carew Steel, Carew Chemical, First Monongahela Bank and Trust and other enterprises founded by Lee's great-grandfather.

She was standing, slightly hung over, in a motel room two hours northeast of the Golden Gate Bridge. The clock radio on the bedstand read 9:13 A.M. Farther north, another two hours up the coast, Clarence Greaves was puzzling over the fact that $11,000 had passed through the account of "d/b/a Thunderbolt" the previous day and cursing his failure to have flagged it. Five thousand miles and four time zones to the east, Don Escobedo's jet was bound for São Paulo to deliver Mona Kurchinski to the overnight Air France flight for Paris.

Lee blew her breath out in a sharp whoosh of disgust, stepped back, turned sideways, then full face, cupped her breasts, patted her bush, twisted her neck this way and that and, in the manner of the swimsuit model she once had briefly been (as a lark), arranged and rearranged herself in a series of expressions and poses and liked none of them.

Her disappointment would have puzzled most onlookers. Indeed, she seemed if anything overendowed with the right stuff.

The truth was, Lee Boynton was a knockout. Her looks were unforgettable: full down-curved lips, cheekbones to dance on, splendid eyebrows framing dazzling, seductive eyes of a surprising dark gray under thick, dark hair, worn "big" for her current assignment although normally suppressed by her man at Elizabeth Arden into a tight, disciplined pageboy, which she thought took some of the drama out of her features. Her figure was no less dramatic, and she customarily wore loose, curve-concealing outfits which she disparaged as "Armani by the yard."

Lee might curse what her looking glass showed her, but most men found the view breathtaking. Even more so when they discovered that along with the face and figure went a 160 IQ, a healthy appetite for sex, and the income ($2.4 million in the most recent tax year) on $43 million in trust funds administered by First Monongahela.

Lee's objection to her looks was that they called attention to her just when she wanted to fade into the background. As a journalist, she would have preferred something more discreet, mousier, less Brenda Starr.

More "our sort," to use the phrase with which her mother, whom Lee genially despised, triaged all living beings. That she resembled an Italian hooker was, as Uncle Henry said, God's joke on Lee's mother, and there was some consolation in that.

Lady Shackelton, as Lee's mother now was called (in her fourth marital incarnation), would definitely have preferred God to have given her daughter a less—well—*Mediterranean* appearance. Straight, ash blond hair, say, instead of a glinting ebony mane; 32B "bosoms" instead of 36C breasts; a ladylike silky pale tuft at the crotch instead of a great blooming black sporranlike thatch. The sort of looks that went with cashmere twinsets, circle pins, and Grandmama's second-best pearls. Farmington looks, Sewickley looks, Junior League looks,

Newport looks. Looks that drew marriage proposals from blond young men with Roman numerals after their names, usually nicknamed "Chip."

If Lee's mother was put off by her daughter's appearance, she at least withheld comment, which was not the case when it came to what Lee did with her life and with her portion of the Carew fortune. Like the dynasty's progenitor, Lee was an entrepreneur, although the venture of which she was coproprietor was one that great-grandfather Carew would have cursed from beyond the grave with a vehemence equal to that expressed by Lee's mother from the head of her great Newport dining table.

For the past nine years, she had been copublisher, coeditor, and sole angel of *Capitol Steps,* a Washington political monthly whose capacity to irritate the rich and powerful was as notable as its financial condition was desperate. It was cordially feared and disliked on the Hill, on Wall Street, in the offices of the big New York and Beltway law, lobbying, and public relations firms, by the suck-up, talk show media, and by everyone in her mother's set. Anyone whose hatred was worth earning hated *Steps.* It was said that in some federal bureaucracies, merely to be seen carrying a copy of *Steps* was grounds for demotion.

Lee found the carrying cost of such distinction was manageable. The magazine lost roughly a quarter-million dollars a year, or approximately 10 percent of the annual income from Lee's trusts.

Steps had been founded in 1982 by Barney Cagel, a fugitive from *Newsweek,* as an antidote to the Reagan administration. That was the year Lee decided to do something with her Bryn Mawr degree, quit modeling, moved to Washington, and got Uncle Henry to fix her up with a staff job on Capitol Hill.

Within six months, she was thoroughly disillusioned with the legislative end of popular democracy, including the pawing to which she was subjected by her congressman. By then, however, she was involved with Barney and with *Steps.* Barney was twenty years older than Lee, and had what initially seemed to her an El Greco quality, although later she would conclude that his ascetic looks were more the result of cigarettes and alcohol than saintliness.

Her affair with the magazine outlasted her affair with its founder. The latter entanglement hadn't ever been for real, she would later realize; the two of them had fallen in love not with each other, but with the notion that two so entirely different people might fall in love, a notion that could only throw off erotic energy for so long. Eventually emotional entropy took over, Barney went back to his old girlfriend, Claire, and married her not long afterward.

But Lee stayed faithful to *Steps*. With her backing, the magazine had gone from strength to strength, at least as she and Barney measured such things. The point of investigative journalism, he liked to say, was to produce indictments as well as stories. So far, *Steps* had inspired two winning antitrust and five SEC prosecutions, precipitated three *Forbes* 400 indictments, and ruined the public careers of one Supreme Court justice, two congressmen, seven Cabinet officers above the level of assistant secretary, and a round dozen CEOs of large corporations. Lee's only real disappointment so far was that she and Barney had as yet failed to bring about the impeachment of a President. Well, there was still plenty of time left for that.

She decided there was nothing she could do about her looks, turned away from the mirror, and began to dress.

The question before her was: Should she stick around? Investigatively, this trip was a bust so far. The President was due to speak in two days, and Lee still hadn't located a patsy, a fat cat ready to tell all in return for the prospect of copping a quick feel or maybe more.

The last time she'd done something like this, she'd come home a winner. That had been when she penetrated bungalow eight at the Beverly Hills Hotel, the playpen reserved for the biggest hitters at the Drexel Burnham-Milken Predators' Ball. She'd been after a particular junk bond artist and she'd nailed him. The guy had been given two years in Allentown after *Steps* brought his crooked world crashing down; Lee hoped that he had used the time well, perhaps in contemplation of the abiding truth of Barney's dictum that the key to a man's mouth is his pecker.

Getting into bungalow eight had been a snap. The guard at the door obviously figured there was no way an SEC or journalistic sting was going to spring for seventy-one inches of Armani at $200 the linear inch, and Lee had waltzed right by him.

Out here, doubtless because of the impending Presidential visit, things were different. The happy campers were staying behind the wire, not thronging the Russian River motels and beaches in search of poontang. The state police were checking registrations at lodging places within a fifteen-mile radius of the Grove. The locals complained that the encampment had never been this sealed up, or business this bad.

The President's appearance was being given the same top-secret treatment as Nixon's first trip to China. Official White House schedules stated that the President would be at Camp David this coming Friday night, but Barney's source said that was a cover-up: The man was coming west to try to sell to the powerful men gathered in the lakeside amphitheater a new economic program, based on a return to noblesse oblige and sacrifice at the top, and the subjugation of private personal advantage to common public good. Few at the Grove knew he was coming. His appearance was to be a complete surprise.

If it was true, it was a major story in about a dozen ways. No President had ever attended the famed Bohemian Club encampment while in office. He must have something huge on his mind—and some specific, dollars-and-cents proposals. According to Barney's source, the Presidential appearance had been brokered by the Vice President, who was tight with the Grove crowd.

She finished painting her lips, examined the result, and shook her head in disgust.

Christ! She looked like goddamn Joan Crawford in *Mildred Pierce*!

No! She looked like goddamn Faye Dunaway in *Mommie Dearest* looking like goddamn Joan Crawford in *Mildred Pierce*!

Well, it couldn't be helped. You played the hand you were dealt.

She threw down the lipstick and clicked on the television for a reflexive CNN check. Against stock footage of a busy securities trading floor, the announcer was saying something about "panic" in the foreign exchange markets. She sounded excited.

Lee watched for fifteen minutes. What had happened was that a consortium of central banks had set and sprung a trap on the arrogant bastards at the currency desks of the banks and investment houses. The French franc, which in recent days had been under severe pressure, both from sellers and speechifiers self-servingly pronouncing it "overvalued," had suddenly taken off, pushed from 5.20 to the dollar to 4.90 by a combination of circumstances engineered by the central banks.

This was a cataclysmic move. The announcer spoke of billions being lost, of major Wall Street and London names being driven to the brink of insolvency. At a press conference, the Chairman of the Federal Reserve had spoken of "restoring order and long-term credibility" to the foreign exchange markets. Apparently the Fed and the rest were prepared to step in, as they had in the 1987 panic, but this time only on the strength of assurances—backed up with hard collateral—that the foreign exchange crowd's rapacious speculative mania would be brought to a once and forever halt.

Score one for the good guys, Lee thought. She clicked off the television, set the fax-modem on her laptop to standby, and went outside. It was another blazing, bluebird morning. She climbed into her rented Tempo and drove west toward Route 101, where she had located a truckstop that served a proper breakfast: no Pachelbel on the Muzak and flavored decaffeinated coffee, no tasteless sixteen-grain muffins the size of Lee's head.

She ordered juice, eggs, bacon, coffee, the works: Big girls need their vittles. She ran through the front page of *The Wall Street Journal* and found nothing to get excited about. She raced through the *San Francisco Chronicle*, checking the sports section, Herb Caen's column, the comic strips. Then *USA Today,* the Oakland *Tribune,* and a local broadsheet. Her craving for ink still raged like a fever. She looked around. *The New York Times* wasn't in yet, the *San Jose Mercury* and *Sacramento Bee* were sold out. A folded paper lay on the counter a couple of stools down. Lee went over and got it.

It was a Mendocino County biweekly, published in Petrolia, wherever that was, dated the previous Friday. A cookie cutter regional giveaway mostly devoted to real estate and the environment. At the bottom right, a subhead caught Lee's eye: BORDRERO BAY "SODOMIZED" BY '80s, SAYS MAYOR IN SPEECH.

The word choice intrigued Lee. She read the story, a report of a speech given by Bordrero Bay's mayor, a woman interestingly named Constancia Browning-Lopez, to the Petrolia Lions Club. What the mayor had to say was old hat to anyone who hadn't slept right through the 1980s. Another one-horse, one-industry (timber in Bordrero Bay's case) town blown to financial bits by the big-city leveraged-buyout crowd.

But *sodomized*? That isn't quite the right word, Lee thought. *Date rape* would be more like it.

She paid up and left the diner. It was searing outside, hard to breathe, as bad as Washington. It would be nicer over on the coast, she thought.

In the glove compartment was a guide to the state. Just out of curiosity, she looked up Bordrero Bay.

It was about halfway up the Mendocino coastline. There was a picture of the town. It didn't look like California; more like New England. In this desert, it seemed awfully inviting.

Back at the motel, her message light was blinking.

It was Barney.

"Bad news, honey," he said when she got him, "but Numero Uno's given the Grove the leg."

"The foreign exchange blowout, right?"

"Nobody's saying, but that's my guess. The shit seems really to have hit the fan. Apparently the Masters of the Universe are lining up hat in hand from the Bowery to the Ginza looking for handouts. You have to figure this isn't the sort of initiative that plays well with the Grove crowd, so Number Two's being dispatched to the sequoias to make nice with the fat cats. Pack up and come on home."

Lee hesitated. She wasn't sure she wanted to head back to Washington. By late July, the nation's capital was a furnace. Anyone sane got out of town by Friday noon, but the only weekend invitation she had was from a guy she'd feel morally obligated to sleep with if she went out to his place at Rehoboth Beach. It was either that, or sit in the air-conditioning, or invite herself to Newport.

Or stay here, and see what happened.

That didn't appeal to her either. The VP was coming west to kiss ass, which meant he wouldn't really have anything to offer, and the only other notable on the bill was Kissinger, and who needed that?

"What's it like in Parnassus on the Potomac?" she asked.

"About a hundred forty in the shade. Humidity to match."

"I may just hang out here, then. Drive over to the coast, check out the vast Pacific. One way or t'other, I'll see you Monday."

What about Bordrero Bay, she thought? It wasn't just the promise of a weekend at the seaside, but a hunch, a sense there might be something worth looking at or into. She booted up her computer, logged onto a financial data base, and went to work. Forty minutes later, she had confirmed her expectation that this particular case of

1980s financial "sodomization" was fairly standard. What she'd forgotten was that Credit Provençal had been a big player in GoldWest, which intrigued her; the French bank was turning up in the goddamnedest places these days.

You're looking for an excuse to go there, she told herself, so go there! Anything had to better than Washington, or grunting and groaning in sweaty sheets at Rehoboth.

Besides, she might learn something. Like most journalists, she had written her share of deplorations of the "excesses of the 1980s," but—like most journalists—she'd done so sitting on her butt in an air-conditioned office. She'd never actually gone out into the field to see what one of these busts did to a real place and real people, to see what the numbers looked like when they had human faces.

A couple of minutes later, she was on the line with Mayor Constancia Browning-Lopez, who not only sounded like a cool sort of lady, but was actually a subscriber to *Steps*.

"Who's running the show up there for Uncle Sam?" Lee asked.

"The occupying power's a guy named Clarence Greaves."

"Nice guy? You think he might be helpful if I decided to write something?"

"Clarence? I would think so. He's basically a decent man. A disenchanted person of color, but very capable. A little bit of a fuss budget, as you might expect, a stickler for regulations, but on the whole, Clarence and I get along just fine."

"Is there a place I can stay?"

"The Cephalod Inn."

"Do you think I can get a room through the weekend?"

"You can. As it happens, I own the inn."

"I'll drive up this afternoon," Lee said.

"Perfect. Come to my house for dinner. Say six-thirty. I'm about a ten-minute walk from the inn. They'll tell you at the desk how to get here."

So away we go, thought Lee, hanging up. She had no idea where all of this might take her, but she would do what her Uncle Henry always advised: She would let the logic of the situation dictate her next move.

FIVE

▼

hen his beeper went off,
Peter Kim was taking a
leak in the bathroom
down the hall.

Well, well, he thought, what now?

He zipped up, washed and dried his hands, and went back to his office, identified on the outer door by a cheap-looking plaque that read DSC/DATA SECURITY CONSULTANTS, INC.

He deactivated the alarm and opened the locks, one electronic, operated by a keypad, the other a two-key manual deadbolt. There was nothing unusual about this: These were precautions normal for a small business in a largely-unrented building in a nondescript office park. An armor expert would have noted that the door was flush-hinged from the inside; a knowing tap or two on its drab surface might have told him that it would take a small missile to break in.

It was Kim's one strictly aboveboard client—a unit of the United States government—that had insisted on this excess of precaution. Kim himself harbored no apprehensions that his premises might be attacked by rocket-bearing visitors, hostile or larcenous. Apart from the occasional FedEx or CourierQuick delivery, he expected no visitors. Peter Kim was a prudent, organized man who took pains in everything he did, but to his mind JEDI System Security's insistence on armoring his small office like a battleship was excessive, foolish, and typical.

From all outward appearances, there was nothing to distinguish

DSC from perhaps a thousand service businesses like it operating within a one-mile radius of Kim's office: one-room firms with high-falutin' high-tech names and marginally high-tech capabilities, and, to judge also by appearances, marginal profits. Like mushrooms after rain, they had sprouted south of San Francisco just north of Silicon Valley, where the big—and real—high-tech action was.

Kim's little business was an exception, however, in that it booked an annual turnover of $5 million in consulting fees and, having only one human employee, was highly profitable. This too would have been difficult to ascertain; in the interests of confidentiality, DSC invoiced from several post office boxes in five Bay Area zip codes, and took in payments via wire transfer at thirty-nine bank accounts maintained under different names in the San Francisco suburbs. Kim had set up these arrangements himself just in case Dun & Bradstreet or some other such outfit ran a credit check. In his mind, this too was unlikely: DSC neither borrowed money, sought vendor credit, nor accepted new consulting engagements apart from the four it had: one with JEDI System Security and three with different entities under the control of a private individual.

He hung his suit jacket on the back of the door, using a stout, highly polished mahogany hanger, which bore a small, oval enamel plaque inscribed with the name of a swank London tailor. It was an article of personal furniture typical of the British, Kim thought: too much for what it was and what it did. Kim had come across it while "sweeping" a Tahoe hotel room where the Client had, with his typical carelessness, left it.

That had been one of the few occasions Kim had dealt with the Client face-to-face. Most of their communications were by telephone or voice mail, conducted through an elaborate network of call forwarding cutouts, which roughly replicated DSC's data transmission facility. Even to himself, Kim thought of the Client as just that: never by name (which he knew as well as his own and which he had recorded in the "insurance policy" he maintained against the contingency that some unforeseen problem, or conflict of interest, or oversight on his or the Client's part, might somehow come violently home to roost). Kim had, so to speak, "taken out" the policy once it seemed clear, on the basis of the terms and objectives of his consulting arrangement, just what sort of business the Client—or (as seemed more likely) the people the Client represented—was in.

He went behind his desk and turned his chair around to face the computer array set up on a console against the wall: three DEC 486 processors with Radius monitors linked in series to a quartet of 486 "clone" CPUs. The system gave Kim roughly the computing power and speed of a small mainframe. To one side sat a specially modified Mac; it was connected via a black box of Kim's own design and manufacture into the main computer complex. On a nearby table was a high-definition Sony television with integrated VCR. It was not part of Kim's professional setup. He watched Japanese pornographic videos on it, along with Tae Kwan Do tapes he rented at a video place in San Francisco's Little Korea. In what had been the office's coat closet was a multiline telephone board with conventional and cellular capacity, and three levels of scrambling capability.

During his brief absence in the men's room, the left hand of the three monitors had become active. It had been some time since an alarm had gone off, and Kim studied the screen intently.

It was nice to have a change of pace, he thought, a little action. Day in, day out, he kept an eye on JEDI for information and now and then for entertainment. Last week, for instance, he'd watched the Federal Reserve lay and spring a $14-billion trap on foreign exchange speculators around the world. It had been more fun than "Jeopardy."

If you knew how to tune JEDI properly, the system was the greatest computer game ever invented. JEDI had been set up to enable a number of federal agencies to access, process, and integrate data in a way that exponentially enhanced their ability to pinpoint and prosecute high-dollar criminal activity. From his desk, Kim could track the various DEA "stings" that were under way at any given time. The names under which field agents in the United States and a score of foreign countries were operating. The status and value of property held by various agencies for sale or disposal. The rates of mortgage redemption at Fannie Mae and Freddie Mac, information that was worth literally hundreds of millions to bond traders. He could browse the secret files of a hundred federal, state, and local agencies, as well as private data bases containing information on tens of millions of individuals. He could monitor CHIPS, the electronic highway along which the bulk of the world's money traveled at the rate of a trillion dollars a day, since JEDI had been made privy to the confidential encryptions that identified each transfer.

With JEDI, a knowledgeable user could ascertain meaningful patterns in a seemingly random universe of transactions and relationships. The system could cull, correlate, arrange, rearrange, and sort to the nth power; if you knew how to ask, it would even draw conclusions and make deductions. There was no haystack large enough to hide a needle from JEDI, no needle too small for JEDI to find. As the Client said, JEDI sure as hell beat steaming envelopes open.

So what envelope had caused his beeper to go off? Kim studied the monitor. JEDI's "banking module" was being queried about an account at the Bordrero Bay Bank, one of a series of accounts that the Client had engaged Kim to keep a watch over, and which he had accordingly flagged electronically.

The querist was obviously someone who knew what he was after but wasn't quite sure how to find it: someone who had a rough idea of what JEDI could deliver but—to judge from the alphanumeric confusion on the monitor—who had little or no experience in actually using the powerful data interface. The Bordrero Bay Bank was a unit of the collapsed GoldWest system —a principal focus of the Client's concern. As a matter of course, data on all financial institutions either in federal hands or under federal surveillance was inputted into JEDI's banking module down to the last paper clip. An eye that knew what it was looking for and how to find it on JEDI would massage the banking module for suspicious transactional and account patterns and timing relationships that might suggest fraud, money laundering, or other fun and games.

But this querist was probing an account that was strictly tertiary or lower in Kim's surveillance hierarchy, a negligible tributary of the main flow, a trickle in a torrent—although it was an account which Kim personally serviced, or so he guessed.

Puzzled, he slid his chair over to the Mac and tapped out a series of commands. The Mac was Kim's magic cloak, his cybernetic philter; it made him invisible to JEDI System Security, let him transform himself digitally, now into a deep-swimming fish, now a hawk stooping from on high, now a vapor, now a monolith. Wholly invisible or partly visible—as he chose.

Within seconds, the screen informed him that the querist had logged on to JEDI using a pass code assigned to the office of the Deputy Attorney General for Civil Rights.

Kim frowned. This made no sense! Why would the Justice Department's civil rights arm be looking at accounts in an obscure California bank?

If it had been the Fed, FDIC, Treasury, the Office of the Comptroller of the Currency, or even the DEA and FBI, Kim wouldn't have got the wind up. These agencies practically lived in the banking module.

But this made no sense.

And what made no sense was, at least to the logically ordered, hospital-corners world of Peter Kim, potentially big trouble.

A few seconds later, his uneasiness had deepened. A second set of instructions to the Mac produced the information that the querist was accessing JEDI from a telephone number in the 707 area code, a number directory-listed for Bordrero Bay Bank.

What the hell was going on?

Kim swiveled and picked up the phone on his desk. He activated protocols that would ensure that any trace of the call he was about to make would run into a wall, then dialed the 707 number.

It rang twice, then a voice, high pitched with impatience at being interrupted, said "Agent Greaves."

"Is Mr. Johnson there?" Kim asked quickly in a flat tone.

Told he was not, Kim apologized for calling a wrong number, and hung up.

Returning to his computers, he initiated a search of JEDI's personnel module. It took a few seconds longer than usual—JEDI had to make a phonetic match for the spelling of *Greaves* before riffling through the electronic equivalent of several million file cards—but Kim soon had his answer. The color monitor displayed the image of a stocky Afro-American man apparently in his late fifties or early sixties, and identified him as Clarence Frank Greaves, a field agent with the Resolution Trust Corporation, with a Civil Service rating of GS-10.

GS-10 was three levels below JEDI Level Four access parameters. And Greaves had nothing to do with the Justice Department and never had, according to his civil service record.

So what was going on?

The personnel module carried family data out to four degrees of connection, to third cousins. A few more keystrokes yielded the information that Greaves had a niece working in the Justice Department. Kim pulled up her file. A pleasant-looking woman of about thirty, she was employed as an executive administrative assistant in the office of the Deputy Attorney General for Civil Rights.

Obviously she had "borrowed" her boss's pass code and loaned it to her uncle.

For an instant, Kim indulged himself in second-guessing. When JEDI was first set up, he had argued strenuously that access ought to be tightly controlled and compartmentalized, apportioned strictly according to legitimate, functional, need-to-know criteria. What the hell need did the Department of Agriculture have for access to a data base whose principal orientation was law enforcement?

But JEDI was hotter than a grandstand seat at Cape Kennedy, and Washington was at bottom about turf and boasting rights. The bureaucratic mentality had carried the day; access to JEDI was made available to any and all agencies at the deputy director level or higher.

Kim put these thoughts aside and concentrated on his options. As he pondered what to do next, the computer beeped. The querist was switching module sectors. A list of CUSIP numbers appeared onscreen. Every piece of negotiable paper issued in U.S. markets carried a CUSIP (Committee on Uniform Securities Identification Procedures) number: every bond, share of stock, savings certificate, certificate of deposit, or commercial promissory note. A CUSIP denotation was the equivalent of a license plate.

As Kim watched, Greaves flailed around aimlessly in CUSIPland for a minute, failed to locate what he was looking for, and returned to the banking sector of the JEDI finance module. He was homed in on four accounts designated "d/b/a Thunderbolt" in Bordrero Bay and three other GoldWest banks in Sonoma and Humboldt counties. These were accounts on Kim's flag list, although he'd never paid much attention to them. They'd been recently added by the Client, almost as an afterthought; in Kim's opinion, they had to do with the Client's personal business. It seemed to him to be mixing apples with oranges, but he wasn't making the decisions.

Now Kim took a closer look. He studied the data Greaves was looking at, did a little quick calculating, and whistled softly. The most recent deposits in the four accounts added up to exactly the amount of Kim's last cash transfer to Courier Services.

Very interesting, Kim thought. Thanks to this Greaves, Kim's stock of knowledge of the Client's operations was usefully larger.

What this new information might mean was something he'd have to consider at length. It would necessitate a modification of one or two items in his "insurance policy." The money exited those accounts as quickly as it went in, Kim could see, wired to several East Coast banks but surely headed offshore. Offshore was where JEDI hit the wall.

Well, he thought, what action should be taken?

He could zap the guy: a dozen keystrokes would send a virus barreling back up the line to crash Greaves's hard disk, take out his system, and obliterate his data beyond the capability of any recovery system yet invented. But this presented problems. At the simplest level, Greaves could always go back into JEDI—he knew what he was looking for, after all—so all that would be gained was a little time Kim wasn't certain he could use to any real purpose. If Greaves read the zap as a glitch in JEDI, which he might, suppose he reported it? If JEDI tech support got in the act and started probing, Kim might have to rejigger his whole setup. On the other hand, it was unlikely Greaves, who was inside JEDI with false papers, as it were, would call attention to himself.

Kim could of course fool with JEDI itself and delete the information Greaves was playing with, but this raised more problems than it solved. Kim was familiar with the architecture of JEDI System Security, which protected the system against unlicensed incursions, but he wasn't sure he was properly up to speed on the protocols protecting the integrity of the data base itself. A misstep might trigger an alarm.

No, he thought, at this point the logic of the situation—that favorite phrase of the Client's—dictates that I do nothing.

And "nothing" included not telling the Client, at least for the moment. The Client was too excitable.

Just to be safe, however, Kim flagged the access code Greaves was using for future surveillance and then went back through the intramodular user log to see if the 707 number had come on the system at any earlier time. It hadn't.

Well, if this was the guy's first shot at JEDI, he had a long way to go. Kim relaxed and turned his thoughts to other business. It didn't occur to him that it might have made sense, just to be on the extra safe side, to check whether any other 707 numbers had logged on to JEDI over the same period. Had he done so, he would have found six other connects, all from a 707 number listed for a Days Inn not far from Bordrero Bay.

JEDI was one hell of a system, Kim thought. It just kept getting better. Like a virtuoso noddling at his Steinway, he loved just to play around in it.

By now, it was at the Mark XII Stage. Kim's intimate involvement had ended between the Mark VII and Mark VIII stages, although he remained a $2,000-an-hour consultant to the system, which was what made the federal government DSC's second-largest paying client.

Kim's specialty was the development and refinement of defensive protocols. After graduating from Cal State-Fullerton, he had done a stint in Vietnam and then been assigned to one of the Tiger Teams assembled in the 1970s by the Defense Department to test Pentagon system security. The teams' mission was to break into the Defense Department's computers.

Twenty years later, he was still doing that. Kim had come to JEDI from the New York Stock Exchange, where he helped refine the exchange's Stockwatch countermeasures against insider and manipulative trading. It was at the NYSE that he'd first met the Client, who was then at the SEC. It was on the recommendation of the Client's boss that Kim had come to Washington when JEDI was finally given the Congressional go-ahead and was funded.

Kim's JEDI consulting contract called for him to continue to work with System Security on refining the protocols in place and on developing new, more secure ones. In another year, existing access safeguards—still tied up in pass codes and digital screening—would be replaced with real-time voice-recognition technology. Until then, the fences and moats around JEDI would remain alphanumeric. Which meant the system remained vulnerable to the one-in-a-million shot, the kid with a closeout 64K Atari and enough change for the pay phone.

The consulting agreement also obligated Kim to attempt to hack his way into JEDI at irregular unannounced intervals, probing here, bashing there, checking the system for water tightness, making sure it was burglar proof. It was an exhilarating business, like playing chess against oneself. Of course, as any computer freak worth his obsession knew, no computer had ever beaten a chess grand master head-to-head. For a state-of-the-art computer to do what the human brain could do would require a machine the size of Alaska.

For a private consultant to have this kind of access to a top-secret federal program was unusual, but so was JEDI. Unlike every other federal computer installation, JEDI security wasn't assigned to the Secret Service arm of the Treasury. The JEDI security managers considered themselves an elite set apart by the impregnability of the system. If Peter Kim couldn't break in, who could? His exorbitant hourly rate was worth it for the comfort factor alone. It was essential that JEDI remain inviolate and unviolatable. To enjoy unlimited access to JEDI was to control a universe of possibility for malefaction on a galactic scale.

Inviolate, inviolable, impregnable. That was what Kim chose to let them believe. The fact was, he had turned JEDI inside out.

His mind returned to Greaves. Something about this whole business profoundly irritated Kim. Something about Greaves.

Perhaps because he was black.

Kim didn't like blacks. Blacks and Koreans were natural enemies, with a hostility born of mutual resentment. Koreans were regarded as "the niggers of Asia."

Blacks had trashed five South Central Los Angeles liquor stores in which Kim had a $50,000 investment, a minichain purchased by a cousin who fronted for a loan from the Dung Yo Emigrant Development Bank, a new outfit in Seoul set up to help Koreans acquire and establish U.S. businesses. Kim's investment was kaput, unless the American government made him whole.

Just thinking about that money boiled Kim's blood. He got up and went to the office's single window. In the distance, a fat airliner lumbered clumsily aloft from SFO International. A dirty haze hung over the bay. On the window ledge was a small stack of foot-long sections of two-by-four lath. Kim stood one on its end, keeping it upright with the flat of his left hand; he breathed in and out levelly, settling into an attitude of total repose, which he maintained for just an instant, body and mind in utter harmony, still and integral as the Koryo vase he often went to the San Francisco museum to admire. Then, in a sudden violent flash of motion, he crashed his right hand into the beam and split it.

He took a series of deep, ventilating breaths until he was himself again, and only a certain wildness in his eyes betrayed the residue of his inner fury. He shot his cuffs; the ornate cuff links, embossed with the Presidential seal, made him think of the Client.

When should he be told about Greaves?

Kim fervently believed that the earlier one started to think about a problem, the better were one's chances of keeping it from getting out of hand. But was this really a *problem*? There were any number of reasons this Greaves might be looking at these accounts, Kim thought. They were cash accounts with a high rate of turnover, pit stops for obviously impatient money. The sort of thing a low-ranking, field-grade GS with a taste for chicken feed would get excited about, waste a fair amount of time and government computing power on, and then give up. The only real question was why would the man go to the trouble of borrowing a pass code; if he got caught, both he and his niece would be in big trouble.

Actually, it wasn't the Client about whom Kim was concerned, but the people the Client was working for, the ultimate recipients and users of the JEDI briefings Kim sent winging off into cyberspace at the end of each day. Where those people might pillow their heads he was loath to speculate, although if someone had handed him an atlas and asked him to guess, he would have pointed to the Andes.

Such people, Kim had heard, tended, like the Client, to over-react—but in a more sweeping, exacting manner. Kim's client was basically a nonviolent type. *His* clients were not. Kim had no intention of risking their exactions; indeed, his "insurance policy" was designed to forestall just such a contingency.

He tapped the window glass, thinking—and then decided to wait for more conclusive evidence that this Greaves really was a problem.

He turned away. The impeccable geometry of his office pleased him—and reminded him that he had housekeeping to take care of.

From a stack of checkbooks on a shelf behind the desk, under a bookshelf containing technical manuals along with *Cyberpunk, The Cuckoo's Egg* and several of William Gibson's novels, Kim selected seven. He removed blank checks from each and made these out for amounts between $1,200 and $3,200, all to "cash." He arranged them in a neat stack in the order in which he intended to cash them.

Every other business day, according to a seemingly random schedule, which the computer had worked out for him, Kim would visit between seven and ten of DSC's banks of account and make cash withdrawals totaling between $10,000 and $15,000. Then, every other Thursday, he would place the cash in a Courier Services bag, seal it, and drive it over to the Courier Services clearing facility in the cargo area at SFO International.

Courier Services would take it from there. The money would presumably end up in accounts such as those which Greaves had pinpointed, presumably as part of a larger transfer operation. A jalopy slipstreaming a formula one racing car.

Kim reckoned he was tangentially involved with very big money movements, although the sums he handled were small. Now and then he found himself thinking he was probably grossly underpaid relative to the profits his surveillance of JEDI could be generating. Well, if he ever decided he was, he judged himself to be in a solid negotiating position for a readjustment: based on his insurance policy, which consisted of a written, oral, and digital memorialization of what he knew.

This was the day's final order of business before he set off on his round of the banks. He copied the previous day's JEDI gleanings onto a fresh floppy disk, attached a Post-it to it, and made a few notes in small precise writing. From his desk drawer, he took out an audio microcassette and added it to the disk. Then he took a small padded mailing envelope, prestamped and preaddressed, placed the disk and cassette in the envelope, and double sealed it with strong mailing tape.

He put on his jacket and went down the hall to the mail chute. As he listened to the envelope skitter on its way, he reflected that this must be what Alexis de Tocqueville, a writer of whom Kim was deeply fond, meant when he spoke of "self-interest properly understood."

SIX

▼

Lee took her time getting to Bordrero Bay. Shunning the fast route via the interstate, she swung diagonally northwest toward the Pacific and picked up the winding coastal highway near Albion. Gradually the atmosphere changed: The sky took on that singular spacious quality suggesting big water. The air and light sharpened—the shimmering Monet landscapes of the heat-stricken interior gave way to crisply defined vistas that reminded her of Rhode Island.

She reached Bordrero Bay just after four-thirty. The town looked just like the pictures in her guidebook. Set on low-lying land on the edge of the estuary where river met ocean, it reminded her of Martha's Vineyard. The bay proper was shaped like an inverted hook; running north from the town, the coastline rose sharply, ending in a swing of high bluffs that defined the bend of the hook. The Cephalod Inn was set in the middle of these, in a low fold of land fringed with wind-battered sea pines.

Lee was given a room that looked back down the shank of the bay, a half-mile stretch of dun beach between the town and the Point Clara headland. It was a bright afternoon; scattered tiny figures picked their way along the ocean's edge. In the farther distance, beyond the town and the river, the land rose rapidly; she could just make out a hazy blur of thickly wooded foothills and beyond them the low mountains that sealed the coast off from the baking interior.

She unpacked quickly and left her room. A broad, rough-mown lawn flowed down to the edge of the cliffs; a GUESTS ONLY staircase zigzagged down the gray face of the escarpment.

It took her about fifteen minutes to walk to town. Halfway along, she passed beneath three identical, wide-verandahed frame houses perched grand as dowagers on the crest of the bluff, seeming to stare down their noses at passersby. The middle one—robin's egg blue with pale yellow trim—would be the mayor's.

She strolled up Bay Street to the ochre brick Victorian mansion that housed the Bordrero Bank. Two bronze plaques were affixed to the pilasters flanking the main door: one dated the building (1886) and identified it as a protected landmark of the Bordrero Bay Historical District; the other named the bank and designated it as an affiliate of GoldWest Financial Group. Below this plaque, a cardboard placard taped to the brick advised that the bank was until further notice being operated under the supervision of various agencies of the United States government.

It was almost five o'clock when Lee returned to the inn. She took a brief nap, showered and made up, dressed for one expectation of the woman she was about to meet, rethought it and redressed, and finally set off for Mayor Constancia Browning-Lopez's house.

Evening was just settling in. In the slowly deepening light, the beach was now an umber slash bordering a sea rendered molten copper by the raging orange sun. The distant hills were already half-lost to darkness. As the sun sank, the lights of Bordrero Bay began to come on: first a series of long strings, like suspended necklaces, which marked the two town piers, then the lamps along Bay Street. Lee's New England ear picked out the familiar noises of a seaside town getting ready for a lucrative summer evening: the clank and click of a breeze in the rigging of moored pleasure craft; a hint of music from a restaurant deck; exuberant voices; the long exhalations of the tide; a foghorn out at sea.

The mayor was not what Lee expected.

Perhaps it was the "Lopez" that had misled her. She should have paid closer attention to the voice on the phone. Lee had pictured a squat, dark woman in early middle age, a sort of female Cesar Chávez with a state college degree. But the woman who greeted her was exactly what Lee wished to find in *her* mirror: blond, cool eyed, slim, small bosomed, perfectly turned out.

Constancia Browning-Lopez sensed Lee's surprise and smiled at her guest; her amused expression said, but my dear, surely two can play at Armani.

She led Lee into the drawing room. Wide windows took in the sweep of the bay and the lights of the town. It was decorated in good, heavy mission Spanish, with a few decent English pieces here and there. Over the fireplace hung a competent oil portrait of a woman who Lee judged from the resemblance to be the mayor's mother. On the tables were family photographs and ill-assorted souvenirs. A real place furnished by a real person out of a real life.

A man sitting on the sofa beneath the windows got up as the two women entered the room.

He had a drinker's face, with a florid nose and cheeks that were a pasty thicket of busted capillaries, the features puffed and roughened by decades of hard duty with the cocktail shaker. His thin sandy-gray hair was oddly yellow at the temples, as if it had been dipped in the same nicotine that stained his fingers. His pink Brooks Brothers shirt was frayed and rumpled; he was wearing what looked to be a club tie, hard used and spotted, and a madras jacket that must have dated from the 1950s. He was gripping his martini glass so tightly his knuckles were white.

Lee "made" the type at once. This man was what most of the men her mother had besought her to marry would turn into. In her life she must have seen a hundred like him, barking like seals for their gin at Bailey's Beach and Piping Rock and Mill Reef, citizens of an order of being at whose shores liquor lapped like the sea. A social order in which alcohol had passed from being an accessory to being an absolute value.

"Jimmy," said the mayor, "this is Lee Boynton. Lee—Jimmy Spalding, president of Bordrero Bank."

"But only for as long as the head nigger'll let me," said Spalding. He cast a sly smile at Lee. Its presumption of familiarity made her shudder inside.

The mayor took no notice.

"Jimmy has to leave tomorrow, and I thought before he does, he could give you a bit of background—"

"On my way to the Grove," Spalding interrupted proudly. "Heap big powwow Saturday. Might I have another of those delicious cocktails, your honor?"

Constancia poured expertly from a silver-topped crystal shaker beaded with frost. Spalding examined the replenished martini with great satisfaction. It was obviously not his second, so Lee skipped the pleasantries and asked him straight off about the bank's collapse.

"Actually," he said, "it was the Encino crowd that went poof! Without the paper they shoved our way, we'd be fine."

He sipped his drink.

"I vas chust taking orders," he added in a bumptious and bad mock-German accent. Why did gin seem to compel WASP men to do dialects? "The money came in and the money vent out. I chust did vat I vas told."

"It seems to have been a lot of money," Lee observed.

"Boxcars of the stuff, m'dear, simply boxcars!" Spalding changed into a bluff English clubman. "D'you know, when our dear Connie's cousin Lem stole me away from Charlie de Bretteville and the Bank of California, away from Montgomery Street and all that, as they say, we had some ninety million dollars in assets. If we did a loan a month it was a big thing. This was a company town, m'dear. Everything belonged to Browning Paper. Then we got sold to GoldWest, who were a very go-ahead, sky's-the-limit bunch. When the head nigger showed up two weeks ago and closed us down, we were at four hundred million dollars and we'd been as high as six hundred! Of course, it wasn't just GoldWest. When they took down the border fences and the greasers started flocking in—"

"These GoldWest deposits?" asked Lee hastily. "Were they mostly brokered?"

"Muchly, muchly, m'dear. Brokered to a fare-thee-well, y'-might say. The big cheese was an outfit in Chicago called Freemark Securities—now, if memory serves, of blessed memory."

Lee nodded; she knew of Freemark. The firm had briefly been a Wall Street comet. Its star had been one Leo Gorton, a cut-rate Milken who'd somehow managed to stay out of jail.

"Wasn't just Freemark, though," Spalding continued. "They were all on our doorstep. GoldWest's doorstep, actually. You name 'em, they were here! Merrill Lynch, Paine Webber, Shearson Lehman. They all had computers that could sniff out interest rates like a bloodhound. Offer an extra half-a-point on your six-month savings certificates and before you knew it, someone'd hit a button somewhere and twenty or thirty million'd come pouring in over the wire from Gestapo HQ. All in neat little hundred-thousand-dollar pieces.''

"And went out just as quickly, I gather?"

Spalding winked at Lee and gave her a thumbs-up.

"Bien sûr, ma cherie! Right the first time! Yours truly simply clicked heels and bowed from the waist, signed what I was told to sign, and Bob's your uncle! All done with faxes, computers, and that sort of thing. Hand quicker'n the eye! Not like the old days, I can tell you! Back then, you dealt with *people,* not some damn machine!"

"All on instructions from Encino?"

"Natürlich! Although from what I heard, it was Alphonse and Gaston who made the big calls.''

"Alphonse and Gaston?"

"Claude and Bruno, actually. Mutt 'n Jeff in berets, the men who would be king. One tall and weedy, th'other short, dark and surly, strictly *pied noir* to these tired eyes. Claude and Bruno are the straws that stir the drink at CP. Surely, you've heard of CP? Credit Provençal? The Banque Provençale de Credit et d'Investissement? When CP whistled, the lads and lasses down at Encino sat up sharp and proper, I can tell you!"

Spalding pronounced the bank's name with exaggerated care. Lee sensed that his decent French accent was one of the few remaining ties to a brave old world, to a better life than he had known since.

"Say this about the Frogs," Spalding went on, "they still do what they do better 'n anyone else in the goddamn world does it!"

"Are you speaking of creative finance, Jimmy," asked Constancia with a smile. "Or cooking?"

"The latter, m'dear, of course. The whole art of living. I've told you about Frogs and Wogs, Connie. Never forget it, by God, I won't!"

" 'Frogs and Wogs'?"

Spalding grinned complicitously at Lee. She tried not to flinch. "Well, there was this fellow Gorgon, hah, hah, hah, the head boy at Freemark—dreadful fellow, although I understand the Squash and Quoit in New York took him in, which just goes to show you that clubs damn sure aren't what they were. Anyway, he used to stage a big annual do for all his customers and rent boys, to which even mere parasites like yours truly were bidden. Always in a top-flight resort: Gstaad, Camelback, the last one I went to was down in Anguilla. Took over the whole damn island! Had all these little boats driven by rentacoons; take you anywhere you wanted to go any time you wanted. Rum punch by the fountainful. I never went to that thing of Drexel Burnham's, but I'm damned if I can imagine it had a patch on this! Money managers and money brokers from the far ends of the earth, all kids of sphinxlike types smelling of garlic, and *beaucoup* Arabs. Hence 'Frogs and Wogs,' you see. Get it?"

Lee got it, but Spalding, pleased with his joke, insisted on repeating it before plowing ahead.

"Well, m'dear, you can imagine the form. These *Schutzenfests* are all alike. Speeches by the world's high and mighty, Kissinger, Bob Novak, Her Grace the former British PM, and much huddling and whispering in dark corners. The humble likes of yours truly were strictly below the salt, far side of the velvet rope. Sent off to seminars to be lectured at by the peach-fuzz crowd about things we didn't understand and never will. A far cry from m'youth, when the only hard decisions you had to make were whether to buy more PG&E and whether to order the sand dabs or the Rex sole at the P. U. Club."

"So who was doing the huddling and whispering?"

"Alphonse and Gaston and assorted foreigners, with Gorgon flitting around the edges. There was definitely an A list and a B list. Circles within circles, as they say. When the Dragon Lady showed up, however, all bets were off and everyone groveled at her feet."

" 'Dragon Lady?' "

"M'dear, don't tell me you're too young to remember a comic strip called Terry and the Pirates. First thing we used to look for in the funny papers during the war. There was a character in it called the Dragon Lady. Dark, sultry, rather like you. Very imposing. So was this one. Tall, about forty-odd, I'd say. Her nose was the thing: a schnozz like Durante's but somehow she got away with it. *Très, très chic.* And tough as a boot, I wot. Reminded me a bit of that woman on 'L.A. Law' who fell down the elevator. Anyway, the aforesaid D.L. would always chopper in the next-to-last day, rather like Brunhild dropping in on Siegmund to tell him he's a goner. Strictly a state visit, d'you see, *beaucoup* kissing of hands, capes spread at her feet, Gorgon—heh, heh—tugging forelock for all he was worth and Alphonse and Gaston wriggling at her size eights like newly whelped puppies! Got another of those perfectly judged cocktails, your honor?"

"But you never met her?" asked Lee. "Did she have a name?"

"If she did, I'm damned if I can remember it. She did not pass among us mere mortals. Oh, thankee, Lady Constance, thankee."

Spalding was clearly approaching capacity. There was something else Lee was curious about.

"Go back to GoldWest for a minute. You say the deposit and loan processing was all automated? The big stuff, that is?"

"Right the first time! Oh, every now and then the phone'd ring and a disembodied voice'd say, 'my dear Jimmy, we're taking a little hundred-and-fifty-million-dollar piece of this deal of Drexel's. They're signing in San Francisco tomorrow so do be an angel and pop down there.' And down I'd go, put my John Hancock where indicated, and truckle along to the P.U., where you still find people who remember when there were white men in this business. But, yes, the money moved back and forth, in and out, untouched by human hands."

He looked at his watch, and took a deep final swallow of his drink. He got up unsteadily.

"Oops," he said, "duty calls."

He set the empty glass carefully on the table, as if it contained a grenade. With exaggerated courtesy, he kissed Constancia on both cheeks, then Lee.

"A pleasure, *mesdames,*" he said, bowing low. Slightly swaying, he made his way toward the front door.

"Poor old Jimmy," the mayor said when she returned. "He's what they call Nob Hill white trash. Now—as for a horse of a different color—I've set you up with Clarence Greaves for breakfast tomorrow. Is seven-forty-five too early?"

"That's fine. Tell me about Greaves. What's your impression of him?"

"He's a good guy. He goes by the book but he also understands the big picture, which most bureaucrats don't. When they took over

the bank, there could have been a panic. Instead, Clarence got people
to calm down, told them it would be business more or less as usual,
and so it seems. Jimmy's still there, at least for the time being, and
Marge, the head cashier, and the old tellers and Joe, the guard. People
who know the customers' names. You can still cash a check and make
a deposit, at least for the time being, and apply for a mortgage. No
more junk bonds, though."

Constancia refilled Lee's wineglass and gestured toward the
porch. "Shall we? We're rather proud of our sunsets out here. I'll
bring the bottle."

The world was a uniform blue-black; only a searing orange
stripe, thread thin, marked the horizon.

"You came across pretty angry in that newspaper article," Lee
remarked. *"Sodomized* is not a run of the mill word."

"Once upon a time," the mayor said quietly, "twenty percent of
the linerboard produced west of the Rockies was FOB Bordrero Bay.
This was a proud town with its roots in honest labor. Then, in the
1980s, Wall Street got hold of it, came in with their siren songs and
junk bonds, and now what is it? A phony Victorian tourist trap that
sells wicks 'n wax to gawkers who come here to watch whales fuck!
Something about that offends my sense of moral proportion!"

She refilled their glasses.

"When the mill finally closed, people around here were ready
to throw in the towel. Write off the town. At least at first. We
thought that without the paper mill we'd have to board the place
up. But people—and towns—are more resilient than we think. I
kid about the whale fucking, but it saved us in the beginning. A
bunch of us with roots here decided to hang tough. What was I
going to do, anyway? My husband had left me for a guy, and the
prospect of moving to San Francisco or New York and hand fighting a crowd of equally desperate women for the few straight men
was hardly inviting. So I bought the inn and got into local politics.
Some people from Santa Fe took over the Chartroom House. Little
by little, we turned the place into a first-class tourist trap. Between
encounter groups, whale watchers, and adulterers, we're making
out like bandits. Are we better off? I'm not sure. People who think
God is an economist at heart would probably say we are, but I just
don't know. Anyway, that's not the point, Lee."

"What is?"

"The fact that the sonsofbitches who bankrupted this town and a thousand others seem to have gotten away with it! That's not right! Maybe that's where you—the press—come in! Or are supposed to!"

After dinner and coffee, and the best part of a second bottle of wine, the women returned to the porch. The night was starless. Lee could feel a breath of inrolling fog on her face.

Constancia produced a carved Mexican box. Inside were three fat joints.

"Now and then I find this helps," she said.

They passed the joint back and forth, the world slowed down and grew agreeably cool, and they talked some more, two solitary people piecing together the intricate yet simple puzzle of new friendship. Lee felt at home. It was close to midnight when she finally returned to the inn.

She slept well and rose early. The news on the bathroom scale was not good. A couple of turns around the inn's exercise trail were definitely called for.

It was bright and clear near the inn, but as she jogged closer to the ocean, the air moistened and suddenly she found herself plowing through a dense, yellowish fog. She slowed to a brisk walk: forward visibility was limited to a few yards; the terrain was root strewn and untrustworthy. Off hidden in the fog, the sea beat loudly against the rocks; it sounded just a few feet away. Lee, thinking of the plunging cliff face, drew back and made her way cautiously, keeping well away from where she guessed the edge was.

It took her ten minutes to make her way back to daylight. She was soaked with sweat; it wasn't just the exertion. For a moment or two out there in the fog, she had been disoriented, frightened.

Fifteen minutes later, after a fast shower, she met Clarence Greaves in the lobby. Her first impression was that he was the blackest man she had ever seen. His skin had the purplish undercast she had noted in African tribesmen. He was built square: squat legged and short armed. With his high forehead, white hair, and thick, heavy-rimmed spectacles, he struck Lee as an unlikely combination of a college professor and a wrestler.

While they waited to be seated, they made small talk. Greaves's mind was elsewhere, Lee sensed. He seemed distracted, anxious to get back to business. She was right. Greaves was distracted. Distracted, puzzled, and frustrated.

JEDI was all of a sudden giving him fits. Until yesterday, he had experienced no difficulties, but now there appeared to be some kind of glitch in the data module; when he queried the file for information on federally-insured financial institutions having "lockbox" or other contracts with Courier Services, all he got back was alphanumeric garbage.

It was weird. With Brinks or any of the other financial transport companies there was no problem. Greaves had enough of a feel for computers to sense a certain artificiality about the module's response timings and patterns. It occurred to him that he might be facing a new kind of anti-incursion protocol. Rather than go through an elaborate investigative procedure, perhaps JEDI System Security had fenced off certain data sectors with make-work and phony glitches in the expectation that whoever was being a nuisance would give up and go away.

Or maybe he'd stumbled into some kind of a setup, a sting that JEDI had demarcated need-to-know for the players directly involved, a sting in which Courier Services was a piece. That would certainly argue for electronic detours and roadblocks with no explanations attached.

Then this morning, things got worse. He'd let himself into the bank at six-fifteen, to catch a quick half-hour on JEDI before meeting Lee, but he'd scarcely logged on before his hard drive crashed. It was as if the operating system had been hit by a virus. A virus nobody knew about, moreover, because the software program was protected by a Norton antivirus program.

Well, there was nothing he could do about it. The machine would have to be reformatted and reprogrammed. Fortunately Greaves had backed up what he had so far, both on his pocket organizer and on floppy disks; the data he'd assembled so far was safe on the hard disk of the laptop in his motel room.

The waiter came over. Greaves put whatever was bothering him to one side and called for three eggs over easy, two orders of bacon and one of sausage patties, a double order of English muffins, large orange juice, and extra cream for his coffee. Real coffee.

My kind of guy, thought Lee, and ordered the same, plus a couple of sides of roast-beef hash.

When the waiter went off, Greaves looked around the dining room.

"Very nice," he said. "Deductible as a business expense, I assume."

Lee said nothing.

"Definitely snazzier than the accommodations we servants of the public are given, but then again we're spending the taxpayers' money like it was going out of style."

"How much of our money do you expect to spend here in Bordrero Bay, Mr. Greaves? Just as a ballpark figure."

Greaves smiled. "Call me Clarence," he said. "As for a ballpark figure, well, insured depositors don't accept those. They want exact change, so I can tell you precisely."

From an inside pocket, he produced a handsome leather scabbard and unholstered a complicated-looking gadget. It was one of those electronic pocket "organizers" Lee had seen in Sharper Image catalogs and airline magazines. She'd often wondered who bought them; she'd never actually seen someone use one.

Greaves's stubby fingers keyed the device. It cheeped faintly, like a baby robin.

"Best darn thing I ever owned," Greaves said. "It's like having a computer in your shirt pocket."

He peered through thick glasses at the minuscule screen.

"As of the close of business yesterday, we're estimating a hundred forty-six million, seven hundred thousand dollars to be made good by the taxpayers here in Bordrero Bay."

"Aren't those amazing losses for such a small bank?"

"Normally, yes. But most of those losses—and deposits—were generated out of GoldWest. The one-forty-six-seven could go lower, depending on how much we can collect on some assets we're currently carrying at zero."

"All in all, the 1980s cleaned this town out pretty thoroughly, wouldn't you say, Clarence?"

"That's the talk on Bay Street, Lee. There's a lot of bad feeling. If I was a Wall Street investment banker, I'd think twice about showing my face in Bordrero Bay!"

His voice intimated that said Wall Streeters should also approach Clarence Greaves with caution.

The waiter arrived. Greaves approvingly contemplated his plate. Lee smiled. This was wheat germ and granola country: They probably hadn't served a breakfast like this in five years.

When Greaves came up for air, he smiled at Lee and said, "I do hope you're not intending to do a hatchet job about how Uncle Sam shouldn't have ever let messes like this happen, or what a pisspoor job we're doing cleaning them up."

"You have my word on that."

Greaves picked up knife and fork and attacked his roast beef hash.

"You know," he said, "we all screwed up. Sure, there have been major mistakes and giveaways on the bailout. That's inevitable. The private sector takes ten, fifteen years to make a mess, and then Congress wants it fixed in ten minutes. And sure, it never should've been allowed to happen at all. But it wasn't just government, you know, or a bunch of bought congressmen. You media people—present company excepted, of course—didn't exactly cover yourselves with glory in the guardians of the public interest department. Anyway, if anyone wants to know exactly how come, or who's responsible for what's been done to whom, I can recommend a list of a dozen books on the S&L and bank crisis and bailout, some of them pretty good, and all easily found on the remainder tables of your friendly neighborhood bookshop."

"I take your point. It *is* the damnedest thing, isn't it? American taxpayers have been taken for a half-trillion-dollar ride and no one wants to hear anything about it!"

Greaves polished off the hash, and looked around expectantly, as if a genii might arrive bearing fresh victuals.

"Well, no point in crying over spilt gold," he said, waving his empty coffee cup at the waiter. "I'm just here to help, as the old joke says. We haven't seized the bank, and it's incorrect to say we have. We're just running it for the time being, under what's called the Accelerated Resolution Program, until things get straightened out. Then we'll try to put it into the right hands."

"I understand. Whose might be the right hands?"

"Hard to say. That French bank that was mixed up in GoldWest has put out feelers about buying Bordrero Bay and the other Gold-West banks up this way . . ."

"CP?"

"That's the one. Frankly, though, it's our feeling that the people who made money creating the problem shouldn't make more money solving it. Especially offshore types."

A noble sentiment, thought Lee sarcastically, but probably beside the point. The question in her mind was: Why would a big, adventurous, action-oriented French bank want to buy a handful of financially decrepit, out-of-the-way country banks?

"When did CP express interest?" she asked.

"Couple days ago," Greaves answered. "Through an outfit called Phoenix. One of those vulture funds." A plate of muffins magically arrived. Greaves split one and slathered it with local sea grape jam. Lee couldn't. She knew when she was beaten.

"Anyway, I'll be out of here in another two weeks top and off to somewhere else to write out more checks on the taxpayers' account. Right now for the S&Ls and the banks. Tomorrow it'll probably be the insurance companies and the collateralized mortgage pools and the pension funds. All those agencies with cute names—Fannie Mae, Freddie Mac, Sallie Mae. Who knows?"

He sounded beaten, too. Clarence Greaves had probably once been driven by public spirit, Lee guessed, but he was now just running on the vapors. She decided to switch topics.

"Not to change the subject, Clarence, but do you think GoldWest was on the up and up?"

"Meaning do I think GoldWest was a BCCI? A Ponzi scheme? A drug bank? No, I don't. GoldWest was a victim of greed, recklessness, and hubris. But crooked? No! Dumb? You bet!"

Somewhere in that assertive tone is a nugget of doubt, Lee thought, not quite knowing why. It was just her reporter's instinct. There's something else going on here, she decided.

She was right. Even as he spoke to Lee of bailouts, Greaves was thinking that there was something definitely fishy about "d/b/a Thunderbolt." The deposits and withdrawals were continuing. He'd run a JEDI trail on the last withdrawal; the money moving out of the account barely lit on the East Coast before taking off again for points offshore. He'd tracked the CHIPS encryption as far as a bank in Aruba.

For an instant he considered telling Lee about "d/b/a Thunderbolt." She was media, after all, and her little paper had a hell of a reputation for investigative work. He decided to say nothing. He could always go back to her if nothing panned out with the big media. A paper like hers was desperate for news; you wouldn't have to sell Lee Boynton the way you'd have to sell Bob Woodward or Mike Wallace.

Lee caught the momentary hitch in their dialogue. She waited a beat before continuing.

"Still, several billion dollars seems to have gone missing at GoldWest," she commented.

"Thanks to the 1980s, we don't consider a few billion as worthy of public attention. GoldWest was nothing special. A bunch of young people on the make who bought a lot of bum deals at wholesale and middlemanned them at retail into its deposit accounts and pocketed the spread. Junk bonds—on which there were probably kickbacks. Lousy real estate loans vetted by quote appraisers you could work with unquote. Quote tax-sharing unquote gimmicks that were really about loss sharing. IPOS that were underwater the day the prospectus was printed."

Greaves's tone was sarcastic, bitter.

"Our reconstruction suggests that GoldWest was probably losing cash money by 1988. But because of the way the regulatory book-keeping worked, they could show paper profits. In most of these failures, there's what we call a 'risk-loss-cover-up-fraud-failure' cycle. GoldWest never got much past the 'cover-up' stage. The 1980s ended too early and the 1990s buried them. They had lousy assets collateralizing good money. When deflation and recession came along, GoldWest was dead!"

"Speaking of 'good money,' and I'm thinking in terms of virtue not liquidity or negotiability, where'd a fly-by-night outfit like Freemark find those hundreds of millions it brokered into GoldWest?"

"From wherever. Offshore, onshore. Freemark was close to CP, which also banked the GoldWest people, and, from what I hear, CP knows all kinds of people with all kinds of cash! It was natural to go through Freemark. Hell, it wasn't just CP! There was a ton of money around in those days, and nobody seemed to give a damn about keeping their nose clean. For instance, Paine Webber brokered six hundred and seventy-one million dollars into Charlie Keating's S&L and Goldman, Sachs was thick as thieves with Robert Maxwell, if you get my meaning. The interesting thing here is that when GoldWest tanked, the deposits brokered by Freemark took a real small hit, comparatively speaking. Call it luck or whatever, but they were moved out before we moved in. I'll bet we don't pay off on more than twenty million dollars of Freemark brokered paper, which is peanuts compared to what they fed in here."

" 'Moved out'? You mean withdrawn?"

"Some. A lot of the time deposits were short dated and they simply weren't rolled over at maturity. Others got discounted—sold—in the secondary market. Whichever way, the timing was exquisite. Anyway, that's neither here nor there: My job is to concentrate on what's still on the books."

Greaves paused and studied his empty plate, as if he was trying to will a third breakfast into being.

Lee gave him a moment, then asked: "All this money brokered in by outfits like Freemark. Tens and tens of billions. Is a lot of that from overseas?"

"The technical term is 'offshore.' "

"Whatever. Anyway, I assume most of those deposits flow out of the trade deficit, from Japan selling us Hondas for dollars, just to take an obvious example?"

Greaves nodded.

"What about drugs?"

"Who knows?" He shrugged, then went on. "Money's like physics. The old 'E equals *mc* squared.' The faster it travels, the more there seems to be. The bank wire, what they call CHIPS, is settling on over three hundred trillion dollars a year! Three hundred *trillion!* Now you and I know there isn't three hundred trillion dollars of real money on earth, at least we feel like we do, but CHIPS says there is. We all think in too few zeros. I read somewhere that you know all the poetry you're going to know by the age of twenty-five. I'm not so sure that it isn't the same for our sense of money.

"For example, you take me. I grew up in Asheville, North Carolina. In high school, I worked as a grocery cashier. So naturally I think I know all there is to know about the grocery business. But I like to keep up, so nowadays maybe I'll be driving around Silver Springs, some place like that, and I'll see a new Food Giant supermart, and I'll ask myself how much a unit like that grosses on a good weekend. Well, I'm pretty good at estimating shelf space and traffic flow, and so I'll work it on my trusty Sharp here what a given store will gross. Then when I get home, I'll log on to the IRS data base and check the sales tax filings for that store—and you know what? I'm usually off by a fifty-to-sixty-percent minimum, almost always on the low side!"

They both thought about that for a few seconds, then Greaves jabbed a finger at Lee and said, "Now you take the mall out there on Route one-oh-one. As malls go, it isn't much. Bunch of fast food, a cineplex, cheap shoes, pretty good-size Tip 'n Take."

"Tip 'n Take?"

"They don't have 'em back East, but it's a big deal all through this part of the world. A kind of downmarket West Coast Wal-Mart with a touch of 7-Eleven thrown in. Strictly cash and carry, no house accounts, very little plastic. Popular with the Latinos. Anyway, make a guess as to what that Tip 'n Take'll do on a good weekend."

Lee figured quickly. Assume five hundred people a day. Assume each spends fifty bucks a head. That's $25,000 a day, or $50,000 for Saturday and Sunday. Greaves was obviously teasing her, so she wanted to be on the high side, so say the same for Friday, which brought it up to $75,000. Just to be safe, she bumped her estimate 20 percent.

"Ninety thousand dollars," she said.

"Try a hundred and fifty thousand!" Greaves exclaimed triumphantly. "Here's another. There's a service station out there. Energy City. Another regional chain. Discount gas. Mostly cash, although they do take Visa and Mastercard. I assumed they pumped a million gallons a month at an average of a dollar forty retail including tax, which is what a big station does these days, and then I allowed for good business in the rest of their lines, and came up with two million dollars total. I figured about a third of that is plastic, say seven hundred thousand, which is the only number I turned out to be right about. So I was guessing a million three cash. But darned if Energy City's monthly cash deposits haven't averaged two million—that's *cash only*—for the last year. I checked the records myself. They must be pumping close to a million and a half gallons a month!"

They shook hands at the front entrance.

"Well," Greaves said, "good luck to you with your story. This town got off lightly. They don't think so, naturally, but let me tell you I've seen others that looked like Dresden after the firebombing when the junk bond boys got through. Anything I can help you with, you know where to find me."

Lee went back to her room. The rest of the day stretched before her like a desert. Maybe she ought to bag Bordrero Bay and head back to Washington. There was nothing here.

Still, it was a beautiful day.

Without really thinking, she got in her car, and drove west. Twenty minutes later, the North Coast Mall appeared ahead.

It was a two-story enclosed complex laid out to catch the winds of trade blowing north and westward from the agricultural and light manufacturing districts that had sprouted along Route 101. About its flanks clustered a compact sprawl of tire and muffler shops; from a distance it appeared to rise from the flat landscape like some massive shelled creature hunkered down among its brood.

Lee was not a veteran "maller." She wandered around inside aimlessly. It seemed inconceivable to her that anyone would buy the stuff on display. In the fast-food section, the conflated smells of nine different varieties of high-grease cuisine made her woozy, and she sought a bench.

Her head ached from the noise, the smell, and the closeness, her feet from the concrete walkways. After a few minutes, she got up and headed for the Tip 'n Take at the north end, thinking she might at least see how the other half spent before heading back to the coast.

A young man asked if he could help. A badge identified him as Arnold Somoza, store manager.

Lee introduced herself as a journalist doing a travel piece. He seemed suitably impressed and pleased to show her around. It was clear Somoza was proud of his store and knew every inch of it, every counter and cranny, every stockkeeping unit from fingernail clippers to canoes.

"So how is business now?" Lee asked.

Nothing like it had been back in early 1987 when he'd started as a stockperson, he told her. Still, it could be a whole lot worse. His customer base was 80 percent Latino, and those people spent what they earned, at least what they didn't send home. Tip 'n Take got most of their action, Somoza said, thanks to price, selection, and

Spanish-speaking help on the floor. Tip 'n Take also took a piece of what they sent home, thanks to a Fastchek check cashing/money order desk just inside the main entrance. Fastchek was another subsidiary of Tip 'n Take's parent company, Nationwide National Enterprises, a conglomerate specializing in small-ticket businesses. To Nationwide, a cash customer was like a hog to a packer: You tried to get everything out of him but the squeal.

"The Latinos work for less, so the recession hasn't hurt 'em as much. They get laid off last," Somoza explained to Lee. "Fact is, a recession's good for us, at least on the hiring end. You'd be surprised, the kind of people'll take a clerk's job after being out of work for a while."

"Exactly how bad has the recession been for you in terms of revenues?"

"Bad but not horrible. Most weekends, which is how I rate our business, I manage to drop seventy thousand, maybe eighty thousand dollars in the lockbox. That's between Friday noon and when we close Sunday night."

Now wait a minute, thought Lee. Clarence Greaves had said something about $150,000 on a recent weekend!

She asked Somoza to explain the "lockbox" setup.

Every couple of hours he swept the registers, counted the money, and bundled it with the register tapes, sealed it in a money-bag, and placed the takings in the lockbox, which was like a safe set in the wall of the building. Sometime after 10 P.M. on weeknights, or 7 P.M. on Sunday, a Courier Services armored truck would make the rounds of the mall lockboxes and transport the cash to Bordrero Bay. Courier Services handled the cash transfers for all of Nationwide National's subsidiary companies.

"Why Bordrero Bay?" Lee asked. "That's fifteen miles away. There must be a closer bank."

"There is. There's a Wells Fargo over in Sundale, and a B of A in Greenmont, but our parent company also has a relationship with Bordrero Bay, so that's where we do our business. What with the computers and all, it doesn't make much difference."

As Lee prepared to leave, she asked, "Just so I can get some feel for how bad things are right now, what's the biggest weekend you've ever had here, Mr. Somoza?"

"Since I've been with Tip 'n Take? That's easy. Christmas 1988. Back before the recession hit. We did a hundred and thirteen thousand for the weekend."

Lee drove over to the Energy City service station. As Greaves had said, it was a big one. She chatted briefly with the assistant manager while the Tempo was filled up and its oil and tires checked.

According to the manager, last month the station had pumped just over 800,000 gallons. The Energy City chain was also a subsidiary of Nationwide National and followed the same tally, lockbox, and collection procedures.

Driving back toward Bordrero Bay, Lee asked herself what the hell was going on here? Somoza and the Energy City guy obviously knew what they were talking about; Greaves was looking at the bank's records. Everyone was using real numbers in real time.

So what accounted for the discrepancy? Between lockbox and bank, it appeared the money was growing.

So what might we be looking at here? A "pizza parlor" scam exponentiated to eight zeros?

Lee did a little quick arithmetic. How many Tip 'n Takes were there, how many Energy City stations? Say three hundred of each. It didn't take long to extrapolate into the tens and hundreds of millions. Legitimate cash flows large enough to hide hundreds of millions in dirty money!

How many times had she heard Barney declare that the objective of money laundering was to break down Everest-size mounds of cash into electronic data packets no larger than pinheads.

It was the cash that was the problem.

In the old days, when the Mob also worked with fewer zeros, you could simply dispatch squads of wiseguys to the local bank with valises jammed with used bills. Crack cocaine and the DEA changed all that. The former escalated the narcotics volume to multibillion-dollar levels just as the latter got tough with the banks.

By 1990, the money was so big it was more efficient to weigh it than count it. Million-dollar bundles were airfreighted to Panama and elsewhere to be converted into electronic impulses. Lesser fry went in for onshore scams like "la Mina," which the feds cracked in Los Angeles. It was a primitive scheme. Drug money was shipped to Los Angeles and cycled through a bunch of wholesale jewelry operations into the commercial banking system, and then sent offshore. From what Lee understood, BCCI, the biggest laundry yet discovered, was just a bigger, more sophisticated, and wider ranging version of the basic scam.

BCCI, Noriega, and "la Mina" were out of business now, but not the drug trade: so someone had to have taken over the money laundromat or opened a new one. The crack kings didn't report to the Commerce Department, so there was no way of knowing whether their gross receipts had been affected by the recession, but even if volume was down, say, 15 percent, there were still tens of billions that needed to be laundered.

Might Bordrero Bay fit into such a scheme? What about GoldWest? Or CP—and "Alphonse and Gaston and the Dragon Lady"? Lee decided she'd better call Barney.

After she finished telling him what she had, there was a moment's silence, then from the receiver came a sound that she recognized as a fifty-three-year-old man with a cigarette cough and chronic shortness of breath whooping in exultation.

"You sweetheart, you!" he wheezed. "You've fallen right into the shit and come up aces! Hot damn! Dust off the mantel and get it ready for the Pulitzer!"

"Down, boy. So far all I have is a hunch and some very circumstantial findings."

"Some hunch, some circumstantiality! Honey, the big problem for these clowns has always been how to move the cash!—how to get the physical moola offshore in order to bring it back in on the bank wire. But suppose someone figures out a way so that cash, in industrial quantities, doesn't have to go offshore?"

He paused to cough. The wracking noise was more like a retch.

"Like Nationwide National," said Lee.

"Exactly! A money Maytag that's both big and totally legit. A mostly-cash business the size of McDonald's. Which means a major up-front bank-scale investment."

More coughing and wheezing.

"The feds may not be brilliant, sweetheart, but even those assholes become suspicious if they see a sixty-seat Mob-owned clam joint on Mulberry Street taking twenty million dollars a year to its bank of deposit. But a chain of two hundred Tip 'n Take stores grossing six hundred to seven hundred million dollars a year—"

"Three hundred twenty-seven stores, according to Value Line."

"Three hundred twenty-seven Tip 'n Takes. Most of the business in low-ticket cash transactions. Who's going to notice a few extra ten millions passing through the registers?"

"Provided you have a well-inclined armored-car service and a friendly bank of deposit."

"Precisely! So enter, stage left, Wiseguy Savings and Loan or Goodfellas First National, perhaps also known as GoldWest or Credit Provençal. My point is, we are talking big, serious money. Bigger than big, bigger than serious: We are talking *huge!* A two-hundred-billion-dollar-a-year industry worldwide! Enough to service the national debt! We're talking GE and Ford and Exxon combined and you can throw in Microsoft! Plus, with that kind of money to put to work, you don't need a friend at Chase Manhattan, honey, you need the whole goddamn bank! You need computers, MBAs, consultants, your own rocket scientists to design your funds transfer program. You can get 'em, because you can be fully competitive on compensation. This size bread, you're bigger than Soros, so you got to be able to play the whole damn spectrum: swaps, options, junk bonds, old masters, program trading, stud farms. You need your own Merrill Lynch, your own Manny Hanny, your own Price Waterhouse! Plus lawyers up the googoo!"

Another coughing spasm seized him. Lee waited. She could visualize Barney on the other end, cigarette in one hand, phone pressed against his thick-lipped mouth, chair tilted back, feet up on the battered desk in the seedy, cluttered office. She could see his narrow, perpetually tired face; recently it had looked less healthy than ever, gaunt and gray under its customary sallowness.

He's sounding different, Lee thought. There's something badly wrong.

"Barney," she asked evenly, "are you okay?"

There was silence.

"No bullshit, please, Barn. Barn!"

Silence for a moment. Then: "No bullshit, huh?" in a weak, drained voice, all its former insouciance gone. Then another brief fit of coughing followed by a terrible phlegmy throat-clearing that sounded as if he was dredging his lungs.

"Okay, honey. Bottom line time. Better I tell you over the phone. Otherwise I might cry and I'm too old for that."

"Just give the news, please," said Lee, trying to hold her voice firm.

"Okay, sports fans, it's like this: The news is not good. Like it's—well—fourth and forty on my own one-yard line and zero on the clock."

"Barney—please."

"Okay. Okay, okay, okay." A pause, then: "The bottom line is, we are talking Shit City. Very definitely."

For a moment, Lee said nothing. Then: "How shitty?"

"Shittiest, honey. As in shitty, shittier, shittiest."

"Where?"

"Lungs."

"Anywhere else? Has it migrated?"

"What do you think I am? Ellis Island?"

"You know what I'm talking about."

He didn't reply, which meant the answer was yes.

Lee started to say something, but Barney broke in. "Hey, what do they know? This is one guy at NIH talking. I'm gonna get a second opinion. And maybe a third, fourth, fifth, and sixth—until I come up with one I can live with. Hey, come on: That's a joke."

"How long?"

"You remember that old John McCormack song 'Mavourneen'?" In a cracked, bad-imitation Irish tenor, he crooned, "Oh, it may be for years, and it may be foreverrrr . . ."

"Cut it out," said Lee. "Have you told Claire?"

"Not yet. And I'll thank you not to, either."

That'll be the day, Lee thought.

"But enough about me," Barney said suddenly, his voice brighter. "Let's talk about you. Let's talk about Bordrero Bay and what we do next. This RTC clown, Greaves—you think we can use him?"

"He's not a clown," she said, trying to sound indignant. She wanted to sit down by the ocean and cry. She forced herself to think about Greaves. "I've spent roughly an hour in his company. A bit of a self-hating bureaucrat, the way all the good ones are, eventually, but honest and smart enough, and devoted to his job. What do you mean by 'use him'? Should I tell him about Energy City and Tip 'n Take? He does seem to be plugged into some magic computer system that has all the answers."

There was a pause, then Barney said, "Not yet. Don't say a word to him. I want to think about it. You understand this could be a major, major story. This isn't some senator with his weewee where it shouldn't be, this is big-time!"

"So do you want to take it somewhere with more horses?" Lee asked. "The *Post* maybe?"

They'd done so in the past with leads too big for them to handle on their own. They had a good relationship with the people on Seventeenth Street.

For an instant, there was silence. Then Barney said: "Nowhere. We take it nowhere. *We* do it. You and I. We, ourselves and us!"

"Barn, we haven't got the resources . . ."

Silence again. If we brought Greaves in, Lee thought . . .

After a minute, Barney spoke.

"You ever hear of a guy named Thurlow Coole?"

"It seems to ring a bell. Refresh me."

"Coole used to be a major hotshot on the Street. An all-American analyst on his way to Cooperstown or Parnassus or wherever Street geniuses end up. His specialty was financial stocks and bonds. Banks, insurance companies, shit like that. A weird person, to hear people talk. Very cranky, independent. The kind of guy people are always trying to get fired. Into mystical thinking, I heard, of the exotic Oriental variety: Kung Fu meditation, the stuff guys study to make their dicks stay hard. Anyway, around '83, I think it was, Coole was nailed by the SEC for passing out inside information to his best clients and got sent to Allentown. What I hear, the clients shopped Coole to save their own asses. When he came out, he wanted revenge on Wall Street, so he set up as a supersnoop. Specializes in what they call 'document-based' crime. Paper trails, book cooking, names behind the numbers, numbers behind the numbers, stuff like that. A lot of computer wizardry. I'd like to hire him to work with us."

"So hire him."

"Well, he's expensive."

"How expensive?"

"It costs ten grand to talk to his answering machine."

"Ouch."

"We're probably looking at half a million minimum, although I'll try to negotiate a rate. I know we're looking at fifty Gs nonrefundable because that's what *Time* paid him to vet their BCCI stuff. Coole usually gets hired by one set of dirtbags to nail another set of dirtbags. He might be willing to cut his price to be on the side of the angels."

Fat chance, thought Lee. She knew the type. On retainer to half the *Forbes* 400 just to keep him out of the employ of the other half.

"As you are well aware," Barney continued, "I don't have half a largest, and neither does the magazine. You do. So either you come up with it, or we lay this one off on Woodward, which since it's likely to be my last real shot at a Pulitzer, I am reluctant to do. It's your money, kiddo, so it's your call."

Half a million is real money, thought Lee. But not as much to her as to most people. That was beside the point.

Her partner was dying. If they didn't go for this one, would there ever be another? She had no choice.

"I'll spring for it," she said softly.

And then she started to get teary and with a choked-off sob thrust the receiver from her face.

"What's the matter," Barney asked, "you okay?"

"You're the goddamn matter," she muttered, swallowing a sob. "Jesus, you are such an asshole! I'm not going to forgive you if—"

"If nothing," Barney said quietly. "Not to worry. Hey, why not sleep on it? Let me know tomorrow. I can call Coole in the morning."

"Call him now," said Lee.

SEVEN

▼

It chanced that Thurlow Coole would be in Washington the week Barney called him. A meeting was set for Coole's suite at the Hay-Adams Hotel that Friday afternoon.

Lee, who was always on time, got to the hotel a few minutes before two o'clock. It was two-fifteen when Barney rushed in, gasping like a drowning man. She hadn't seen him since she'd returned from California. He'd been in New York all week talking to various oncologists, chasing alternative opinions and therapies.

She knew at once that the consultations had yielded no hope. Barney seemed utterly changed. Perhaps because his illness was now an inescapable fact, the life seemed to be going out of him second by second. He seemed deflated and shrunk, sapped and beaten.

The countdown—the death watch—has begun, she thought. Could she handle it? Hey, she admonished herself: If he can, you must!

The door of suite 1006 opened promptly to her knock, almost as if Coole had been lurking on the other side, waiting and listening. He was extremely tall, extremely thin, and completely bald.

For an instant, the three of them stood there, sizing one another up, then Coole said, "Miss Boynton, Mr. Cagel? Won't you come in, please. How disagreeable this weather is. I can't imagine how anyone can live in Washington."

The voice was cadenced and accented in a fashion that Lee's mother would have instantly (and approvingly) pinpointed as "our sort." Deep but not plummy, the words carefully articulated, the pronunciation clipped; only a faint spreading in the vowels hinted of Boston or New England origins. It was a voice capable of deepest gravity when required, Lee thought, serious tones in keeping with serious money, especially at Coole's going rate of $3,000 an hour.

The body type was pure Yankee. Spindly at first glance, but in tiptop shape for his age, which Lee took to be about forty-eight: wire and sinew, the product of countless hours on the squash court and hockey rink. His features were as narrow as the rest of him: long, straight nose, slightly down-curving thin-lipped schoolmasterish mouth, sharp, devilish chin, candid gray-green eyes that knew a thing or two. A face that tended—at rest—toward the morose, but when animated capable of a sly smile.

If the face is mirror to the mind, she thought, Coole's is prehensile, studious, exact, long of memory, wry. A man who rations his laughter.

The hand that took Lee's was large enough to palm a basketball. His grip was firm. Without really thinking, she found herself wondering whether that long, strong nose, those long, strong fingers might be an earnest of other aspects of the man. Lee as a rule didn't go for bald men, but there was something quirkily sexy about Thurlow Coole.

For a person of sober mien, Coole's attire was surprisingly lighthearted, suggesting an undertaker in motley. He was wearing a well-worn suit of old-fashioned wide-striped puckered seersucker, slightly yellowed at cuff and lapel. A bright gentian-hued handkerchief peeped from the breast pocket. A yellow Brooks Brothers button-down shirt and pink bow tie speckled with tiny pale green amoebas completed the ensemble.

Really very Harvard, Lee thought as Coole gestured them into the sitting room of his suite.

The place had an unmistakable personal touch. A pretty good Hepplewhite sideboard took up half the far wall; it held a color fax equipped with all the latest bells and whistles, along with an array of video display terminals and other devices. The coffee table sported a Colonial silver tea set that looked like the Revere service Lee's Uncle Henry had donated to the Smithsonian when he quit the capital. On the facing wall, above the sofa, was a portrait resembling the Copley that Lee's mother liked to pass off as being of an ancestor.

In the middle of the room stood a waiter's trolley with the remains of two club sandwiches. Off to one side was a card table with a chessboard. At the card table sat a black youth whom Lee guessed to be in his midteens. He was not studying the pieces on the board, however; he was engrossed in a Nintendo Game Boy and didn't lift his eyes when the three adults entered the room.

"Up, please, Du Bose," said Coole to the boy in a quiet voice that had the authority of a marine drill instructor's shout through a bullhorn.

The boy slouched up from his seat. He was wearing a red and black Chicago Bulls warm-up jacket, at least two sizes too big, with matching sweatpants and enormous, black, loose-laced Nikes. On his head, back to front, sat a purple velour baseball cap.

He shoved the Game Boy into the recesses of the warm-up jacket, and limply shook hands with Barney and Lee. The slackness of his grip was just to show "cool," Lee thought, not an indicator of strength.

He was about as tall as she was, but still just a kid; for all his cool, a little boy inside. Something about him told her he hadn't yet been ruined by the street life. This one might have a chance.

"We need to talk, Du Bose," said Coole. He nodded toward an open bedroom door. The boy went off. Coole gestured Lee and Barney to the sofa under the portrait. A gilt label verified that it was indeed a Copley: *Portrait of Artemis Coole,* Litt. D. (1711–1767).

Coole waved a long hand at the bedroom door.

"Quite a story, Du Bose. The name is a perversion of that of the late, great W.E.B. Du Bois. He's just seventeen. Five months ago, he was discovered wandering around inside the Pentagon computer banks, which he had contrived to access from a pay phone near the housing project where he and his five siblings live with their grandmother in two rooms. He broke in at a level of access theoretically off-limits to anyone below the Joint Chiefs. The Secret Service was all for sending him to prison. Fortunately, I have friends, and they told me about Du Bose. I persuaded the Service to petition the court that he be remanded to my custody. Are either of you familiar with Boys Harbor, Tony Duke's camp for inner-city children out on Long Island?"

"I know it," said Barney.

"Well, I have something similar on the North Shore of Boston near Pride's Crossing. A sort of computer version of the Duke operation. Mine is for wayward young people with computer skills—delinquent hackers, you might call them. I hope you'll come and see what we do with our young people. It's pretty impressive, if I do say so myself."

Barney looked at Coole.

"The kid broke into the goddamn Pentagon mainframe? Jesus? So what are we talking about here, Mr. Coole. Some kind of Mozart? Or idiot savant?"

"A bit of both, possibly. And let us not forget our Darwin: The power of species to adapt. For reasons of opportunity as well as sheer survival. Otherwise how can we explain why young black men grow up in the inner city, on diets that a Somalian orphan would find malnutritious, to be big and strong enough to play for the Celtics or the Redskins? It's the same with our computer instincts, as we might call them. When it comes to computers, children today, even toddlers, are light-years ahead of old fogeys like you and me, Mr. Cagel. You might almost say it's in the air; they seem to grasp intuitively what you and I, using all our reason and instincts, can only barely begin to comprehend. I suspect video games have a great deal to do with it. They instill a feeling for the rhythms and patterns of computer thinking that becomes almost reflexive. Provided the host—the mind—is properly attuned to begin with. In most people our age, it isn't, no matter how bright we are. Have either of you ever attempted Nintendo or Sega?"

Lee and Barney shook their heads.

Liar, she thought, looking at her partner with amusement. On dull afternoons a counterpoint of beeps and oaths could be heard in Barney's office as he once again sought vainly to master Super Mario. He kept a Game Boy in his desk—he claimed he had bought it for his son and that Claire, full of attitude as always, had forbidden it in the house.

"Well," said Coole, "I have. Strictly in the interests of research, of course. I am a Phi Beta Kappa from Harvard with a magna cum laude in mathematics and logic. I am not without a certain physical and digital dexterity: I was squash champion of my house at Harvard, as well as having had a national court tennis ranking since I was eighteen, and I play the piano passably. But the highest score I have ever been able to manage in Tetris or Super Mario, the only Nintendo games whose parameters and structure I begin to understand, is derisory. Indeed, my efforts reduce my young people to laughter.

"On the other hand, when Du Bose came to me, he could not spell his surname, let along a word like *derisory*. It had been four years, according to his grandmother, since he attended school with any regularity. In every area of life, with the exception of the cost of certain status-laden articles of clothing endorsed by basketball players, he was abysmally ignorant. And yet he routinely achieves the highest possible score on his Game Boy, and—since we have had him—on games infinitely more complex and serious on much, much larger machines. It would appear that the logic underlying computer games is first cousin to the architecture of larger data bases."

"Once he's in," asked Lee, "does he know what to do with what he finds? Or what to look for?"

Coole smiled.

"No, but we do."

He let that sink in, then said, "Now, to business. What is it exactly that you think I might be able to help you with? I know only from Mr. Cagel that you wish to engage us in connection with some investigative reporting your magazine is considering doing about the collapse of GoldWest Financial Group. Are you interested in having us dig into the figures, to perform what my associates and I call 'forensic accounting'? As you know, we do not come cheap, and the more closely we define our role, the better value you are likely to find us."

He looked at Lee as he said this, obviously aware whose signature would be on the check.

"We're not quite sure how you fit in," she said, and for the next twenty minutes, filled him in about Bordrero Bay and Clarence Greaves.

When Lee finished, Coole steepled his long fingers and gazed at the wall behind Lee like a physician contemplating a particularly dire X ray.

"Very interesting. The GoldWest collapse, of course, is the least of it. That was probably essentially centrifugal in nature, although I am intrigued by what your Mr. Greaves implied about what sounds a very prescient hemorrhage of deposits brokered into GoldWest by the late Freemark Securities. Then there's the connection with Credit Provençal . . . hmm . . . I wonder . . .''

Muttering to himself, he picked up the phone at his side and, after a moment's pause, began speaking in a low voice, evidently over an open line. In the next room, Lee could hear Du Bose's Game Boy cheeping like a tree frog.

"Now then," said Coole, hanging up, "logic suggests that we first focus on Courier Services, since it is during the transition from lockbox to bank that the apparent mysterious growth in cash deposits uncovered by Miss Boynton must take place. Are you familiar at all with Courier?''

"Only to the extent that it's kind of a cross between Brink's and Federal Express and that it's big," said Barney.

"And that it belongs to Nationwide National," Lee added, "which I understand is also connected to CP.''

"Indeed. NNE—or "Nanny" as it is called in the stock market—bought control of Courier Services out of a 1983 railroad bankruptcy, using a loan from CP. Through incestuous arrangements with its own subsidiaries as well as with CP affiliations like GoldWest, Nanny has dramatically expanded Courier's customer base.''

"You said 'control of Courier.' Who owns the rest?''

"I believe various clients of CP.''

"Does CP have a piece of NNE as well?" asked Barney.

"Only about five percent directly. The balance of the shares, all but a few hundred thousand, that is, are as far as anyone knows held in an interlocking jigsaw puzzle of offshore interests domiciled in jurisdictions ranging from Macau to Bermuda. CP manages the position and votes their proxies.''

"What actually is CP, Mr. Coole? A kind of baby BCCI?''

"Alas no, Mr. Cagel. How much easier our task would be if it were. CP is a very sophisticated operation, which BCCI was not, although it got away with its rather crude malefactions for far longer than it had a right to do, thanks to regulatory corruption and stupidity.''

"Still, you hear things. CP's supposed to be not totally on the up and up.''

"That may be so. What we do know is that Banque Provençale

de Credit et d'Investissement, to give its full and rather ponderous proper name, was a sleepy Avignon bank with a long and decent pedigree dating back to the reign of Louis-Napoleon. It was acquired ten years ago by two ambitious young Frenchmen, Claude Vertreuil and Bruno de Fried, who had made names for themselves at the Credit Lyonnais, a bank with a taste for financial adventurousness, facilitated by the fact that it is a semigovernmental institution, so that its adversaries end up banging their heads against the walls of the Élysée Palace."

"Vertreuil and de Fried would be Jimmy Spalding's 'Froggies'?"

"I expect they would be, Miss Boynton. At Lyonnais, Vertreuil covered the Middle East and de Fried liaised with the Swiss banking community. Claude is more of a strategist while Bruno is essentially a front man, good at marketing and massaging. He brings in the money, Claude puts it to work.

"The financing for the takeover of CP was provided by Middle Eastern interests, at least that's the gossip. Beyond that, little is known of the bank's internal workings. It would appear that their stint at the Lyonnais left Vertreuil and de Fried with an obsessive concern with secrecy and security. They operate behind more veils than Salome, and their security is entrusted to a cadre of former Foreign Legion types, everything from Senegalese to Scotsmen. In a way, one cannot blame them. CP is widely assumed to number among its largest clients people known for reacting extremely violently to unforeseen shifts in fortune, including innocent missteps by their money managers. If I had such clients, I too would make sure that my personal security arrangements were first-class."

"You're talking drug lords?"

"Who can say, Mr. Cagel? We live in an era marked by violence in so many areas of human endeavor."

Lee looked at Barney sharply. This was an angle she hadn't thought about. This could get dangerous.

"Since its founding, CP has grown to be truly global," Cole continued. "Were I to diagram it for you, it would look exactly like the large, *rayonnant* sun the bank uses as its logo. Think of the rays as symbolizing all the usual high-secrecy, low-tax jurisdictions: from the Cayman Islands to the French Hebrides, from Macau to Willemstad."

"What the tabloids call 'an octopus of international finance.'"

"Exactly, Miss Boynton. You might say the sun never sets on the CP sun. Onshore, in the United States, that is, CP's presence is limited. There are various small direct investments, like NNE. There is a tiny private banking operation headquartered in a New York brownstone with a branch in Beverly Hills. These are irreproachable, squeaky clean operations, providing highest-net-worth individuals like film stars and *Forbes* 400 types with custody and trust services, investment management and useful addresses offshore. They also do a little wholesale and interbank lending. Then there is United Eagle Investors Services, which CP bought three years ago; those are the Eagle funds, twenty-eight of them around the world with aggregate assets of sixteen billion dollars, of which ten are sold in the United States: funds with names like Eagle Balanced Growth, Eagle Emergent Technologies, Eagle Mexico, Eagle Biogenic. Here again, CP appears as the direct owner of less than five percent; the controlling balance is tucked away in friendly pockets hither and yon. Finally, CP is a twenty-percent limited partner in Phoenix Capital Associates, a so-called vulture fund run by one Leo Gorton, who at one time was the driving force in none other than Freemark Securities, GoldWest's favorite money broker."

"This Phoenix, it's what they call a 'TNT,' right?"

"I beg your pardon, Mr. Cagel?"

"TNT: Trafficker in Tragedy. An outfit that buys up busted junk securities for pennies on the dollar? Paper that then mysteriously triples in value?"

"Exactly so. The irony, of course, is that the worthless securities for which Mr. Gorton is now offering pennies on the dollar were in many cases originally sold to the public at one hundred cents on the dollar by none other than Mr. Gorton's old firm. In many cases, the deals themselves were personally overseen by Leo Gorton. The issues of commercial morality this raises are, at the very least, subtle."

"When CP puts an investment syndicate together," Lee asked, "who typically are the other players?"

"A wide range. It's hard to say exactly, because they mask themselves behind entities with names like 'Argos S.A.' or 'Helios NV,' care of banks and law firms and accountants in jurisdictions with airtight secrecy laws. But one guesses certain Arabs, certain Greek shipowners, at least one Korean bank, some Taipei currency-exchange interests, recently a great deal of Spanish capital. This is mostly 'black money,' mind you, which is at least technically different from 'dirty money,' although once the two are commingled, they're indistinguishable."

"How would you characterize the difference?" Lee asked.

" 'Black' is money fleeing regulation, taxation, or disclosure. 'Dirty' implies criminality of origin. Drug money. The proceeds of embezzlement. That sort of thing."

"Either way, it's happiest offshore."

"Only up to a point. Offshore is where it seeks and acquires anonymity. Of course, you must not think of 'offshore' as having a defined physical geography, as an exotic setting for a Paul Erdman novel. Offshore is no longer of our geography: it exists in what is called cyberspace, its cartography is digital. You can be in the bar of this very hotel, and if you have a palmtop computer and a phone jack you can make yourself every bit as 'offshore' as if you were sitting on a Swiss mountaintop or a beach on Vanuatu."

"Isn't it difficult for 'black' money to get in and out of the United States?"

"To get out, yes. To get in, no. Over financial immigration we seem to have no control. Over emigration, we retain a vestige, thanks to surveillance systems and institutional cooperation, as well as the sheer physical bulk of the cash—black or dirty—which needs to be moved. Hence the importance of what you may have hit upon at Bordrero Bay. Tip 'n Take and Energy City—and Courier Services, of course—may be components of a huge and sophisticated money-laundering operation: enormous in scope, admirable and creative in conception, deft in execution. State-of-the-art, as they say. A better mousetrap which permits cash to be effectively laundered in industrial quantities without ever having to cross the border."

He paused to let this sink in, then continued.

"The larger point is this. Just as water runs downhill, money will tend to head for America. Not only do we revere money as much as the Swiss, but our markets are infinitely more capacious. They constitute the largest money hotel in the universe, if you will. The 'vacancy' sign is never extinguished; there is always room to accommodate another ten or twenty or a hundred billion dollars. As a result, just as has been the case in the legitimate financial markets, a host of exotic investment products have been developed for the sole purpose of getting money into the States from overseas: straw borrowers, shell companies, *hundi* chits, Dutch sandwiches . . ."

"Jesus," said Barney, "and only yesterday, we thought pizza parlors were the latest thing. What in God's name is a Dutch sandwich?"

"The technique is believed to have originated in Rotterdam. Say you're an American manufacturer who has sold ten million dollars of widgets in Taiwan. You want the cash in the U.S., but you don't want to report the transaction and pay taxes. So you contact CP-Netherlands, where you open an account in the name of a newly formed Netherlands Antilles subsidiary; you now transfer your ten million dollars from Taiwan to The Hague. Then CP-Netherlands Antilles lends you, directly, ten million dollars, using the funds on deposit in The Hague to offset the Antilles loan as collateral. The proceeds of that 'loan' are then wired free and clear of U.S. taxes to your account at Chase Manhattan in Manhattan. Ergo: Dutch sandwich."

"More like a cake you both eat and have," Lee commented.

"Ah, but suppose your ten million dollars isn't in Taiwan. Suppose it's in Brooklyn. Suppose that instead of widgets, it's crack cocaine you've sold for a pile of currency. What then are your options? How do you get rid of the telltale ring around the collar? The banks are watching out for large cash deposits, especially after BCCI, and Uncle Sam is watching the banks. You can physically send the currency out of the country, to be washed in Panama or somewhere else, but to do so puts you at the mercy of someone else's stupidity or cupidity. The best solution would be to find an efficient, repetitive way to feed it into the domestic capital markets."

"Ergo: Tip 'n Take or Energy City?"

"Precisely. Your ten million dollars is picked up at a Brooklyn drop by Courier Services, taken to a counting house, and from there disseminated around the country by being commingled with the 'normal' deposits of a controlled network of legitimate cash businesses like Tip 'n Take, Energy City, Uncle Noodle's, or any of a score of NNI subsidiaries that transact their businesses mainly in cash. This is an operation entailing considerably less risk and infinitely greater ultimate secrecy than would be involved in moving the cash to Panama. Once washed, the money can be placed as fully insured term deposits through the good offices of a money broker or simply deposited as the proceeds of business in the ordinary way."

"The money broker would break the ten million dollars into insurable pieces, right?"

"Exactly so. Probably in collusion with an institution like GoldWest. One hundred or more pieces of a hundred thousand dollars or less apiece."

"What about taxes? If these are supposed to be the profits or cash flow of legitimate businesses, isn't the IRS going to want its pound of flesh?"

"Indeed, and to some extent it will probably get it. But even at full present corporate tax rates, the result is still favorable relative to the risks of trying to move great wads of cash out of the country and then back in again. Like other people of wealth, these entrepreneurs will have clever accountants scheming to reduce their tax burden. And consider this: Let's just suppose that with your right hand you've placed ten million dollars in insured deposits with, say, GoldWest. Now, with your left hand, you borrow that ten million back again, through straw borrowers. Less the usual fees and commissions, plus let's just say a million-dollar override to persons within GoldWest as the price of their complicity, you'd net, in round figures, $8.5 million in loan proceeds, which could be wired anywhere in the world and from there made to vanish in the limitless caverns of the offshore financial markets, never to be repaid. Do you see where I'm going with this?"

"I think I do. You've got $8.5 million cash from the phony loan plus you're still on GoldWest's books with ten million dollars in insured deposits. In effect, you've turned $10 million into $18.5 million."

"Precisely. So, Miss Boynton, even if you do pay, say, $3 million in taxes, you've still turned $10 million in black or dirty money into $15.5 million that's as pristine as if it had been minted in Washington yesterday."

Barney emitted an appreciative wheeze.

"Wow! Fifty-five percent on your dough with zero risk! Except to the American taxpayer, of course. Whoever came up with that is a genius!"

"The scenario is as old as the Romans," said Coole drily. "You can find it in Juvenal. The Fifth Satire, I believe."

He looked at his watch.

"I'm afraid Du Bose and I will have to be off shortly. I have to deliver him back to the Granary—as we call our bucolic little operation—and then get myself to Cambridge for a meeting at the Fogg Museum. So we'd best turn to practical and tactical matters. You're familiar, I assume, with our fee schedule?"

"Only that I know you don't come cheap?"

"Indeed we don't. In this instance, however, I propose to bill you at a thousand dollars an hour against a minimum retainer of fifty thousand dollars. That's for our standard package of services. Any others we subcontract and bill at cost. We do not paw through people's garbage, unlike some of our competitors. The exception being their electronic scraps, of course. We do not provide what is generally called 'muscle,' although I do have an associate, one Mr. Lenchin, who has considerable practical experience in this area, and he will be available for contingencies."

He noted Lee's surprised expression.

"Miss Boynton, the further you—and we—go with this, the likelier it is that our investigative efforts may come to the attention of people of a decidedly violent turn of mind. It's only prudent to anticipate that."

"I was actually wondering why you are willing to cut your hourly fee."

"I find the puzzle tantalizing, Miss Boynton, hence the discount. Indeed, I would pay to be able to work on this one. The fee I propose roughly splits the difference."

"How do you like to be paid?"

"Any way that suits you, although we don't take American Express."

Lee wrote out a personal check for $50,000, making a mental note to have the Monongahela Trust cover it Monday morning. Coole slipped it into a jacket pocket without looking at it.

"Now," he said, "to the tactical side of things. Until we have a better idea of what's what, I think for the moment it might be useful if your Mr. Greaves were to make the running for us. After all, he has a head start."

"In what way?" asked Lee. She suddenly felt uneasy. Events

seemed to have taken an unexpected, sharp, and ominous swerve.

"Although it involves certain risks, I think you should disclose to him what you came across at Tip 'n Take and Energy City. I think you should make him privy to your suspicions. Keep me out of it, though. If your characterization of the man's on the mark, he'll take the bit in his teeth, and he may be in a better position than we to turn our suppositions into evidence."

"I'm not sure I follow you."

"Didn't you say that Greaves intimated that he had privileged access to a high-level federal data base."

"Yes."

"That could very well be JEDI. The acronym stands for Joint Expedited Data Interface. JEDI's hot stuff, Miss Boynton. My people would give their eye teeth to access JEDI and—without putting too fine a point on it—it hasn't been for lack of trying. If Mr. Greaves can get into JEDI, which I must say I find surprising, given his relatively lowly civil service level, he has a head start worth light-years. It would be silly of us not to trade on that advantage."

Lee nodded. With a thin smile, Coole added: "Of course, if Mr. Greaves were to hand over his JEDI access codes and pass code, we'd be happy to take over."

Maybe Greaves was talking about JEDI, Lee thought, or maybe it was some other system, but one thing she knew: from her impression of the man and his view of the sacrosanctity of the taxpayers' property, there was no way he was going to let any pass codes out of his safekeeping.

There was something else that bothered her: a vague feeling that they might be setting Greaves up.

"Don't you think this could put Greaves at risk?" she asked.

"From JEDI System Security? I should think not. Getting into JEDI's three-quarters of the battle—at least as my people understand it. Once you're logged on, it's assumed you have every right to be there."

Lee was not reassured. She started to speak when Barney, sensing an impasse, changed the subject.

"One other thing, Mr. Coole. Just out of curiosity. Let's assume we're right about NNE and CP and GoldWest and the rest. This's a very elaborate setup, and very expensive. You don't spend five hundred bucks on a washing machine to do ten bucks' worth of laundry.

How much dirty money do you think we could be talking about?''

"Good question, Mr. Cagel. I've heard it said that money laundering's a form of art limited only by imagination, but its cost has to be considered as well. What we may be looking at has already involved a significant outlay. CP's acquisition of NNE, the financing of GoldWest, the expansion of Courier Services, and so on. These required several hundred million dollars of investment capital. How much can be justified by those entities' legitimate businesses, and how much is attributable to the illegitimate business-within-business? I'm not in a position to estimate just yet. But it's safe to say we're talking serious money. I've seen estimates that place the domestic drug traffic at upward of two hundred billion dollars a year, but for purposes of discussion, let's assume, say, a market of one million addicts with a fifty-dollar-a-day habit. Those figures appear supported by most of the data. That's fifty million dollars a day, which, times the standard accounting year of three hundred and sixty days, comes to eighteen billion dollars. Let us halve that to arrive at a wholesale price, and halve *that* number to allow for production and related costs, and we come up with a bottom line of $4.5, say $5 billion divided among roughly a dozen players, of whom the smallest nets something on the order of two hundred million dollars and the largest a billion or so. Over a period of years, that can add up.''

Barney whistled.

"Money worth killing for, huh?" he said, sticking his forefinger into his temple and pulling an imaginary trigger.

"You'd be remiss not to consider the point," said Coole, smiling thinly. "Until recently at least, killing journalists was not an acceptable form of censorship in this country, even by organized crime. The sad case of Mr. Danny Casolaro and Sr. Manuel de Dios in Queens seem to've been exceptions, not the rule, although how much longer this will be the case I can't say. Certainly, elsewhere in the world no such scruples apply.''

Lee was only half-listening. She couldn't get her mind off Clarence Greaves. It seemed to her that Coole proposed to leave the man out there without a net. It was all very well to sit here in a $500-a-day Washington hotel suite formulating plans as if reality were some kind of a board game, but life had an ugly way of turning real.

"Mr. Coole," she asked, "given what you just said, if you were us, would you press ahead with this investigation? It sounds like some of us could end up getting killed!"

"Miss Boynton, I don't tell people what to do. I discover facts and formulate patterns and outcomes for my clients. That's what I'm paid for. I leave it to my clients to decide on their own course of action beyond that. You are looking for a story. I hope to furnish you with the information you need to write it."

"I don't think that's much of an answer."

Coole scratched his cheek.

"I've been an admirer of your magazine for some time now. You've an emotionally vested interest in the same principles I do. Your investigative reporting has been creative. How did you like the Predators' Ball? It might amuse you to know that I had an operative working bungalow eight the same night as you were there. For myself, I find the problem of money laundering intriguing. Like Mr. Milken's so-called junk bond daisy chain, I crave to see my theories about how something works confirmed. Real *proof*, not just an advanced form of conjecture. In today's 'paperless' world, the technology of speculation and evasion is light-years ahead of the technology of detection and prosecution. JEDI's said to be a giant step forward in redressing that imbalance, and that is why I'm anxious to use Mr. Greaves. It's entirely possible, however, that at the end of the day, we'll know everything and yet nothing, that we may find ourselves adrift on a sea of circumstantiality, without a case that will convince a judge and jury, or a story that you, as responsible journalists, feel you can publish."

For a moment there was silence. Lee looked at Barney, then at Coole, and nodded. Coole quickly picked up the thread.

"Good. Let's go forward bravely, then. Albeit with a certain prudence. I suggest we reconvene in Pride's Crossing in a fortnight. By then, thanks to Mr. Greaves, we should have a clearer idea of exactly how the lines and dots might connect. Shall we say the twenty-first? In the meantime, I must ask that there be no freelancing. Other than by Mr. Greaves, of course, who'll be left to pursue matters as he sees fit. If anything happens out of the ordinary, call me immediately and first. I can be reached day or night through my office. That's it, then? Fine, and now, if you'll excuse Du Bose and myself . . ."

He summoned the boy back into the living room. As if on cue, just as Du Bose entered, still fingering his Game Boy, the fax squawked into action.

Coole took the newly arrived sheet from the tray, examined it, and handed it to Lee.

It reproduced two color photographs, surprisingly clear, one full face, the other three-quarters right profile, of a woman in a sable coat. Lee guessed she could be anywhere from late thirties to midforties

She was the sort who would be called "handsome" rather than "beautiful." Her darkish hair was pulled back from a high, brainy forehead. The high collar of her coat was pulled up around her chin, and she wore large, wide-rimmed sunglasses, so that most of her face was concealed, but not her fleshy, prominent nose.

The nose was the giveaway. This woman must be Jimmy Spalding's Dragon Lady.

"What's her name?" she asked Coole.

"Mona Kurchinski. The so-called Mata Hari of global finance, although I hasten to add that there's never been a scintilla of proof that she'll barter physical favors for comparative market advantage. She's expert in moving money around clandestinely, and so she should be: She was one of your Uncle Henry's prize pupils, Miss Boynton, some say his best."

She'd be good then, thought Lee, really good. Her uncle had a genius for financial hugger-mugger. At the CIA, he'd been in charge of fiscal dirty tricks: destabilizing economies; disemboweling central banks; debauching currencies; corrupting markets.

"For the last ten years roughly," Coole continued, "Mona Kurchinski has been involved in private finance, associated with Middle Eastern interests principally, although more recently one hears other names as well, some pretty discreditable. It was her clients who initially backed CP; some say the deal was her idea to begin with and that she remains the power behind the arras. If the trail should lead to Avignon, she may turn out to be our nemesis."

The word seemed to recall Du Bose from cyberspace. Putting aside the challenges of Tetris Level 10, he looked questioningly at Coole.

"Nem'sis," he asked, "what that be?"

"Trouble," said Thurlow Coole.

EIGHT

▼

Soaked through, Oltington slogged back to his car through the slanting downpour and hurled himself into the driver's seat. Christ, he thought, Kim and his damn secrecy! Most of the time, the security procedures were a nuisance. On a night like this, they were a crime against humanity!

Well, there was nothing he could do about it. It would take several minutes for his message to be bounced to Kim's pager, and several after that for Kim to get to a secure phone to call back.

Oltington flicked on the overhead light and picked up that morning's *New York Times*. As he pawed through the damp paper, it occurred to him that perhaps he hadn't heard Kim's message correctly. The rain beating on the roadside phone booth made it difficult to hear. Yes, he told himself in a momentary burst of optimism, I heard wrong, I'm sure I did.

But he knew he hadn't. They had a problem. Their first real problem, and it was a big one.

On the newspaper's Op-Ed page, his eye lit on William Safire's column. The columnist was on a BCCI tear again. "The leaders of three major nations are implicated in a criminal conspiracy," Oltington read; "first, to misuse taxpayer funds and public agencies in the clandestine buildup of a terrorist dictator; then to abuse the intelligence and banking services of those nations to conceal the dirty deal; finally, to try to thwart the inexorable cause of justice."

Ah Bill, thought Oltington, if you only knew the half of it!

On the surface, Safire could be describing the Project. But the Project wasn't BCCI. Not by a mile. BCCI was like a child's drawing; the Project was pure Rembrandt.

At least until now.

Rain sleeted against the windshield. Oltington checked his watch. Seven minutes had passed. Time enough.

He flung the door open and slogged back across to the phone booth and called his district V-mail number. Kim had called. Oltington's plump lips pursed into a sulk as he listened to Kim's oral shorthand. Damn! Damn, damn, *damn!* He *had* heard the fellow correctly!

All of a sudden this fellow Greaves was assembling information—sales tax comparisons, account splitting, and balance transfers—about Tip 'n Take and Energy City! This was a revolting development! It was possible, Oltington guessed, to infer cash receipts from local sales tax payments, depending how these were collected.

Greaves was also querying JEDI about Courier Services. It was evident, however, that he wasn't sure what he was after.

The only bright spot was that Thunderbolt no longer seemed to concern him.

All in all, this was bad, Oltington thought. Heretofore, the Project had been a closed loop of understanding between himself and Kim; now that circumference was in danger of being pierced. Something would definitely have to be done.

A flash of anger at Kim rose in Oltington. Why hadn't the man told him about Greaves when he first appeared on Kim's screen asking about Oystermen's and Thunderbolt Video?

The names were in fact new to Oltington. According to Kim, they had been added to the JEDI Watch List when Oltington's private arrangement had been set up by Mona. Obviously these were intermediate stops on the route plotted by Mona which took the cash that Kim handed over to Courier Services to Oltington's numbered account at CP-Aruba. Oltington didn't know any of the names on Kim's watch list. He didn't want to. He had conceived the Project and beyond that his function was simply to slip Kim the keys whenever the locks on JEDI were changed.

Mona's thinking was clear. Kim was the logical conduit, and he was based in San Francisco, so the first stop should be somewhere around the Bay Area. In forty-nine states out of fifty, Thunderbolt Video stores were as ubiquitous as gnats in June. She'd probably picked Oystermen's out of a hat, but it was the bank of choice for Maryland's rich folks, and was used discreetly to dispatch good-size sums hither and thither in search of a few extra pennies of current return or avoided tax.

Well, so much for all of Kim's talk about foolproof, fail-safe system architecture, about "electronic roadblocks and detour signs"! Kim had assured him that the Project was both airtight and invisible. Foolproof, heh!

Now it was up to Kim and himself to plug the hole in the dike being bored by this Greaves.

Above all, Mona must not know! Thank God Kim had had the wisdom to check with Oltington first. The damage could still be controlled.

The engine started up, Oltington mashed the accelerator down, and the rented Dodge fishtailed onto the road.

If Mona found out about Greaves, he thought, peering into the streaky darkness, she might pull the plug: not simply on Oltington's personal action, but on the Project itself.

That must not happen! More than ever, now that Oltington was planning to move onshore, the continuation of the Project was essential. It was one thing to finance a few riots in Bangladesh, but a Senate race in a big state cost real money.

Fortunately, the Project had thrown off real money. In the last two and a half years, $260 million had been paid into accounts around the world, available to be deployed at a snap of Oltington's fingers. It gave him the powers of a magus: able with a flick of the wrist to create private armies, foment rebellion, destabilize a regime, or cause it to fall. He knew how Kissinger must have felt: exalted, superhuman, on a level with God.

So far he had spent $170 million. All offshore: in Japan, Kosovo, the Ukraine, and Myanmar, the former Burma. Only $90 million remained, but the semiannual settlement date was approaching. Mona had let slip that her clients were having a good year; Oltington anticipated an infusion of an additional $40 to $60 million. He could use the money. He was about to open a domestic theater of operations.

This autumn there were four key Senate races in which party

regulars strongly identified with the President were being challenged by candidates the media once dismissed as "fringe." A Senate race cost roughly $10 to $12 million. It would be money well invested. Voters were confused, nervous, ignorant. As the Master taught: People who know nothing can be made to believe anything, provided you can finance their continued ignorance. The loss of these seats would be a significant rebuke to the President. It would encourage the party to begin looking within itself for a new leader. It represented a politicial investment Oltington should not, could not, would not, pass up!

The Project had really gone quite satisfactorily. There had been stumbles. Tokyo, for one, was sharply over budget. Anyone who thought members of Congress cost a lot ought to try shopping the Japanese Diet! He had thrown $30 million into Yugoslavia and $15 million in Somalia before deciding never again to invest in tribal confrontations.

Oltington had no qualms or second thoughts about running a vigilante foreign policy. The American Century was worth fighting for. If the only source of finance available was drug money, so be it. In JEDI, he had something the drug lords were willing to pay for; they had the money he needed.

The rain seemed to be slackening. Oltington increased his speed. He should be home in another ten minutes.

So: What now?

Like a reflexive mantra, as had been drilled into him at Langley, Oltington silently recited the lessons of the Master.

Precept one: Let the logic of the situation determine the course of action. Precept two: The way out of problems is often the same as the way into them. Precept three: Neither cry over spilt milk nor linger on the scene to mop it up. Think only in the present and future. Precept four: Make haste slowly.

In his mind, Oltington spread out the elements of the problem with which he was confronted and examined them like a spinster sizing up a jigsaw puzzle, trying to shape the elements into some kind of general equation.

Three weeks ago, according to Kim, someone had begun querying the JEDI banking module about an account at Bordrero Bay Bank in the name of a straw firm "d/b/a Thunderbolt Video." This account was on the surveillance roster furnished by Mona directly to Kim and regularly updated. The querist was identified by Kim through the JEDI personnel module as an RTC field agent named Clarence Greaves; he had apparently accessed JEDI with a pass code obtained—in contravention of federal regulation—from a niece who worked in the Department of Justice. According to Kim, Greaves was merely thrashing about, which was why Kim hadn't bothered to notify Oltington at first. Kim had no idea how or why this account had attracted Greaves's attention.

Thunderbolt was no problem. But then, again for no apparent reason, Greaves had shifted his attention to Tip 'n Take and Energy City, two more of the roughly seventy names on Kim's Watch List, and then to Courier Services. According to Kim, Greaves was swinging wildly most of the time, so Kim had pitched him a series of electronic curveballs such as crashing the computer he used at the bank where he was on assignment and laying down a series of megabit red herrings. He hadn't bothered Oltington with any of the stuff, Kim reported. It hadn't seemed necessary.

Until this week, when Greaves had started to compare Tip 'n Take and Energy City's deposits with local sales tax filings and percentage rental payments. The shift in approach was so pronounced, Kim reported, so focused, that it was almost as if the guy was being coached. To Oltington, that notion was so threatening, he simply pushed it out of his mind. The problem had escalated to where a fundamental solution must be concocted. In terms of short-term response, Kim could throw a snare net of glitches over Greaves, but not indefinitely. Someone else might log on to the same data base sector, encounter these glitches, and alert JEDI System Security or Tech Support.

That, at least, was something Greaves wouldn't do, in Kim's opinion. The guy was in JEDI illegally, with a pass code he had no right to use. If System Security came down on him, Greaves—and his niece—would be in major deep doodoo.

Moreover, Kim was pretty sure that Greaves hadn't reported his activity to anyone, at least not through normal E- or V-mail channels. Kim had patched into the phone lines at the bank and was monitoring them.

At this point, the neat geometry Oltington was trying to impose on his thinking fell apart, as it often did, and his temper again took charge.

"Damn you, Mona!" he muttered. Damn you, damn you, damn you!

This was another example of Mona being too clever by half! he stormed. The Thunderbolt–Oystermen's gimmick had been her bright idea. If there was any justice in the world, *she* should be the one to sort it out.

The Master had warned Oltington about Mona. She was too clever for most people's good, he'd said, including her own.

The Master said this, but he was as infatuated with Mona as anyone else in the CIA back then. Mona was his prize pupil, his best operative, for whom he reserved the choicest plums.

Oltington had met her back in 1974, toward the end of his unhappy stint at Langley. The Master was moving her operational focus from Central America to the Middle East, and she had come back Stateside for briefing.

Even if she hadn't been teacher's pet, Mona Kurchinski was the right agent for the job. Lebanon born, the illegal offspring of an Austrian diplomat and his German mistress, she spoke several dialects of Arabic and knew the territory cold, geographically, culturally, psychologically.

Her first stop was Vienna, where she ran a bear raid on the Israeli shekel as part of a secret deal with the Shah of Iran. She also oversaw the implosion of a couple of East African central banks. When OPEC flexed its muscles in the 1970s, and it suddenly seemed that the towelheads had all the money there was, Mona was sent to Beirut to liaise with Saudi intelligence.

She and the Arabs took to each other on sight. The first thing anyone at Langley knew, Mona had quit the agency and set up in Geneva, running her own little *banque privée* from an elegant lakeside villa. It was said she managed the personal portfolios of several members of the Saudi royal family. The sum mentioned had ten zeros.

The Master had been furious. Mona knew too much; he had urged that she be treated "with extreme prejudice." His fit of vindictiveness soon passed, however. Mona might someday have her uses. It was also possible, Oltington thought, that Mona's knowledge of certain dark Agency doings had been memorialized, to be made public in the event anything untoward should befall her, and that the CIA and the Master had been made aware of this.

Oltington himself left Langley not long after Mona did. When JEDI became a reality and Oltington conceived the Project, she was the first person he thought of, although it had been almost fifteen years since he'd seen her.

Old friends from Langley brought him up to speed on her activities. As always, Mona had moved in opportunistic phase with the shifting tides of economic fortune. On behalf of her clients, now substantially richer than when she'd taken over their accounts, she'd acquired a substantial piece of an aggressive new bank, Credit Provençal. Oltington's CIA friends hinted that Mona had brought the bank a number of big clients with major agricultural interests in Colombia and Peru: in Medellín, Cali, Bogotá, the Upper Huallaga valley.

It figured, thought Oltington when he heard that. Drugs were now where the big money was. The Master frequently criticized Mona to her face for her thirst for excitement. It was disproportionate, he would fume, and—in this business—a lack of proportion was what did you in. Mona would listen, and then gaily go on her way. To her, being left out of the action was the one true torment.

She was pleased to hear from Oltington again. It was arranged for them to meet in Paris, under the cover of an official visit by Oltington's boss.

Acquaintance was renewed in a grand apartment CP maintained on the Rue de Grenelle. When he told her about JEDI and outlined the Project, Mona responded with a warmth and enthusiasm most women reserved for love and sex. She met him for dinner in a private room at Taillevent—arriving and departing separately—where she flirted outrageously with him. He felt tipsy when he left—and although he would tell himself it was the wine, a fatly perfumed Clos Vougeot, that had done it, he knew it was Mona's company that was the real intoxicant. He made a mental note always to be on mental alert when alone with her.

When he telephoned the next morning, he was told she had left Paris. That afternoon, when Oltington returned to his hotel, a parcel from Charvet awaited him. It contained the most beautiful shirt he had ever seen, just his size, exactly to his taste, along with an unsigned computer-printed note to the effect that his proposal was now under review.

He next spoke to Mona thirteen days later, from a pay phone on M Street. The number he had been instructed to dial had a Chicago prefix, but he guessed that his call had been patched through three or four other exchanges before ending up wherever it was that Mona was speaking from.

Her people were very interested in the Project, but . . .

"You know how it is now, Russell. No one works on a handshake. You and I remember when millions changed hands on the assumption that people were who they claimed to be, and a person's word was a person's bond. These new people, they don't."

In other words, before anyone she dealt with could consider his proposal seriously, a meaningful earnest of his ability to deliver would be necessary.

Such as what?

Mona told him.

He would have to give it some thought, he answered.

Take as long as you need. Her people were patient. They took a long view. If he decided to go forward, here was what must be done. If he had any questions, he knew where to reach her.

Oltington thought long and hard about what Mona's clients required as a good faith deposit. At any other time, what they were asking would have been unthinkable, but now, as he saw it, the national interest itself was at stake. Critical overseas initiatives were being discarded for lack of funding; spheres of interest that should be maintained were on the verge of being abandoned.

Was the American Century to be abandoned for want of a nail? he asked himself.

The answer had to be no, not when he knew where to find the money to buy nails by the ton!

Shortly thereafter, a parcel arrived at a *poste restante* in the eleventh *arrondissement;* it was addressed to a "M. Hamadi" in a handwriting that any competent graphologist would have identified as Oltington's.

The parcel contained an inexpensive paperback. On the back flyleaf, in the same hand as the address, was recorded certain information retrieved from JEDI. Underneath, Oltington had scrawled his signature. He had put himself up as additional collateral.

Unlike most late 1980s collateral, moreover, his was good.

A week later, the marine detail opening the gate of the American embassy in Bogotá found a bloodstained plastic bag hanging from the flagstaff. Inside was the severed head of the DEA's principal deep-cover agent in Cali, a woman who had operated successfully for three years without arousing a breath of suspicion. Her loss was a major setback for the DEA, or so it was characterized afterward by the agency's Director in his weekly report to the special drug war task force chaired by the Vice President.

"A terrible business, terrible," murmured Oltington, seated against the wall next to Di Maglio; his eyes filled with tears, and he blew his nose loudly in his flamboyant silk kerchief. Di Maglio looked at his associate without much sympathy; people like Oltington never got the point—that this was a tough business and a few eggs were going to get broken no matter what.

Six days after the meeting, a Cessna Citation took off from Houston's Hobby Airport and was never heard from again. The aircraft was registered to the Willis Oil Company of Pass Christian, Louisiana, but in fact belonged to the U.S. Customs Service. The four agents on board were engaged in an elaborate sting operation known to those involved as Operation Post Oak, after the Houston bank that was cooperating in the effort. They were bound for Miami to spring the trap.

Twenty-four hours later, Oltington was advised that he had himself a deal.

That had been thirty-seven months ago, and—until now—everything had gone as smooth as anyone could ask.

Up ahead, his lights picked out the giant, spreading birch that marked the entrance to the estate on which Oltington rented a small, isolated cottage. He turned in, glad to have finally arrived. He would think better after a whiskey or two.

His house was secluded, set off by a heavily wooded rise from the main estate buildings at the end of an unmarked driveway that was little more than a grassy track. The life he lived here on weekends was simple, even humble. Now and then, it occurred to him how much grander his life might be if he'd taken what he'd learned from Henry

Carew to Goldman, Sachs or Morgan Stanley, or George Soros. He would probably be a millionaire several times over by now.

The trouble was, Wall Street lacked the ultimate thrill. On Wall Street, all you could do were deals with companies and stocks and bonds; in Washington, if you got yourself in the right position, you could turn entire political and market systems inside out the way the Fed had just done to the foreign exchange crowd. Ideologically, Oltington had hated the Fed operation, but in terms of technique, he had to admit that it had been breathtaking.

He strode across the strip of soaking unmowed lawn, fumbling for his keys. His clothes felt like they were shrinking with each step; the smell of damp worsted mixed with perspiration was nauseating. He poked his key at the lock, blinded by a rivulet streaming from the unguttered roof. At last it opened, and he stumbled into the house, stripping off his raincoat, suit jacket, and tie, which he threw onto an armchair. With clumsy fingers, he pried open the stiff white collar of his flame-striped shirt. The collar button popped off and Oltington cursed out loud. This was a brand-new shirt from Turnbull and Asser.

He marched over to the bar, poured himself a double measure of sixteen-year-old Lagavulin and drained it neat. The strong, peaty whiskey burned his throat going down, but he didn't mind. Almost he began to feel an inner easing, a slowing of his rapidly racing internal flywheels. He knocked back a second shot. That's better, he thought.

He poured a third and carried it over to the sofa, sat down heavily, and kicked off his shoes. His mind was now moving at a manageable speed. Making haste slowly.

Could this man Greaves be part of a sting? he wondered. Acting as bait in a snare being laid by JEDI System Security? It was possible, wasn't it, that System Security might have hit upon Kim without Kim's knowing it?

No it wasn't, Oltington told himself. Kim was privy to JEDI's innermost secrets. Kim had helped design the goddamn thing! Thanks to the bleeding hearts out there promoting the Big Brother Is Watching You syndrome, anything that had to do with changes in JEDI's surveillance architecture or scope had to be cleared by a three-man panel headed by Oltington's boss. Oltington sat in on those sessions and kept Kim informed.

Kim had scanned JEDI from one end to the other, and there was no sign of a sting that Greaves might fit into. God knows, every agency seemed to be running one. Customs had C-Chase, and another jointly with the IRS called Greenback; the FBI had Cashback Expressway; the DEA had Pisces and Polarcap and had just closed out Swordfish II. Not that there mightn't be exceptions, something off-JEDI, eyes-only at the very top, but was it likely whoever was running it could—would—have bypassed Oltington's boss?

No way.

So if Greaves wasn't part of a sting, thought Oltington, that meant he could be stung.

He began to formulate a plan.

A plan that would leave intact and undisturbed both the Project and Oltington's personal action.

The latter was the consequence of a love affair, an expensive one. The objects of Oltington's affection and desire were not human, however; not created by God or biology, but by a squat, plain Dutchman who had been dead for 321 years when Oltington first encountered him, one Rembrandt Harmensz van Rijn.

To carry on with Rembrandt took a great deal of money, money Oltington didn't have. He lived on his government salary, eked out with modest savings and the income on a small legacy.

"Barely enough to buy a frame," he'd told Mona.

The affair had lasted eighteen months now. It had begun when Oltington had traveled up to New York for a state dinner at the Council of Foreign Relations. Mona had arranged to be in New York at the Carlyle. After seeing to the *placement,* he had on the spur of the moment trotted across Park Avenue to pay a quick visit to an art show at the Seventh Regiment Armory.

He had made the rounds quickly; he was due back at the Council in an hour.

Then he stopped dead in his tracks, as Dante must have done when he first saw Beatrice on the Ponte Vecchio. He had spotted something he knew at first glance he must possess.

It was a superb impression of the fourth, to connoisseurs the most desirable, state of *The Three Crosses,* perhaps Rembrandt's most famous and dramatic etching. The work dated from around 1660. It was priced at $1,700,000. Oltington had never seen anything so marvelous. He was smitten. He must have it!

But the price!

"I almost wept," he told Mona the next morning, "it was more money than I could *pronounce!*"

"So," she said, "if that's what you want, Russell, why not 'borrow' the money from your accounts?"

By her lights, $1,700,000 spent on a Rembrandt etching was a hell of a lot better investment than blowing up some no-account Central American *prefectura.*

Borrow from the Project! Oltington was shocked.

And in the next second he thought: Why not? What was a lousy million seven out of two hundred million? So far, he had taken nothing for himself. Wasn't he entitled to a reasonable fee?

"But how?" he asked. It was a plea for guidance and help.

After a moment, she said she thought she saw a way.

It was arranged that a numbered account on the Macau branch of Credit Provençal would be debited in the amount of $1,700,000, bringing that particular balance down to $23,237,000. The money was wired to an accommodation account at a Baltimore bank.

Oltington called the dealer back that afternoon. The dealer was apologetic. Out of the blue, he had accepted an offer from a Towson law firm acting for an overseas collector.

Oltington's vocal chagrin was heart-rending. The dealer expressed his profound regrets. He knew what it was like to miss a great opportunity, especially for a new collector writhing in the sweet agony of initial infatuation.

When Oltington hung up the phone, however, he grinned and danced a little jig. The next afternoon, a van bearing the logo of CourierQuick, the overnight-delivery arm of Courier Services, drew up to his P Street apartment building, and the Rembrandt was his.

It would be inaccurate to say that Oltington's joy in its possession was wholly unmixed. He felt that he had betrayed a trust. But he could not help himself, and it was only a small betrayal.

Over the next fifteen months, *The Three Crosses* was joined by impeccable impressions of Rembrandt's *Self Portrait* of 1629; the *Portrait of the Artist's Father* of the following year, and of the artist's mother of the year after that; the *Ecce Homo* of 1635–1636; the *'Great' Jewish Bride* of the same period; the *Three Trees* of 1643, the *Faust in His Study* of 1652, and the *Saint Francis* of 1657. The collection was as good as any in private hands. It had cost something over $12,000,000 to assemble.

With each acquisition, Oltington's remorse lessened, although by now the sum he had siphoned off could have bribed a left-leaning sub-Saharan democracy back onto the path of political righteousness.

He was not utterly without guilt. He would resolve to quit, like a cheat resolving to give up an affair, or an addict his cocaine, and then another incomparable etching would come on the market. Affecting the manner of an impecunious amateur, he haunted the New York print dealers; they showed him everything, told him all the gossip, including that a serious unknown collector, rumored variously to be Greek, Swiss, Argentine, was buying up every choice Rembrandt etching that came up. It never occurred to them that the mystery man might be the chubby, wasp-tongued man sitting across the desk.

Oltington reckoned that he needed $5,000,000 a year to feed his habit properly. Unwilling to invade the Project's capital further, he cast about for a second source of personal funding, and thus the sub-rosa Committee for Market Democracy was born.

It was never known by that name, of course, nor did the rubric ever appear on a letterhead or in any form of published or written communication. Oltington conceived the CMD along the lines of Skull and Bones, the Yale secret society to which the Master had belonged, whose name was never uttered by its initiates—except to one another.

The Committee consisted of twenty people, men and women who didn't like the way things were going in the country, who were upset by what they heard and saw. The man they had successfully backed for President was no longer himself; he had become someone else, someone threatening to the way they wanted things run. It was time to finance an alternative.

To avoid inconvenient publicity or inquiry, it was arranged that contributions to the Committee's work would be routed through Kim's Data Security Consultants and appear on the contributors' books as payments for consulting services. By this device, Oltington hedged himself against any unpleasantness that might arise should a contributor discover that his money was in fact diverted to Oltington's personal use.

Having come up with the money, Oltington sought Mona's assistance about how and where to hide it. They met in Mexico City, in the Ethnographic Museum, over a weekend when the Vice President was standing in for Number One at an OAS conference. Oltington told Mona he needed to move some money, not much, less than half a million a month. Would she help?

Whose money? Mona wanted to know.

A domestic slush fund, he told her. A sort of unregistered PAC.

Mona wasn't crazy about that. Still, she was inclined to accommodate Oltington. He had delivered the goods with JEDI. By her own estimates, access to the system had saved Don Escobedo and his clients close to $400 million in losses they had been able to sidestep, on top of yielded real cash profits of close to $800 million. More important, of the $7 billion the clients had placed in various U.S. capital markets, close to $2.6 billion was "JEDI sensitive": in situations where the sort of foreknowledge Oltington provided could literally reverse risk-reward ratios.

She told him she would see what she could do.

Not without some unease. To help Oltington in the way she intended was a clear violation of her understanding with Don Escobedo. Mona was under no illusions as to what happened to those who crossed the Don.

On the other hand, the machinery required was in place and purring smoothly. And she had this to consider: Oltington was clearly obsessive about his etchings. Obsessives left to their own devices tended to do foolish things. If she failed him, he would look elsewhere.

So Mona had initiated a procedure whereby the money was routed via Kim to Courier Services, which took it from there. Oltington knew nothing more about the money's travels. When he needed cash, he advised Mona and deposits were wired from overseas into whichever account he designated.

Until now, it had gone flawlessly.

"Until now . . . ," he muttered to himself and poured another whisky. He was beginning to see how to deal with this. A doggerel formed in his tipped-over mind: Greaves the stinger. Sting the stinger. Sting the sting. The stinger stung.

An hour later, he shrugged unsteadily into his still-damp Burberry and went out. The rain had stopped. He drove slowly to a service station on the outskirts of a nearby town where he knew there was a pay phone.

There was no one about, few cars on the road. He pulled up close to the booth, dialed Kim's pager with the signal that he needed to speak personally, then sat in the car with the window down, waiting for the phone to ring.

When Kim called back, Oltington outlined what he had in mind. He knew his voice sounded slurred, but his mind was sharp.

"Makes sense to me," said Kim. If he noticed anything odd in Oltington's tone, it wasn't apparent.

"You have everything you need? Documentation, badges, whatever?"

"I have what I need. Can you cover your end if . . ."

"If what?"

"Suppose the guy tries to check up on me?"

"You're covered at my end," said Oltington.

That was the whisky talking. He had no cover arranged, no fallback. Would Kim sense that?

"And if he doesn't bite?"

"He will," said Oltington confidently. "But whatever happens, do what you have to do."

Kim was silent for an instant.

Then he said "no problem" in a quiet voice that was almost a murmur, and hung up.

NINE

▼

The caller identified himself to Greaves as Special Agent Arthur Chung and said he would arrive in Bordrero Bay late that afternoon. No one should know he was coming; he needed to speak with Greaves urgently, on a matter of utmost confidentiality. It shouldn't take more than an hour. He was on a very tight schedule: he planned to return to Washington that evening on the overnight flight.

Could Greaves suggest a meeting place? Someplace discreet. Not the bank or anyplace where they could be seen talking together. Perhaps Greaves's hotel room?

Greaves paused before answering. He felt uncomfortable. For some reason, maybe because it was his private space and Special Agent Chung was obviously coming on official business, he didn't like the idea of meeting back at the Days Inn.

How about the observation site at Point Clara, he asked; the place was generally deserted on a Monday.

That was a lie. It was a beautiful day in Bordrero Bay, which promised a fine sunset. When the weather was good, you could count on people coming out to Point Clara. For some reason, Greaves thought it would be a good idea to have company.

That sounded fine, said Chung. How about five-thirty?

When Greaves hung up, he was in a sweat. Apprehension hit like an angina twinge. This was not good, not good at all. He had crossed a line and they were coming after him. In Special Agent

Chung's voice was a gravity that any veteran federal employee would have recognized, a gravity that Greaves himself had projected on many occasions. Its meaning was unmistakable: a sin had been committed, and now the full weight of official opprobrium was about to come slicing down like a guillotine blade.

Best to be prepared, he thought; try not to panic. He did something he had never done before during working hours. He exited the liability spread sheet he'd been putting together, pass coded into JEDI, logged on to the personnel module and tapped out his caller's surname.

The minute the Chung profile came up, Greaves knew he was in big, big trouble.

Because there was none. No picture, no text. Only Chung's name and federal serial number. And the entry: "File Sequestered/Special Assignment."

Holy mother of God, Greaves muttered to himself. Whatever Chung was connected with, it was so secret that his file had been taken off JEDI! He banged at the keyboard, suddenly anxious to get out of JEDI, mistyping the Exit sequence like a kid stumbling in headlong flight from a broken window. In his haste, it didn't register that it was odd, assuming he was in trouble with JEDI System Security, which seemed the most rational explanation, that the pass code he'd been using for almost four weeks was still valid.

The bank logo finally came onscreen with a comforting glow, and Greaves reaccessed Lotus. He pretended to study the wavering digits, but his mind flew elsewhere.

So of what unit was this Chung a special agent? Probably JEDI System Security, Greaves figured, although there had been a heaviness to his words that suggested something bigger. God, Greaves thought, could the guy be from SMERSH, the top-secret interagency security outfit that some joker had nicknamed after the archcriminal cabal in the James Bond pictures? If SMERSH was on your case, the cafeteria gossips proclaimed, you were in shit deeper than the Mariana Trench!

"Chung." Now what kind of name was that?

Chinese? Maybe, also possibly Korean. Computer-literate Asiatics were flooding the agencies these days, squeezing out career people like Greaves, not to mention ordinary applicants. Sooner or later, there wasn't going to be a real American left in America, Greaves thought. The slopeheads might be good with computers and numbers, but somehow it didn't seem right, not with so many indigenous Americans out of work.

Anyway, what difference did it make whether the guy was white or yellow?

The big question was: What was Chung after? Put another way: What kind of trouble was Greaves in?

One of two kinds, by his estimate. It was possible that he had wandered into a part of JEDI he wasn't supposed to be in. Or he had somehow been detected using someone else's pass codes.

It occurred to him now that the second was unlikely. If that had been the case, they would have started with his niece, and he'd have been warned. Which meant he should alert her.

He decided to call her when he went out for lunch. Use the pay phone across from the coffee shop. The phone on his desk suddenly looked like a steel-jawed trap. Was he getting paranoid? Seen too many spy pictures?

Maybe, but it didn't hurt to be careful. He was pretty sure he was on to something big. Tip 'n Take's and Energy City's local sales tax filings, which he'd checked out with the town receiver of taxes, who worked from the actual register tapes, didn't square with the size of their deposits. Either they were stiffing the Bordrero Bay Consolidated School District or their actual cash takings were being padded. Was this some kind of tax cheat? Then there was something funny about the way the deposits were split and shifted before being wire-transferred out. Greaves hadn't made sense of this yet, but instincts honed over thirty years suggested the footwork was complex and fancy, which indicated a major scam of some kind.

He had just about figured out how exactly to instruct JEDI to massage its megamillions of data bytes to give him the information he needed. He was beginning to be comfortable with the system, really comfortable, which made Special Agent Chung's appearance on the scene doubly vexing. JEDI was complicated, high-strung and temperamental. You didn't just march up to it and ask it to dance.

He was satisfied that Thunderbolt Video was a separate, small potatoes deal that he could safely write off. Probably one of the store managers out at the mall had a friend at Courier Services, and they'd decided to do a little business together, skim a few hundred grand and piggyback it through a lockbox.

Courier Services was obviously in the middle of whatever was going on, but so far Greaves hadn't hit the right JEDI buttons. Courier serviced nine shopping center lockboxes. The logical thing would be to stake out each of the nine and see what was what. That was obviously beyond Greaves's means. It had occurred to him that maybe Lee Boynton, who had put him on the Tip 'n Take–Energy City scent, would be interested in hiring a private surveillance firm. She was due back in D.C. Wednesday; maybe he'd suggest getting a PI. After all, so far he was doing all the work for half the potential glory.

What he was itching to go after now were all those Freemark-brokered deposits that had been withdrawn from GoldWest before Uncle Sam moved in. The timing had been incredible! It was as if $300 million had been given the order to pull out just hours after GoldWest had been put on the Watch List; certificates of deposit that hadn't budged for three years suddenly decided they should move to other institutions. Several hundred million departed in such haste that a few million dollars were left on the table as penalties for early withdrawal.

Freemark was rotten, that seemed clear. When GoldWest tanked, a photo of Gorton, the guy who ran Freemark, went up on the Director's bulletin board next to photos of Milken and Keating. Those two were down; Gorton was proving harder to nail.

What Greaves had so far he'd considered too preliminary, too theoretical to inform Lee Boynton about. But now, with this guy Chung suddenly hoving onto the scene, he thought he better fill her in. Modem her the raw data stored in his laptop back at the motel and brief her as to his sense of what it might mean. There'd always been talk of moles in the agencies handling the S&L–bank crisis. These withdrawals seemed to confirm it.

He reached for the telephone, then drew his hand back. If this guy Chung really was SMERSH, it was certain they'd bugged his line. Probably at the motel, too. He was suddenly glad he'd gone to the extra effort of downloading his JEDI stuff from the bank computer to his Sharp, and then—back in his motel room—uploading from his Sharp to his laptop. If he'd modemed directly from the bank to the Days Inn, the data flow coursing over the phone line could have been monitored.

What could this guy Chung do to him anyway? Give him a hard time, that was about it. This was America, after all, not some banana republic where they dragged you off to a dark cellar and hot-wired your testicles.

When he went out for lunch, he crossed Bay Street and placed two calls to Washington, one to Lee, one to his niece's apartment. In both cases, answering machines picked up. On Lee's he left a message to call him ASAP. On his niece's machine, he left a terse alert.

As he ate his sandwich his mood improved. It seemed obvious what had happened, why Chung was coming. He'd wandered into a sting that he might queer if he kept asking questions. That had to be it. They wouldn't send a special agent all the way out here to bust him for unauthorized entry to JEDI.

And then he had a terrible thought.

Suppose this wasn't a sting. Suppose it was a scam. The risks on a sting weren't mortal: stings were run by guys in white hats, and were about law and justice. Scams were black hat propositions involving big money. The number of people who got killed for reasons of rectitude and justice was about a tenth of those who got killed for money.

God, he thought, feeling the perspiration starting to come. If it's a scam, I could be a dead man.

He needed a rabbit to pull out of the hat if he had to, a cavalry troop to whistle up if it got sticky.

When he spoke with Lee Boynton, he would tell her about "Chung."

And he would tell "Chung" about Lee Boynton.

On the way back to the bank, he stopped at the pay phone and called Lee again. Still not home. He called *Capitol Steps* and got a machine there. He decided not to leave a message.

The afternoon passed anxiously. Greaves spent most of it fidgeting, his mind elsewhere. He now assumed the bank's phone, fax, and computer lines were all tapped. SMERSH would have triple A1 priority when it came to high-tech cloak and dagger. There was probably a microphone in the lid of his water thermos, a scanner built into the rubber plant in the corner, a fiber optic audiovisual bug in one of the pencil erasers.

At three-thirty he went out for coffee again. The day was less luminous, the sky lightly brushed with a dull haze. En route to the coffee shop, he stopped now and then and used the reflection in shop windows to check his rear. On his way back to the bank, he placed another fruitless call to Lee, this time taking pains to shield his dialing with his body. He added a message asking her to get in touch with his niece.

When he came outside at quarter to five, he saw to his consternation that the day had completely changed. One of the region's noted fogs had swept in like a squall. Bordrerans liked to boast about their "three-star pea soupers." This one was a five-star.

On the way to the rendezvous with Chung, he stopped at a Chevron station and tried Lee again from the pay phone, then checked his motel for messages. None. He thought about turning back. He could claim car trouble. Then he told himself to cut it out. He had to assume the guy was legit. He was "on" JEDI, after all.

By the time he pulled into the Point Clara parking area, the fog had become so thick he banged the low stone retaining wall with his bumper. The mist was like a solid sheet of gray-yellow metal; somewhere on its other side, the sea thrashed the cliffs with a thunderous roar.

He didn't like this at all. It was like a Hitchcock movie. He changed his mind, decided to go back to the bank, let Chung find him there; they could get together in some bright, well-lighted place.

He switched on the ignition. As he did, lights emerged from the fog and shone blindingly in his rearview mirror. He froze.

A blue Mercury Sable with rental plates nosed into the adjacent parking space. Even this close, he could barely make it out. He heard the door open, and saw a trim figure move toward him. Greaves rolled his window down.

"Clarence Greaves?" A slim hand reached in. Greaves shook it; the fingers were like steel cable. "I'm Special Agent Chung."

A face appeared in the window opening, flat planed, the eyes cool and faintly almond shaped.

"Here are my credentials."

Greaves examined them. Everything looked in order. The seal embossed on the agent's photo was Treasury. Secret Service, no doubt. Greaves relaxed. This was probably a JEDI security check.

Dollars to doughnuts, it was a dispute over turf. Everyone in the participating agencies knew the Secret Service was really burned about being frozen out on JEDI. Normally, the security of federal computer installations was the service's responsibility, but for JEDI, a separate System Security had been set up. Obviously, Greaves guessed, the Secret Service had set up a probe—"File Sequestered/Special Assignment"—to catch JEDI System Security nodding; they had somehow spotted him while the JEDI watchdogs had not. Now they were probably going to use his penetration as a club with which to beat the JEDI boys, to enlist his cooperation in return for an all-is-forgiven.

"Mind if I get in?"

Chung slid into the passenger seat. Next to Greaves's bulk he seemed almost tiny.

"So, what can I do for you, Mr. Chung?"

"You can start by calling me Arthur." The agent's grin flashed white in the gloom.

The agent explained. It wasn't exactly as he'd surmised, but Greaves still felt a flush of relief. It *was* a sting, after all. A DEA sting. Chung was DEA, not Treasury.

Thunderbolt Video was part of it, but the real target was Courier Services. They were setting Courier up for a bust. From what little Chung said, Greaves inferred that the DEA had infiltrated Courier, gotten someone into the counting house with a Minox. As the agent explained, to have Greaves thrashing around in the electronic underbrush was just something they didn't need right now.

"So Tip 'n Take's also a player?" Greaves asked. "I figured it was." He gave the other man a comradely nudge.

Behind the affable smile on the face of "Arthur Chung," Peter Kim's mental temperature rose a few degrees. He hated to be touched.

"As to that, I'm afraid my lips have to be sealed." His voice was controlled.

"Come on," Greaves said, "you don't need to give me the old BS. We're all working for the taxpayer."

Kim-Chung thought fast. Maybe he could fold this guy up in a different way. Make him think he was part of something. Take him on board. Greaves didn't seem like a bad guy. To hit the "delete" key on Clarence Greaves would be a waste of energy.

"The thing is, Clarence, that this operation's pretty inner circle. First things first."

First things first. Precept five. Another of Oltington's treasured crumbs of wisdom.

"You're on the right track, however. It's occurred to the people back home that it might make sense for you to work with us on this, seeing as how you've bumped up against it."

"How?"

"I'd propose we start by seeing what you've got, and how it interfaces with our operational matrix, and see where we go from there. I assume you've kept your findings to yourself?"

Greaves nodded, but inside, his alarm system was going crazy. Something wasn't right here. The last thing that the people running a big sting ever did was wing it, which is what this guy was doing with him. Especially when it was about to go down, as Chung implied it was, because that was when people started thinking medals, and bonuses, and kisses on both cheeks from the President, stuff they weren't about to cut field-grade types like Clarence Greaves in on.

He checked the mirror. There hadn't been a car go by in ten minutes and there probably wouldn't be, not on a night like this. At over twenty miles an hour, the twisting coast road was treacherous even in bluebird weather; tonight it would take five minutes to negotiate a mile. Time was all he had, Greaves thought. He decided to try to buy some more.

"What do you guys have, some kind of monitoring setup hooked into JEDI that their System Security doesn't know about? Is that how you picked up on me?"

Kim grinned.

"Hey, Clarence, come on! You know I couldn't tell you about that if I wanted to."

The needle on Kim's emotional thermostat began to quiver again. He was on edge, tired. San Francisco-Washington-San Francisco in thirty-six hours had been a brute, given what he had to do. Anyway, he was within minutes of completing the second phase of his job. The Washington end was all taken care of, but he had had to get rough with the girl, and now she was quietly decomposing in the trunk of a car parked at the farthest end of the Dulles long-term lot. It could be weeks before the stink attracted enough attention; by then, this problem should be history.

Come on, Clarence, he urged silently, buy my story. Buy it and save your life. Don't be an asshole.

Greaves continued to stare out the windshield. Chung's representation definitely didn't ring true. Still, so what if it didn't? Why not cut his losses, go along, say okay? Then he'd be free to go.

Except he had a sudden feeling he wouldn't. Something was terribly wrong here. All his instincts said so.

He needed to play for time: time for the fog to lift, for another car to show up, for something to happen.

"I suppose you wouldn't mind if I asked to see your ID again?" he asked.

Kim's needle entered the red zone. It was as if the space in which he and Greaves sat had been compressed to its square root, to a terrible intensity.

"Not at all."

He smiled, pulled out his credentials folder, and passed it over. He pushed the button to lower the window and let in some outside air, but Greaves had turned off the ignition and the window didn't move. In the sealed car, the air was terribly close.

Greaves put on his glasses to study the documents. He switched the ignition back on, then the overhead light, and held Kim-Chung's ID up to see it better.

The movement exposed his throat. At that moment Kim hit him.

Hit him with microsurgical precision using the stiffened side of the hand that could split a two by four. The blow shut down Greaves's neural machinery. A second blow sliced into his throat, right under the chin, smashing his windpipe, rendering him senseless, eyes open and staring, mouth agape, dribbling. The third, lower down on the neck, six inches below the right ear, killed him.

For a few moments afterward, Kim sat very still, trembling slightly, taking deep ventilating breaths. Finally his systems eased back to normal speed.

The fog remained dense. The invisible sea beat at the rocks. There were no lights on the highway.

Kim got out, went around behind the car, and manhandled

Greaves's body into the passenger seat. He started the car and let down all the windows. The heavy moist air seemed to cleanse the interior. When Kim felt completely calmed down, he finished the job.

Two hours later, he was seventy miles southwest of Bordrero Bay. This far inland, the night was clear and furnacelike.

On the seat beside Kim lay Greaves's electronic organizer. Kim had taken it off the body just before he consigned Greaves to the roaring fogbound Pacific.

He had hoped to find a hotel key on the body, but there hadn't been one. This bothered Kim; good tradecraft prescribed that the guy's room be checked. But without a key, he'd have had to bullshit his way in, which could cause more trouble than it was worth.

Roughly abeam Petaluma, Kim stopped at a Route 101 service area for gas. While the tank was being filled, he idly picked up Greaves's organizer. A pretty neat little gadget, he thought, examining it in the pallid light. He'd check it out in the morning. He could probably figure out how it worked by himself, but if he had a problem, he could always get a replacement book from the manufacturer.

He got to SFO International with forty minutes in hand, plenty of time to telephone a Washington number to leave word that both meetings had gone well.

Not exactly as foreseen—but well.

TEN

▼

Lee had never been good at waiting.

For the fifth time, she put down her magazine, got up and walked over to the floor-to-ceiling windows that looked out on the airfield. Nothing yet. No landing lights, no pilot-to-tower gabble on the lobby squawk box. As she watched, a USAir DC-9 moved slowly away from the main passenger terminal on the other side of the field, ran up its engines, and lumbered off into the darkness.

She was the only one in the Carolina Airmotive waiting area. Charleston was not a busy airport even at its most active; over here at the general aviation terminal, where private aircraft arrived and departed, things were really dead. In the hour she'd been waiting, the only traffic had been a Citation deplaning a foursome of what looked like investment bankers: presumably for a weekend of golf; Lee doubted there was much banking business in the jewel of the Confederacy.

For perhaps the fiftieth time, she shot an irritated glance at her watch: Coole was now twenty-six minutes late.

This is unlike him, she thought; and then, But how would I know?

It was his manner. Coole's bespoke precision and punctuality, an old-maidish, Boston and Cambridge, seersucker-and-bow tie, Somerset Club-Eliot House-Hasty Pudding-Porcellian Club fussiness. In her day, Lee had been to enough Harvard football weekends to know the type.

A type not without charm, she thought, if you were lucky enough to find one with a brain in his head.

On the flight down, Lee had found herself thinking about Coole again and again. It had been months since she'd been made love to; could that be it?

Now she felt like a young girl on her first date, half-apprehensive, half-angry, wondering if she'd been stood up.

Where the hell was he?

Coole's instructions had been to get herself from Washington to Charleston, rent a car, drive around to the far side of the airport to Carolina Airmotive's terminal, where he would be arriving by private jet at around 9:30 P.M. He sounded all business; Lee inferred that a late dinner by candlelight and adjoining rooms in a charming, romantic inn in Old Charleston's historical district were not on his agenda. As to the purpose of this expedition, he had been cryptic; Lee knew only that they would be investigating something to do with the Phoenix fund.

The thought of Phoenix reminded Lee to try Greaves again. They had been missing each other all day. She went to the pay phone and dialed his motel. No answer. Well, it was still early out there: 10:05 in Charleston translated to 7:05 in Bordrero Bay. She called her answering machine in Washington. Nothing new since his last message.

That had been at around five-thirty coast time. The message had struck Lee as peculiar: instructions to call his niece—Lee didn't know he had one—and tell her there had been "system problems." Greaves had sounded rushed and harried, a man with a lot on his mind.

Lee had tried the niece, gotten her machine, and hung up without speaking. She didn't like the idea of leaving her voiceprint on machines she didn't know.

Has Clarence hit pay dirt, she wondered as she hung up. That idea of Coole's about rental percentages might have paid off. Just then, the loudspeaker above the service counter emitted a noisy babble. The duty clerk listened, then looked over at Lee.

"That'll be them, Ms. Boynton, just coming on final approach."

Several minutes later, a Falcon 90 marked with the legend UNITED STATES OF AMERICA rolled up to the gate, and Thurlow Coole, in the ugliest madras sport jacket Lee had ever seen, uncreased khaki trousers, and a lopsided Panama that looked like it had been at San Juan Hill with Teddy Roosevelt came down the ramp carrying a much-used attaché case in one hand and a small canvas duffel marked with the seal of Harvard College in the other.

He shook her hand gravely, thanked the air force warrant officer who had accompanied him from the plane to the terminal, and followed Lee to the car. He got in the driver's side and they set off.

They drove for approximately two hours, stopping after forty minutes at a Big Boy Bar-B-Q for fatty ribs and starchy fries drenched in a hot reddish sauce. Coole seemed to relish every bite.

He had flown in from Coral Gables, he told her while they ate. He was helping Uncle Sam sort out an especially tangled can of S&L worms.

"It must be a pretty big case," she said, "to warrant a personal jet."

"Big enough," he said in his best Sherlock Holmes voice. "About eight hundred million dollars. A malefaction, moreover, with very interesting ramifications."

She asked where they were headed.

"South," said Coole.

The faint green glare from the dashboard gave his attenuated features a raffish and seductive cast. Lee could see he was still mentally working through the problem he had just left: adding, subtracting, classifying, trying it this way and that, so she remained silent: a well-brought-up young woman who waited to speak until she was spoken to.

"Amazing," he said at length.

"What is?"

"What people will do for money," he replied.

Lee said nothing.

"I fancy I've learned most of life's great lessons," he continued, "but about that one I've been rather backward. I must say, though, when I was a younger man I was greedier. I suppose that's what it was."

"It" presumably being what sent you to jail, Lee thought. She said nothing. It was said Thurlow Coole had gone into prison on the side of the devil, but had come out on the side of the angels. He had lost his hair and gained righteousness.

They traveled for a while longer in silence, then Coole asked, "Do you ever see your uncle? How's he enjoying his retirement? He's at New Haven, isn't he?"

"He is."

When Henry St. Albans Carew left the CIA after thirty years, he struck a deal with his alma mater: He would donate $50 million to Yale to build St. Albans College, a new residential and tutorial complex, provided that he could remain as its Master for life and run it on his terms.

"He sounds as if he's thriving," she added, "although I haven't seen him for quite a while."

"Quite a change, I should think: from ravaging the Chilean economy to teaching Yale sophomores how to drink port."

"I don't think Uncle Henry actually *teaches* anyone," said Lee, trying not to sound testy. "From what I've seen up there, he devotes his time to keeping the late twentieth century at bay; to seeing that St. Albans maintains—well, a certain style."

Coole smiled. "That's what I meant. Anyway, if we find Mona Kurchinski is mixed up in whatever it is, you may be wanting to pay your uncle a visit. She was his star pupil. Ah, here we are."

He turned onto a narrow paved road. Lee sensed they were somewhere near water.

"This is a private shooting lodge maintained by clients of mine in the interest of good governmental relations," he explained. "It also happens to be extraordinarily convenient for our purposes."

The lodge was a comfortable, sprawling cabin decorated in nineteenth-century American macho.

A steward greeted them, confirmed to Coole that Mr. Lenchin had arrived a while earlier and had already retired, and offered coffee. Coole declined. He went to a sideboard that held an array of bottles, examined them in an unimpressed manner, and finally selected a cognac. He poured two snifters, handed Lee one without asking if she wanted it, drained his, pronounced it tolerable, and said good night. She would be called at six-thirty for breakfast at seven. Their mission would be made clear at that time.

Before turning in, Lee tried Greaves again. Again there was no answer. She checked her watch: It was just after midnight, which meant nine and a bit in California.

You're making quite an evening of it, Clarence, she thought, maybe you got lucky. But she was beginning to worry.

She awoke sluggishly to the steward's knock, and was trying to figure out where she was when an awful clattering racket outside her window made the glass shake. A single-engined Cessna seaplane was taxiing noisily down the finger of a marsh creek on which the camp sat. Its prop wash scattered the tendrils of mist, which rose like yellowish, evanescent stalagmites from weedy gray water. It was like being in some Southern Gothic jungle, all pale grays and greens: mangroves bent low to the creek, willows like berobed mourners, a tall waterbird, a heron or egret, pacing the far shore, vigilantly stalking its own breakfast.

She dressed quickly in jeans, Nikes, and a rough, waxed-cotton Barbour jacket. Coole had indicated that this was to be an outdoor adventure.

The two men were drinking coffee in the dining room. They rose when she entered.

Coole was attired as if for a committee meeting at the Harvard Library. His companion—who he introduced simply as "Lenchin"—was a hard-eyed man so deeply tanned his skin might have come from a saddlery. Built like an ape—squat, bandylegged, long armed—he was wearing an extravagantly stitched lightweight suit of an improbable shiny fawn color. Its trousers were stuffed into calf-high Gokey boots.

A map was spread out on the table; it showed a wide-waisted chunk of earth roughly kidney shaped connected to the South Carolina mainland by a narrow causeway.

"Margaret Island," said Coole. "The jewel in the crown of Dunbar Realty and Development. Does Dunbar ring a bell, Miss Boynton?"

"A faint chime, somewhere," said Lee, "no more."

"Margaret Island lies approximately forty minutes' flying time from here, just off the coast. It was acquired by Dunbar for approximately a hundred million dollars in 1988 from a group of Middle Eastern investors who had earlier purchased it for roughly a fifth of that sum from the family that had owned it for several generations. It was to be the site of a three-hundred-million-dollar luxury resort development. This, along with the land purchase, was financed with a four-hundred-million-dollar issue of Dunbar junk bonds placed privately in this country and offshore by Freemark Securities. Of that amount, sixty-eight million was taken up by GoldWest. Bordrero Bay Bank was allocated eighteen million.

"The Dunbar bonds proved to be less than sound investments. Dunbar defaulted nine months after issue and took a bankruptcy chapter. The entire issue had to be written off without a penny of interest or principal having been paid. To the extent the issue was placed with federally guaranteed institutions such as Bordrero Bay, the American taxpayer will of course make up any losses."

"Losses being the difference between what GoldWest, etc., paid for the bonds and what Dunbar's assets can be sold for today?"

"Precisely. It is those assets that you and I and Lenchin are now going to have a look at."

They flew northeast for about an hour, Coole in front next to the pilot, Lee and Lenchin squeezed into the backseats. Finally, Coole pointed ahead to a scrub-covered amoeba spread flat on the horizon.

For forty minutes, they crisscrossed Margaret Island in low swooping passes. It was virtually in a state of raw nature. What little development had taken place was obviously a matter of a few fleeting gestures, random scars inflicted on earth and brush; here a paved road ran a few hundred yards flanked by perfunctory house lots, there a half-dug sewage ditch went nowhere. In the center of the island an area of several acres had been cleared: in the middle was a cluster of low buildings, looking abandoned, surrounded by regimented stacks of sewer piping, giant coils of heavy electrical cable, palleted sacks of cement arrayed battalion strength, and an irregular platoon of yellow construction machines. Off to one side was a cement helipad; the red-and-white painted bull's-eye was already fading.

Lenchin kept busy with a Nikon equipped with a fierce-looking lens, now and then muttering into a pocket microcassette recorder.

Suddenly the pilot tapped Coole, shouted something in his ear over the noise of the engine, and gestured with his thumb toward the east. Lee made out something hovering in the strong morning light like a giant Japanese beetle; it hung briefly, then shot forward and emerged from the glare: a helicopter marked with the logo CSS. It looked the seaplane over, then swung away sharply, and disappeared to the west.

"Big Brother is watching us," shouted Coole over his shoulder. He grinned at her. Neither he nor Lenchin seemed the slightest bit worried.

They were back at the lodge by eleven. Lee excused herself, went to her room, and tried Greaves again, first at the Days Inn, then at his direct number at the bank. No answer either place. "Where the hell are you, Clarence," she muttered, then told herself that he must be en route from his motel to the bank, or perhaps taking one of his constitutionals out near the Cephalod Inn. She decided to try again in an hour when she could be certain of catching him at work. The vague concern of the previous evening was giving way to genuine apprehension.

She called her machine. No word from Greaves or his niece. Ordinarily she would have gotten Barney to hunt up the niece, but he'd taken his family off to the Blue Ridge Mountains, and Lee didn't want to disturb what might be their last vacation together. Hanging up, she heard the seaplane depart. She went back into the living room. Coole and Lenchin were talking over coffee. Lenchin's bag stood in a corner. He was obviously on the point of leaving.

Coole looked up. There must have been something in her expression, because he asked if there was anything wrong.

"I can't raise Greaves anywhere. He called me—my machine, that is—several times yesterday, and now I can't get hold of him. There's a niece in DC who might know where he is, but I can't find her either."

Coole frowned and shrugged.

"Well, you'll just have to keep after him," he said. "Now: Lenchin here's about to be off. He'll give us a full report, of course, with photographs and so on, but I think you'll find his conclusion interesting. Correct me on this, Lenchin, but it's his professional judgment that the sum total of infrastructural and other investments made to date on Margaret Island, at least what can be seen, amounts at best to five million dollars. That right?"

"That's the eyeball number, sir. And obviously it don't include the cost of the property, which they book in at a hundred million dollars even."

"The bottom line," Coole continued, "is that what we looked at this morning is nothing more or less than the equivalent, in terms of real estate development, of a salted gold mine."

"A salted gold mine worth four hundred million," Lee remarked. "Less the out-of-pocket money spent to set the scam up. So what was Dunbar, just a front?"

"That we'll have to look into."

"Four hundred million dollars up in flames, just like that!" Lee snapped her fingers. "And no one's asked any questions? No one's come out here to see where their money went? Dunbar just defaulted, took a chapter, and that was that? Jesus!"

Coole smiled.

"The mysterious ways of junk bond finance, Miss Boynton. You must be careful when you say 'no one.' The instructions to cut the checks that bought the Dunbar junk bonds were given by money managers; the actual money behind those checks wasn't theirs, however; it most likely belonged to pensioners, mutual fund stockholders, trust beneficiaries, and others whose sense of where their appointed managers are putting that money isn't perhaps what it should be."

"In other words, the old 'OPM' ploy, right?"

"Spoken like a true child of the television era. But you're right. It's Other People's Money that makes the world go round for Wall Street. Round and round and round. Don't forget, as well, that Dunbar, like many such speculative transactions, paid extravagant fees and commissions. Freemark was paid seventeen million dollars for structuring and placing the bond issue, and Freemark in turn passed out choice baubles and sweetmeats from Leo Gorton's cornucopia to participating or cooperative money managers."

" 'Baubles and sweetmeats' such as . . . ?"

"Warrants to buy pieces of other, more solvent Freemark deals, trips to Boca Raton, perhaps a Land Rover or two, at the least a lucrative stock tip. Very much in the style of Mr. Gorton's idol, Michael Milken."

At this point, Lenchin excused himself and left. He was on his way to California and Texas, Coole said.

"I want him to have a look at a wind turbine project in the San Gregorio Pass, and an agricultural chemical plant at Ingleside, near Galveston. I doubt either will bear scrutiny. Between the two, they absorbed some six hundred and fifty million dollars of capital in the form of junk bond offerings underwritten by—"

"Let me guess. Freemark Securities?"

"Correct."

"And both are in default?"

"Correct."

"Leo Gorton seems to have been a terrible judge of businesses."

"Not as bad as his customers were with respect to Mr. Gorton's offerings."

By twelve, they were on the road back to Charleston.

"So," said Lee as Coole pulled onto the highway, "the sixty-four-dollar question is: Money, money, who's got the money? Dunbar, whoever they were? Gorton? Shadowy persons unknown? I have to say I find it absolutely mind boggling that anyone could pull off a scam as obvious as this one seems to have been."

"Obvious is as obvious does. It wasn't entirely crude: There were some nice touches. To buy the land, a hundred million dollars was borrowed from an Atlanta bank that is a paragon of respectability; that loan was repaid in good order on its due date, a fact that made reassuring reading in the offering circular. A light compost of respectability is an essential first stage in preparing the ground for a really first-class defalcation."

"So what's next? How do things stand with Dunbar as we speak."

"That's the interesting part. Until two days ago, the holders of Dunbar's junk paper, including the government as heir and assign of GoldWest and other busted 'investors,' have been engaged in the usual bankruptcy squabbling over which piece of paper gets how much of what's left."

"What's left being roughly zero. Plus the land."

"I like that, Miss Boynton. Five million in infrastructure and equipment, and you call it 'zero.' You're starting to think like a true 1980s financier."

"I take that as a compliment. And you might as well call me Lee."

"Very well, Lee. As I was saying, until two days ago Dunbar was merely a corpse being pecked at by lawyers. But a jackal has now drawn up a seat at the dubious feast. Phoenix Capital, which is associated with CP, which is associated with GoldWest, has offered fifty million dollars cash, or twelve and a half cents on the dollar, for the Dunbar junk bonds."

"And Phoenix is now run by Leo Gorton, who used to run Freemark Securities, which is the firm that placed the Dunbar junk in the first place, right?"

"Correct. As for 'running' Phoenix, let us say that Mr. Gorton is Phoenix's public aspect, the hand we see on the tiller. My guess is that other more resolute and clever hands may be guiding his."

"Not a bad deal: fifty million dollars for a hundred and five million dollars' worth of land and infrastructure?"

"In this real estate market, more like fifty million dollars for fifteen million, if you ask me. Like everything else in high finance, the value of property is a creature of its moment. Just ask the Japanese about Rockefeller Center. Still, you've asked the right question."

"To wit?"

"To wit: The common assumption is that so-called vulture funds like Phoenix have as their sole purpose the acquisition of assets at far less than their going value: to buy for cents on the dollar what is really worth dollars on the dollar. But suppose we stand that assumption on its head. Suppose we imagine a vulture fund that is set up to purchase for cents on the dollar assets that *it knows to be worth only mills on the dollar*. Then we are speaking not of making money, but of preserving money already made. We are speaking, essentially, of damage control."

"Buy up the junk bonds and you buy up the evidence. Is that it?"

Coole nodded and shot Lee a quick glance. The bright blank stare of his mirrored sunglasses was unnerving.

"A cash offer is a healthy disincentive to curiosity. Especially if Uncle Sam has become a bondholder by default. One would not want some overambitious civil servant from the Resolution Trust Company, say, taking a hard look at exactly what the Margaret Island Development consists of, coming to approximately the same conclusion as Lenchin, and pronouncing the whole affair a monstrous fraud implicating important institutions and individuals in this country and offshore. Better by far to forestall that possibility with a little cash on the barrelhead."

"Is this something Leo Gorton's masterminding?"

"From what I know of Mr. Gorton, no. Greed and ambition have dulled the man's perceptions, both the moral and the numerate. He's like a horse in blinders. My guess is that he's convinced he is offering pence for pounds."

"So who isn't? Who's behind him?"

Coole's look told her she should know the answer to that. The image of a striking woman in sable flashed in her mind.

Coole drove on for a moment in silence.

"I think we spoke earlier of connecting up dots. Seen in the conventional way, Phoenix is just a dot. Viewed the way I suggest it might be, it could be a line. It's just like money. In finance, every number has two dimensions: the absolute and the proportionate. It helps to keep that in mind."

They reached the Charleston airport with plenty of time to spare. Lee went straight to a pay phone. She started to dial Greaves's direct number at the bank, then stopped and called her machine in Washington instead. There was one message, from Constancia. The machine's robot voice said it had come in at 11:03.

The mayor's voice was agitated. Lee was to call immediately! Instinctively Lee knew that something must have happened to Greaves.

She was right. Greaves was dead. According to the mayor, he had gone out to Point Clara the previous evening for his regular turn around the Cephalod Inn exercise circuit. In what had been the thickest fog most people in those parts could remember. He had either stumbled, or missed his footing, perhaps while edging around the inn's boundary fence, or lost his track and wandered too close to the cliff. Whatever had happened, Greaves had gone over, headfirst apparently, because the fall had snapped his neck. His body had finally lodged on a low shelf, snagged between rocks which kept it from going into the water, where it was spotted just after first daylight by a couple of abalone divers.

This makes no sense at all, Lee thought, surprised—and a touch disappointed with herself—that her first reaction was not to mourn, but to calculate. Clarence Greaves was a hypercautious man. Not in a million years would he have gone within five miles of a cliff face in thick fog.

Unless, of course, he had a gun at his back.

She told Constancia to hang on, left the phone dangling, and went to find Coole. He was browsing a nearby magazine rack. Lee told him what had happened.

"Tell her we'll be out there sometime tonight. We'll call back and tell her when after I've dealt with our arrangements."

He started to move away, thought of something, and came back just as Lee was about to hang up.

"This is most important. I believe you mentioned Greaves carried a pocket organizer? Tell the mayor to sequester his personal effects, including whatever's in his hotel room. She should lock them in her office or her home. If Greaves owned a personal computer, the mayor should make copies, *immediately,* of all its files."

He paused, pulled out a small pigskin notepad, and wrote a number.

"Give her this. The best thing would be if she could modem Greaves's computer files to my office in Boston. This number's on twenty-four-hour standby. The transmission protocols are all plain vanilla. I'm sure she can find someone to do it if she can't. Tell her not to use the bank line, however. Has Greaves's agency been notified? I assume the Bordrero Bay police are treating this as an accident?"

"I don't know."

"Well, find out! Regrettably, Washington will have to be informed, but not necessarily immediately. Tell her to wait two or three hours if she can. We'll need all the headstart we can manage."

Lee passed Coole's instructions to Constancia. The mayor said she'd do her best to delay formal notification to the RTC, but this was a small town, Greaves's associates at the bank already knew, and so on, and so on. As for modeming Greaves's computer files, Constancia was sure she could handle that herself. She and a police officer would head for Greaves's motel pronto.

Coole found a charter outfit in Savannah that had a Lear available. An hour later, they were wheels up, bound for Eureka, the airport nearest to Bordrero Bay. Coole reckoned they would reach their final destination sometime around 10 P.M. PDT.

He had put the Learjet charter on Lee's American Express card. Speaking of which, he added, there was something else she should know.

"You'll recall the helicopter back at Margaret Island? I'm certain it noted the stabilizer number of our chartered seaplane, which by now will have been tracked to the charter service from which the aircraft was hired, from which there may have been ascertained the credit card number used to settle the account: yours. The CSS marking on the helicopter, incidentally, stands for Courier Security Services, which is the custodial arm of Courier Services, whose other associations you know."

Something in his tone of voice stung Lee.

"For Christ's sakes, Coole, are all of us just bait to you? That's what Clarence was, wasn't he? You set the poor SOB up! Just like you've set me up!"

She bit her anger off in mid-phrase. There was a lot else she could say, but what was the point?

Coole smiled.

"Not at all. Clarence Greaves, alive, was a dot; dead, he too may turn out to be a line. I'm heartsick at his passing, but what more can I say? What we need to know now is: why. Why did he go to Point Clara? What or who lured him there? A need for exercise? Hardly! And if his death wasn't an accident, it seems clear that persons unknown felt he was coming too close."

"Too close to what?"

"That's what we need to find out. It's our task to see to it that Clarence Greaves shall not have died in vain. The best way to do that's to work things out so that his bad luck becomes someone else's worse."

You sound just like Uncle Henry, Lee thought. What was it Uncle Henry was always saying about luck: that luck was the residue of design. But whose design?

"When people resort to violence in white collar situations," Coole was saying, "they've ceased to think rationally. People in that state make mistakes."

"To err is human. What about the divine part?"

"I'm afraid where very big money's concerned, there's no such thing as forgiveness. Even the gods can count. Greaves's death may have been their first big mistake. Our effort must be to help them make others.''

After that, Lee fell into a fitful half-sleep, alternating stretches of near-wakefulness with deep, violent dreams. She was aware of Coole talking incessantly on the telephone, like a general in a bunker. They were starting their descent into Grand Island, Nebraska, to refuel, when she came fully awake.

Coole was just finishing a conversation. When he hung up, he saw Lee looking at him, and smiled triumphantly.

"As they say, the game's afoot!"

He explained. The Bordrero Bay police had received a call from an Agent Arthur Chung of the Secret Service. The agent was calling from Spaghtville, a town an hour southeast of Bordrero Bay. He was on his way from San Francisco to take possession of his deceased colleague's computer files, which were believed to contain sensitive information.

Sensitive information?

"We'll only know when we see them. The important thing is that Greaves *did* possess a laptop computer and that the mayor has dealt with the files as I requested. The odd thing is, the pocket organizer, which was so conspicuously a part of Greaves's personal apparatus, seems to be missing. When his body was found, a scabbard in which he apparently carried it was there, but not the organizer.''

"Couldn't it have fallen out, into the ocean?"

"That was my first thought. The call from 'Agent Chung' obliges me to change my thinking. For one thing, he claims to be from Washington—a trope designed to impress the locals and enhance the likelihood that no questions will be asked—but there hardly seems to have been enough time for Washington to react. The mayor managed to delay her formal notification to the RTC until almost 2 P.M. Washington time.''

"What do you expect to find in Greaves's computer files?"

"I'm not sure. A complete record of his researches is my hope. People addicted to electronic gadgets, as Clarence Greaves seems to have been, tend to use them to the fullest extent of their capabilities. Gadgeteers leave no capability unexploited; it's against their nature. I have a friend who insists on watching five or six sporting events simultaneously simply because the Japanese have produced a televi-

sion set that permits him to do so. The selling point for pocket organizers is such gadgets' capability to interface with computers. My
guess is that Greaves transferred his enquiries to his organizer, and
then in turn retransferred that data to his laptop in his motel. That data
would include whatever it was that ultimately drew him to Point
Clara. If someone else has looked at Greaves's organizer, they would
want to see what else might be on the laptop."

"You're saying that assuming Clarence was murdered, whoever
killed him got his organizer, read it, and figured out he'd probably
uploaded to another computer? And has dispatched this Agent Chung
to get it?"

"Precisely."

"God, it all sounds so farfetched."

"To repeat myself, Lee, when the money involved's large
enough, nothing's too farfetched. The preposterous and the prosaic
are sisters under the skin. Who could ever have believed an Ivan
Boesky?"

For the rest of their journey, after leaving Grand Island, Lee and
Coole talked of this and that. She probed Coole's perimeter defenses,
trying to work deeper, but it was hard going.

She had done what Coole homework she could; he might look
sixty, but he was only forty-six; born Cambridge, Massachusetts, father a professor of economics at MIT, mother a translator of Leopardi
and D'Annunzio; Coole had graduated from Boston Latin, Harvard,
Harvard Business School; he had spent ten years on Wall Street, the
last seven as a security analyst-investment strategist at a famous mutual
fund and money-management firm. For five of those seven years he
had been ranked number one on *Institutional Investor* magazine's all-
American research team in the financial institutions category.

Then came disaster. From something one of its executives had
let slip, Coole deduced big trouble in a specialty insurance company
that was at the time one of the Street's hottest favorites. Coole had
slipped a sell recommendation to certain big clients, cautioning that
the information was on the verge of being "inside," so that it should
be used with utmost discretion. A couple of the clients hadn't. They'd
put their money where Coole's mouth was, and banged the stock
hard on the short side. The company's ensuing collapse severely em-
barrassed the insurance commissioners of seven states.

The SEC came down hard, alleging a conspiratorial manipulation and insider trading: the clients gave back some of the money, and Coole and six portfolio managers drew ten months in the federal minimum-security correctional facility at Allentown.

When he came out, Coole didn't return to Wall Street. He had an idea for a new service. He went straight to his old clients, who from whatever motives were only too glad to finance his new venture. A man with Thurlow Coole's talents was always worth betting on.

Of his personal life, Lee knew little. There had been a divorce; she gathered there was an ex-wife living on the South Shore.

Coole was obviously not going to discuss his private life, so he switched the subject to Mona Kurchinski.

"Don't think of Mona as Moriarty to my Holmes," he continued. "She isn't and she won't be. I've never laid eyes on her. She's said to be extremely clever—obsessively so—and has a great ability to think ahead, which is rare for a woman, if you'll pardon my saying so. Of course, she's had the benefit of absolutely first-class training from your uncle. A virtual Ph.D. in financial manipulativeness. There's no doubt she fits in here somewhere, probably through Phoenix and NNE, but we'll just have to see."

They reached the Cephalod just before eleven. The inn itself had been taken over by a Microsoft regional sales gathering, and all that was available was an outlying bungalow. It consisted of two bedrooms with no view, a living room, kitchenette, and small patio with a hot tub. Lee noted Coole eyeing this curiously, like a Brahmin tourist contemplating an aboriginal ziggurat. Without asking, she took the better of the two rooms. After all, she told herself, it's my dollar. About thirty thousand of them, so far.

After calling room service for sandwiches and coffee, Lee phoned Constancia. Agent Chung had come and gone, carrying away Greaves's laptop. Arrangements had been made to ship Greaves's body to Washington; there had been difficulty reaching his next-of-kin, however, a niece who worked in the Justice Department. She had not appeared for work for three days.

When Lee reported this to Coole, he said he doubted the niece would ever reappear.

There was a knock on the door. A bellperson handed over a

manila envelope which contained a videocassette. There was no VCR in the bungalow; Coole stuffed the tape in his duffel impatiently, muttering that they could view it in the morning.

He went into Lee's room and returned with her laptop. He hooked it up to the teleport on the room phone, booted it, and set it on Receive mode. He dialed a number and issued a series of terse instructions, then sat back, studying the small glowing screen intently.

It took about three minutes for the data he was expecting—six screens' worth—to download. He unhitched the phone line, moved the computer to the coffee table where Lee could see it more easily, and began to scrutinize the confidences imparted by the late Clarence Greaves to his electronic diary.

It made little sense to Lee—merely screenful after screenful of disparate combinations of numbers, letters, and amounts, but Coole seemed to know what he was looking at.

She was pouring them a second cup of coffee when Coole exclaimed, "Aha! Now this will interest you," and chuckled grimly.

He tapped the screen with his pen. There was her name, and her home phone number, as well as the name and phone number of *Steps*. Coole ran through the screens. That was all there seemed to be about Lee, he said with satisfaction; that, and a notation in the organizer's appointment book that Greaves had met Lee for breakfast on July 19.

"They" have me two ways now, she thought. Tied into Phoenix through the seaplane charter, and now to Bordrero Bay and Greaves. She made a mental note not to walk under ladders or next to cliffs.

Coole switched off the computer, stood up and stretched. He gestured through the open patio doors at the hot tub.

"I don't suppose you know how to work that thing out there?"

"As a matter of fact, I probably do." A minute later, the water was aswirl, and the first fingers of steam rose from the surface.

Not a bad idea, she thought. She ached with fatigue. It had been an interminable, exhausting day, and now it was three in the morning for her. The Jacuzzi sounded like a good idea.

She went into her room and stripped. She dumped the contents of her bag on the bed and pawed through them three times, looking for a bathing suit. She usually traveled with one—she liked to get in her laps in hotel pools—but apparently this time she'd forgotten.

She put her underwear back on and examined herself in the full-length mirror. The effect was reasonably maidenly; she didn't look like a fugitive from a Victoria's Secret catalog. There was a terry cloth robe in the bathroom. She put that on and went outside.

Coole was standing by the hot tub. He was wearing a faded pair of madras trunks, unfashionably long and roomy, drooping almost to his bony knees, the sort of garment snatched up at Brooks Brothers at the last moment on the way to the Cape or East Hampton.

"I must ask you to avert your gaze," she said in an exaggeratedly ladylike voice, sounding just like her mother and hating it.

They stayed in the tub for twenty minutes, talking. Coole wanted her and Barney in Boston the following week for a strategy session. A date and time were agreed.

Lee felt drowsy as she clambered out of the tub. While Coole looked off into the night, she stripped off her wet bra and panties, drew the terry cloth robe around her and stretched out on a deck chair. She closed her eyes. Above the splashing of the hot tub, she thought she heard Coole talking to himself.

She must have dozed off. When she opened them again, Coole, now clad in a terry cloth robe twin to hers, was standing looking down at her. She followed the direction of his gaze and saw that her robe had parted, exposing the black curly mat at her crotch. In the white moonlight, her legs looked like parchment; a few drops of water that still clung to her bush sparkled. She moved to cover herself, then thought, oh hell.

"So what are you looking looking at?" she asked.

Coole's long face remained impassive.

"I hesitate to give it its technical name," he said, "for fear of destroying the magic of the moment."

She had no idea what then got into her.

"Then perhaps you'd better kiss it," she heard herself saying, "and make it feel all better." She reached for him. The robe fell all the way open.

"I think I'll kiss you first," said Thurlow Coole, moving toward her, his own robe parting. As she closed her eyes and lifted her face to receive his kiss, the last thing she noted was that Mr. Coole could by no stretch of the imagination be called snub-nosed. With agility that seemed to her miraculous, he entered her just as their lips touched first time. She began to come almost immediately, one screaming, racking, long-waved orgasm after another; it had never happened to her like this: as he slid up inside her to his full enormous length, and then withdrew in a slow, excruciating outward stroke, first a tiny shriek was torn from her, a gasping bird note of absolute excitement, followed by a cascade of fierce deep moans, another, then another and another and another; she felt as if he had turned her inside out.

She drifted off before he climaxed, never felt him finish, just lay there for what seemed like a few minutes until she awoke and discovered she was in her own bed. A glance at her watch told her it was 7:14. She shifted her head and saw that the room was flooded with early sun, and that Coole, dressed for a day at the bank, if still jacketless, was standing at the end of her bed. His button-down today was a sort of grayish beige, she saw, not a bad color for him, but not his best.

She had to say something, but anything that came to mind sounded embarrassingly trivial. She rolled over on her stomach, then back again, mumbling like a six-year-old being roused for school. Never, she thought, never in my life, never anything like that—and hers had not been a sheltered life.

"We have four o'clock flights out of San Francisco," he said.

Matching flights, isn't that sweet, thought Lee. And we've only just met.

In a voice still rough with sleep, she pointed out that it was barely seven-thirty and that it was only a three-hour drive to San Francisco.

"So, Coole, why hurry?" she said in a deliberate little girl's voice, and pushed aside the sheets.

E L E V E N

▼

Ten days later, Lee was ushered into Coole's office. He was seated behind an approximate acre of Regency cherry wood: a huge, neatly organized partner's desk.

"Miss Boynton, sir."

Coole's assistant withdrew. Lee heard the door close behind her.

Coole got up and came around the desk. His attire was as crisp as the day outside: a lightweight tweedy jacket mixing a half-dozen autumn tints, the usual button-down, apricot this time, the bow tie burgundy with orange polka dots. He was naked below the waist and completely aroused.

"How are you, Lee?"

He kissed her lightly on the lips and in a smooth movement lifted her on to the edge of his desk. She tilted back slightly, legs splayed wide like an animal in heat presenting herself. She was wearing no underwear.

Coole slid into her and sweet reason vanished down a vortex of pure, moist sensation . . .

"Miss. *Miss!*"

The insistent voice yanked Lee out of her reverie.

"Your seat back, please, Miss. We're beginning our descent into Boston."

▼ ▼ ▼

The offices of Coole Research Associates were located on a renewed
stretch of Boston waterfront, in a flamboyant Michael Graves building with an aggressive polychrome facade that would have evoked
envy in a Tuscan archbishop. Lee, alighting from the airport cab,
shivered in her light dress. New England was in the grip of a sharp,
unseasonal cold snap, although Labor Day was still weeks away.

She glanced down at herself. Her nipples were sticking out like
flashlight batteries. It wasn't just the chilly weather. She had spent the
entire cab ride from Logan trying to pull herself together, but she still
felt so lit up with sex that she might have been wearing neon instead
of taupe Armani silk.

So what is this all about, she asked herself as the elevator as-
cended. Is this what critics call "gratuitous sex," as in "gratuitous sex
and violence"? Could what was real also be gratuitous? What about
the violence that had swallowed up Clarence Greaves's life? What she
felt—assuming there was such a thing as vulval hunger pains, she had
it—was real enough.

But was it love? Could you call it "love"?

Or was it just "an affair," "a fling"? She still hadn't made her
mind up how to address Coole other than "Coole." How could you
be in love with someone you still called by his last name?

The funny thing was, "Coole" sounded right. She couldn't call
him "Thurlow," and a "Sweetie" he certainly wasn't. It would have
helped if she'd known what his friends called him. Did he have some
dreadful boyhood nickname dating back to a boyhood of yacht clubs
and tennis courts, a name—God forbid!—like "Chip"?

"Chip" Coole? Give me a break!

The elevator halted at the fifteenth floor. Stepping out, Lee
wished Barney had come to Boston with her. She could have inter-
posed her partner between herself and Coole, so to speak. But Barney
wouldn't fly; he said it was the effects of the chemo.

A receptionist led Lee back to Coole's office. The firm appeared
to take up about half the floor. In offices opening off the hallway, men
and women spoke quietly on the phone or worked intently at desktop
computers. The atmosphere was very Boston. Huge amounts of capital were run out of this city, Lee knew, but the traffic along Boston's

corridors of high action always seemed to move at a dignified pace—not with the pelting, blaring frenzy of New York or the smooth and sneaky calculation of Washington.

In the anteroom to Coole's corner office, high windows opened on Boston harbor; the view was spectacular, taking in the whole north-south panorama from Charlestown to the Narrows. Against the opposite wall stood a Chippendale secretary that looked identical to the four-star piece Lee's grandmother had bequeathed to the Newport Preservation Society. Another, very similar, had recently sold at Sotheby's for $3.8 million. Coole Research Associates, Inc., was evidently prospering.

"Miss Boynton? Mr. Coole will see you now."

Lee was shown into Coole's office. When the assistant withdrew, he came around his large, square desk and shook her hand gravely.

"How nice to see you, Lee. Everything well?"

"As well as it can be, I guess. And you? How goes the chase?"

"We're getting there."

"So, what's on the agenda?" She was determined to keep things crisp, all business.

"This morning I thought we'd review the bidding with one of my associates. Recapitulate what we know and what we don't. That should occupy us until lunch. I've booked a table at the Ritz on the late side. Afterward, I thought you and I might drive up to Pride's Crossing to see the Granary and I could bring you up to speed on our JEDI endeavors. Mr. Greaves's files have proved immensely useful in getting us up and running. We could stay there overnight and have you out of here on an early shuttle."

Now you're talking, thought Lee. And then her pleasure was dashed. She was due in Pittsburgh that night for two days of family trust conferences. An audience with the Pope was easier to get out of.

When she told him, Coole seemed genuinely disappointed. Better still, she gloated.

She heard the door behind her open. The room was suffocated in a billowing rush of Yves St. Laurent's Opium. There was a clunk of heavy jewelry and the unmistakable whoosh of presence.

Lee turned to greet the arrival and recognized her at once. Any reasonably regular viewer of television financial shows would have

The hair, the turnout, the style were unmistakable.

This was Shirley Greenacre, better known on Wall Street as "Short the Shirt" Shirley.

What the hell is she doing here? Lee wondered. Shirley Greenacre was hardly Coole's style.

The woman in the flesh was even more overwhelming than on television. Every aspect of her seemed proportionately twice the size it did on the screen. Her hair was the "biggest" Lee had ever seen on a white woman, a frizzy, henna-rimmed Watusi "do," half halo, half mop, that must have been a yard across. The gold jewelry at her neck, wrists, and ears must have weighed three pounds; spread on a Dolly Parton bosom was a multistranded gold neckpiece that would have drawn gasps of envy from a pharaoh. The woman was surprisingly slim at wrist and ankle, and her carriage was firm and straight. She was sheathed strikingly if not altogether successfully in an outrageously patterned, ass bustingly tight outfit that had to be Versace. Lee had never seen anyone actually *wear* Versace. The modiste who unloaded that one deserved a bonus from Bergdorf's.

Shirley Greenacre looked younger and fresher than she did on television. She was in her early forties, no more, with a plain, slightly ruddy face, level green eyes, and a sexy mouth—notwithstanding that it was painted a wholly unsuitable pale pink. She had very good skin.

She was a legend in her own time and mind, created by herself with no little help from Louis Rukeyser, "Adam Smith," and Lou Dobbs. She was a fixture on the Wall Street television circuit, notorious for her frankness. Not long before, on "Adam Smith" Lee had watched her characterize the chief executive of a thirty-billion-dollar bank, in his presence, as a "brainless asshole!" Public television switchboards had lit up everywhere as viewers called in with salty characterizations of *their* bankers.

Greenacre was by profession a stock and commodities broker. She did her own research and followed her own drummer. She wouldn't pick up the phone for less than $100,000 in "soft dollars" or take an account worth less than $5 million. The commission business she splashed around the Street put her at the top of the priority or "first call" lists of every firm from Goldman, Sachs down to two-man bucket shops in the Florida panhandle.

She touched all the fashionable bases: value analysis, market timing, stock picking, arbitrage, and hedging, but it was her "Short the Shirt" theory that had made her famous. Its premise was as simple as its results appeared to be infallible: If the CEO of a large industrial or financial company appeared in public or in the media in a shirt with a colored or striped body and white collar and cuffs, it was a sure thing that his company's earnings were about to go right down the toilet.

Her theory had first hit pay dirt with Citibank. Walter Wriston had appeared on "Sunday with David Brinkley" in the requisite shirt; Shirley decided the time had come to test the theory—which was in fact based on protracted study of Wriston's shirts and Citicorp's financial reports—and hit the phones; the "Greenacre Gang," as they came to be called, had sold Citicorp stock short right down to the basement, taking out profits of more than $400 million.

The single greatest winner had been American Express. Over four different selling cycles, the gang's short sales netted a half-billion. Shirley sent the AmEx chief executive a $10,000 gift certificate to Sulka, a preferred source for such shirts, along with a gift card expressing heartfelt wishes to keep up the good work. When he stepped down, she became despondent and took herself off to the Golden Door for a week.

The previous autumn, the British Chancellor of the Exchequer had appeared outside 11 Downing Street in such a shirt and pronounced the pound to be solid. Shirley promptly led a bear raid that cost sterling 15 percent of its value and the Bank of England 40 percent of its reserves. One Hong Kong client alone was reputed to have made a billion dollars.

Hardly Coole's style, Lee reflected. So what was Shirley doing here?

Coole read Lee's mind.

"Shirley thinks variety is the spice of life," he said, "so now and then I can persuade her to commit her undoubted genius to the pursuit of virtue rather than lucre. When it comes to paper trails, she's a veritable Comanche scout. Her association with us is both ad hoc, and—I need hardly add—very much on the QT. Now, shall we get down to cases?"

Shirley began with a run-through of the CP-NNE-GoldWest-Courier relationships.

"The name of this little game is see if you can find out who owns what."

With that, she led Lee and Coole through a maze constructed from no fewer than 105 entities. It struck Lee as a gigantic spiderweb, some filaments readily visible to the naked eye, others apparent only in refracted light.

"I really get off on this offshore shit," Shirley observed in a deeply appreciative voice. She tapped her chart with a gem-studded gold Cartier pen. "Whoever put this together had major smarts. Just look at these interrelationships! You got to love it! Nothing's obvious and nothing's left out. Bahamas Asset Protection Schemes, Montserrat 'Mirage Companies,' Lichtenstein Grantor Trusts, Sark PLCs, they're all here. Jersey, Guernsey, Isle of Man, Vanuatu, you name it—and in all the best vintages."

The only new development, she reported, was that CP seemed to be upping the ante in its Korean involvements. Newest was a $75 million investment in a joint-venture P'yongyang bank. The French bank had also underwritten a facility of convenience in Andorra, to act as registrar for exotic offshore mutual funds, domiciled on Pig Cay in the Bahamas, which were going to be sold in Eastern Europe and the former USSR.

"That's Mona, I'll bet," said Coole.

"Whoever thought it up, it's a nice touch. Apparently they're using old KGB and Stasi types to peddle the funds, which is an idea they stole from Ross Perot. Hey, Coole, remember when he tried using ex-marines as customers' men when he took over DuPont-Walston?"

Coole nodded.

"Andorra's a new player in the offshore game, isn't it?" asked Lee.

"They've been in for about a year now. It's like a dance craze: doin' the Offshore." Shirley snapped her fingers in quick syncopation. "Everybody's doin' it, doin' it, doin' it. I hear Jamaica's next. Anyway, this CP-Korean deal's probably been set up to finance ice."

" 'Ice'?" asked Lee. "You mean diamonds?"

"She means crystal methamphetamine," said Coole. "A drug of choice in West Coast markets. A new processing laboratory is said to be under construction near Pusan."

Shirley now took them back onshore, and ran quickly through

NNI, Courier Services, GoldWest, and Phoenix.

"It seems to me," she said, "that although Nanny's the milk-shake, Courier's the straw that stirs the drink. Nanny owns about fifty businesses like Tip 'n Take and Energy City. Cash businesses. There's Cashachek, Shopbrite, which is very big in the Midwest, Uncle Noodles, Mister Burger, American Cineplex, Video Vector, which tries to compete with Thunderbolt in the Deep South, and so on. Dull businesses but steady, the kind of crap the Street'd never look at unless there was enough stock around to do an LBO or a greenmail with, which there isn't. Hardly chickenshit, however: Tip 'n Take has nine hundred and twenty-seven stores grossing twenty-three billion dollars across the Midwest; Shopbrite's six hundred and forty-two markets grossed fourteen billion dollars in the Middle Atlantic and South Central states; the theater chain operates two hundred eighty-six screens in Florida. What's interesting is: None is really what you'd call 'national.' They're all what the analysts call 'regional' or 'subregional.' Obviously Nanny likes it that way."

"But Courier Services does operate coast-to-coast and border-to-border."

"Correct. From sea to shining sea. And services every single Nanny subsidiary with everything from armored car services to over-night express delivery via 747. What a business! Totally unregulated; you can steal as you please. You remember that chickenshit outfit on Long Island, Coole?"

"You're thinking of Revere."

"Yeah, Revere. Well, multiply Revere, which only stole a cool forty mil from its customers, by a factor of about a million and you get some idea of Courier's potential. Hell, they even have a detective agency. You better watch out, Coole!"

Coole flashed a thin, quick little smile.

"Nanny bought all of these companies between 1984 and 1991, paying a total of $1.4 billion," Shirley continued. "They paid high prices, higher than I would've paid for this kind of crap, but my guess is that they saw synergies that I wouldn't."

"Such as laundering money?" Lee asked.

"Could be. You see, these businesses are already pretty good at what they're *supposed* to be doing, which means they lend themselves to what the chin scratchers in the B schools call quote the efficient incremental processing of substantial amounts of cash unquote. Namely, you can sneak a few million into the cash flow and no one's the wiser.''

"Still, you'd think someone would've noticed they were over-paying.''

"Hey, Lee, get with the program! When Nanny was buying, it was still the 1980s. Everybody overpaid. You could hock that waste-basket, or get Drexel or Leo Gorton to do you a junk deal against it. So everyone was buying and selling everything. Nanny was doing exactly what KKR or Forstmann Little were.''

"Where'd they get the money?''

"The usual places. Freemark sold eight hundred million dollars of junk bonds for Nanny, and the banks ponied up another billion or so. Through CP, Nanny hit up the Euromarket for five hundred million dollars. Money grew on trees, don't forget! Cash was the last of Nanny's problems. And you have to give them credit. Nanny's still alive and kicking.''

It seemed like a good point to take a break. Lee went to the ladies room. She had been in there a couple of minutes when a click of heels and a clunk of jewelry, and a great deal of rustling, announced that Shirley was in the adjoining stall.

A moment later there came a hiss: "So how was it?''

"How was what?''

"Coole. Obviously he's done you. You have that look. Once you've been done by Coole there's a certain something a girl never loses.''

Really, thought Lee; and does it take one to know one? She said nothing.

"You ever seen anything like it,'' Shirley hissed; "it's unfuck-ingbelievable! This girl I know at Bear Stearns says he went to some monastery when he was at Harvard, one of those king fu places where you learn how to keep it up for about fourteen days at a time plus add a few inches. I'll tell you, if Coole could bottle what he's got, the Street'd pay fifty times Year 2000 earnings for it! It'd sell at a price that'd make Merck look like a cyclical.''

Lee said nothing. Neither, for a few beats, did Shirley.

Then, apparently having gotten the point, she said, "Anyway, no offense meant. You been up to the Granary yet?''

"No."

"You got to go, Lee! It's a trip! All these teen-age cyberninjas playing table-stakes Super Mario. Bowling for billions, I call it. The place is a dump, as you would expect, *très vieux* New England with a decorating budget of about eight bucks, and that was during Grover Cleveland's administration, but what they do with these kids is dyn-O-mite! And the kids are great! Outside of when he's in the rack, Coole may come across like the all-time tightass, but underneath that rigid backbone, et cetera, beats the heart of Mister Softee. If he invites you to see the Granary, which he does with about one percent of one percent of the people he meets, you gotta go!"

When they reconvened, Coole turned the subject to Thunderbolt Video.

"This tiny discrepancy was the anomaly that first animated the late Mr. Greaves's curiosity," he said.

Lee looked puzzled. Greaves had never said anything about Thunderbolt Video to her.

"It was Thunderbolt that inspired him to borrow the JEDI pass code from his niece . . . who, I gather, seems to have vanished from the face of the earth . . . ?"

Lee nodded.

"On the basis of the files that we abstracted from his personal computer, Greaves came across an active account at Bordrero Bay 'd/b/a Thunderbolt Video.' It turned out to be a business that does not exist, and very likely never did."

"My clients own six million shares of Thunderbolt," Shirley commented, "it's a great company and one reason it is, is that they've stayed out of California."

"Quite so. There are no Thunderbolt Video outlets, either company-owned or franchised, west of the Sierra Nevada. In any case, the deposit pattern at this mysterious Thunderbolt roughly resembles what Lee came across at Tip 'n Take and Energy City. Money from nowhere, transported by Courier Services. It was this last consideration that led Greaves to expand the scope of his JEDI inquiry."

"What is this JEDI, anyway?" Shirley asked.

"It started out as an exponentiation of the National Crime Information Center data base but has grown into much, much more."

He gave Shirley a quick run-through of JEDI's properties and capabilities. When he finished, she whistled and shook her head.

"They ever put that in the stock tip business, I'm OB. It must be a bitch to crack. You got the kids working on it?"

Coole nodded.

"Thanks to Mr. Greaves, we have a start. Not much of one, but a start. The encryption algorithms are more difficult than CHIPS codes, but the underlying logic is starting to look manageable. Freddy thinks we're making progress."

"To get back to Thunderbolt," Lee asked, "is Courier the only link with Tip 'n Take, et cetera?"

"The only obvious one. Our Mr. Greaves was resourceful, however, or possibly it was just rational free association, but for whatever reason, he seems to have made—entirely on his own—a leap of the mind that springboarded him from Thunderbolt-Courier to the much larger, more complex universe of GoldWest-Freemark-CP. In particular, he started looking at certain deposit withdrawals that must have struck him—because they certainly so strike my people at the Granary—as downright suspicious in their timeliness. In that area, we're building on Greaves's work; standing, as they say, on the shoulders of a giant."

He took the two women through the process. Greaves, and now the Granary, was using JEDI to compare the timing and pattern of deposit and withdrawal of large GoldWest accounts with similar accounts at roughly comparable institutions. The focus was on time periods, usually a week or two, that encompassed occurrences a sophisticated depositor or investor would consider "material"—*if he had known about them.*

These would include contemplated changes in the federal funds rate or unannounced, substantive alterations in the policies of the Federal Reserve and banking and thrift authorities, such as the recent abandonment of Too Big to Fail or the more recent decision not to pay off on all deposits exceeding $100,000 per account. The identification of an institution as "a problem" would also qualify. Persons in command of this information were in a position to save themselves money, and, depending on what kind of money was involved, considerable inconvenience, by getting out early.

"Comparing GoldWest with other institutions," Coole concluded, "suggests that certain depositors had a crystal ball. The timing with which these deposits—mainly brokered in from offshore by Freemark, chose to fold their tents and silently steal away was uncanny. Clearly, someone knew something."

"Maybe had a mole at the Fed?"

"Or was himself privy to JEDI?" Lee said. "JEDI's where Clarence got his raw material. Why not someone else?"

Shirley nodded at Coole, then looked at her watch, whooped that she was overdue at Fidelity, and got up.

"If you guys need me, just whistle. I'll be in Houston tonight with Fayez, Fort Worth tomorrow with Sid and Lee Bass, and then Beverly Hills. You can reach me at the Spellings' or at CAA. Nice to meet you, Lee." In a raucous counterpoint of clanking gold and clacking heels, Shirley departed.

Coole studied the door with the manner of someone contemplating the path of a recent tornado. Then he picked up a remote and switched on the integrated VCR sitting on a corner stand.

"Now for a little show and tell."

The first image to flicker onscreen was familiar: the woman whose photograph Coole had received on his Washington photofax. Mona Kurchinski.

"For whatever it's worth, we have positive identification from your friend Jimmy Spalding that this is his Dragon Lady. He has also confirmed, through the good offices of Mayor Lopez, that these gentlemen were present on Mustique."

He clicked the remote. On the monitor, Mona Kurchinski was replaced by two men standing on the steps of an elegant old building.

"Those knights errant of the magic kingdom of Offshore, Monsieur Claude Vertreuil and Monsieur Bruno de Fried. You know about them. Here's one I'm not sure you do know."

Click. A middle-distance shot. Lee recognized the location: the north end of Broad Street, just south of the old J. P. Morgan Building, across from the Stock Exchange. Click. The screen filled with the full-color image of a well-dressed, dark-haired, slickly good-looking man in his middle forties standing by a limousine. A candidate for Shirley's short-sale list, Lee thought; he wore a shirt with a white collar and bold pink body. Although his face bore an expression of high confidence, he nervously fingered his necktie, an affair of thin navy and scarlet stripes on a paler blue background. Lee recognized it as the tie of the Knickerbocker Squash Club.

"Leo Gorton," said Coole drily.

"I guessed it might be."

The screen came alive. The camera followed Gorton across the sidewalk and through high bronze-framed Art Deco doors.

"Is this recent?" she asked.

"Last week," said Coole. "Outside the former offices of Phoenix. They are moving to new quarters outside Princeton. Mr. Gorton's enthusiasms, apart from high finance and clubs, are said to include young men of a certain comeliness, with which Princeton is well supplied.

"Mr. Gorton is expert in having it both ways," Coole continued. "GoldWest was a particularly good client. He brokered sixty-three of GoldWest's acquisitions, including—it may amuse you—the merger of Frontier Life and Annuity, which was the instrument for looting the Browning pension funds. Without putting too broad a point on it, it would seem that between 1985 and 1990, GoldWest constituted a veritable piggybank for Leo Gorton's deals."

"Margaret Island—Dunbar—was his too, wasn't it?"

"Of course. Currently he's proving that what goes round comes round. Lenchin's currently looking into certain of Mr. Gorton's other financings, deals in which some seven hundred eighty-seven million dollars in junk bonds and equities posing as bonds were sold. Those securities, by the by, are currently quoted in pennies on the dollar. Lenchin's making me a report on the hard values underlying that paper; I should have his report tomorrow. What is interesting is that, like Dunbar, all are being bid for by Mr. Gorton's Phoenix Capital: at prices ranging upward from fifteen cents on the dollar and averaging out at around thirty cents, which is considerably more than Lenchin's estimate of the going value of the underlying assets."

"Which supports your theory about damage control. Or maybe we could call it 'hush money.' "

"However you wish."

"I'm surprised Phoenix hasn't gone after GoldWest, at least the Bordrero Bay end."

"Frankly, that's puzzled me too. These people do tend to keep their affairs tightly compartmentalized. But CP's as mixed up in

NNE and Courier as it is in Phoenix. Of course, GoldWest does have significant holdings of some of the issues for which Phoenix is tendering."

That's not the same thing, thought Lee.

Coole clicked Gorton off the screen.

"Now—here's someone you've never seen, but of whose existence you're aware. Let's see if you can put a name to him."

Click. The moving image had clearly been taken by a bank surveillance camera. The fixtures shown were Victorian. A fern loomed out of an urn next to a low balustrade.

Bordrero Bay, thought Lee. So that's why Coole had Greaves's stuff moved from the mayor's office to the bank. Cle-*ver!*

A slender figure, quite sharply dressed, entered the camera's field of vision. He engaged a teller, then Jimmy Spaulding, in conversation, produced credentials. The teller disappeared off camera, returning with a small Lands End suitcase, which she handed over. As the newcomer turned to leave, the camera caught him full on and zoomed in. The face was flat, Oriental.

"Special Agent Arthur Chung?"

Coole nodded.

Korean, she thought. Koreans were said to be the coldest-blooded people on earth, with a low regard for human life. Koreans were famous for breaking bricks in half with their bare hands. She couldn't help her next thought: Was the neck of a sixty-one-year-old, overweight civil servant tougher than a brick?

Coole clicked the screen off, went over to the VCR, ejected the cassette, and handed it to Lee.

"Given that Agent Chung presumably knows about you," Coole said drily, "you may want to study him. Your associate Mr. Cagel should see this too, just to be safe. How's he doing, anyway?"

Terrible, thought Lee. "He's quite sick, I'm afraid."

Coole made a grim face. When people of Lee's sort described someone as "quite sick," that person was usually dead by suppertime.

"I'm sorry to hear that. We'll do our damndest to bring this to a satisfactory conclusion while he's still with us. As a going-away present, if no more."

"Barney'd like that."

Lee took the cassette and shoved it in her bag.

"I'm hungry," she said.

"The Ritz awaits," said Coole.

Lee felt bold. She felt shameless.

"I don't suppose that the Ritz could rent us a room for the afternoon? I feel this terrible craving for room service."

This time, Coole's smile was warm. "It's already been taken care of," he said.

TWELVE

▼

When the Washington summer reached the sticky nadir of August, it was Oltington's inflexible policy never to go out of doors. Like a hyperallergic child in a sealed bubble, he could survive only in a permanently air-conditioned environment, abandoned only for the seconds it took to race across the infernal, unclimatized spaces that separated the chilled chambers of his existence—marked "home," "vehicle," "office," "meeting place"—as if across the embers of hell. Even in the fetid blaze of late summer, he dressed for a life conducted at around sixty-six degrees Fahrenheit.

But even the most carefully laid plans can sometimes be forced astray. The President had dragooned the Vice President for a spur-of-the-moment turn of the White House rose garden, and Oltington found himself boiling inside a double-breasted Anderson and Sheppard suit cut from twelve-ounce worsted. His personal thermostat had gone beserk. Sweat gathered between his shoulderblades into a mucilaginous rivulet that threaded ticklishly down his backbone into the cleft of his fanny. His shirt felt glued to his body; the splendid mauve pima darkened by perspiration to inky purple, the snappy white collar, a perfection of starch only minutes before, wilting by the second. Filthy, clammy, and unkempt, he stared longingly at the Executive Mansion, yearning to be back in the icy air circulating behind the splendid creamy walls.

It wasn't just the heat, he knew. It was frustration and fear. Frustration and fear that had kept him awake right through the night even with the air conditioner turned all the way up.

Frustration at Kim's latest news. With a little apprehension mixed in, too.

And now Mona had called for a meeting. "Instantest!"

Ahead, the President and Vice President, heads close together, began another circuit.

What the hell could Mona want? What could be so urgent?

Well, in two days he would know. A meeting had been set for Berlin, where Oltington would be accompanying the boss on an official visit. The trip had been publicized as purely ceremonial, but was really a cover for some turkey-talking with the Krauts about monetary policy. The last thing anyone wanted right now was an exchange rate war with the Hun, as Jim Hoagland in this morning's *Post* had surmised with an accuracy that could only mean Craxton had been busy on the leak-o-phone again.

He squinted through the shimmering light at his boss and his boss's boss. The President's arm was draped easily over Number Two's shoulders; most onlookers would have seen men bound by common purpose and a shared view of what America was supposed to be about and how to get the nation there. The fact was, Oltington knew, the projected mutuality was slowly dissolving in the acid of ambition and political possibility.

"Ambition." That was what the Beltway called what Oltington saw as his man's clear-sighted staying of the course in opposition to Number One's woolly-headed drift toward a politics of sentiment, a view shared by the hard-eyed men of affairs whose checks Kim processed each month.

The two men resumed their stroll. Oltington, following, put aside grand thoughts of politics and resumed his deliberations about how to deal with the latest bad news.

The irony was, the problem Kim had been dispatched to resolve had turned out to be no problem at all, now that they knew for a fact what the fellow actually had come up with. They should have left him alone.

But they hadn't, and now the problem had escalated. *Metastasized* was probably a better word, thought Oltington.

Footsteps pattered on the asphalt track behind him and Di

Maglio came scooting past, clipboard in hand. Oltington watched as the Vice President's domestic policy aide interrupted their chief's conversation with the President. Di Maglio was full of himself these days, sporting a smug grin and a new red Porsche. Oltington thought he knew why. Di Maglio had intervened on behalf of a bigtime Beltway fixer who represented a Wall Street group who'd wanted to buy a bunch of busted banks out of an FDIC seizure. The deal had gone down, the banks had been "cleaned up"—inside talk for shoving their bad loans and lousier branches back to the taxpayer, d/b/a Uncle Sam—and flipped to a New York holding company for three times what the Texans had paid. Oltington was certain Di Maglio had taken a cut, hence the Porsche.

It occurred to Oltington that he might have done the same with Bordrero Bay. Dip into the Project for $20 to $30 million, run it through a scrim of dummy companies—willing front men were thick on the ground—buy the bank, have Kim scrub its computer files Rinso-clean, and Bob's your uncle. But he hadn't, and now it was too late.

But there was no time for might-have-beens. Kim's new bad news was that someone had taken over from the late Mr. Greaves.

Whoever it was—Kim had dubbed him or her "UQ" for "Unknown Querist"—was good, Kim said. Very, very good. A pro. And he appeared to know he was being tailed. He stayed on line only so long, and he threw up screens behind him when he left. He was an artist at vanishing around corners. Kim's traces either banged up against walls of electronic brick, or petered out in a vast black wilderness of random and meaningless impulses.

It was like two Nintendo Life Masters—Oltington supposed that by now there was such a thing—going up against each other: the Kasparov and Karpov of Super Mario or Sonic 2. He detected frustration, professional humiliation, lethal rage, in Kim's reports. But it was the frustration of the games player, and this wasn't a game.

So Kim had taken drastic steps. Like an actor impersonating a drunk, he had shambled into JEDI through several doors, banging into furniture, making all sorts of digital noise, leaving clues, attracting the attention of System Security—but leaving no traceable footprints of his own—with the objective of causing a "global" change in JEDI protocols that would freeze UQ out.

To a degree, he had succeeded. A number of agency heads had been called on the carpet. Kim himself, in his "public" guise as a highest clearance consultant to JEDI, was even summoned to Bethesda for an emergency meeting. Stern warnings were issued to all users. Passwords and access codes were changed every forty-eight hours now.

But UQ was still in there. It was as if he had cracked JEDI's DNA.

Fortunately, UQ seemed to be making no more real progress than Greaves. At the end of the day, Oltington told himself over and over and over, JEDI might sharpen suspicion to the point of certainty, but you couldn't put the damn thing in the witness box!

Had Oltington been ill-advised to send Kim to scare off Greaves? He had assumed a threatening word or two would do the trick. How in the world could he have known Kim would kill the fellow? Still, there was no indication that Greaves's death ·was regarded as anything but an "accident." As for the other termination, it turned out the woman had a record of flightiness, was prone to no-shows and tardiness, and had no pets, relatives, or particularly close friends wanting to know what had become of her. She hadn't been liked; she wasn't missed.

Then there was the matter of Lee Boynton. How odd that the Master's least favorite niece should have turned up on Greaves's electronic date book! That idiotic little magazine she supported—probably the only way she could get a job as a journalist—had caused a great deal more trouble than it was worth. Without the Carew money, it would have disappeared long ago.

So what was she doing in Bordrero Bay? Greaves's record was no help. "7/19 B 0745 Cephalod—Lee Boynton, *Cap. Steps.*" That was the extent of the entry: nothing about what had been discussed or why they'd gotten together.

The sun beat down relentlessly. The men ahead paused under the shade cast by a beech.

Next: Mona.

Mona, Mona, Mona, what troublest thou, my sweet?

Why had she pressed so urgently for a meeting? Could she have learned of the strange developments at Bordrero Bay? About "UQ?"

Was Kim talking out of both sides of his mouth, reporting to her, playing a double game?

Well, Oltington would know soon enough. She was coming to Berlin, at great inconvenience she had made clear, breaking off important discussions in Peshawar, because she needed—instantest—to see him.

She would have her agenda; he should have one of his own: a counteragenda. Should he tell her everything, anything, or nothing?

The answer had to be nothing. The Project must move ahead! Each passing day in Washington made it clear how absolutely vital it was that the money be there. Not to mention that in three weeks, an especially fine impression of the second state of Rembrandt's *Hundred Guilder Print,* as snappy and crisp as if the artist had put aside his burin only the day before, was coming up at Christie's in London.

So many problems, so little time, Oltington reflected glumly. He felt as if the top of his skull had been removed and pure liquid bile were being poured in.

Nor was his frame of mind much improved three days later when he stood under gray skies on the narrow bridge over the River Spree, keeping an easy watch on the Friedrichstrasse, waiting for Mona to appear.

In Washington it had been the heat and the humidity; now it was the chill and the humidity. A dank piercing wind had blown down from the Baltic; Berlin gasped in great, gelid exhalations. Oltington shivered; he had neglected to bring anything but a light raincoat, and when he priced a more substantial Burberry on the Kurfurstendamm, he almost fainted at the money being asked.

It was Mona's idea that they attend a matinee performance of *Die Dreigroschenoper* and discuss their business at the intermission, continuing afterward if necessary. He would find the play culturally enlightening, she told him, a view of the true German soul. He doubted he would. The German soul didn't interest him much.

A westbound elevated train rumbled into the S-Bahn station down the way. A few moments later, Mona, in head-to-toe sable, advanced up the Friedrichstrasse. As she swung rakishly past a crew chipping at the pavement, the men stopped what they were doing and followed her progress. An instant later, Oltington was enveloped in billows of *Je Reviens* and soft, deep fur. This is not, he thought as he hugged her, what masters of espionage tradecraft would regard as a rendezvous conducted with suitable discretion.

"Darling Rusty."

"Mona, m'dear."

"You had no trouble finding your way here?"

"None at all."

Which was a fib. Mona had insisted that he make his way to their meeting by public transportation; something about not wanting a record in the embassy vehicle log. So Oltington had found himself standing on a wind-ripped street corner three blocks from the embassy wrestling with an intractable foldout map, the infamous *Falkplan,* trying to figure out the rapid transit routings while the map flapped with the fury of a spinnaker whose halyards had parted. In the end, he had come by taxi.

The performance proved every bit as ghastly as he anticipated. At the interval, Mona bought them coffees.

"I want your help on something, Russell," she said quietly.

"Mine is yours to command."

This must be serious, he thought. For the first time ever, there was a catch of disquiet, of unconfidence in her voice. Just a whiff, but it blew through his awareness like a line squall.

"Do we have to talk here?" he asked. "All these people!"

"Not at all. Come on. I know a place."

They walked down the Friedrichstrasse in silence and took the second right. Suddenly Mona snatched his hand and pulled him into a narrow alley and through the heavy door of a Turkish café with impenetrable leaded glass windows.

Now this is more like it, thought Oltington as they were led to a table. The place was dim, with wailing, singsong music drifting scratchily out of a loudspeaker, the air perfumed with sweet coffee and strange spices, people talking in low voices across tables faintly lit by red-bulbed brass lamps of an astonishing and ornate cheapness. This is the real thing: a set out of a Le Carré novel, where in the old days the "joes" would have sat for hours, smoking cigarette after cigarette, sipping bad Spanish brandy, waiting to try to cross over.

The menu was unintelligible, so he let Mona order. The waiter brought two glasses of clear liquid that smelled like fusel oil and tasted worse. Mona leaned toward him and clinked her glass to his. Exotic ululations drifted from the sound system.

"So, darling, how's the trip been? *Grand succès diplomatique?* Should we be looking forward to another great fiscal initiative? If so, I hope it'll prove as profitable as the last."

Without letting him answer, she went on. "I had a most entertaining morning. Went out to the old East German security headquarters to get a line on some more mutual funds salesmen. Have I told you about our Red Bloc funds? Anyway, while I was there, I had a look at my Stasi file."

Stasi—*Statische Sicherheitsdienst:* the East German KGB.

"And . . ."

"And nothing, darling! *Nada, niente, rien du tout!* I've never been so insulted in my life! A fortnight ago in St. Petersburg, I got to see what the KGB had. Now that was a triumph! I felt quite like Bernhardt!"

Like all prima donnas, Oltington reflected, Mona's favorite subject is herself. Which is okay as long as the voice and legs last, or are valued for what they once were. In Mona's circles, the latter was seldom the case.

"Anyway, darling, to business: Does the name Phoenix mean anything to you?"

"You know it does. It's that vulture fund you set up for CP."

"That *CP* set up. Accuracy is everything, Russell, you know that. In any case, you also know who Leo Gorton is?"

"The penny-ante Milken who runs Phoenix for you . . . Sorry, for Claude and Bruno. Those junk bond deals he did, all garbage now. Ashes to ashes, junk to junk. I also hear he's a raving pansy."

Mona looked at Oltington with amusement. She knew his own sexual tastes to be a matter for speculation along Embassy Row.

"Don't be censorious, Russell, it doesn't become you. It's true: Leo was very actively engaged in leveraged finance in connection with a number of projects that failed to meet projections. But he was hardly alone in this. Times changed. If there's an explosion in a refinery, whom do we blame: the spark or the fumes?"

Oltington sipped the Turkish brandy. It was like undergoing a tonsillectomy without anaesthetic.

"If you wish to debate the pros and cons of the 1980s," said

Mona impatiently, "we can do that another time, but I have a four-forty flight from Tegel and I have other things to do."

"I'm sorry. Please, do explain Phoenix and Gorton to me. I can hardly wait."

"Such sarcasm! It simply happens to be my and Leo's conviction, shared by certain of my clients, that a great many defaulted securities have an attraction considerably in excess of the price at which they can be bought today."

"I thought that was the theory of vulture funds. Buy the junk cheap, sell the underlying assets dear."

"It is. Customarily. In our case, however, the word *attraction* has a somewhat different meaning."

She smiled confidingly at Oltington. Now he felt like a saucer of cream.

She explained. From 1985 to 1990, Freemark Securities had presided over the issuance of some $800 million in junk securities now rendered virtually valueless by the collapse of the enterprises they had financed. Many of these bonds and preferred stocks were in the portfolios of investment and depositary institutions now also insolvent and in the hands of the government. To be blunt about it, it would be most unfortunate if federal authorities—or anyone else stuck with the worthless paper—should scrutinize the assets underpinning the paper, or the associated enterprises, too closely.

"It struck some of us with knowledge of the particulars that simply from the viewpoint of . . . let us call it prudence . . . it makes good sense to buy back these securities very cheaply."

"And send them to the shredder?"

Mona merely smiled.

"Hence Phoenix?"

She nodded.

"And Gorton fronts the swindle?"

She put her forefinger to her lips.

"Does he know what's going on? I'll bet he doesn't!"

Again the forefinger.

Or would Gorton even care? Oltington wondered. These types were all the same. Obsessed with being seen to be where the action was, any action, so long as it put you back at the right table at "21," in the right courtside seats at Knicks games, at the right table at breakfast at the Regency Hotel, trading noogies with Bob Tisch. Gorton was just another snout at the trough, too busy eating to notice.

From Mona's point of view, Gorton would make a convincing enough front. Oltington had seen a flattering profile in *Forbes*. There had been other stories, appearances on television with Rukeyser, and Adam Smith, and McLaughlin.

"So what's the problem you need my help with?" he asked.

Before answering, Mona took a sip of her drink, stirred her coffee, affected to listen to the music from the loudspeakers.

Something's really eating at her, thought Oltington. It was something about the set of her mouth.

He was right.

It started almost a month earlier. Mona had awakened in her suite at the Oberoi Hotel in Delhi moaning and sweat drenched, shivering so violently she wondered at first if she'd picked up an Afghan dengue. She had dreamed she was wandering on the cobbled banks of a filthy, sluggish river winding through a haunted, surreal town. The night was moonless, dank, unbreathing. Ahead was a ruined bridge, oddly familiar. As Mona drew near, she became aware of something hanging from it. At that instant, the spatial arrangements of the dream altered and she was standing on the surface of the river, face-to-face with the dangling apparition. It was wrapped in a shroud of black, which was also red, red-black, the color of dead blood. The face was veiled at first, then the shroud fell away, revealing a skull or was it a face? A skull with a moustache, with glaring eyes, yellow Doberman pinscher eyes, killers' eyes. The face of Death, the face of the Don.

What did it mean?

A week later, while Mona was still in Delhi, other troubling portents materialized.

One of the corpses on Phoenix's list was a real estate developer called Dunbar, which had been looted of roughly $300 million. Dunbar's principal asset was a resort development, Margaret Island, off the Carolina coast. Margaret Island was guarded by CourierGuard, Courier Services' plant and facility security arm, which was providing patrol services at key locations and facilities of various enterprises for whose worthless securities Phoenix had launched bids.

There had been an incursion at Margaret Island. A Cessna seaplane had made a number of passes, covering the island from one end to the other. A CourierGuard helicopter had been sent up; the trespasser's stabilizer identification number had been noted.

The seaplane had been traced to a Savannah leasing and charter service. On the date in question, it had picked up three people—two men and one woman—at a corporate fishing-hunting camp southeast of Charleston. The charter fees—which came to $1,137.50—had been charged to an American Express card issued to Leonore M. Boynton at a Washington address.

Mona recognized the name at once. Leonore—Lee—Boynton was the Master's niece: the one with the sultry looks and what Henry—the Master—called "detestable egalitarian politics." She owned a magazine in Washington, a rich girl's plaything.

Sitting on the edge of her uncomfortable bed, now and then looking out the window at the Hooghly flowing to the sea, Mona had logged onto Nexis and screened up a five-year recapitulation of articles with the byline "Lee Boynton." Most were on financial topics. Scandals and swindles.

So had Boynton tumbled onto Margaret Island? How? How could Mona find out? The thing to do was to put CourierSurv, Courier's investigative arm, on Boynton's tail, see what they turned up. She decided to take that course of action under advisement, at least temporarily; to wait and see.

Like all information relating to Phoenix "enterprises" generated by Courier Services, the Margaret Island report had been transmitted as "eyes only" E-mail to the Avignon headquarters of Banque Provençale de Credit et d'Investissement, to an office and a computer to which Mona had exclusive access, and which she checked daily from wherever her business took her.

The following week, there was more. Another incursion.

This time at the Texas NutriChem facility, four hundred acres near Galveston on which, according to the offering documents issued in connection with a $375 million junk bond financing underwritten by Freemark Securities, would be built the world's fourth-largest liquid phosphate processing facility. Plumb in the center of the tract was a three-acre plot on which was stacked an impressive array of turbine and compressor equipment, tubing and girders, and other physical evidence appropriate to a giant industrial construction project that had fallen somewhat behind schedule. This plot, set off behind a high

fence topped with razor wire, was permanently illuminated by powerful spotlights and swept constantly by a battery of video cameras.

It was an elaborate security-surveillance setup, justified by the
investment to date in site, equipment, and other materiel of some $23
million of the $375 million which had been raised. The balance had
long since disappeared.

The watchman on duty had noticed suspicious activity shortly
after midnight and went to investigate, arriving just in time to see a car
spinning its wheels in the muddy dirt before careening into the night.
He got enough of a look to take down the license plate, which was
traced to an Alamo Rental desk at Houston Hobby airport.

The vehicle had been rented to a Mr. O. B. Smith. "Mr. Smith"
had presented a Louisiana driver's license, which proved to be a fake,
and had settled the Alamo bill in cash. A check was made of motels
lying just off I-45, the Galveston-Houston interstate, and, sure
enough, car and driver had bunked for a few hours at a Budget Inn
some twenty miles south of Hobby. On checking out, "Smith" had
again paid cash. The clerk remembered him as a squat, swarthy man,
a rugged type, probably a roughneck from one of the fields down near
Beaumont, all dressed up for a time on the town.

"Smith" had not, however, swept the sand behind him entirely
smooth. Hotel computers nowadays record all calls, whether or not
charged to a room. "Smith" had called, collect, an unlisted number in
the 617 area code at 2:14 A.M. CDT. Further investigation established
that the number, now disconnected, had been billable to Coole Research Associates, Inc. at an address in downtown Boston.

Coole! The name chilled Mona.

Chances were, he could have been one of the two men with Lee
Boynton on the Margaret Island overflight. Mona faxed CourierSurv
urgentest to find out whether one had been tall, thin, bald. The identification was confirmed within hours.

Coole!

If he had "made" Margaret Island, and "made" Texas Nutri-
Chem, it was likely his people had also had a look at Port Aranses
Shores and Aeolus Energy.

She had to move quickly, although it was likely if he was
working for Lee Boynton, there would be more time than if Coole
had been hired by aggrieved bondholders. Journalists were obliged

to get their facts right before publishing; lawsuits could be launched on a hunch.

And then came Gorton's call.

He had been contacted by a journalist named Bernard Cagel, the editor of a small but influential Washington magazine, with a request for an interview about Phoenix. The man had dropped threatening proof of "irregularities" at Phoenix.

Gorton had refused out of hand. But what was this about "irregularities," he demanded of Mona.

Just a journalistic trick to get you on the defensive, she told him.

So should he go ahead and see the chap?

Not just yet. She wanted to think through just how this should be handled.

Leo is a weak link, she reflected after breaking the connection. Like most hypocrites, overimpressed with his own imagined probity. Confronted with the evidence Boynton, Coole, and now this Cagel seemed to be gathering, he might break down. Gorton didn't know too many specifics, but he did know some names.

And then there was the Don to be considered.

The Don had never liked the idea of Phoenix. If Phoenix should blow up, compromising everything else, the Don would be deeply displeased, lethally displeased.

The thing to do must be to wind up Phoenix in an orderly fashion.

Starting with Leo Gorton.

But Mona didn't do "wet work," and it struck her that to call on either the CP network or—certainly—the Don would be to raise questions she had no wish to answer.

Which left Oltington and his man Kim. According to Russell, the Korean was a regular little killing machine. Special Forces, that sort of thing. Hands like axes.

She leaned across the table and said in a low voice, "The fact is, despite what I said earlier, I'm afraid you're right *au fond* about Leo. I fear he *has* let us down. But I don't wish to act hastily. So what I need you to do is have Kim incorporate Leo into his surveillance landscape. Phone, as well as voice- and E-mail. I have all the Phoenix phone numbers, scramble codes, and passwords in my bag. I have to know what Leo's really up to before I can decide what to do."

"What do you think it is?" Oltington's question was disingenuous; he didn't believe a word she was saying. Something was wrong,
really, really wrong; it wasn't simply silly Leo Gorton who had got the
wind up in Mona.

"I'm going to be straightforward with you. I have reason to
believe that there may have been an unauthorized diversion of funds.
If this is true, my people are going to be most unhappy with Leo."

And with you who selected him, thought Oltington.

That she was lying didn't bother him. She was merely going by
the Master's book. If you found yourself in deep trouble, went the
gospel, lie and don't stop. It buys time, and sometimes help does arrive before they kill you.

He decided not to divulge his own bad news. What was the
point? Whatever was on Mona's plate left no room for anything else.
Anyway, they were all in this together—up to a point. Events seemed
to be drawing tight around them. Gorton might be predictable, but
who could have figured on some low-level GS coon hitting on
Thunderbolt? In the end, any way you looked at it, whatever had
gone wrong was Mona's doing; it was she who should be handed
the bill.

After a second cup of thick Turkish coffee and a second round of
raki, Mona paid the check from a thick wad of deutsche marks. Outside, a light drizzle just this side of sleet was falling and heavy, late-
summer twilight was settling in.

Oltington felt her slip a folded piece of notepaper into his
pocket: Gorton's phone numbers.

At the mouth of the alley, they separated. Oltington headed on
down the Friedrichstrasse toward the Grand Hotel, where he could
be certain of finding a taxi. Mona watched his pudgy figure disappear
into the gloom. Their conversation troubled her. As little as Russell
had been allowed to say, she couldn't help feeling he had something
on his mind he hadn't told her. She should have done less of the
talking.

Diagonally across the avenue, the lights on the Unter den Lin-
den, resplendent neon evidence of the new German order, were
coming on. In another twenty years Berlin would be back to what it

was when Mona's mother had come here after the Anschluss. All would be restored: Alexanderplatz and Potsdamerplatz would again vie with Piazza San Marco; the fine neoclassical buildings on Museum Island would recover their noble rose-marbled glow. From one end to the other of the vast city, the last footprints of the conquerors would be effaced. The Reich would truly have risen again.

And will I live to see it, Mona wondered.

THIRTEEN

▼

Clanking and swaying, the Metroliner sped north. To Lee, looking carelessly out the window, it was as if the right-of-way was a channel cut through a waste of rubbish, much of it human.

Through the translucent grime, now streaked by a light drizzle, the landscape seemed monochrome; one depressing gray and shattered vista after another: a dreary succession of stubbled fields interspersed with the Darwinian margins of broken-backed cities: stretch after stretch of boarded or shattered windows giving on lightless rooms and lives.

Lee leaned back, shut her eyes, tried to sleep, couldn't. She was too keyed up.

This encounter with her uncle would be the first in five years. Could it have possibly been as long as that? She counted on her fingers. It had been.

Six years earlier, Henry St. Albans Carew had "stood down," as he put it. Furious with the administration, he had packed it in at Langley, sold the famous Georgetown house, and took himself off to New Haven to oversee the building of St. Albans College.

He departed Washington at flank speed, in a single weekend, leaving not a wrack behind. One moment his Georgetown home had been its notable familiar self, rivaling the Alsops' and Pamela Harriman's as the place at which one wanted—one *needed*—to be seen. Then, just like that, the famous Federal house was nothing but a tired brick and masonry shell, a weathered husk with a realtor's sign out front and four rough holes in the brick where the brass number plate with the St. Albans coat of arms had been.

As far as Lee knew, her uncle had never once returned to Washington. He had disliked Reagan; he had nothing but contempt for Bush, whom he characterized as "a traitor to our sort," the same epithet he had applied to his niece when, a year after Henry Carew quit Washington, *Capitol Steps* published an exposé that drove six of his intimate Metropolitan Club circle into retirement and disgrace. When he advised Lee that he intended never to speak to her again, he had quoted at her Forster's lines about rather betraying his country than his friend.

That was all so much WASP crap and she told him so. He affected to be deeply insulted—after all he'd done for her! They were both stubborn. Weeks passed while Lee waited for him to call and he for her, then months. And then, in the fashion of such quarrels, it now seemed impossible for either of them to make the first move toward reconciliation.

She missed him. Her father had died young and wasted, her mother was hopeless, and it was Uncle Henry who had stood in loco parentis. When Lee's father, despondent and hopeless, had put down his fourth martini of the afternoon and decanted himself into Park Avenue from the fourth floor of the Racquet Club, Henry St. Albans Carew had without hesitation stepped into the hole poor Billy Boynton—always "poor Billy Boynton"—had left in his eleven-year-old daughter's life. He had taught Lee most of what she knew to be useful in the great business of life: principally how to get out from under her mother and her money. When she'd first arrived in Washington, and for a long while afterward, indeed right up to the day he left Washington for good, Lee and her uncle had eaten together two or three times a week, at his clubs, at Duke Zeibert's, at the Lion d'Or, Germaine's, Tiberio. If she was in town, Lee served as hostess at the off-the-record luncheon buffets he gave every Sunday in Georgetown. His departure from Washington had left a bigger hole in Lee's life than her father's suicide.

She had heard he was utterly absorbed by his new Yale life. It was very high table, she gathered, very Brit: St. Albans Anglophilia given opulent reality by Carew money.

Now she was going to see him again. Coole had insisted.

The train clattered out of Trenton. The depressing Jersey flats rushed by. The day was gray and angry; the high dirty overcast was faintly streaked with orange, which made it look inflamed, infected. In the far distance heavy-bodied jets rose and sank at Newark Airport.

The previous week, she had spent two days with Coole. There had been no repeat of her first visit, the afternoon at the Ritz—the late afternoon light seeping thickly through muslin undercurtains, the two of them naked on the ravaged bed, the afterscent of lovemaking in the air like musk, one empty bottle of Pol Roger on the night table, another on the way.

This time Coole had picked Lee up at Logan and set out immediately for his farm at Pride's Crossing.

As they drove north, he reviewed the bidding.

It was exactly as he had feared, he told her. The pieces were on the table, they knew what the puzzle must look like when completed, and yet were helpless to put it all together in a way that others would find comprehensible and indictable.

"It's really pretty impressive. Here's Nanny, with sixteen billion dollars a year in consolidated revenues, ninety percent in cash. It can swallow a couple billion dollars a year in dirty cash easily, provided the cash is fed into the system in an orderly, consistent manner. Here's Nanny's cousin Courier Services, with six hundred operating centers spread over fifty states and thirty-six jurisdictions offshore, with a fleet of armored trucks larger than Brinks and the fourth-largest flotilla of cargo jets in the world, which has the capability to do just that. Courier has an exclusive contract to process the lockbox deposits of every Nanny subsidiary, although here and there other firms have been given a piece of this or that Nanny unit's business. Purely as window dressing, I think we can assume."

"So where does this leave us?"

"In a thriller, we would try to put someone inside Nanny or Courier. Infiltrate. If it could be done, which I doubt, it would take time and very possibly resources that we don't have."

"So . . . ?"

"About the only thing we can do is let the opposition prove our case for us. Do a few things in the hope that they'll react foolishly."

"Who's 'they'? Courier and Nanny? The Dragon Lady? Special Agent Chung? Persons unknown?"

"Any of the foregoing, I should think. Whoever's in charge. I doubt anyone at field level knows enough to make a mistake large enough for our purposes. You know those Oriental effigies with a hundred arms?"

"Sure."

"My guess is that Nanny and Courier resemble those. No one hand knows what any of the ninety-nine others is up to."

"So where do we start?"

"With the one discordant note that's been played so far."

"You've lost me."

"Think it through, Lee. What we're looking at is obviously an operation conceived and implemented at the highest level of white collar professionalism. It is also, however, a criminal enterprise, involving vast sums of money. Let me give you a hint, tell you about a dog that curiously hasn't barked in the night. My people have been combing police and insurance records, looking for chinks we might get a piton into. They've noticed one rather odd coincidence. In the last five years, every major armored transport service in the country has been the victim of a stickup or hijacking or has had employees involved in violent episodes suggesting criminal activity. *Every* major armored transport service, that is, save one."

Lee could guess which one. "Meaning what? The word from on high is 'hands off' on Courier? So where's 'on high'? Medellín?"

"Possibly. Possibly Palermo. Possibly Phnom Penh. Possibly the Ravenite Hunt and Fish Club in Brooklyn, or any of a dozen coffee houses in Little Italy. Possibly Kingston, Jamaica. And possibly the lovely old city of Avignon, jewel of Provence."

"In other words, Nanny-Courier could be washing money for all the big boys, or most of them. The cartels, the posses, the Mafia?"

"Why not? From what I know of Mona Kurchinski, it makes sense."

"Still, am I missing the point? What's your 'discordant note'? I give up."

"The killing of Clarence Greaves, of course."

He drove on in silence now, letting this sink in. He could see Lee was puzzled. They passed Suffolk Downs racetrack. The grandstand was deserted; it somehow added to the bleakness of the day.

"Lee," Coole said at length, "in finance, all things ultimately regress to the mean. White though its collar may be, the financial activity we're looking at here is criminal. In crime, the mean is violence. There's been one killing. If we continue to apply pressure, there may be more."

That "more" could include us, thought Lee.

"Which is why," Coole continued, "it is vital that we learn why Greaves was killed."

"Presumably because of what he found out?"

"He found out nothing."

"What're you talking about? What about Thunderbolt, Courier, the deposit-withdrawal highjinks at GoldWest? Plus the stuff I fed him?"

"All pretty good stuff, Lee, except that if you look at it closely, it's worth very little. That's what Shirley informs me. Answer your own question: Would you publish on the basis of what Clarence had?"

"No."

"So let's take a hard look and see if we can come up with any anomalies that might point us in the right direction."

Lee had the feeling she was being coached through a carefully prepared script.

"First, there's no doubt that Greaves trespassed on some fairly sensitive areas, assuming that our general premises about Nanny, et al., are correct. But the way to deal with trespassers is to get them in your sights and cover them until they either become a real problem or they go away empty-handed."

"How about frightening them off? *A la* Special Agent Chung?"

"Possibly. Don't forget, also, that what's a problem for one person will hardly give another a moment's pause. Keep that in mind while you consider something else. List for me the situations Greaves was looking into. Just to refresh your memory."

"Tip 'n Take. Energy City. The nonexistent Thunderbolt Video. GoldWest. Courier. I think that's it."

"Now: Imagine you're doing one of those puzzles where you're shown a list of five items and asked which one doesn't belong. Which one in Greaves's list would that be?"

Lee thought for a few seconds.

"Thunderbolt. The others're all real, going businesses."

"And big businesses in the bargain. Thunderbolt is not only nonexistent, but it is pro forma a penny-ante swindle by comparison. Now, I'm going to tell you something you don't know, something I didn't know when I saw you in Boston. We've analyzed Greaves's computer files—the man saved everything, God help us—including his JEDI sessions; think of these as transcripts of conversations between Greaves and JEDI. Now that my people have a handle on JEDI, they're certain that very early on, well before you met Greaves and handed him Tip 'n Take and Energy City and, by extension, Nanny, someone was making life difficult for him on JEDI, presumably with the objective of making him throw up his hands in frustration and go off about his other business."

"Are you saying that when Greaves started asking about Thunderbolt, the alarm went off?"

"It certainly looks that way."

"But that it wasn't until he started in on Tip 'n Take, et cetera, that drastic measures were called for? Such as Special Agent Chung?"

"So it seems. My people say that the further Greaves went, the more radical were the countermeasures employed to frustrate him. Think of JEDI as a video game. A game combining Dante's *Inferno* with Wagner's *Ring,* based on circles of information concentrically disposed in a need-to-know hierarchy, separated by barriers that're the cybernetic equivalent of Wotan's fire. The bed of flame that moats off the innermost circle. The obstacles at circle two'll be more difficult to surmount than at circle one and so on."

"With Chung being circle whatever? Lucifer himself."

Coole smiled. "I believe that circle is called Game Over."

Night was mercifully coming on. The tiresome strip malls lining the highway became featureless.

A few miles farther on, Coole left the main road. The countryside became hilly. Great trees hulked against the deep, starless sky. The warm lights of houses punctuated the darkness. Lee cracked her window. It was definitely cold now; the air had that special nip. Autumn in New England. Cozy fires and apples in a basket. Love under the comforter.

But first things first.

"So if Clarence really didn't find out anything," she asked, "how come he was killed? Because he might find out something? The word you keep using to describe this operation is *professional*. I'm not a crime reporter, but I have a definite sense that pros don't kill people on spec."

"I wouldn't push that too far. Chung or whoever killed Greaves knew what he was doing. What we're trying to get a handle on is: Why was Chung there? My guess is that Thunderbolt'll turn out to be the key. It doesn't fit in one way—as an enterprise—so it may not fit in others. It's obviously tied in to Courier and the rest—look at the methodology—and yet it simply doesn't feel right. Do you follow me?"

"I think so."

"Which means we have to follow our sense of the situation, our instincts. JEDI is a peerless information source, but it can't do our thinking for us. It is not Sherlock Holmes. That may have been Greaves's mistake; he thought it was; in certain Washington circles, the system has that reputation. What's certain is that JEDI, in the wrong hands equipped with the right keys or combination, is the informational equivalent to Fort Knox."

"So what do we do?"

"We step into Greaves's shoes. Let them know we're about. Let them see us on JEDI. As a matter of fact, we've been at it for some time now, albeit with a nimbleness I doubt Greaves possessed. This should provoke them. Scare them. Draw them into making the big mistake that'll bring down the walls. Ah, here we are . . ."

The Granary occupied nineteen well-wooded acres looking back across a finger of Salem Harbor at what she was told was Hawthorne's House of the Seven Gables. Off to the west, in the distance, the lights of Pride's Crossing glowed faintly. Closer to starboard was a splotch of illumination that Coole identified as Great Misery Island.

Coole lived in a rambling clapboard house not unlike Constancia's set on a slight rise looking down on several outbuildings. The housekeeping and cooking were supervised by a pair of Irish spinster sisters who were waiting on the porch when they pulled in.

The interior of the house was of a piece with its exterior. Rumpled, comfortable, faded. Lee was pleasantly surprised. The place was full of eccentric touches: in the conservatory, in a splendid Victorian cage, was a piebald mynah bird rocking on its perch, alternately intoning in strangulated croaks, "Loveliest of trees" and "When I was one-and-twenty" over and over and over until Lee finally made Coole cover the cage.

"I'm trying to teach him the poetry of A. E. Housman," said Coole. "Housman was my favorite poet at school. So far, it has not been a success."

It figures, thought Lee. Housman was a huge favorite of Uncle Henry's. His poetry went with squash and rowing, port on the sideboard, the inhibited heart.

In the dining room, one wall displayed a suite of elegant Piranesi prints. On the opposite wall were hung a half-dozen photographs in ornate period frames. Four were pristinely restored old sepia portraits of young men in Civil War uniforms posing bravely. One showed a stained bronze statue, another a worn marble relief.

These, Lee guessed, would be Coole ancestors. She was right. What surprised her was how matter-of-fact Coole's voice was as he led her from picture to picture. She had once been pursued by a Richmond banker of obstreperously good family; his Confederate bragging was wearisome. Coole's New England restraint was invigorating.

"This is Ephraim Coole, who served with Colonel Robert Gould Shaw's black regiment, and died at Fort Wagner. His cousin Adolphus, dead at Antietam. *His* younger brother Augustus, likewise. This is my Maine great-great-grandfather on my mother's side, John Homer Winslow, killed at Gettysburg, on Little Round Top. His brother John Horace Coole, dead of the typhus in a Confederate prison camp after being taken at Shiloh, is the pigeon target. You can find the statue on the village green in New Winslow, Connecticut. The *faux*-Donatello is Morris Cole, my great-great-great uncle. He served with Sherman, and was killed at Atlanta."

"And where is his monument?"

"In the chapel at Groton School."

Coole studied the portrait. " 'Life, to be sure, is nothing much to lose,' " he said, " 'but young men think it is, and we were young.' "

"I beg your pardon?"

"Housman." He returned his gaze to the photography. "Do you suppose this is the meaning of history . . ."

"What is?"

"That the Union be preserved, all these young men die, so that a Leo Gorton might thrive?"

"If they'd lived, they might have ended up doing deals with Jay Gould and Jim Fisk."

He stared down his long nose at her, and for an instant she thought she caught a twinkle.

"So they might have," he said.

There was something about Coole at his Granary that reminded Lee of her uncle at his Rhode Island summer place, Little Meadow, perched at the tip of Sakonnet Point, a tall flagstone house that glowered across the five-mile reach of Narragansett Bay at the frivolous pretensions of Newport. At Little Meadow, Henry Carew put aside the urbane, overread, epigrammatic Georgetown seigneur and adopted a taciturn, on-the-cheap, Yankee simplicity. He did it very well; less than sharp-eyed visitors failed to grasp that the simple muslin slipcovers were by Colefax & Fowler and the red wine being poured into dime store jelly glasses was '47 Lafite-Rothschild. It was the same here: How much was the real man, how much the actor? Or was there a distinction?

When Lee came down for dinner, one of the sisters informed her that Mr. Coole was on the phone to Paris.

She poured herself a drink and inspected the drawing room. She had hoped in her short stay to nose out something of Coole's sense of himself: what people put out told you how they liked to think of their lives. Rows of scrapbooks covering childhood to yesterday might be too much to hope for, but she had expected the odd bit here and there, the stuff you found in other old houses, in the homes of people who had been long on the ground: photographs on the Baldwin baby grand in the library, or on side tables, an engraved cigarette box, an ashtray from a Paris bistro or a framed menu in the powder room, a yellowing school certificate in the upstairs corridor, a meaningful inscription in one of the books in her room, something, anything with a hint of private history, an inference of personal choice. But as she prowled from tabletop to tabletop, shelf to shelf, she became aware of something odd: there was no middle life on exhibit here. Everything was either old—from Coole's youth at the latest—or spanking new and impersonal.

After dinner, they repaired to the library. Coole offered Lee a choice. The cognac was best quality, and the Armagnac quite up to it, Coole asserted, but she felt like something sharp and cutting on the palate—dinner had been a hearty stew accompanied by a big Burgundy—and she asked for malt whiskey instead.

Might as well get in training for Uncle Henry, she thought. Lee guessed Coole was going to ask her to get back in touch with her uncle, presumably on the subject of Mona Kurchinski.

The malt on Coole's silver drinks tray was Glenmorangie, which Uncle Henry would have dismissed as suitable for serving with tea sandwiches; he liked peaty Islay malts, which tasted of rough wet salt air: Lagavulin, Bunnahabhain and Bowmore. "Tweed on the tongue," he called them.

The whiskey wrapped her in a blanket of warm contentment. The fire sent crackling shadows dancing across the varnished surface of the Inness landscape above the mantel. The heat, the faint tipsiness, the pools of soft light cast by the table lamps: Lee felt on another planet. Coole talked, what about she wasn't quite sure, and she answered dozily.

Then Coole lowered his thin shanks from the needlepoint footstool with a discernible thump, squatted by her chair, and, in a voice with not a little cognac in it, said, "You know why we're doing this, don't you?"

Lee made herself focus. The Coole speaking was not a Coole she knew.

"Come again?"

He tilted his head up, stared at her hard. In the firelight he looked cadaverous, mysterious, Elizabethan. Instead of a crewneck sweater, he should be in black, she thought: doublet, a stark white ruff, a dirk at his hip, paying his last obeisance to his queen before heading off to Walsingham to root out a nest of Papists.

"This chase we're on," he replied. "You, Bernard Cagel, Greaves, Her Honour the mayor . . ."

There was a pause here, a long beat. Say it, Lee urged silently, say it. Then, at last: ". . . myself. We're simply chasing down a pack of money launderers, a good story. For us, it's a crusade."

"For what: truth, justice and the American way?" The smart

answer was out of her mouth before she could help it. That's the booze talking, she thought.

Coole didn't seem to notice.

"You might say so. We have larger game in view, an entire decade. To help history at last wield the lash on Mr. Reagan's era."

Speak for yourself, Coole, thought Lee. The 1980s put you in the slammer, ruined your great 1980s career, took you out of the game. Me, I'm just a reporter on the track of a big story. No that's not true. I hated the 1980s, too. Hated them so much I tried to pretend they weren't there.

But she wasn't going to argue the point. She was relaxed and complacent and desire was welling up within her. She shook her hair loose, licked her lips, unbuttoned her cardigan. Gave her man the full Yvonne.

She saw it register. In a moment he'd rise, pick her up, bear her off upstairs, plunge her into his fat four-poster, and love her until dawn.

"So's that what it is for you?" she said, her voice easy, blurred, coming from a great distance. "Avenging fury, like? On whose side?"

"Those young men in my dining room, I expect. What this country's supposed to be about—trite as that may sound. Hating to see the crooks and . . . and the mediocrities get away with it, although sometimes I wonder if that's not envy talking. I prefer to call it intellectual frustration."

Lee wriggled in her chair, stretched like a cat. This is getting heavy, she thought.

Coole was under a full complement of sail, however. Jibs, Genoas, staysails, the works. She let him plow on.

"Sitting by knowing that what was going on was either crooked or evil or just plain stupid and yet no one lifted a finger, that was the worst part. Seeing you press types turning your backs. Watching all those second-raters coming out on top. It was a sickness, a dementia, this compulsive, obsessive need to be in on the action, whatever the action was. It ought to have a clinical name."

Cognac-driven, he went off on a tangent, fiddling with Latin prefixes and suffixes, -philias and -phobias, finally coming up empty.

"Fellow from Cornell I played squash against. Dumb as a post.

Ended the decade worth a hundred million dollars with his picture on the cover of *Forbes*. It was that kind of boom. Made geniuses of fools.''

Lee closed her eyes. Call it anything you like, she thought, it's us—pardon me, *our sort* versus *them*. The old against the new. You can call it the good guys versus the bad guys, but it all depends on which side of the table you're sitting at and when you opened your account at Anderson and Sheppard.

Coole had stopped speaking. Lee became aware of a new sound in the room. Music. Piano music.

She opened her eyes. Coole was playing the piano. To her ears, it sounded wonderful; he might have been Horowitz, although afterward he apologized for playing thick-fingeredly, for missed notes and memory lapses.

Nothing as romantic as this had ever happened to her. Forget that she and Coole had already shared half-a-hundred orgasms. This beat all. Tonight, she decreed, 'll be our "official" first time.

When he finished, she asked what he had been playing.

"Schumann. The C-Major Fantasy, the third movement."

She wanted to know more, but gave up. Ignorance was mystery and what was love without mystery? The room seemed to waver; she reached out and steadied herself on the back of a chair, suddenly feeling incredibly sexy.

"Hey," she said, "Coole. C'mere." She held out her arms. "Beddybye. Come to Mommie Dearest!"

He towered over her, seemed a hundred feet tall. Right out of Cocteau, she thought: Beauty and the Beast.

"Carry me upstairs," she commanded in a voice faint with excitement.

Just as she knew he would, he lifted her effortlessly. She was a big girl, but he bore her as if she were a feather.

Then they were in bed. His? Hers? Did it matter?

Suddenly, she didn't feel drunk at all. She knew what was happening, what her part was, at least until she came for the first of about ten thousand times. Just before she drifted into a deep sleep, she looked at him and murmured . . .

"The next station stop is New Haven! New Haven—the next stop!"

The parlor car squawk box jerked Lee back to reality. She shook her head, scattering the strands of her woolgathering in every direction, and looked out the window. The train was slowing. In the middle distance Lee made out Yale Medical Center and Grace New Haven Hospital. The crisp day was perfect for this first big weekend of the Ivy League football season. Yale was playing Brown. She supposed Uncle Henry would make her go.

On the platform, she looked around; Uncle Henry had said there would be someone to meet her. She saw, coming toward her, a black man in a light gray chauffeur's uniform. Extremely tall and extemely thin, he reminded her of the warriors in *King Solomon's Mines* and the skinny seven-foot African who used to play for the Bullets. Whatever else you might say about this business, she thought, it was certainly producing its share of interesting black men. He addressed her in a deep, Caribbean voice. Creole, she guessed, probably Haitian, probably ex-Ton Ton Macoute. Haiti had been one of her uncle's favorite test tracks.

"You're Miss Boynton, m'am, excuse me, please. I am sent from the Master."

Lee smiled. Don't tell me he's still pulling that "the Master" crap? That was what her uncle encouraged his agency acolytes, the kids who writhed at his feet and filled in the chinks and crevices of his lunch parties like human plastic wood, to call him. Had Mona Kurchinski called Henry Carew "the Master"? Not bloody likely, thought Lee.

The driver picked up her bag and led her through the station out to where the well-remembered bottle green Bentley was parked, watched over by a squad of what used to be called "street urchins" before they started arming themselves with Uzis and dealing crack. The chauffeur distributed ten-dollar bills from a fat roll. The Bentley nosed into traffic and began the fifteen-minute drive across the expanse of mean streets that lay between the station and Yale.

They remind me of Du Bose, Lee thought. The Du Bose of that first meeting at the Hay-Adams, with the Bulls gimme cap, the oversized jacket, the giantkiller Nikes, the sullen expression.

Nowadys Du Bose looked like he'd stepped out of a J. Crew catalog and did nothing but smile.

The morning after Coole played Schumann for her, Coole showed Lee through the Granary proper. As they walked down the rise through the yellowing remnants of a heavy fog that had accumulated overnight, Coole filled her in.

The kids worked a full day. Mornings were given over to formal academic studies conducted by moonlighting teachers borrowed pro bono from top schools in the Boston area. In the afternoons, the kids earned their keep.

"It's not a complete break from their past, however," he said. "Look at this."

On the far side of the Granary, another large structure, almost as high as the original, had been added. It housed half a regulation basketball court, with parquet flooring and glass backboards.

"I don't want to take one hundred percent of the street out of my charges," said Coole. "There's a tradition there of sorts, you know. So this seemed the best solution. Once a week one of the Celtics comes up for a clinic. On weekends, the young people'll play for hours at a stretch. And we have a schedule of outside games."

"Whom do you play?"

"Whoever. Local schools. Amateur teams. Swampscott Beverage gave us quite a tussle last week. The fact is, we haven't beaten anyone by less than thirty-seven points. We cut quite a swath."

He sounded enormously pleased with himself.

"Who coaches? You?"

"Only in a manner of speaking. I arbitrate any internal disagreements, which're blessedly few. By and large, they coach themselves. The boys—and our one young lady, who also plays—have proven surprisingly apt at picking up team spirit, at learning how to fit into each other's existence."

He led her through a door and down a hall to an office where he greeted a man staring angrily at a computer ensemble.

"Ah, Freddy, good morning!" He introduced Lee.

The man who returned Coole's greeting by dipping his chin and touching two fingers to the bill of his flat tweed cap looked as if he'd stepped out of Harrods' window. He looked to be a few years the far side of sixty. Stocky, red-cheeked, tweeded, and flanneled from head to toe, as English as plum pudding to the casual eye—except for the pungent cigarette with a quarter-inch ash dangling precariously beneath a graying, nicotine-stained moustache.

This gave the game away. French, Lee guessed. No one worked

harder at emulating classic English male style than the French, with the possible exception of the Italians.

The man greeted her in good Oxbridge English that was obviously the product of many hours of hard, careful practice. His full name was Frederic-Marie Celeste Auber, but he had never been called anything other than "Freddy" in the twenty years Coole had known him. Paris born, he had joined IBM Europe after graduating from the Polytechnique in the early 1960s, and had helped Jacques Maisonrouge build Big Blue's giant share of the Continental market. He had been sent to MIT on an advanced training program which put him in touch with Digital Equipment, which convinced him that big mainframes were headed the way of the dinosaur. He had also developed a taste for Boston and Cambridge. He sold his IBM stock and options for close to $200 a share and set up as a consultant, which was when he made Coole's acquaintance.

"He's a great reader of spy novels and technothrillers, Freddy is," Coole later told Lee. "Le Carre, Tom Clancy, that sort of thing. He saw very early that computer security was going to be hot, and he made something of a specialty of it. That's how I got to know him. He's very good."

"As good as whoever you're playing against at JEDI?"

"Better."

"I'm surprised he wasn't in on JEDI at the outset."

"Actually, he was invited to participate, but he won't travel. Like most Frenchmen, he finds America barbarous, outside of Cambridge that is, and maintains that civilization ends at Route 128, although he'll make an exception for Tanglewood and certain parts of Maine that remind him of Brittany."

"How'd you snare him?"

"Location, location, location. And he loves to teach young people."

That was plain to see when Freddy showed them around. It was equally plain that the young people responded.

Lee was impressed by the physical plant. It consisted of a series of classrooms radiating off a single large space, which resembled a small Wall Street trading room, with twenty computer workstations, each with several screens and CPUs and multiple phone lines. Each station also boasted an array of joysticks and game controllers.

Along one wall stood a row of sophisticated arcade videogames. At one end, three rows of chairs with writing rests faced a blackboard and projection screen. At the other, desks and chairs formed an open-space study area.

A short, narrow staircase led to the living quarters: ten double bedrooms opening on a corridor and separate boys-girls facilities. The rooms were modest and marine-neat. Only seven were currently occupied: six by boys doubling up, the other by the Granary's solitary female camper. Freddy occupied a separate suite, rather grandly furnished, with its own bathroom.

A bell signaled an end to class time. When they returned to the main room, the young people were at their workstations.

"Du Bose," said Coole, "you remember Miss Boynton. From Washington. When you first came to us."

The change in the boy nearly knocked her over. It wasn't just the clothes—a dark blue polo-colored shirt under a plain white sweatshirt, neatly pressed chinos, with only a pair of major Nikes to bespeak the old "attitude." It wasn't just the handshake, or the open gaze, or the smile, or that the caketop "do" had been replaced by an orderly haircut. It was the sense of wholeness. This boy—a Humpty-Dumpty of the streets—had been put back together.

"Du Bose is discovering that 'by your side' produces easily as much self-esteem as 'in yo' face'," murmured Coole as Du Bose, having shaken Lee's hand and acknowledged her presence, sat back down.

"Du Bose and Freddy're concentrating on JEDI," Coole said.

"And the others?" Lee gestured at the rest of the room. The campers were busy at their stations. Freddy circled the room ceaselessly, checking, suggesting, interfacing.

"Just now, we're on a crash program for another client. One even more remunerative than you."

"Who's that?" Lee asked jokily. "Nintendo?"

"As a matter of fact, yes. They pay us three million dollars a year for game development and testing. It keeps the place going and more so. Shigeru's coming in next week."

"Shigeru?"

"Nintendo's chief designer and game architect. The man who gave the world Super Mario. He's heard rumors that the SEGA-

Genesis people have made overtures to us—which in fact they have. I anticipate a most profitable renegotiation."

"You said something about 'more so.' Who gets that?"

"Half goes into a college fund for the young people, half goes to the Harvard library endowment. It seems only fitting. Freddy, Du Bose, would you be kind enough to show Miss Boynton your three-minute tutorial on JEDI."

As Du Bose logged on, Freddy explained to Lee that JEDI's basic System Security syntax was effectively a Boolean variant of Super Mario. Once they understood that, it was easy for Freddy's experience and intelligence and Du Bose's computer instincts to reconstruct the vocabulary and timings.

"Usually, you have to hang about trying to poach PBX codes and such," Freddy said, "but thanks to the pass codes we pulled off Mr. Greaves's computer files, it wasn't much more than putting two and two together. To the nth power, of course."

"Here he comes," said Du Bose, scanning the monitor for the infinitesimal hitch in transmission readup that would betray the presence of the unknown watcher. His fingers danced across the keyboard.

Lee said it reminded her of a dogfight.

"Oh, it's certainly a bit of that," said Freddy. "The trick is to keep moving, not stay in one place long enough to let him activate his sights and zap us with a virus our software isn't prepared to recognize and defend against."

"Can you get into JEDI without him spotting you?"

"We're pretty sure we can . . ."

"But there wouldn't be any point to that," interrupted Coole. "What we want to do is get the opponent in *our* sights by getting in *his* sights and then keep him there long enough to pinpoint his PBX coordinates. The way we do that is to go after the sort of data that Greaves was chasing. That gets his attention and the chase—or the dogfight, if you prefer—is on. Think of whoever it is as sitting in the dark in a dim room, shotgun across his knees, watching a door. The knob slowly turns. Then it stops. He rushes to the door. By the time he opens it and looks out in the direction of fleeing footsteps, the corridor is empty. But in the shadows at the other end is someone with a camera."

"And so you're sure he hasn't identified you already and is just holding his fire until he has a better picture of you?"

"He may have, although our electronic impersonations are first-rate. That's one reason we're staying within the information parameters Greaves staked out."

"What about JEDI System Security?"

"They're overmatched," Freddy replied. "JEDI's universe is too big for surveillance other than random spot checks. The systems security managers tend to concentrate on in-process material, DEA stings, and such. We've stayed away from that, although our guess is, whoever's observing us, can observe anything on JEDI he damn well pleases, and System Security won't have a clue he's there."

For the next minute or so, Du Bose scrambled from one data path to another—pursued, he said, by the unknown observer. Lee thought it was like squirrels chasing each other in the treetops. Except that at least one squirrel had fangs like a cobra.

"Quite something, isn't it?" said Coole later, on the way back to Logan.

"Amazing. It gave me the shivers. And not just because of Clarence or the thrill of the chase. Those aren't just screens of data, Coole, those're Big Brother's eyes we were looking into."

"You have a point. There're aspects of JEDI that strike me as walking a fine fiber optic tightrope between legal and illegal. We're starting to know too much about each other. Or making it too easy to do so. Between the FBI, say, and private credit police like TRW and Equifax, and the credit card companies selling us out, and now this, there's a veritable data Gestapo in this country!"

"God help us when the computer generation gets in the White House."

When they reached the shuttle terminal, there were still twenty minutes to the next Washington flight. Coole parked outside and handed Lee a fat brown envelope.

"Lenchin's dossier on the collapsed enterprises whose securities are being tendered for by Phoenix Capital Associates. Mr. Cagel'll want these for his interview with Gorton. Has he been able to get a date yet?"

"Not so far. They're stonewalling."

Coole's plan was to sic Barney on Leo Gorton. Confront him

with Lenchin's dossier if necessary. Threaten a story, exposure, prosecution, imprisonment. Get him to blow the whistle, name names.

Mona Kurchinski was Lee's assignment. The place to start was with Uncle Henry. Read her mind through his.

She checked her watch. Time to get a move on. She started to lean toward Coole, then halted. He was not the sort of man one kissed in public. Not even in the semiprivacy of a parked car.

She drew back, kissed the tips of the fingers of her right hand, reached over and brushed them lightly down Coole's cheek. He smiled, put his hand up to cover hers, and left it there for a moment.

When she turned back at the door of the terminal to wave, his car was gone.

The bottle green Bentley stopped suddenly, throwing Lee forward. The driver cursed out loud in a strange patois. A bunch of ghetto kids had darted in front of the car. They grinned at the driver and struck big-man poses, full of threat and wiseass. Lee saw the driver's shoulders hunch in anger. If this were Port-au-Prince, she thought, they'd be dead. They probably would be soon enough, anyway, even if this wasn't Haiti, but New Haven, Connecticut, home of Yale.

The moment passed, the kids moved on, the car turned up Chapel Street. A few minutes later, the prestressed crockets and battlements of St. Albans College loomed ahead.

So here I am, she thought. Step one on the road to Mona Kurchinski. Would Uncle Henry help? Mona was his creation. She might also be his creature.

FOURTEEN

▼

It had been said of Lee's Uncle Henry that if knowledge had calories, he would have been the size of a brontosaurus.

Physically, the Jurassic beast had been all body and not much brain, while the Master was just the opposite. His head seemed extraordinarily large for his short, slight frame, with features that managed to be both robust and sinister; his friend the pundit Joseph Alsop had called Henry St. Albans Carew "a roast beef Episcopal version of Torquemada."

Like Napoleon, Bernard Berenson, and other vast and ambitious egos compressed within small physiques, Henry Carew turned his stature to advantage; emanating from this delicately built little man, his mind and personality seemed amplified, like a tiny loudspeaker capable—through miraculous engineering—of sounding the highest trebles, the deepest basses.

In other respects, nature and destiny had been lavish. His mental capacities were awe inspiring—or regarded as such by most of those with whom he came in contact. He was a masterful schemer, with an innate flair in matters of manners and taste. Finally, thanks to peculiarities of the family trust arrangements, he was the richest of the Carews.

Money, he liked to say, wasn't everything. Those who knew him, however, also knew he didn't believe a word of it. If pressed, he would cheerfully confess to hypocrisy. Other men similarly situated might insist that their own wealth counted for not more than, say, 20 percent of the personal chemistry of success. Other ingredients easily outranked money, they would spout: character, intellect, personality. Not Henry Carew; if you had money, he asserted, you were obliged to use it—as a club, if necessary, or a goad, a prod, a stick, a carrot. It was in the nature of things that money would talk as loudly as it could; if it could shout down all other voices, well, so be it.

He considered his point entirely proven by the 1980s. How many staunchly upright people he knew who once loudly disparaged lucre in the smoking room of the Cosmos now fell silent and tugged forelocks when it became clear that Big Money would like to say something! How many, like his old friend Clark Clifford, simply sold out.

But one was only obliged to face facts, he liked to say, not to make friends with them. The stink of money was the principal reason he left Washington, he told people. It was worse and more pervasive than the humidity. Influence had become 90 percent a matter of cash to hand. Everything in political life tasted of money, smelled of it, bore its stamp and its stink. What would happen when there wasn't enough to go around, as the Reagan fiscal policies guaranteed would happen? Henry Carew, for one, didn't want to be around to see.

Motivated as he was by a sense of public obligation—his great model was Colonel Stimson—he couldn't simply retire and grow roses.

His compulsion to continue in influence combined with his distress at the course his alma mater had taken gave him the answer: St. Albans College at Yale University.

Like Don Escobedo, it amused Henry Carew to see just how far people and institutions could be bent for money. The terms on which he offered Yale $50 million for the construction and endowment in perpetuity of St. Albans College and its Mastership, along with another $50 million to be added to the university's general funds, should not have been acceptable to a great, or self-respecting seat of learning for a gift of anything less than a billion dollars. People who put a price on everything grumbled that old Carew had got a great bargain; he riposted that, since the Metropolitan Museum in New York was peddling trusteeships to junk bond traffickers for a lousy $10 million apiece, he felt he'd been taken to the cleaners by Mother Yale.

The deed of gift was cleverly written. It was damned variously as chauvinistic, racist, homophobic, and elitist, and indeed it was all of those things, although to the dismay of the enforcers of political correctness at Old Eli, only between the lines, and not on the dotted line. The Master's vision was that St. Albans would be an island of manly civility in a sea of know-nothing, limp-wristed barbarism. A beacon of intellectual rectitude in a world that considered "attitude" a substitute for knowledge, and opinion a synonym for fact.

Architecturally, St. Albans was a scaled-down version of Pembroke College, Cambridge, with features of Trinity and King's thrown in, along with a bit of Azay-le-Rideau in the Loire. Life within its walls was predictably Anglophile; the *Yale Daily News* regularly referred to it as "Brideshead Reborn." The fellows of the college—there by personal invitation of the Master—affected academic dress and kept a cordon bleu high table while elsewhere on campus full professors slouched about dressed like wharf rats and lined up with trays for cafeteria slops.

It was an era that regarded confidentiality as a form of discrimination; expectedly, the rough generalities of the arrangement were leaked before the ink was dry. There was something about St. Albans to offend almost everyone who wasn't a member of the college. Hardly a day passed when the pavement outside the main entry wasn't occupied by protesters: placard-waving environmentalists (it turned out there was a "spotted owl" aspect to the dining hall paneling), shrill gay splinter groups, stolid lesbians clomping back and forth in workboots, egalitarians, Native Americans, blacks, and just plain troublemakers.

The day being fine, they were out in force when the Bentley carrying Lee drew up outside the Master's Gate. When the car slid to the curb, they fell silent, obviously impressed by the sight of a quarter-million dollars of coachwork and engineering. When Baptiste emerged, they fell back, murmuring nervously.

The driver got Lee's things out of the trunk, came around and held the door for her. The gate was opened by a uniformed, armed guard, who then took up station beside the car. Through the shadowed passage, Lee caught a glimpse of a patch of well-tended lawn, suspiciously emerald for this late in the year. Behind her, the picketers resumed their noisy circumambulation.

As she followed Baptiste across an inner court, it occurred to her that Henry VIII would have been quite at home here, as would Evelyn Waugh. Sunlight danced on stained-glass windows, moved with stately pace across the pale ochres and gray sandstone surfaces, spread its warmth across dappled lawns and into deep-shadowed arbors. In the bay of a handsomely mullioned second-floor window lounged a young man, pale and blond, tweeded and flanneled, so appropriate to the setting that Lee for an instant wondered whether he might be a mannequin.

A Filipino manservant admitted Lee and the driver to the Master's chambers and showed them into his study.

Her uncle bounced up from an enormous leather wing chair, casting aside the magazine he had been reading. Lee saw with amusement it was the latest number of *Covert Action Intelligence Bulletin*.

He raised himself on tiptoe to kiss her, then led her to a chair near the hearth, dismissing Baptiste with a few curt words in what Lee guessed was Haitian Creole. Henry Carew spoke fifteen languages, not counting patois and dialects.

Lee jerked her head at the sound of the closing door.

"Ton Ton Macoute?"

"A very good man, Baptiste. He was of service to us, so when the Duvaliers went down, I had the Swiss ambassador get him out."

Lee shook her head. She'd never shared her uncle's enthusiasm for dictators, but then she wasn't a geopolitical animal.

Niece and uncle examined each other. It struck Lee that Uncle Henry was in a way a reduction of Coole. When Coole was seventy-five, and shrunken by age, this was how he might look.

"What in God's name is *that*?" she said, pointing to her uncle's chin. He was sporting a scraggly goatee, lopsided and uneven. It looked glued on. Most of Henry Carew's affectations came off, but not this one.

"You don't think it makes me resemble Sir Thomas Beecham?" The Master picked up an ivory-handled looking glass and examined himself. He shook his head, then turned his frank gaze on Lee. "Handsome is as handsome does, my girl. Anyway, I'm bound to say you're looking less tarty than usual, my little Yvonne."

He leaned forward and peered at her. "Definitely. Rosy cheeks, a distinct dermal flush—a cruder mind than mine might say 'postcoital'—although I can't imagine that sort of thing happening on Amtrak. Train travel, even in first-class, is not what it once was. Fellow who was with me at Langley took the Orient Express to Venice the other day. Never again, he swears. Full of Nip stockbrokers drinking indifferent champagne. But that's neither here nor there. Why the glow, my girl? Don't tell me you're in love! Not again!"

Lee wasn't going to let him get away with that.

She looked around and pointedly examined his study article by article, then said, "I thought that English country house exhibition finished in Washington. I didn't know it was coming to New Haven. I must say it looks quite well, if a bit cramped. Or are you opening a Ralph Lauren boutique?"

She was careful to mimic the exaggerated, meticulous diction her uncle invariably adopted when he was launching a verbal rocket from on high.

He threw up both hands in a gesture of mock surrender.

"Well, all in all you look pretty well! I'm pleased to say I don't see or hear a jot or tittle of your mother in you. I should think you're now well past the age when contamination is still possible and that there is virtually no chance of your becoming a socialite."

He frequently referred to his sister as if she were a strain of chicken pox. He claimed Chekhov as his authority; the Russian writer had characterized the Moscow upper crust as "a form of fungus."

They passed the afternoon talking. He wanted news of "the Rialto": of Capitol Hill, the chanceries of Constitution Avenue, the White House. How was the new man? Had to be better than "Dorothy's boy," as he referred to the last President. Or perhaps not.

"One hears whispers the fellow's a closet FDR. That he's going to keep hammering the boys on the Street. That this foreign exchange stunt was only a first step. Bloody well done, too, if you ask me; I was positively green! I tell you, if we'd had these computers in my day . . . anyway, the Street's not going to like it. They've had the country pretty much their own way for too long to give it back to the common man without a fight."

"Meaning what? A coup? A junta in pinstripes?"

The old man shrugged.

"Just things one hears. Tell me, how's my friend Bernard keeping? You should have brought him along. I just got some new Islay from Caidenhead's. Marvelous stuff. Close your eyes when you taste it and you can practically hear the great Rabbie Burns's voice."

"Barney's not well. Not at all."

The old man heard her clear. He paused for a beat, smile gone. "That bad, eh?"

"I'm afraid so. Both lungs. And it's spread."

"Ouch. How long are they giving him?"

"He won't say and I'm not asking. Months, perhaps. Who knows?"

Outside, twilight fell, the room became chilly. Winter was on the way. The houseman laid a fire. Tea was brought.

"Tell me," asked Uncle Henry, "do you ever run into Russell Oltington in the course of your rounds?"

"A glimpse now and then. He's sort of the Vice President's valet. The little shadow that goes in and out. Picks up the towels and so forth. And a great favorite with gossips of Embassy Row. And the First Lady."

Her uncle's face darkened, as if he disapproved of what he was hearing.

"Poor Russell, I'd had rather better hopes for him. But then, his appearance and general deportment do him little credit, make it rather easy to be dismissive of him. People thought I kept Russell around for entertainment, or as a favor to his father, who was in Scroll and Keys with me. That may have been true at the beginning, but I soon learned better. Babbling brooks can also run deep. Russell has imagination—most gossips do—and more than a touch of cruelty, and he's very adept with figures."

"That *is* surprising. I would never have guessed."

"That's Russell. He chooses to keep his brightest light under the basket. He comes from a long line of bankers. Cleverer with other people's money than their own, I have to say."

"Most people in Washington write him off as a silly little man."

"I suppose they do. On the other hand, when there's serious work to be done, who better than someone whom no one takes seriously? That was my theory. Potentially, he was one of the two best people I ever had."

Lee seized the opening. "The other being Mona Kurchinski?"

"My goodness, my dear, you do keep up! Yes, Mona, ah, what a woman! Of course, she's gone on from strength to strength. Such energy! She never stops, never even winds down! Why, when we sank the cruzeiro back in 1980, even I had to pack it in after forty-four hours straight on the phone, but not my Mona!"

He got up and stirred the fire, then looked at his watch.

"Speaking of which, I don't suppose anyone has told you, my dear, but I've become an old man. I need me nap. So I shall arise and go now, and catch a few winks. Thanks to union regulations agreed to by this university's spineless administration, we are obliged to dine at six-thirty, which is heathenish, but there you are."

"I assume you dress for dinner."

"We do. Have you something suitable?"

Lee had brought along something suitable: a long-sleeved dress that a nun would consider prim. On impulse, she had also packed her slinkiest Armani. She knew which she was going to wear.

"I do."

"Good. Even in this day and age, it won't do to give the young men dangerous ideas."

When she entered the anteroom in which the high table had gathered for a preprandial cocktail, her uncle took one look, grinned, and hissed, "You did this on purpose, you devious little bitch!"

"Of course I did," she hissed back.

His were the only complaints, however. According to the Sterling professor seated on Lee's right, a Nobel laureate in biochemistry, the testosterone count during the meal was certainly the highest registered in St. Albans's brief history, even surpassing the levels of the night Jodie Foster dined at high table.

How could he tell, Lee asked. Did he have the estrogenic equivalent of a Geiger counter?

The professor smiled. He said he considered himself a competent scientist, but in this matter he spoke purely as a dirty old man.

After dinner, high table regrouped in the adjoining Fellows Lounge. Henry Carew, mollified by the powerful impression Lee had made, took her on a tour of the walls, which were hung with a first-class collection of English prints from Hollar to Lucian Freud. Before Hogarth's *The Rake's Progress,* he paused and said something that would cause Lee to lose that entire night's sleep.

"You know, damn it, speak of the devil, seeing these prints reminds me of Russell Oltington."

"How is that?"

"It was about two years ago. Around this time of year. The college had been open about six months and I was most anxious to secure a set of Hogarth for the lounge. Can't have a proper English college without a *Rake's Progress,* can you?"

"I wouldn't think so."

"Well, the boys over at the Mellon Gallery hadn't any to lend, but they said there was a pretty good set with a dealer in New York and not too badly priced. Said this chappie was the best when it came to old master prints. Fellow named Tumick, Tarick, something like that. So I duly made a date, and on the appointed day, down Baptiste and I went. It was pissing rain, no day for a walk-round, and being a Monday, the Morgan Library was closed and I didn't feel like whiling away an hour in the Links Club and running the risk of being bored to death, so I headed right to Tunick's—that's the name—figuring that, in the worst case, he could stick me in the cloakroom or somewhere.

"Sure enough, the man was the soul of courtesy. He couldn't see me right away—had someone coming in, a very big prospect, I was told—but I was welcome to wait in this sort of anteroom. Hung ceiling to floor with Degas, it was, so it wasn't like being consigned to Purgatory, and anyway I had my book with me. I settled myself in, looked around and then settled down with Boswell and the doctor in the Hebrides.

"A few minutes later I heard the door buzz and then voices coming down the hall. One of them I knew as well as my own, so I jumped up, popped my head out and said, 'Well, Russell, m'boy, what a surprise!' "

"Russell Oltington? In New York, at a big-time art dealer's? What was he doing there?"

"Well, he was with a Japanese—he introduced him as a Mr. Owata from Tokyo, with the Bank of Japan Art Fund, as I recall—and said they were there to look at Rembrandt etchings. I must say Russell didn't seem all that pleased to run into me, but then it was business, and he was very much in his bow-and-scrape mode, trying to keep the grisly Oriental in good humor and yours truly has never been the flavor of the month of the BoJ, not since 1968 when we had some fun with the yen. Anyway, I gathered Russell's lord and master was down on Sixty-eighth Street at the Council on Foreign Relations trying yet again to persuade the yellow peril to open its domestic markets to American rice, and that our lad had been seconded to accompany Owata, although what Russell knows about Rembrandt you can put in a thimble.

"In the event, there was no opportunity for Russell and me to have a chinwag, so after another cordial grasp of hands, and the usual insincerities about seeing each other soon, I retreated to my little room and tried to get back into Boswell, but I couldn't stop puzzling out something."

"About Oltington?"

"No. It was this fellow Owata. The fact is, I'm damned if he was a Jap! I've known my share of sons of Mother Nippon, and if this Owata was Japanese I'll eat an entire tuna's worth of sushi. If you ask me, he was Korean. Flat-faced, straight black hair, eyes three miles apart. Sort of one step back on the evolutionary chain from Brother Nip. So that set me to wondering: Why would Russell try to put one over on me? He knows how I dislike that!"

Lee said nothing. Korean! It couldn't be, must be sheer coincidence! How many Koreans were there in the world: fifty million? But then again, she had that feeling she'd known before in other unlikely situations, that journalist's sense, that presentiment that it all somehow connected.

"Then there was something else."

"Yes?"

"I went in and did my business with Tunick, and while I was in with him I asked how it had gone with Russell and his Mr. Owata. The dealer was of course the picture of discretion—I wish I'd thought to recruit more art dealers in the old days—but he did let drop one thing which I found interesting."

"And what was that?"

"Well, it turns out that when it comes to Rembrandt etchings, I couldn't be more wrong about our Russell; apparently the lad really knows his oats. You'd have thought the man was talking about one of his best clients or the director of the Rijksmuseum. Not that Russell Oltington's about to collect Rembrandt etchings on his salary. He probably steers business Tunick's way, gets free catalogs, that sort of thing."

When they went back to the Master's rooms after a second glass of port, Lee's mind was still spinning. Was it conceivable that Russell Oltington's "Mr. Owata" might be "Arthur Chung?"

If only she had the tape Coole had given her! She could have her uncle make a positive identification. Where was that tape anyway? Come to think of it, she needed to show it to Barney, too.

Henry Carew decanted another bottle of the 1963 Dow.

"Now," he said, in a manner that reminded her of Coole, "shall we get down to cases? You said you needed my help. How?"

How much should she say?

She wanted a lot from him. Not merely a way to Mona Kurchinski, but a better sense of how this half-lit world into which she'd wandered really worked. Her uncle knew that realm cold. Knew its geography: its concentricities, indirections, parallelisms. How to read its connections and tangentialities. Nothing was direct or straightforward here, except now and then a crude punctuation mark like the death of a Clarence Greaves, perishing in affairs beyond his understanding, like a dolphin drowning in a gill net. It was a boundaryless half-world of vaguely defined sovereignties in which orders were hissed from the shadows, where movements were hinted at, where nothing was quite what it should be, where everything was something else.

She decided to tell him everything.

She started with her trip west to scout the Bohemian Grove and moved on to Bordrero Bay, to Greaves and to everything since. She left nothing out. No fact, no speculation, no clue, no blind alley, no red herring. She gave him Thunderbolt Video, Phoenix Capital, Tip 'n Take, Nanny, Courier Services, JEDI, Margaret Island, GoldWest, CP, the lot.

It took her about forty minutes. He didn't interrupt, except to get this fact or that absolutely straight.

When she finished, he let her sit there for another five minutes while he pondered. The hands on the Thomas Tompion long-case clock behind the desk were inching toward eleven. The port in the flat-bottomed ship's decanter was down to its dregs.

Lee got up and poured three fingers of Lagavulin, neat, into cut-crystal thistle glasses. She handed one to her uncle, who took it wordlessly.

Finally, he spoke.

"It's an operative's worst nightmare."

"I beg your pardon?"

"What you've described. There's a rogue operation somewhere here. Someone trading for his or her own account inside a larger scheme. The thing we used to fear most; whoever's behind it is trying to glue it back together."

He thought some more, then asked, "What is it exactly you want me to do?"

"I want you to arrange for me to meet Mona Kurchinski."

"You think she's mixed up in this from top to bottom?"

"We think CP is. She seems to be CP. Besides, she was your protegée. You know how she thinks."

"You flatter me. I'm not so sure I can deliver the goods. One thing I will do, I'll arrange for you to have her agency dossier. It'll be at the Jefferson tomorrow."

He sipped his whiskey.

"Odd how things work out, isn't it?"

It certainly is, thought Lee.

"I don't suppose you know this, but one of my fondest dreams was to make a team of Mona and Russell. Between them, they could have taken over for me. They complemented each other. I used to think of them as my Bobbsey Twins."

"Tell me about Mona."

"What's to tell? She is blessed with a very high level of financial ingenuity, a good strategic intellect, a terrific feel for markets. Her judgment of risk is refined, although she *can* sometimes be too clever by half: too daring in her conceptions and a bit offhand in her calculations, with not enough margin for error. She tends to fall in love with the idea of her ideas, if you follow me."

"Could this Thunderbolt thing be her idea?"

"It might be. Except that Mona detests working with small amounts of money. When we destabilized Zaire—what a sweet little operation that was—it was all I could do to keep her mind on it!"

"What about killing Clarence Greaves?"

"Not in a million years. Oh, Mona's got a bit of blood on her hands, we all do, but she's no Lady Macbeth. From what you've told me, killing this fellow Greaves makes no sense in terms of relative risk and return. It's the sort of thing nonprofessionals do. It suggests panic. Only amateurs panic. Mona is a professional. She never panics."

Yet panic was what Coole had in mind for Mona, Lee reflected.

The clock struck the hour. The old man put down his glass.

"Gracious, Jacob Marley will be coming to call soon. Now, as I'm no good at all after eleven-thirty, that leaves you half an hour— just in case you want to tell me about your new love life."

"What's there to tell?"

"Don't be coy with me, young woman. Start with Mr. Coole."

Lee's mouth dropped open.

"You should know by now," said Henry Carew, "that I make it my business to know everything. When you suddenly pop back into my life after all this time, this long silence, I naturally wonder why. Niecely affection rearing its head? I ask myself. Not bloody likely! So I make enquiries. Now: Tell your dear old uncle everything."

It had to be Barney, Lee thought. Damn him!

But she told her uncle anyway. Told him selectively. She left out the sex, and it frankly shocked her to see how little there was without the sex.

When she finished, he said, "You should know that I at one time urged my former colleagues to try to recruit Mr. Coole on at least an ad hoc basis. That was after he ceased to be a guest of Uncle Sam. He's very good. Very good. It seemed unlikely that his sojourn at Allentown would have affected his abilities, and indeed it doesn't seem to have done so. But the boys on the sixth floor wouldn't go for it. The business about his son, I imagine . . ."

"What business about what son?"

"I'm sorry. You didn't know? You did know he was married? To a Lowell, I believe, a rather dour woman who lives on the Cape?"

"The South Shore."

"Wherever. She and Coole had one child. A son. A boy about fourteen or fifteen. Be in his twenties now. He was away at school— Groton, as I recall—when Coole went to jail, I gather the boy was ragged pretty badly by his schoolmates. You know how cruel children can be?"

Lee nodded.

"Well, the boy hanged himself. I gather Coole went quite off his head. Fortunately, he was where he couldn't do any harm to himself or anyone else. When he got out, he'd calmed down, at least on the surface, but I guess the headshrinkers at the agency worried about the reliability of the inner man. They might be right. There are people who know him who say his current line of work is a protracted act of vengeance on the world that sold him out. What do you think? Personally, I never thought much of vindictiveness as an operating philosophy."

"I don't know."

Lee felt exhausted, drained. She got up and kissed her uncle good night. There was no more talk left in her.

She didn't sleep. In the blackness above her face, her mind projected a wall on which were attached names, some with photographs, others without. She let her imagination draw lines between them, known and speculative connections. Oltington was connected to Mona. Oltington was connected to Chung. Was Chung connected to Mona? Greaves was connected to Thunderbolt. Greaves was connected to Courier Services. Chung was connected to Greaves, and must be connected to Courier or to Thunderbolt or both. Mona was connected through CP to Courier. Was she connected to Thunderbolt via Chung through Oltington? Was Oltington connected to Thunderbolt via Chung through Mona? Gorton and Phoenix were connected to Mona and to Nanny, and Courier was connected to Nanny. Did Chung connect to JEDI? Could Oltington be connected to JEDI through the Vice President? How, how, how, how!

Circles within circles, melding into a vortex down which Lee whirled helplessly, deeper and deeper until the gentle hand of her uncle's houseman drew her back to safer realities with a cup of coffee.

While she was putting on her face, she heard the phone ring, and her uncle's voice, first murmuring, then rising in pitch. When she went into his study to say good morning, he was sporting a triumphant grin of such gloating candlepower that it seemed to light up the room.

"You'll never believe what's happened! Talk about sheer coincidence!"

"Fill me in."

"Well, my dear, that was none other than Mona herself on the blower just now! Asking me if I would arrange for *her* to meet *you*! Can you believe it?!"

Lee could. She let her mouth gape in surprise, but she could believe it. This was no coincidence. Coole had warned her to assume she was under surveillance. Now she knew for certain.

"Did she say why?"

"Something about a transaction in which she's involved that she gathers you're looking at. That Phoenix thing you told me about last night with the fake assets. Good thing you got to me first. Mona'd have me believe it's strictly legitimate, that all she wants to do is chivvy you a bit. Which makes sense in a way: these days, manipulation of the press appears to be a key element in speculative finance."

Just give the news, please, thought Lee.

"She wonders if it's possible we might meet her in Edinburgh next week."

" 'We'?"

"Well, I shall be joining you, of course: You can hardly expect I'd miss a trip to Scotland. Edinburgh is one of the glories of mankind. I'll enjoy showing you round, my poppet. Moreover, my old friend Jock MacSturgis from MI Five has retired to his ancestral keep, and I'd like to pay him a visit, but I gather it's a bit of a push. You can drive me. Are you a good driver?"

"Perfectly adequate."

"Good, then that's settled. Baptise is competent, but he'd look out of place in the Highlands, which would quite spoil my visit. And let's not forget that you and Mona may require the services of a referee when you get down to cases. Now: Will you do about the tickets or shall I? Not the Concorde, please. I couldn't bear looking at the sort of people I hear you find on it nowadays."

Lee said she would.

"One last thing," said her uncle, "that we need to have clearly understood between us. Absent proof of a threat to the national interest, I'll expect you to mind your manners. Unless requested by both parties, I shall remain essentially neutral with respect to whatever you and Mona find to talk about. To do otherwise would be a gross discourtesy, considering that I'll be a guest in her house. Of course, as my niece, you have a claim on my blood loyalty in extremis."

"Meaning what: if she tries to have me killed?" Lee shook her head. Seventy years after adolescence, her uncle was still pulling the wings off flies.

"There's always that possibility," said Henry Carew cheerfully, rubbing his hands together. "We used to say that Mona ought to carry a warning sticker, that she could be dangerous to one's health. I'm looking forward to a most exhilarating visit!"

FIFTEEN

▼

It was good thinking weather, Mona reckoned, high-skied and crisp, the sun not long up. She steered the Ford Estate Wagon through the castle gates and headed for the M8 motorway. At the Bonnyrigg intersection, a gray Toyota parked in front of a newsagent pulled out and took up station a few hundred yards to her rear.

She checked the mirror and smiled. Normally, she travelled inside Scotland without cover, but as these men were here at her request, she might as well use them. Among his Scotsmen, Bruno said this pair was the best for what she had in mind. Former Guardsmen, set adrift by a regimental consolidation, no records, clean passports, the right skills. Her intentions for them were still unexact, at this stage still somewhat vaguely based on something the Master had casually said over the phone. She would have to see how things developed, if the right opportunity presented itself. It might not, it might come to nothing, in which case she'd simply send the two men back to Avignon and devise a plan B.

She had an hour's easy driving to Glasgow Airport, plenty of time to prepare herself for her arriving guests. And she had much else on her mind.

These Dominican Republic "Brady Bonds," for instance. Would Don Escobedo have read about them? Just imagine! The Dominican Republic was proposing to offer bonds serviced by "remittances from abroad." That's what the prospectus said. Its cover bore the names of two great and famous New York investment banks. "Abroad" was the United States mainly, and the "remittances"— everyone knew—deriving principally from drugs and prostitution, although the accompanying press release hinted at a stream of small contributions mailed home by green-carded Dominican maids and gardeners.

If Wall Street pulls this off, she thought, money laundering would have become a regular-way function of global capital markets. South American central banks would take over as agents of exchange. It would change the institutional character of drug finance, that was clear. But what effect would it have on existing networks? On CP's role? On her own situation? On the Don's? These matters would have to be carefully thought through.

Then there was Eastern Europe, the Balkans and the old Soviet Union. Her recent swing through the area—she had gone as far east as Tashkent in Uzbekistan—had made clear to her that the deposed *nomenklatura* had been busy emptying the coffers: $350 million out of East Germany, $5 *billion* from the old Soviet Union ($3 billion in gold alone), hefty sums from Rumania, Bulgaria, even Albania. From what had been Yugoslavia, flight capital that spoke a half-dozen dialects and claimed as many nationalities: Serb, Croat, Montenegrin, Bosnian, Muslim. Most of it was marking time in Switzerland, awaiting more creative and lucrative deployment.

Mutual funds would be the right vehicle, she thought. Just now, mutual funds were hot, hot, hot—taking in money at the rate of a billion dollars a day worldwide! Mona's soundings indicated that, properly marketed, she could count on $2 to $3 billion coming her way, as an initial minimum. In Eastern Europe, she was a known quantity, and CP had a good reputation for ingenuity and discretion. Farther east, she could count on her friends in the Middle East putting in a good word with the people who were illegally diverting roughly 80 percent of Russian gold and oil production, and the same would be true of her Southeast Asia connections when it came to getting tight with the Uzbek poppy growers.

A family of funds, that would be the way to go. Guernsey registry with double books of account in Lichtenstein and perhaps Curaçao, and physical custody under "street name" in Zurich to keep the Swiss happy and the customers feeling safe.

The money would be managed out of Avignon, of course, for CP's standard fees, with pieces farmed out here and there subject to a juicy override. The funds would buy stocks and bonds mostly, in financial markets from New York to Beijing, with U.S. and Eurodollar derivatives, a little real estate, and now and then a special situation. High-rate bridge finance would also be possible: if the Don's clients needed fifty or sixty million in short-term capital for their Karaghastan joint venture, she could feed it to them through one set of funds and be repaid via another.

It would take careful salesmanship, she reflected. This new money was unrealistically greedy. These people seemed to think you could take Rubens drawings or imperial vermeil filched from Tirana or Kiev and turn the stolen treasure overnight into a choice office building on the Paradeplatz or several million in bearer bonds in a Lichtenstein vault. These days, however, there weren't nearly enough good deals or acceptable properties on offer—not by Mona's standards. But it did seem you could sell anything these days. Perhaps the Don's prediction was correct: He had said the 1980s would be back and they seemed to be.

Speaking of which, what exactly was she going to do about Phoenix?

Well, that was one reason she'd invited the Boynton woman to come over. She'd been nosing around Phoenix, she and Coole, and a man working for Coole.

Compared to Coole, Mona regarded Lee as no real threat. Mona was accustomed to dealing with the press, and she had made it her business to learn all she could about Lee Boynton. She knew what toothpaste and panty hose she bought, knew what Washington restaurants Lee favored, knew whom she saw, who her friends were, knew Lee was sleeping with Thurlow Coole. For the last month, the special unit of Courier Services that reported directly to Mona in Avignon by coded E-mail had kept Lee Boynton under limited surveillance: no break-ins, phone taps, bugs, close tailing. Presumably Coole would be watching Lee's back, Mona guessed. The objective was to keep as far away from Thurlow Coole as possible.

When the surveillance reported Lee had gone to New Haven to see the Master, it was too good an opportunity for Mona to let pass.

She couldn't resist telephoning the Master to ask to be put in touch with Lee.

As usual, she'd been manipulated by the old man. To have him along was the last thing she wanted, but once he invited himself, what could Mona say? There was no point in getting his back up. Aroused, he might make trouble. Retired he might be: But around the world, there were powerful men and women who still clicked their heels at the faintest dry snap of those spidery fingers.

His coming shouldn't make any difference. What was one more casualty? To everything there is a season, Mona thought. What must be, must be; whoever must go, must go.

The problem right now was Leo Gorton.

He had called Avignon again yesterday, nearly hysterical. This reporter Cagel was bugging him again, dropping hints of additional "gross irregularities."

What the hell was going on! Leo had demanded. What should he say!

Mona had begun to wish she'd never thought Phoenix up. For the first time in any of her careers, a major gambit was sputtering, a theoretically seamless weave of manipulation was starting to fray.

If Phoenix blew up, how would she deal with the Don?

He hadn't liked Phoenix from day one. He thought it too clever by half and told her so. He didn't like Leo. Initially, she had put that down to the Don's generic dislike of investment bankers, but now she saw that his objections were grounded in the man himself. Leo *was* weak, Leo *was* self-indulgent; he lacked, as the Don put it, "the courage of his greed."

And if the Don somehow found out about Boynton and Cagel and Coole . . .

She felt a sudden need for air and rolled down the window. Sheep-speckled fields losing summer's green swam by. She saw that snow had dusted the crest of the distant Pentlands.

It pained her to contemplate the winding-up of Phoenix. The concept was admirable, the irony sublime. Only on Wall Street could one make a huge profit cleaning up the very messes one had earned a huge profit making. But the Don was not a forgiving man.

Leo had become a definite liability. As a front man, he had certain qualities; he was glib, well connected; he had made a name for himself on Wall Street. But he was also a publicity hound. His young men were hardly the sort to keep secrets. And now he was scared.

Up ahead, Mona made out the sign for Glasgow airport. In the distance, light glinted on the wings of a descending airliner, very possibly the plane carrying Henry Carew and his niece.

She put aside Leo Gorton—she'd cope with him later—and prepared herself to meet Lee Boynton.

It might have been helpful had she been able to get Russell's take on the woman. He surely knew her; he knew everyone in Washington. But he would have wanted to know why she was asking.

She pulled up to the main terminal, ignoring the signs prohibiting stopping, and got out. The gray Toyota slid by and entered the short-term parking lot. A uniformed security guard bustled up and started to make difficulty, but Mona gave her a sharp look and a five-pound note, and the woman shuffled off.

She waited inside for ten minutes. Finally a porter appeared pushing a trolley piled high with expensive luggage, followed by Henry Carew with a tall, dark-haired young woman on his arm.

Mona gave a little cry of delight and hastened toward the Master, sizing up the opposition from behind her sunglasses: noting Lee's big frame, dramatic looks, intelligent mouth, bosom to die for.

Embraces and introductions ensued. From behind *her* dark glasses, Lee studied Mona. In the flesh, truly a distinctive-looking woman, she thought; a little heavy in the butt maybe, but I should look so good in ten years! And the nose is dynamite!

The station wagon was loaded, tips dispensed, and they were on their way, the Master in the front passenger seat, Lee squeezed in the rear. The gray Toyota watched them leave, then waited another few minutes, checking the traffic to make sure their party of two wasn't in fact a party of three. Satisfied that Mona's tail was clean, they pulled out of the lot; in a few minutes they were again ensconced on the estate wagon's flank.

They had paid no heed to two men loudly and anxiously asking directions to the Edinburgh bus. Americans obviously, a mismatched Mutt 'n Jeff in garish golfing caps and sweaters, probably visiting Scotland on a ten-day class C golf package, and almost certainly tipsy; most Americans visiting the birthplace of whisky usually deplaned in that condition. Given directions, they manhandled hideous self-wheeled valises and hooded golf bags toward the bus stop.

The tall, thin one wore a hideous greenish blue cap marked with the emblem of a public golf course in Bakersfield, California. He had refused to remove it for the entire flight, which was understandable, since beneath it he was completely bald. His companion, squat and dark, seemed unduly attentive to his golf bag: also understandable, since among the shafts rattling inside it were the components of a specially designed high-powered rifle, along with three dozen golf balls that were surprisingly malleable.

The bus they boarded was only halfway to Edinburgh when Mona turned into the imposing gates of Rosskill Castle, some twenty miles southeast of the Scottish capital. A moment later, the Toyota went by, continuing on the narrow road to Loanhead.

Lee was impressed. The castle seemed right out of *Macbeth*. It had "a pleasant seat," tucked away in a sunny glen in the center of a thickly forested park of—according to Mona—some fifty acres boasting some forty kinds of trees. At the castle's rear, the land fell away sharply; steep, rocky palisades ran down to the burn, or stream, that gave the place its name. In most years, the Rosskill was fairly fast-flowing, Mona said, but it had been a long dry summer, and the water was down to a mere whispering trickle feeling its way through stones and tangled brush toward the distant Firth of Forth.

The architecture of the place was, well, eccentric. It was a little bit of everything. The earliest part, the tower, or "keep," dated from the late fifteenth century, the latest from the mid-twentieth. Each succeeding Earl of Rosskill had added a bit here, a bit there, in the style of his times, right up to 1965—the swimming pool at the far end of the garden. CP had bought the place in 1985 as a retreat and research center. It made sense for the bank, Mona observed, since everyone in finance seemed to want to play golf in Scotland.

The castle's interior was as dramatic as its setting. As Mona explained, she wanted to preserve a Scottish feeling, "but without all those awful Balmoral antlers." She had taken Abbotsford, Sir Walter Scott's house, as her model, and used a Milanese decorator, a protegé of the great Mongiardino, to refine it and take out the fustiness. Lee's first impression was that it worked marvelously.

Angus, the castle butler, showed them to their rooms. Lee was given a large chamber near the keep, with a view looking up the

Rosskill toward Loanhead. She unpacked partially, then went down-stairs, leaving the rest for the maid. As she passed the door leading to the keep, she noted a small NO ENTRY sign. The tower was locked and cordoned off. Lee guessed it contained the computer and communi-cations arteries that connected Rosskill to Avignon.

In the drawing room, she found her uncle looking disappointed. "Mona has bad news for us, I'm afraid. We are to be deprived of her splendid company. She has to leave tomorrow afternoon. Business calls."

"Such a bore, but now I have to be in Hong Kong Friday. You know how it is, with the Chinese taking over there, and it is necessary to stop in Dubai on the way. You and I can talk in a bit, Lee, if you're not too tired from your flight. And, Henry, you must be my guests as long as it suits you. Are you still planning to try to go to Gryme? To see your friend MacSturgis?"

"I am."

"It's a very bad drive, as you may have been told. The direct road is often closed. You can go round by Inverness, of course, but that adds hours. Let me send you in the helicopter."

The old man wouldn't hear of it. He detested helicopters. They shook his tired bones to death. As for the easier Inverness routing, nothing doing! The direct way ran through some of Scotland's most spectacular country; mountain-locked Loch Gryme was said to be one of the wonders of the British Isles; if they went by Inverness, they'd miss the loch entirely. Lee was a big, healthy girl with good reflexes, said the old man; she would be only too happy to drive.

Mona looked at Lee, who replied with a helpless shrug that said: what can we do with him?

After lunch, the two women adjourned to the sun room.

It was a smallish square chamber that had been decorated in the late 1930s with improbable surrealistic murals by the eleventh earl, who considered himself a Scottish Dali. It had a splendid view of the glen and the rocky escarpments tumbling down to the burn. Sunlight shone bright on majestic stands of chestnut, ash, and beech.

After a moment's awkward pause, Mona set the conversation in motion. Her tone was friendly, her manner relaxed, her words to the point.

"Miss Boynton, I'm not a woman who plays games. It's come to my attention that your magazine has been investigating Phoenix Capital Associates. Your associate Mr. Cagel has been in touch with Phoenix's managing director, casting what I'm informed are veiled aspersions of an almost libelous nature. A seaplane chartered by you has conducted an overflight of Margaret Island, which is a property in which Phoenix is interested. This constitutes rank trespass and there have been similar incidents at other properties that can be traced to Thurlow Coole's firm. Can I assume you have engaged Coole to assist you in your journalistic enquiries?"

Lee said nothing, nor did she offer any other sign of admission.

"Very well. As you know, Miss Boynton, I'm both a senior consultant to Phoenix and to its managing sponsor, Banque Provençale de Credit et d'Investissement in Avignon. My client's concerned that you may know something that we don't. We have made a substantial commitment to Phoenix's acquisition program, based on Phoenix management's assessment of certain properties—properties that it believes it can acquire on a basis so advantageous that it would be economically foolish not to do so. Your appearance on the scene suggests we may be mistaken to rely on that assessment. Am I on the right track?"

Lee thought quickly. As Barney would say, Mona was "handling" her. Obviously the woman knew they didn't have enough to go on, certainly not enough to publish—otherwise why would Barney be hounding Gorton? She decided to take the offensive.

"All I can say," she replied, "is that you know how it is, Mme. Kurchinski. You hear things, and as a journalist you try to check them out. Perhaps if you can help me, I can help you."

"If I can, I will, Miss Boynton. What are the 'things' you say you hear?"

Lunge, parry, riposte, thought Lee.

"Oh, just this and that. You know: typical Street gossip."

They fenced this way for two hours, with Lee mainly on the offensive. This was fine with Mona. Someone else's questions often gave you the answers to your own.

It was not just Phoenix in which Lee was interested, Mona saw to her chagrin. It seemed to be CP and everything in which CP had an interest: including GoldWest and NNE.

In a general way, the woman was on the right track. Still, when

Lee dwelt on NNE's concentration on high-cash-volume businesses, Mona's response was hard to argue with: In a U.S. and global economy of lowered expectations, the most reliable growth areas would be inexpensive or bargain-priced goods and services; transactions in these sectors were overwhelmingly conducted in cash. NNE was simply taking advantage of economic realities.

All we're doing is playing poker with B school buzzwords, thought Lee. She ceased to pay attention to Mona's words, and reoriented her journalistic radar to catch the pause, the hitch, the undertone that would tell her as surely as an exclamation that she had hit a nerve.

As they went along, Mona's confidence expanded. There was nothing to worry about. They really didn't have enough to go with. Roll up Phoenix pronto, cancel the tenders, have Gorton continue to stonewall, and that would be that.

The afternoon wore on. Lee began to lose heart.

And then she hit pay dirt.

Almost casually, at the end of a series of questions about Bordrero Bay Bank, Lee mentioned Thunderbolt Video. The barometric pressure of the conversation dropped sharply. Mona was too quick to respond—Thunderbolt Video? At Bordrero Bay? That had to be a mistake! Anyone who knew anything about the stock market knew that Thunderbolt had nothing in California! Lee sensed a tightening under the other woman's glibness, a faint, fugitive note of tension.

It was the sort of thing a man would probably have missed completely, but women are more careful listeners—especially with other women.

"I don't suppose the name Clarence Greaves means anything to you?" Lee asked next.

Mona paused to consider the question. Greaves? The name was utterly unknown to her. She shook her head. " 'Greaves'? How do you spell it, Miss Boynton?"

Lee spelled it. Mona made a small, puzzled face.

"I can't say I've ever heard of your Mr. Greaves. Who is he?"

Lee was almost knocked over. She knew at once that Mona was telling the truth!

Lee had been lied to by the best. Washington was the world capital of prevarication. In her time as a journalist, she had been spared no shade of falsehood. She expected untruth, and she had adopted the practice in interviews, following Barney's example, of visualizing the dial of an imaginary lie detector located in the air by her subject's face.

All afternoon with Mona Kurchinski, the needle on Lee's invisible polygraph had been fretful and jumpy.

Now it hadn't stirred.

She's on the level, Lee thought. She really doesn't know who Clarence Greaves is!

Mona's sudden honesty was like an abrupt key change from minor to major. Lee doubted Mona was aware of the signal she had given of a significant shift in voltage. She would have been straining all morning to put over the false as the true; the chance to speak truth itself would have been easy, reflexive, welcome, offhand, effortless, unconscious.

Then Lee thought: If Mona doesn't know about Greaves, who in her circle does? Or are we talking about two circles?

She forced herself to stay on the track.

"Clarence Greaves was an RTC agent overseeing the federal bailout of Bordrero Bay Bank."

" 'Was'?" asked Mona.

"He fell off a cliff. The local police have written it off as an accident. Such occurrences are not unknown on that particular stretch of coast. But we think he was murdered."

Mona managed to maintain a puzzled expression.

"Murdered? By whom?"

"We think by someone posing as another federal employee."

Lee thought about leaving it at that, then decided what the hell, and pushed the rest of her chips into the pot.

"We think the murderer may have been an impostor posing as a U.S. Treasury agent named Chung."

"Chung? What is that—Chinese?"

"Actually, we have excellent reason for believing him to be a Korean."

"I see."

Mona turned away and gazed out at the landscape, showing Lee her best profile. Auburn flames seemed to dance in her hair. The effect was splendid.

Lee tried to keep the hand going.

"Our guess is that Greaves stumbled on something, some irregularity at Bordrero Bay perhaps. We know he was looking into various accounts—including one in the name of Thunderbolt Video—that didn't smell quite right. As you say, there are no Thunderbolts in California. Someone may have found out and decided to liquidate him."

"What an extraordinary story."

Mona smiled indulgently and renewed her study of the glenscape. The light outside was fading. Lee saw no point in prolonging the interview. She folded her cards.

"You've been very patient, Mme. Kurchinski, I guess there's less of a story in Phoenix than we thought. You won't mind if I come back to you with any further questions that might occur to me?"

"Of course not. I'll give you my direct number in Avignon. Ah, Angus, is it teatime already?"

That night, shortly after midnight, Lee was awakened by a sound that came from inside the thick walls. These old castles were full of secret passages and crannies, she knew, boltholes where Papists, royalists, partisans in the Stuart interest, followers of Knox or Montrose, Covenanters, and such had in their time been hidden. Mice had probably nested in one.

Lee's surmise as to a secret passage was correct, although the narrow way along which Mona was hastening in bare feet was of recent construction and did not appear in the plan of Rosskill in the most recent edition of *Scottish Castles*. It led from Mona's private apartment to the communications center in the tower.

As she hurried along the narrow, dim walkway, Mona was in a state of considerable agitation.

It had been difficult enough to make light conversation with the Master and his niece in the drawing room after dinner. In the hours since the interview with Lee, Mona had grown inwardly rigid with rage at Oltington.

It must have been his Korean who had murdered the agent Greaves. What was Russell up to? Had he lost his mind?

Then Angus had appeared to say Mr. Gorton desired urgently to speak with Madam. He turned out to be close to hysterics. The reporter Cagel was talking about taking what he had to the SEC. Mona told him to stay by his phone; she'd call back later.

At ten-thirty she bade her guests good night and went up to bed, wanting to sleep a couple of hours before dealing with her problems. She dozed off at once, and then came the nightmare, the same she had experienced in Delhi, Death with the Don's face, and she awoke shivering. It was barely half-past-eleven.

In the keep, she called Gorton first. He was near panic.

Mona managed to calm him down. Yes, of course he could agree to meet Cagel. Mona might want to come to Princeton and sit in, but she couldn't possibly do that for another week. By then she would have thought through exactly what they would want to say. Gorton should be thinking where a meeting might be held. Remember Ivan Boesky and his body microphone, Mona cautioned.

She next placed a call to an inn in nearby Delkeith and spoke for a good twenty minutes. Her instructions were precise and technical. This was the most difficult decision she had ever made, the most difficult command she had ever given, but she felt she had no choice: the opportunity was there; it must be seized. She was at a crossroads; the few options she had left had better be exploited now—before she had none.

Next: Oltington.

He wasn't in.

Out on the party circuit, she thought sourly. She left a call back message at his phone drop.

She waited through the night for his call. Gradually, she calmed down, started to think rationally. Before she decided how to deal with Russell, she needed him to do one last errand for her.

It was nearly 5 A.M. in Scotland when he called; he sounded a bit tight and very full of himself. He had been to a black tie dinner at the Danish embassy, he reported; she could imagine him basking in a halo of broad-faced Scandinavian attentiveness, the ambassador's wife and her cronies straining to catch every acidic crumb spilling from those rosebud lips.

He sobered up sharp enough when she told him what she wanted, what had to be done and why and when.

About Greaves and "Chung," she said nothing. Those matters could wait.

He assured her he would see to it. Immediately.

This time, when Mona fell asleep, her repose was deep and dreamless.

The next morning, Lee pleaded a need to do some shopping and had the castle driver drop her in George Street, in the heart of Edinburgh's New Town.

She toured the stores for an hour, picking up souvenirs for family and Barney, Wellington boots for herself, and at Waterstone's buying a road guide and several Royal Ordnance maps for the drive to Gryme along with the American and London newspapers. At eleven, needing a cup of coffee, she ducked into the George Hotel. She scanned her haul of papers and went through a second cup.

When she went to reclaim her coat and parcels, a squat man was struggling to get out of a vast Inverness cape of improbable tweed. In the course of his contortions, he managed to thrust a narrow package into the pocket of Lee's raincoat, shielding the exchange from a red-headed woman seated near the door who was watching the proceedings with amusement.

Lee left the hotel and walked two blocks to the back entrance of Jenner's, Edinburgh's premier department store. She knew she was probably under surveillance but she didn't much care. She made for the ladies room. As expected, there were three capacious stalls with full thick wooden doors. All were unoccupied; she took the middle one.

The package Lee had been given at the George Hotel contained a miniaturized Motorola cellular telephone. The "3" key had been brushed with red marker. She powered the phone and pressed the marked key. An extended series of beeps indicated a patch was under way, probably through the Granary and a series of cutouts and scramblers.

Her call was received by a tiny transceiver pinned to the underside of the lapel of a Harris tweed jacket worn by a slender man in a flat cap of matching material. He was sitting approximately five hundred feet from Lee, on a bench in Prince's Street Gardens marked with a metal plaque engraved: "In memory of Isabella Grant Mackenzie: who found in these gardens companionship and peace."

The man was reading that morning's *Scotsman,* nodding appreciatively in time to the music coming from the earphones evidently connected to a pocket cassette player or radio. He was intently reading a report on salmon aquaculture when Lee called. Moving the newspaper closer to his face, he listened as Lee ran through her interview with Mona Kurchinski.

When she had finished, he spoke briefly, then got up from the bench. Tucking the newspaper under his arm, Coole took a reflective couple of turns around the park, pausing each time to study the monument to the Scots Guards with its roll call of famous campaigns.

Lee had said she would bet her last nickel that Kurchinski had no idea who Greaves was or that he'd been killed. But the Korean connection had hit home, and Lee sensed that Mona also knew about Thunderbolt.

Puzzling, thought Coole.

When he had considered the matter sufficiently, he walked to Princes Street, crossed the busy Bridges intersection and entered the Central Post Office. There he placed two calls: one to America, to the Granary, and one just across the street to Lenchin, waiting in his room at the Balmoral Hotel. When he hung up, Thurlow Coole was as keyed-up as he could ever remember. He sensed that the battle was at last truly joined, although possibly in ways he could not anticipate, of which he had no experience.

When Lee returned to Rosskill, her uncle was out walking with Mona on the high path that wound around the castle and along the palisades, the so-called Mistress Walk, named after the wife of the seventh earl, who had hurled herself off the heights after her husband was executed in Edinburgh's Grassmarket after the Montrose Rising.

Henry Carew might have stepped down from one of the Ramsay and Raeburn portraits that graced Rosskill's dining room. He was wearing a stalking outfit made for him before World War II by the famed Highland tailors Blacknalls of Inverness, set off by an ashplant walking stick topped with a sterling silver grouse.

He was giving his hostess a hard time.

"My dear niece thinks something's rotten with the Phoenix thing of yours."

"Apparently. She's completely wrong, of course."

"Is she now?"

They walked on a bit, then he said, "I must say it does strike me as rather crude. Hardly worthy of you. I supposed you pinched the idea from Juvenal. The Roman satirist?"

Mona's expression said she had no idea what the old man was talking about.

"I believe you find the swindle described in his third satire. Let me see if I can recall it. Oh, yes: 'So farewell, Rome! I leave you to men who land all the juicy contracts to build a new temple, or to drain the marshes, then pocket the cash and fraudulently file their petition in bankruptcy.' That's more or less it, I believe."

"You have an extraordinary imagination, Master, to go with your extraordinary memory."

"Yes, I rather do, don't I? Of course, when it comes out, I expect that embarrassment at having plagiarized from the ancient Romans'll be the least of your difficulties, dear child."

Mona smiled sweetly.

"*If* it comes out the way you say, Master, I expect it might be, but alas, there's nothing to come out. Your niece strikes me as very capable, but I fear she and whomever she's working with have got Phoenix completely wrong. Ah, hello!"

The car returning Lee from Edinburgh was just drawing up. The old man waved his stick vigorously in greeting.

Mona left after lunch. An Emirate G-5 was picking her up at Edinburgh at five-forty-five to speed her to Dubai and thence to the Orient.

Lee and her uncle spent the next two days exploring Edinburgh. Everyone told them they were crazy to drive to Gryme by the high road, the roads were so bad, so Lee rented a Range Rover. On Friday morning they set off.

The first three hours of driving after crossing the Forth Bridge were routine. Well after entering the Grampian range at Callander, Lee wondered what the excitement was about. Two hours later, inching at ten miles an hour along a series of narrow switchbacks roughly tracing the shoreline of a gorge-bound loch two hundred feet below, she knew.

It was desolate, lonely country, reserved to red deer, those who stalked them, and a few hermit shepherds. The road seemed to turn on itself every hundred yards. The primitive guard rail couldn't have stopped a lamb.

At least they weren't alone. From time to time, a quarter-mile or so back, Lee would catch a glimpse of another Range Rover snailing through the switchbacks rising. Also making for Gryme, she guessed; from what she knew of Jock MacSturgis, it would be like him to organize a weekend houseparty around her uncle. Well, whoever it might be, it was a comfort to have them back there.

"Another half-mile, I should think, and then we take them," said the man in the passenger seat, studying a Royal Ordnance Survey Map spread on his lap. The map, to a scale of 1:10,000, showed the road and surrounding terrain down to the last pebble. Beneath the map, across his lap, lay an H&K semiautomatic machine pistol. On the backseat, outfitted with a 4X telescopic sight, was a .308 caliber stalking rifle.

"Right," said the driver.

They were the pair who had shadowed Mona in the gray Toyota. Since being scrambled the day before, they had tracked the route by helicopter, setting down three or four times to establish the absolute optimum place at which to deal with the car ahead. They had lain in wait at Auchterbank, the last town before the Gryme turnoff, putting up at the Grape and Feather, the best inn. At this time of year the town was full of sportsmen dispersing into the fanfold of deep-gouged foothills.

Lee and her uncle left Auchterbank after a quick lunch at the snug in the Grape and Feather. Ten minutes later, the second Range Rover turned off on the twisting twenty-mile road to Gryme. Shortly afterward, barriers closing the road for the day were set up by "work crews."

A bit ahead, the road switched back three times in the course of a vertical drop of eighty feet compressed in a third of a mile, then straightened and ran gradually downhill along cliffs that fell straight off to the icy blue glare of the southernmost finger of Loch Gryme. On the map, this section of road resembled an intestine; its colonic twisting required drivers to throttle down below ten miles per hour. Anything above that would be suicidal.

They planned to halt on the highest level, about even with the end of the triple switchback and the beginning of the runout along the cliffs. From there, the man in the passenger seat—who had a chestful of sharpshooter's medals—would have an easy shot with the sporting rifle. Its clip contained special explosive bullets capable of dislodging a tank tread. Shredding the other Range Rover's inboard tires would slew it round and over the edge. Not even a Hollywood stunt driver would be able to hold it on the road. After that it was a thirty-story straight fall into freezing waters, which local legend held to be bottomless. If somehow that didn't come off, it would be a simple enough matter to finish off the occupants of the other vehicle, and push the lot over the edge. A special jack had been brought along for that contingency.

"Any time now," said the passenger. Ahead, the lead Range Rover disappeared into the descending curve of the first switchback.

The driver gently increased the pressure on the accelerator. The other man began to fold the map.

And then the car phone rang.

The two men looked at each other, startled. The driver lightened his foot on the gas pedal.

The phone rang again.

The passenger shrugged, picked it up, grunted acknowledgment, with his other hand instructing the driver to continue to press forward.

"Don't even think about it," said a strange voice—a flat, cold, American voice.

"There is approximately nine ounces of C-4 explosive, I take it you know what that can do, under your friend's seat," the voice continued. "I'm going to count to five, at which point I shall give you another earnest of my seriousness, and then continue on to ten. If at that point you have not come to a complete stop, then you and your friend will be reduced to extremely small bits of human matter. One . . ."

High above the roadway, behind a half-destroyed cairn that Lenchin had picked out, Thurlow Coole counted while he watched the second Range Rover; it was moving almost imperceptibly now, almost at the elbow of the first switchback. When he reached five, he nodded to Lenchin.

The squat man shouldered the skeleton-framed rifle that had crossed the Atlantic in his golf bag, adjusted for windage, aimed, and fired.

The shot pinged off the Range Rover's hood, tearing a gash in the metal. The men in the car looked at each other.

". . . Seven," said the voice on the car phone.

Discretion is the better part of professionalism as well as valor. Coole had banked on that. As his count reached nine, the two men looked at each other again, the passenger nodded, and the Rover jerked quickly to a halt. Ahead, Lee's vehicle cleared the second switchback.

"Out of the car, please," he said in a level tone, "and no weapons. My man is extremely good with a rifle. So let's have a proper show of hands, and when you clear the car, please start walking in the direction of Inverness. If you move out briskly, you should make the main road by sunup, or, at worst, by the time the pubs open."

He hung up.

The second car's driver looked at his companion and switched off the ignition. He gestured mutely at the automatic pistol in his belt. The other man nodded and slid the H&K under his Barbour coat as he turned to open the door.

They got out, hands high, squinted briefly up the hill, and headed off down the road. Ahead, the first Range Rover was halfway through the last switchback.

As the walkers moved into the first sharp curve, Coole thought, better now than later, and said, "Okay!"

Lenchin pressed a button on his radio control and there came a tremendous crack, a violent explosion shook the ground, and they were pelted with a stinging hail of dirt, pulverized schist, and atomized Range Rover. The blast knocked the two walkers down.

After a few seconds, the stony downpour ceased, they got up, and Coole realized he had made a terrible mistake.

Below he saw Lee, startled by the explosion, bring the Range Rover to a halt, and get out. Henry Carew came around from the other side of the car and joined his niece, looking back up the hill.

The two men who had followed were a mere forty feet above Lee and her uncle, looking down on them as from a third floor balcony. They took in the situation at once and acted.

The man who had driven whirled, pulled out his pistol, and loosed a series of shots back up the hill, pure covering fire, designed to give his mate time. The second man jerked the H&K from under his coat and swung round to fire on the pair below.

In the extreme sudden tension of the moment, Lenchin's movements seemed almost languid. He might have been taking the first brace of the grouse season. The rifle went to his cheek like a fine, milled machine element chonking into place.

Lee heard a single sharp echoing crack and saw the nearer man's head jerk, surrounded for an instant by a scarlet dewburst—just like the JFK film, she thought—and then disappear.

From above Coole watched the second shooter stare for a second at his partner's body and start to run downhill. He nodded again.

Lenchin took his time with the runaway, let him get halfway through the second switchback, and then knocked him over the side with two shots in the chest.

Lee and her uncle crouched by their Range Rover. The sudden silence was as confusing and shocking as the last explosive few minutes.

Then a lanky figure came trotting down the road, trying to maintain balance on the steep, uneven grade.

Coole.

She could make out only the upper part of his tall frame. As she watched, he paused and exerted himself, evidently kicking at something to move it. Then a body rolled over the edge and bounced down the brief vertical angle that separated the upper from the middle switchback. A minute later, he repeated the process, and now there were two dead bodies lying in the roadway.

As they watched, Lenchin joined Coole and the two men manhandled the corpses over the cliff. They watched as the bodies took the long fall and splashed into the loch.

Then Coole was at Lee's side. He was carrying a cellular phone in his right hand like a pistol.

He explained what had happened quickly, telegraphically. There was no time to be wasted. Lee and her uncle must carry on to Gryme Lodge as if nothing had happened. Coole and Lenchin would clean up the battlefield, sweeping the more obvious debris and "shrapnel" over the edge. The Scottish winter would take care of the rest.

Their rented helicopter was parked in a vale beyond the topmost ridge. They would fly it back to Edinburgh and return to the United States. The next move would be up to the ungodly.

Henry Carew seemed to pay no attention to Coole. He stood glaring out into space, quivering with fury.

"That was really very disloyal of Mona," he said at length, "disloyal and inhospitable. I shall have to have a word with her about her manners."

SIXTEEN

▼

Once he got started with the interrogation, Barney figured it would take him no more than fifteen minutes to fold Leo Gorton up like an accordion.

These white collar hotshots were all the same. Soft as cheese inside. Talked tough—Gorton in his public utterances favored marine lingo that let you think he'd been in 'Nam—but their idea of combat was bidding up an eighth for a hundred thousand shares or outtipping another guy to get a better table at "21." Wall Street or Washington: It was all the same. Bucks instead of bullets; it might hurt, but at least you didn't bleed real blood.

If Gorton hangs tough, Barney reflected, staring out at the New Jersey landscape and seeing neither forest nor trees, I can always play the pansy card: the rumor that Gorton's idea of a *really* good time was to get it on with the torn T-shirt set, young guys with wild hair and chins out of *Dick Tracy*. The sort you saw in Guess! jeans ads, but who weren't there yet so they needed the money and what the hell.

Provided you were vivid enough, the card was trumps with guys like Gorton, especially now that the new Attorney General had laid it down loud and clear: no more sweet time in Allentown for bilking the taxpayers. Which meant chances were no more Lompoc or Pleasanton playing tennis and calling your broker between sets, but the strong likelihood of hours on the yard in Leavenworth being reamed up the butt by a three-hundred-pound serial killer. It was a prospect all but the most determined masochist found unappetizing.

Barney had hinted as much to Gorton over the phone. He had hinted a lot of things. It had taken time, but finally something had clicked, and so here Barney was, plunked down in the backseat of a perfectly restored, wood-bodied 1949 Buick Hydromaster station wagon being driven through the polite scenery of New Jersey's exurban waist on his way to interview the managing director of Phoenix Capital Associates.

According to Coole, Barney should figure Gorton's script would have been written in Avignon. You could bluff a Gorton, Coole said, but Mona probably knew what facts you actually had.

And the facts were zilch, Barney thought ruefully. It was turning out as Coole had predicted. They had everything and nothing. The evidence they had proved diddleysquat. It supported a series of rational suppositions, that was all. It touched the further edge of circumstantiality, was almost at the point of proof—except that "almost" didn't suffice. But the most promising paper trails had petered out in cyberspace. And what they had simply wasn't saleable—to a judge and jury, or to the earthshakers in the big media: *The New York Times,* the *Washington Post, The Wall Street Journal, Forbes, Business Week,* or "60 Minutes."

Even what had happened at Gryme proved nothing, anymore than the fact that the deposits to the Thunderbolt account out in Bordrero Bay continued as regular as night and day every other week: into the bank via CourierQuick and out again on the bank wire—first to Maryland, and from there to disappear offshore. Coole's people watched it happen just as if they were watching a television show. This JEDI setup was pretty amazing, Barney had to admit, but you needed a badge to put on it. Otherwise you were just a spectator with a handful of printouts.

Of course, they could always take what they had to Uncle Sam, and see what the Feds could make of it. Let the DEA or whoever flag Thunderbolt, take it from there. But no one wanted to do that yet, especially not Coole. The guy's pride was on the line; he took the Thunderbolt continuation like a slap in the face. And of course now you had the old man in the act, howling like a banshee for revenge after what had happened at Gryme. Old man Carew was majorly pissed off at the Dragon Lady, no doubt of that; at the end of the day,

Barney suspected, trying to take him out was likely to prove to have been a decidedly bad idea.

"Almost there, Mr. Cagel. That's the Institute for Advanced Study on our left."

The kid driving the car had one of those semiprecious, clipped voices you found in art auction houses.

Too bad, Barney thought. She was a pretty girl, a junior at Princeton who worked four afternoons a week shuttling the VIPs who came calling from Princeton Junction to Phoenix's headquarters. Like most youngsters in an age of celebrity, she was impressed by names. Only last week, she told Barney in a thrilled voice, she'd had Alan Greenspan in the car, and the week before that, the cute man who used to run American Express, and Henry Kissinger three times.

Well, he thought, she'll learn. If Princeton gives her an education worth a damn, someday she'll know how to tell the real thing from the assholes.

"So what's your major, dear?" he asked pleasantly.

"Art history, sir."

Figures, he thought glumly, and returned to his contemplation of his surroundings. Absently, he ran his hand over the old leather seats. Original, he thought. Carefully patched and lovingly oiled. He guessed he was sitting in $50,000 worth of restoration.

That kind of money would buy two Geos, he thought, maybe three. But to guys like Leo Gorton, vintage was virtue. Minted yesterday, they were willing to spend a bundle to buy patina. To Barney, the idea of trying to live inside someone else's life and taste was ridiculous, but guys like Ralph Lauren made a billion dollars peddling the notion, so what did Barney Cagel know!

He resented people like Gorton who turned their back on who they really were. It was like changing your name. A few pulled it off, but most didn't. You might try to give the impression you were practically born in Le Cirque, but anyone with a shred of acuteness would always make you for who you really were and the place you came from. You might wash your hands for hours, scrub them with a wire brush, but as Lady Macbeth and Herod found out, some stains are indelible.

The car passed through whitewashed gates and by a spread of horse meadows, with a half-dozen good-looking animals grazing behind pristine fences. On the left Barney noted stables and a training ring. The gravel drive wound along a shadowed track, which ran in a long twisting sweep through a thick stand of scrub pine and emerged in a circular clearing embraced by the wings of the two-story brick house that Phoenix had recently moved into.

There was no other car in the parking area. Coole must be running late.

The plan was for Coole to fly into Newark, rent a car, and meet Barney, traveling up from Washington on Amtrak, at Phoenix. Afterward, Coole and Barney would drive together back to Washington, where Coole had a meeting at the Riggs the next morning.

Gorton wasn't expecting Coole. To bring him in had been Barney's idea. It would emphasize to Gorton the depth of potential trouble they wanted him to think he was in. To be confronted with the famous Thurlow Coole might cause Gorton to plotz, Barney hoped, to literally shit truth.

The visitors' receptionist reported that Mr. Coole had called a few minutes earlier. He should be there by eleven-thirty, twenty minutes from now. Would Mr. Cagel prefer to join Mr. Gorton in the health club now, since Mr. Gorton was already waiting there for Mr. Cagel. Twenty minutes in the life of a person of consequence like Leo Gorton, her tone implied, was worth eons in the miserable existence of a worm like Barney.

Health club? Obviously a precaution against body mikes. Barney beamed appreciatively at the receptionist.

"Why don't I start with Mr. Gorton? You can send Mr. Coole along when he arrives."

"Fine. I'll just notify Mr. Gorton."

She tried twice, then hung up and smiled at Barney.

"He must be in the sauna or the steam room."

She led Barney to a back door and pointed across a strip of perfect lawn to a low shingle building perhaps fifty yards away at the edge of the woods.

Barney walked gingerly across the lawn. A storm front of pain now hung permanently over the landscape of his physical existence. Sometimes it was merely low and ominous: a dull, numb presence. At others it spat alive, was stitched with thunder and lightning: jagged streaks of agony. The most ominous thunderhead had settled at the base of his spine; at its worst, it immobilized him, at its least, made him tend to his movements like a man with a pinched nerve. Today he was moving like he was a hundred.

The health club door bore a brass knocker in the shape of an oar crossed with a squash racquet. Barney gave the knocker a sharp rap, then another, heard no response from within, and went in.

Beyond a narrow mudroom was a changing area: very piss elegant with tall, varnished wooden lockers marked with bronze numerals and small brass card frames. On number three the card was inscribed MR. BERNARD CAGEL in a sawbuck's worth of a professional calligrapher's time.

There was no one about. Barney hung up his jacket, took off shirt and tie in one piece, and sat down heavily on the bench, which ran the length of the bank of lockers. When he got his energy back, he took off his shoes and began to shrug out of his trousers. How long Oh Lord, how long, he grunted, trying to push off his right trouser leg with his left foot. At length, he finished, and sat there in T-shirt and skivvies, panting.

"Messaw Cagar?"

Barney turned. An Oriental attendant was standing there.

He had a flat, quince-colored face, coarse, straight black hair, and dead eyes. A Korean, Barney thought. The man, dressed only in a pair of loose-cut, short-legged white gym shorts, was lithe and fit.

"Messaw Cagar?"

The Asiatic accent was so thick it came close to parody.

"That's me," Barney said.

"To forrer me, prease."

Barney stripped off his underclothes and grabbed a terry cloth robe from a hook. It was marked with the Phoenix logo: a fat flame-tailed bird with a beak like a scythe.

"Messaw Golto za," said the attendant. He pointed to the last door down the hall, obviously the steam room or sauna.

"Okay," said Barney. He started up the passage, the attendant close behind, then stopped.

"I'm expecting a Mr. Coole. Would you send him in when he gets here?"

Trying to be helpful, he pidgined the name: "Coor, Coor."

A light of understanding spread across the attendant's impassive face. He nodded vigorously.

The last chamber on the right was marked STEAM ROOM. The rubber-gasketed door was heavy. When Barney finally grunted it open, a great cloud of medicinal-smelling steam gouted out. He pushed through it; the door clunked shut behind him. As it did, he heard a phone ring. That would be the receptionist announcing Coole's arrival. It rang four times, then stopped.

The room was dead dark; its light evidently burned out.

"Mr. Gorton?"

No answer.

Barney tried to get his bearings. He was still wearing his glasses and they'd fogged up, which made it worse.

"Mr. Gorton?"

He thought his voice sounded all wrong: tentative, squeaky. Scared. He cleared his throat, tried again.

"Mr. *Gorton!*"

Silence.

He took a step to one side, feeling his way like a child in the dark, hands moving here and there, fingers spread, sliding his feet carefully one in front of the other along the slimy floor.

And then he touched something.

First with his ankle, then with his left hand. Touched something soft but swollen, something that felt tumescent. He wanted to pull his hand back, but somehow couldn't. His fingers defined the shape and he realized what it was.

A tongue.

"Holy shit," he gulped, heart in his throat.

As quickly as he could, he felt his way to the door, found the handle, pulled it open and stumbled into the passage.

From the dressing room came sounds of someone bustling about. Barney rushed back up the hall and found Coole was slipping out of his boxer shorts.

Even as he shouted "Gorton!" in a strangled voice, Barney couldn't help noticing the sonofabitch was hung like Secretariat.

Coole snatched up a towel, wrapped it around his middle, and rushed up the corridor. He jerked open the door and irritably brushed aside the escaping steam.

As Barney watched, Coole felt along the wall until he found what he was looking for. He screwed the light bulb back in and the room sprang alight.

Puddles of condensation spotted the floor. Glistening beads stood out on the rough insulated surface of the angrily fuming steam pipe.

Leo Gorton was on the far bench, leaning all the way over on his right side, head on chest. One leg was pressed under him, the other extended straight out, his arms hung limp at his sides.

Gorton's eyes protruded from the sockets like piebald grapes. His tongue, swollen and already blackening, spilled from his gaping mouth. On his face was written a horror Barney never wanted to see again. He guessed Gorton had been strangled with the lights on.

Around his neck, pulled so tight it had sunk into the skin, was a cerise-colored strip of fabric worked with the emblem of the Knickerbocker Racquet Club.

"Nothing we can do for him," said Coole. He looked down at the body. There was nothing in his expression to suggest an atom of sympathy.

"At least he died wearing the tie." Coole looked sharply at Barney. "Now—before we call the Princeton police—you better tell me everything."

It was close to nine before Barney and Coole were allowed to start back to Washington. Not that Barney's interrogation, first by the Princeton police, and then by a lieutenant of the New Jersey State troopers, didn't go smoothly enough. It was clear from the spirit of the interrogation that Leo Gorton had not been a favorite of the authorities. His tastes were well known. Apparently, the back door to the Phoenix health club opened on a narrow path that led back through the pines to a pulloff. On Saturday nights—and others—the lieutenant hinted, traffic to and from through the pines could be heavy.

Barney's story was taken at face value. No one seemed to know how selective it was. At Coole's suggestion, Barney had omitted the Korean attendant from his account. No one discorroborated him.

When they were finally on the lower reaches of the Jersey Turn-pike, Coole looked over at Barney.

"The masseur was Chung, of course, or whatever his real name is."

"The Chinaman who offed Greaves?"

"That's my guess."

"Uh, uh. You're wrong about that. Chung's a Chink name. This guy was a Korean! Believe me, I was out there in 1953, I can tell the difference!"

"Whatever you say, Barney. The important thing is that you recognized him from the security video?"

"What security video?"

"The one I gave Lee Boynton to show you. Weeks ago! The bank cameras took it when 'Chung' showed up to claim Greaves's computer."

"She didn't show me any video. Maybe she forgot."

Then it hit Barney what might have happened if he had recognized "Chung."

"Holy shit!" he exclaimed and drew a finger across his throat.

"Exactly." Coole grinned at him, then fell silent and stayed that way all the way to the Camden exit. The guy's ass is burning, Barney thought. When Coole finally spoke again, however, his voice was cheerful.

"On reflection, I think we should forgive Lee. If you'd seen the bank video, as you suggest, you'd have recognized Chung and proba-bly would have shown it, and he'd most likely have killed you as well."

Barney shook his head.

"Given the way I am these days, that might've been the best for all concerned."

Coole turned and smiled at Barney.

"You didn't say that. Or if you did—I didn't hear it."

They smiled at each other. Outside, in the sweet darkness, the miles rushed past.

SEVENTEEN

▼

A big storm had rushed up the Gulf of Mexico, hammering the spine of Florida before blowing itself to pieces off Bermuda. Its slipstream lashed the western Caribbean like the tail of a giant, dying reptile; for three days now, driven by a wind swirling out of the northeast, the sea had been heavy and turbulent under dishwater skies.

The indifferent weather hardly affected Don Escobedo's annual Jamaica sojourn. He was not one for the beach, and he played neither golf nor tennis. He confined his outdoors exertions to brief, brisk constitutional paddles in the villa pool before breakfast and at teatime.

He spent his days in his "rented" villa. Although, as "Señor Montanez," he was a reasonably active participant in Turncoat's Cove's active evening social life, he did not "do" lunch, nor did he entertain.

His principal pleasure was to sit under the awning on the verandah, reading, sipping cup after cup of matchless Blue Mountain coffee, and now and then letting his intelligence float free in keeping with the easy rhythm of the breakers combing the beach below.

Today, the weather was six or seven degrees cooler than usual for late November, and the Don had knotted a light sweater loosely about his scrawny shoulders. To his satisfaction, the sea was visibly calming down at last. In the far distance, rents of pale blue gashed the gray moiré sky. By teatime, he reckoned, the day might turn warm and fair.

The villa he occupied was located on Jamaica's northwest coast, roughly twenty miles due west of Montego Bay. Turncoat's Cove, named after the scoop-shaped, protected bay over which the Don gazed, was built on rolling land that had once been a sugar plantation; the common facilities consisted of a first-class golf course, tennis and water sports, the refurbished Manor House, now a decent small hotel with a very good restaurant and bar, and a security equipage—embracing every form of protection from radar to rottweilers—which would have satisfied the requirements of the most insecure Balkan dictator. Turncoat's Cove's members occupied sixty villas erected within cannon shot of the Manor House, some down by the beach, others perched on two sea-facing hills known as "East Egg" and "West Egg."

The villa occupied by the Don was the highest on East Egg, topmost of a stepped rank of four reachable only by golf cart. It was virtually impregnable. On three sides the hillside tumbled away precipitously and was covered with an impenetrable savage tangle of vine and flowering thorn, brilliant flame-flowered bushes whose nettles could flay an armadillo. The house belonged to a Vaduz-based lawyer, a specialist in the jurisdictional problems of capital, irrespective of nationality or pedigree. On the urging of certain clients based in Kingston, he had bought the house in the mid-1970s, when Jamaica was going through bad times and even diehard overseas Jamaicaphiles were selling up and getting out.

He had met the Don, whom he knew as "Señor Montanez"—a Cuban refugee of means variously resident in Madrid, Mallorca, and Santa Barbara, California, with a Curaçao business address—through Mona Kurchinski. In the course of a meeting on Mallorca to finalize domicilary aspects of certain "Montanez" interests, he happened to mention his Turncoat's Cove house. The Don had shown interest. The lawyer, who had an excellent ear, and thought he detected more of Cali than Castile in his client's Spanish, which meant seriously big money, had pressed the matter: although the villa usually rented for $10,000 U.S. a week, staff and service *compris,* he would be honored if Señor Montanez would take it as his guest.

It sounded just the thing to Don Escobedo. November was dreary in the Andes, and the violence in the cities was insupportable. He accepted the most kind and generous offer of his friend the advocate.

The arrangement was an unqualified success. Each year, at around the time of the American holiday Thanksgiving, when the Turncoat's Cove season got under way, the Don occupied the villa for ten days, notionally as a tenant but in fact as the lawyer's guest. He reciprocated by helping the lawyer with difficult negotiations, and with a week each autumn of partridge shooting in Spain.

In Jamaica, he was left in peace. People in Kingston had been advised who Señor Montanez was; he was perhaps the only visitor to the island who was never hustled or cheated.

Today, however, the Don's mood was troubled, the improving weather notwithstanding. Forty-five minutes earlier, an Air Jamaica A-300 had lumbered overhead: presumably the plane bringing Mona from Miami. If the delays Third World immigration and customs inflicted upon First World tourists as an affirmation of bureaucratic dignity were no more extensive than usual, he could expect her to be on his doorstep within the hour.

He expected that Mona's arrival would cause talk—in ten years, "Señor Montanez" had never had a house guest. But Mona had urgent things on her mind, the Don on his.

He had recently reviewed his clients' investments and holdings. Times were changing. Look at Italy. For years the Don had been envious of his Italian associates' situation: so all-embracing and widespread was Italy's corruption that even the most arrant, enormous speculation seemed as unremarkable as a pigeon feeding in Piazza San Marco. Now that was no longer the case. Adjustments in the Milan portfolio were called for.

He was equally concerned about the United States. He had a sense that some form of populist reaction might be brewing. This would require significant shifts in their holdings and procedures, shifts that Mona was not going to like. Henceforth the emphasis must be on consolidation instead of accumulation; preservation instead of augmentation. The strategy must now emphasize stability, discretion, safety, moderation, restraint, even dullness.

Creativity, flair, daring, boldness, flamboyance, inventiveness would not merely be deemphasized, but would be discarded—at least until the political weather changed back for the better. Investment operations characterized by those qualities must be terminated or wound down, which meant that Mona herself, in whom these qualities were so splendidly manifested, would have to be reined in.

She had done her job well, no doubt of that. The U.S. end functioned like a marvelous petrochemical complex: the raw funds moved smoothly along the pipeline; ingenious processes distilled, fined down, cracked, and catalyzed the flow. The thing now was to leave it alone, running on its own momentum, not to tinker with it, or seek to improve it. The same was true of CP.

He proposed to offer her another assignment. Now that Hong Kong's outlook was uncertain, closer attention must be paid to Korea. A Seoul-Pyongyang-Palermo-Medellín axis, with the Persian Gulf as the fulcrum, seemed to make sense. That sort of financial architecture was Mona's specialty: an entire arterial structure to facilitate the payments flows would have to be devised; no one came close to her genius in this area.

The fact was, this Phoenix business had shaken his faith in Mona. She should have told him at the outset that Gorton was a pederast. Had he known, he would have killed Phoenix at the outset. Pederasts were unreliable in sensitive operational situations. The American Chief of Staff was correct in his assessment: brave though such men might be, they couldn't control their appetites, and this might put others at risk.

The Phoenix business was also causing him to re-evaluate all U.S. commitments, including "Washington," although for no good reason.

"Washington" had yielded pure gold, value beyond calculation—whether measured in treasure, opportunity, comparative advantage, or blood. Still, how long could this high level of accomplishment be maintained? To everything there was a season. No enterprise was invulnerable; often it bore within itself the seeds of its ultimate destruction.

"Washington" was high-technology. High-tech meant constant change. Change implied instability. Instability meant trouble.

The other principal U.S. operation was by contrast stable almost to a fault. Fast-food, dry cleaning, unleaded gasoline, videotapes, cheap dry goods were steady; alteration consisted of minor pricing adjustments, menu changes, managers' specials. These were businesses, to paraphrase Mao Tse-tung, that swam like minnows in the great sea of consumerism. NNE dealt in money actually in hand. "Washington" dealt in money of the imagination. Its possibilities were limitless, but its exposure to risk was large.

Well, he would also talk to Mona about "Washington."

As he tucked away this thought, he was struck by an irony that made him chuckle out loud. So intensely had he focused on what he wished to say to Mona, he had almost forgotten that it was *she* who had asked for this meeting.

What could be on her mind, he wondered now. What could be so urgent?

Probably some incredible new idea, he thought, which would only make things more difficult. If only Mona could shut her mind down for a month or so! Last month it had been Balkan mutual funds. God knows what she had in mind now.

"Hello, there!"

The Don could tell at once that she had had an exasperating trip. She looked well, especially in the shorts and incredible Versace shirt into which she'd changed for the Miami-Montego Bay leg of her journey, but her face seemed thinner, her eyes larger and deeper cut.

Mona knew she looked tired; she had a right to be. In a fortnight, she had traversed thirteen time zones and put up in places that were among the true sinkholes of the world. That went with the territory: You did business where the money was.

Both Mona and her host felt, however, that she looked most alluring when pushed to the limit of her physical and mental energy. Exhaustion did to her what grief did for other women: lent an ethereal, a transparent quality that could be breathtaking. She would be the star of the Sargeson-Milnes's cocktail party this evening, thought the Don; he looked forward to showing her off. In order to preserve the bloom of her beautifying fatigue, he decided to plunge right into business and keep at it right up until it was time to dress and go out.

What news did she bring?

Important news. From "Washington."

It seemed that the successful bear trap that had been sprung on the foreign exchange markets in July, along with a recent frontal as-

sault on the oligopoly that controlled the Treasury Bond market, had
gone to the President's head. People close to the Oval Office were
speaking openly of a new "politics of retribution" replacing the old
liberal politics of redistribution. JEDI was to be the key in drawing up
new maps of the domestic economy.

It was like a search for financial DNA, Mona said. Step one
would be to match ten years of domestic account activity—bank and
thrift deposits and withdrawals, along with transactions in all significant securities, commodity, and currency markets, whether traded
cash basis or futures—with CHIPS flows—offshore and back on—
and with RTC and IRS data bases. The Group of Seven was within
weeks of signing a protocol to make available encryptions data and
hitherto secret account information. Even the Swiss were said to be
willing to join in.

"And what does 'Washington' think? What about his man?"

"He thinks the President's mad. *His* man, of course, is in a terrible position, caught between the White House and a demanding private clientele. For the time being, he is zigging and zagging, buying
time."

Behind her words, Mona was thinking: Let the Vice President
handle his own damn problems! She had enough of her own.

How had it come to this? Only months ago, her masterpiece had
been intact: sumptuous, beautiful, flawless. Now like a great Louis
Seize *bureau-plat* left outdoors through a Jamaican summer, it was falling apart: joints buckling, ormolu chipped, veneers cracked and
sheering off. Was it past restoration?

It all depended on the Don. Her first task was to get him easy in
his mind. Keep him from reading her mood. Play it with a poker face.
It wouldn't be easy.

Play on their closeness, their long relationship. Hell, they were
as good as married to each other. Only death could them part.

The fact was, Mona was experiencing uncertainty of a kind
she'd never before had to deal with. Not indecision arising from vacil-
lation between reasonable alternatives, but outright perplexity flowing from great, basic gaps in the information she required to cope
with a situation. Plain and simply: For the first time in her professional
life, Mona Kurchinski did not know what the hell was going on.

To begin with, what had happened at Gryme? Lee Boynton and

her uncle were by now supposed to be in the bottomless depths of the loch, but the day after Mona returned from Hong Kong, Lee had telephoned to thank her for her hospitality, and the next day, the Master called! The two Scotsmen had never reported in, indeed they had not been heard from since, and of their Range Rover, there was no trace.

Mona had considered sending someone up to Gryme to look around but decided against it. There was no point in arousing anyone's curiosity.

"Now," said the Don, "as to Phoenix. I assume Mr. Gorton's demise closes the matter?"

"It does."

"Bad luck for Gorton but good luck for us, you might say, my dear Mona."

"It happens all the time, *mi Don*. Leo obviously picked up too rough trade."

Her answer struck the Don as too glib, too confident. He pushed his glasses down his nose and looked at her over the frame. It was the ophthalmic equivalent of a Doberman's growl; Mona, enjoying the warm afternoon, missed it. After a moment, she turned to him, smiling.

"Anyway, *mi Don*, it's all behind us now."

Mona inclined her head and touched her forehead with a twirling gesture of courtly submission. She turned a thousand watts of personal incandescence on her host.

And very smoothly too, she thought. Half-page advertisements had already run in *The Wall Street Journal* mourning Phoenix Capital's untimely loss of its peerless leader. From Avignon, a CP spokesperson had issued a statement that Leo Gorton's brilliance and knowledge of the tertiary high-yield market was, quite simply, irreplaceable and that, with regret, Phoenix would cease operations forthwith, although tenders in hand would be honored by CP's New York representative office. A leading Princeton real estate brokerage had been given an exclusive listing on the Phoenix headquarters. In six weeks, the high-flying firm would be just a name from the past. No one buried its dead and went on with its own life with the supersonic dispassion of Wall Street.

But if only she could be sure it was over. The press coverage of

Gorton's murder nowhere mentioned an Oriental being sought for questioning, and yet Oltington had reported that Kim had encountered Cagel, whom every story identified as having discovered the body in company with Thurlow Coole. Kim had intended to kill Cagel, but Coole had arrived unexpectedly, and Kim had fled out the back door to avoid being seen.

Kim cut it too close, Mona told Oltington angrily. But why had Cagel said nothing? And what was Coole up to?

And what about a man named Greaves? Mona had demanded to know. He had purportedly been killed by a Korean. Was it Kim?

Oltington said he knew nothing about anyone named Greaves. Mona was sure he was lying.

So what had he and Kim been up to? she wondered. And what should she be doing about it?

And did her host know any of this?

Please, God, let him not! If he did, someone was going to be in terrible trouble.

So better that someone be you than me, Russell, Mona had already decided.

A maid materialized, bearing a tray of island *amuse-gueles:* breadfruit, tiny kabobs of jerk pork and chicken, smoked fish sliced fine.

Mona ate greedily; she was ravenous; it was dinnertime in Avignon. Rum punch was brought, and coffee.

From behind their respective redoubts of tinted, mirrored, polarized, optically-state-of-the-art glass, Mona and Don Escobedo studied each other while they ate. Something was in the air. Both knew it.

Lunch arrived. Lobster salad, island greens, chocho, tropical fruits.

When they had been served, the Don began to lay out to Mona how it was going to be. His disquisition took them through most of the afternoon. When teatime came, Mona tried to excuse herself for a lie-down, but the Don insisted she join him in his constitutional paddle. The saltwater would wake her up, he insisted.

Six hours later, after three cocktail parties and a dinner, she finally got to bed, too exhausted to sleep. After an hour, she drifted off; her slumber was tossing and troubled, full of old nightmares.

Around three, a great storm blew up at sea. A bank of thunder-heads swelled above the horizon, lit flashingly from behind by stac-cato, sky-wide bursts of lightning. As the storm moved majestically toward shore, the rumble of thunder became continuous, and great fiery stalks of lightning splintered the night. It was as if God had taken an opaque brush to the bowl of heaven; every star vanished; a heavy deluge pelted the house.

Mona awoke feeling feverish and sticky. She slipped out of bed and went to the window, naked. The rain was blowing nearly hori-zontal to the earth; the lightning was now up in the hills. The wind crackled the palms, whistled through the wide-leaved elephant plants, and set up a deep, creaking obbligato in a nearby stand of bamboo.

She felt a desperate need to get into the storm, to recharge her-self with its fierce residual energy.

She wrapped herself in a towel and went outside. Something black and vile hopped across her path. She fell back, saw it was a giant toad, let it pass. The rain was drenching. The towel was useless; she let it drop, let the downpour strum her naked body.

There was something erotic about the moment, highly arousing. People who knew no better might paint Mona as a seductress, but it had been a very long time since she had put her body in the service of her ambition. Now she dealt with her erotic yearnings by herself.

The rain seemed to penetrate her inner being and wash her mind clean of the confusions of recent weeks. Suddenly it stopped, the clouds flew from the sky, and the three-quarter moon blazed white. A fresh, light breeze came quartering out of the west. The sky was again full of stars. Way out at sea, a widely spaced flash now and then sound-lessly lit the edges of galleon-sailed clouds scudding in the direction of Cuba. The Dipper bent low. Insects and frogs, knocked silent by the gale, resumed their uproar. The soaking earth recuperated.

Mona stood by the pool, letting the moisture evaporate. She felt cool inside and out. In control again.

Her mind played with the equation of the situation, using in-dividuals instead of integers, circumstances instead of functions; it tried varying combinations until she had the answer. It had the same elegant inevitability that scientists attributed to the great proofs and theorems; Mona had noticed the same thing in deal making: when a transaction was right, all the elements suddenly seemed to fit together just so.

From his window, invisible in the shadows, the Don studied Mona. What a superb woman she was. How well she had fought off time's exactions! Her bosom seemed high and solid; her hips and bottom unpuckered. Only a slight extra fullness of belly, girded by an all but unnoticeable belt of additional flesh, betrayed her age. The whitish moonlight spilled down on her like Danae's gold. Her skin seemed burnished; her auburn hair, by day brilliant and glinting, seemed a softer brown, the streaming triangle at her crotch almost black.

Without thinking, Don Escobedo's hand slid inside his robe and he began to fondle himself. As he began to harden, it occurred to him that he need only go out on the terrace and that she would be on her knees before him, would yield in any fashion he fancied. And then he quickly took his hand away and drew his robe back about him. She was no longer his.

He had never felt this way about Mona before. There were things he knew about her, things of which he was certain, but this was a wholly new certitude. It had nothing to do with sex, everything to do with trust.

As he watched, her hand brushed her pubis; she twitched, as if a mild electric shock had been administered; trailing her soaking towel, she went back inside.

A few minutes later, the Don switched on the monitor that the villa's owner had thoughtfully provided for his own viewing pleasure. The image conveyed by the fiber optic scanner concealed in the shaft of the guest room's overhead fan was remarkably clear. The Don was surprised Mona hadn't spotted the bug. Perhaps she had. Perhaps she didn't care.

Like a contortionist performing a routine, Mona was arched backward on her bed, knees bent back under her, weight resting on shoulders and the balls of her feet, muscles and sinews standing out in sharp, corded relief. She was moving a small vibrator, its low hum barely audible, in and out of herself, holding the instrument delicately, between thumb and fingers, the way a cabaret singer holds a microphone. She was breathing hard, gasping for air; she obviously knew how to make herself come quickly. An instant later, she gave a great obscene purgative grunt and collapsed flat on the bed.

The Don watched her lie there for a few seconds, then switched off the monitor. He found what he had just watched not the least bit exciting; it had been purely functional, a technical catharsis.

It is different now, he thought, picking up his book from the night table. All afternoon, while he talked, the sense of change had been coming on, the feeling that there was a play-within-a-play being enacted by Mona just out of his range, just the far side of understanding. There had been a shift in their relationship. No outsider would have seen it, would have known to sense it, but the Don himself was sure. He felt a flash of sadness.

The next morning, Mona seemed her old, ebullient self. Obviously, the night's release had hardened her outer shell and patched its chinks and weak links.

At noon, the day being splendid, he suggested a stroll along the beach. They walked in silence to the far jetty, faces in deep shadow under wide-brimmed straw hats. There, Mona looked around, then at the Don, and said, "Something has come up. Something very disturbing, I'm afraid. So personally upsetting that it's very hard for me to discuss."

"Really? Tell me about it."

A few yards out, a pelican crashed headlong into the sea, then rose laboriously with its catch. In the distance, an airliner swung round onto the approach for Montego Bay. A bank of dark clouds was forming over the foothills.

"It's 'Washington,' " she continued. "I have reason to believe he's gone into business for himself. In a fashion that might conceivably compromise the Project."

"Really? What's he been up to?"

Unauthorized use of the system, she told him. Transfers for personal reasons employing channels reserved for the Project.

She's lying, the Don thought. Again he felt sad. Lying like a child.

Her voice was full of outrage. What she said sounded genuine, and doubtless certain details were, but it was a myth she was spinning, because she was involved somehow—of that the Don was certain—and she had edited herself out.

It was a good myth, too—designed to play on the Don's operational phobias: his detestation of unauthorized variations of routine, of procedural free-lancing, of any sort of "winging it" that threatened to break down the Project's functional cohesiveness and consistency.

As they walked back to the golf cart, Mona continued to embroider the story. She is selling out "Washington" to save herself, he thought.

Over a lunch of cold barbecued jack, cucumber salad and fresh pineapple, he asked her how she intended to deal with it. Or would she prefer that he handle it?

No, it was her responsibility. He nodded; in Don Escobedo's order of battle, generals were expected to win back whatever territory they lost.

If he chose to let them live to try.

"Do you have in mind something dramatic like Calvi," he said with a wide smile. "Perhaps to hang 'Washington' from the Key Bridge?"

Mona grinned back; she looked very relaxed.

She thinks she's made the sale, thought Don Escobedo.

"Nothing as dramatic as that, *mi Don.*" Then she told him how she saw it happening. There were to be two prongs. The Don might wish to see to one, although Mona would set it up. The other would be her sole responsibility, although she would look to the Don for logistical support.

"You're certain you wish it this way? I would be pleased to handle that end as well."

"Not at all!"

Do I sound boastful? she asked herself. Greedy? She felt alive again: once again Daddy's best girl, the Master's prize pupil, the Don's indispensable *eminence grise.*

"It's better if I take care of it," she added. "Easier that way, more natural."

It was a good plan, not least because it would finish Lee Boynton and Thurlow Coole. The best way to derail a story is to eliminate its subject. Leave nothing and no one to write about, to question, to suspect.

"There is something 'Washington' is desperate to have," Mona said, "something he has his heart set on. I know how to get it for him."

"Really," said Don Escobedo, chuckling.

She is at her best now, he thought. Alive, positive, confident, sailing over all difficulties as if she were mounted on a sixteen-hands hunter. Poor, too-clever child.

"And what would that be?" he added. "Another masterpiece?"

"You might call it that," said Mona.

EIGHTEEN

▼

By early December, they were convinced they were going nowhere. Stuck, stonewalled, stalemated. Everyone's mood turned as lousy as the weather.

Coole passed through Washington a month after Leo Gorton's murder. The killing had been a three-day tabloid flurry. Eleven young men had been identified as "acquaintances" of the deceased, questioned and released. Gorton and Phoenix were both consigned to the "inactive" file.

There had been no repercussions from Lee and her uncle's Highland adventure, but Coole hadn't expected any. In the opposition's place, he told Lee, he would have swallowed his losses, taken the write-off.

The depressive tension of stalemate made them all impatient with each other. Coole spent an afternoon with Lee in her apartment. It was a disaster; the sex—no way Lee would dignify it as "lovemaking"—was perfunctory and effortful. Lee had trotted out every trick she knew, which only made her feel like a hooker.

Too many key pieces were missing from the puzzle. The only consolation, Coole said, was that the opposition must be as frustrated as they were. Perhaps their frustration would inspire them to do something foolish.

Each knew what the other was thinking. Barney knew it, too. Go to the Jersey State Police, tell them about the Korean attendant, or "Chung" as everyone now called him, and let the cops run with the ball.

If they did, however, they would lose control of the story and probably the story itself. Barney would be in deep shit with the police and might be charged with obstruction of justice. Certainly all the time and money expended to date would be out the window.

So they waited. Coole still had a couple of long shots he thought might yield something.

He went back to Boston.

Five days later, he called, voice full of excitement, and summoned everyone to an all-hands "council of war" in Pride's Crossing.

This time, Barney insisted on going. Lee wasn't so sure it was a good idea and told him so. He looked, literally, like death. He was in bad shape. Just getting out of a chair took all his energy. His skin looked dry and fragile, like a dead insect's husk. He wouldn't discuss prognosis, and Lee got the distinct impression that his latest radical "treatment" consisted of waiting.

Well, she told him, if you want to go, we're going to fly. She couldn't contemplate a seven-hour train trip with him.

When she picked him up at his house on Albemarle Street, in the far northwest corner of the District, he was waiting on the porch with his wife and son. He came down the stairs with painful slowness, pausing every other step to regain his breath, looked back up and waved. It was heartbreaking. Another couple of months tops, she thought. Maybe less.

The weather was lowering, the wind picking up. When they got to National, an occasional snowflake signaled the approach of the storm CNN had warned was tearing at the Great Lakes and moving east. It wasn't due in the Washington area until evening, and in New England until the following day.

The Boston shuttle got out on time, but an hour and a half later they were still circling, and then the captain came on the intercom to announce that Logan's radar had shut down and that they were proceeding to Nashua, New Hampshire.

They landed in Nashua in a driving blizzard. Score another for the weather man, Lee thought, watching the snow stream by as they taxied to the terminal. Weather forecasting seemed to be one instance where the fancier the technology got, the worse the results were.

We are not going to get out of here *ever,* she thought, when she got inside. This was what her Aspen friends called "a dump," at least a foot of snow, maybe more. Making up her mind, she headed for the Avis counter, carrying both their carry-on bags.

Avis had one Tempo left, a piece of crap for these conditions, but Lee had it outfitted with chains and they set off for Massachusetts. In normal conditions, she reckoned the drive would take a couple of hours; today, she figured she should double that estimate.

The actual driving time was five hours. Ten hours door-to-door for a trip that should have taken three. When they finally pulled into the Granary around seven, Barney looked readier for a coroner's slab than a guest room.

They weren't the last to arrive. Her uncle had left New Haven at noon and still wasn't there. The last Coole had heard from him, the Bentley was in a snowbank near Westerly, Rhode Island, awaiting a tow truck. Since then, nothing. According to Coole, the storm had shut down cellular traffic from Montreal to Richmond.

Lee looked at Barney. Every minute's wait was costing him. She suggested to Coole that they go ahead.

He shook his head. He wanted everyone to be present. You're on to something, Lee thought, something big.

About eight, lights pierced the snowfall and the Bentley crunched up to the main house, Henry Carew at the wheel. He bounced out of the big car, full of beans, clad in a voluminous seal-skin parka cracked and stained with age. It had been worn by Scott on his last, fatal expedition, he announced. Behind him loomed Baptiste—looking, Lee thought, really terrible, as if he had con-fronted horrors worse than any voodoo. The driver's eggplant skin actually looked pale.

"Baptiste's absolutely useless in the snow," the Master told Coole, "so I did the driving. Now, how about a whiskey? Got any-thing decent? And I think Baptiste here better have something. A rum perhaps. Got any Barbancourt?"

His exuberance picked everyone up after the long hours of wait-ing. You had to admire the old boy, Lee thought. He could be a perfect prick, but he was officer class to his bones.

The bottle of Glenmorangie was produced, eliciting a sniff from the Master, but he drained one dram and then another. Baptiste sipped tentatively at a glass of Bacardi. Fresh tea and coffee were brought. At length Coole, obviously itching to get going, called them to order. Everyone bundled up and struggled down the drifted path to the Granary.

A semicircle of seats had been set up facing a forty-inch Mitsubishi color monitor. This was hooked up to an impressive array of electronic equipment on which tiny green and red lights and multiple digital and oscilloscopic readouts put on a continuous and impressive light show. Freddy was bustling about, checking connections with the nervous concentration of a vacuum cleaner salesman. Du Bose and a girl about his age, a shy exotic creature, evidently part Oriental, part Hispanic, stood to one side. When he saw Lee, the boy waved and smiled.

Coole took the stage.

"A great man once observed that luck is the residue of design. As you know, Freddy and his young people here have been working night and day since August to penetrate JEDI's secrets. Based on what we pulled off Clarence Greaves's computer, we possessed the necessary building blocks to reconstruct the logic of JEDI's security system and how to beat it if we chose. Those exercises frequently took the form of an exponentiated videogame, at which I pit Du Bose and Soo-Maria here against anyone in the world. Collectively you might think of them as our Mozart to the other side's Salieri.

"During much of this, we knew we were being observed, but not by JEDI System Security. Had we been spotted by System Security, our incursions would have been terminated. But as we were soon aware, ours was not the only unauthorized penetration. The question was: What was our opposition keeping a lookout for? For intruders? Was he or she maintaining a vigil on specific JEDI sectors? Had Greaves simply the bad luck to stray into one of these? And then to make enough of a nuisance of himself that the opposition felt it had to do something? If so, my guess is that they simply intended to warn— or scare—him off, but that for whatever reason, events got out of control and he was killed."

"Simply for trespassing, then, not for anything he found out?"

"Lee, I think so. In the course of pondering the matter a while back, a metaphor occurred to me that is somewhat vulgar but does explain what's been going on. Imagine posting a security guard in the produce department of a supermarket, with instructions to mind only the Boston lettuce, the kiwi fruit, the arugula, and the leeks. And not to get excited even if he sees someone making off with oranges or Swiss chard by the bagful, or even the cash out of the register."

"Are you saying that Clarence picked up a head of iceberg lettuce and the opposition mistook it for arugula?"

"I think it's possible. But there's another aspect that bears thinking through. Don't forget that JEDI was conceived as an adjunct to the nation's law enforcement effort. Without the backing of the legal and police powers of the nation, which have the right to enter and search, to break down doors, to haul before grand juries, to exert pressure on other nations, JEDI had little *applied* value. It's just data. Theory without application. That's been our problem as well. We lack the power of application. We are simply trying to get a story."

"Are you implying that the opposition has this 'applicative power?' That there's something real in it for the bad guys?"

Coole smiled at Barney.

"I am. The proverbial pound of cure, I should think. What's useful in the cause of absolute good can be just as useful, in a completely inverted way, of course, in the cause of absolute evil! After all, the two often aren't all that far apart!"

Especially on Wall Street, Lee thought. She glanced at her uncle, who was listening, eyes closed. He sensed her attention, opened a sleepy eye and nodded.

"To acquire some applicative potential of our own, we needed a break," Coole continued. "Some stroke of luck, or inspiration, or, as I had thought was both a realistic alternative and a real possibility, some piece of foolishness on the part of the opposition that would make all clear. I'm happy to say we've gotten it. At last!"

"So," asked Lee, "which was it? Luck, inspiration, or stupidity?"

"The second. Freddy, would you like to take over?"

The Frenchman explained. On Saturday nights, he rented a video and played it for the kids. If he could, he tried to find something with a computer angle. Not long after they began to work on JEDI, he'd rented a fairly silly spy film, starring Kevin Costner as an unlikely Russian undercover agent. In the film, a key plot point was a computer reconstruction of a virtually unrecoverable image taken from a crushed Polaroid negative.

Weird, thought Lee. This whole business had started with video—Thunderbolt. Was it going to end with video?

"We also had an image, not unrecoverable, happily, but basically unidentifiable."

He clicked a remote. Onscreen appeared a freeze-frame taken from the bank security film of Agent Arthur Chung.

"No federal employee named Arthur Chung is to be found among the ninety-six million individual files in JEDI's personnel module," said Frederic. "Which is not to say that he wasn't in the module earlier. From the JEDI logs that Greaves recorded in his computer, it would appear that he queried the module about Agent Chung and encountered a roadblock, presumably placed in the module by the opposition, and activated only by a certain type of query. Subsequent to Mr. Greaves's death, the roadblock and related activation protocols were deleted."

"So you're saying there's no 'Chung' on JEDI?"

Freddy shook his head. A quarter-inch of ash fell to the floor.

"What about the Korean angle?"

"No luck there either. It would appear that JEDI is politically correct. It does not cross-reference by race or color."

"Damn foolishness," Lee heard her uncle mutter.

"But the personnel module does incorporate record photographs, the same as appear on identification badges or driver's licenses," the Frenchman continued. "It was Du Bose who suggested perhaps we could try to make a face match between our bank video and what JEDI has. What basically we did was to create a code for the gray scale, from the lightest to the darkest, and then we 'drew'—you might say—the Chung face from the video in that code. This gave us a sort of overlay against which we matched the images in JEDI."

"Sort of a digital version of Cinderella's slipper?"

"Exactly, Miss Boynton."

"You did all of this here? On these machines?"

Frederic looked at Coole, then at Lee.

"Well, some friends at MIT were very kind, but, yes, the idea— which is what counts—was born here, with Du Bose . . ."

His voice was filled with pride as he looked at his protegé. Du Bose stared at the floor and rocked nervously on the balls of his feet, obviously ill at ease at being the focus of attention of all these important white people.

"Hey, kid, way to go!" Barney dragged himself to his feet and slapped Du Bose with a trembling high-five.

"So are you going to keep us in suspense, or are you going to show us what Cinderella looks like?" asked Lee.

"No time like the present." Coole gave his aide the high sign. "Actually, I've had Freddy and the young people work up a demonstration tape. You'll forgive us if it takes a brief interval to get to the point. Genius is entitled to its hour."

The image from the security tape dissolved onscreen, becoming a nebula of minuscule points and dashes of light. For a minute or so, these rearranged themselves kaleidoscopically, acquiring color, consolidating and batching, gradually forming an image. Finally the monitor displayed—in bad, rather yellowed tints and in full frontal view—a face whose flat, impassionate features were familiar to everyone in the room. It was indelibly the same man whom the Bordrero Bay Bank security camera had captured.

"Jesus!" said Barney, the only person who had seen him in the flesh.

"Permit me to introduce Mr. Peter Kim," said Coole. "Mr. Kim is the proprietor of a small data security consulting firm in South San Francisco. For the moment, that's neither here nor there. What is important is that Mr. Kim was a member—on secondment from the Securities and Exchange Commission—of the original interagency working party that created the basic architecture of JEDI and was responsible for the system's implementation through the Mark VI stage.

"Mr. Kim has an extraordinary resume. He was born in Los Angeles to first-generation Korean immigrant parents, attended local high schools and California State College at Fullerton, where he majored in computer science and was a member of the karate team, which competed informally with other area schools. He served in Vietnam with the Special Forces, and after the U.S. withdrawal was assigned to the Department of Defense. Does the phrase 'Tiger Teams' mean anything to anyone here?"

There was a general shaking of heads.

"In the mid-1970s, so-called Tiger Teams, small working parties of military and civilian computer experts, were given the assignment of trying to break into top-secret systems installations in the Pentagon and elsewhere. Kim was a member of one of those teams. In 1977, he left the army and joined the Treasury, then the New York Stock Exchange, where he'd worked on computerized trading systems and helped the exchange's Stockwatch surveillance program. He left the Exchange in the early 1980s to go to the SEC. When JEDI was mooted, he was seconded by the Commission to the original planning group. After four years, he quit and went off to San Francisco, presumably to cash in on his knowledge in the private sector."

Henry Carew had been following Coole's recital closely.

"You say he was seconded to JEDI from the SEC?"

"Yes, sir, apparently at the specific request of the Vice President, who'd known Kim both at the Treasury and later at the SEC itself. It's all in the JEDI file."

"I see."

The old man fell silent, his face grim.

"Kim, needless to say, is a specialist in system security and countermeasures. Are you familiar with JEDI security protocols?"

"Only that you keep talking about System Security."

"Quite so, Lee. Well, there are two levels—correct me if I err, Freddy—of security at JEDI. Applied, day-to-day patrol and surveillance, what we might call the guard dog and searchlight sweep level, is the responsibility of what we have referred to as System Security with initial caps. This entity also rotates access and PBX codes and passwords and conducts random checks on a module-by-module basis. Then there is Security Architecture Group, SAG, which is responsible for technical oversight. On one level, SAG operates much as the old Tiger Teams did, attempting unauthorized penetration of the system. On a higher level, it reviews, quarterly, JEDI's external defenses and internal compartmentalities, working with System Security to ensure that JEDI's defenses are state-of-the-art."

"And Kim is on this SAG—or is a consultant to it?"

"The latter. Membership on SAG is rotated among JEDI's dozen superprivilege users, six at a time, with the Vice President as permanent chairman. The committee is advised by a number of independent consultants in and out of government. Included are some of the system's original architects, presumably on the theory that those who put something together understand best how to take it apart."

"Okay," said Barney, "so you've made Kim. You think Kim knows it?"

Coole looked at Freddy. The Frenchman shrugged and said, "We just can't be sure."

Coole looked at the tired faces ranged before him. He signaled Freddy to shut down the monitor.

"I think that's enough for this evening. It's after ten. I suspect we could all use a soak and a drink and a good night's sleep. Tomorrow we can think through what we should do about Kim, now that we know who he is. Obviously, he's now the key."

"Just one thing, Coole."

"Yes, Professor Carew?"

"Could you give me a printout of this chap Kim's CV? I'd like to study it."

"Certainly, sir."

It was still hellish outside. The wind continued to lash with a low, insistent moan. Gusts of snow whirled through the cones of light cast by the spotlights illuminating the walkway. Thick drifts shouldered against the path, making passage difficult. To Lee—and she hoped, to Barney—the prospect of hot water, a drink, and something to eat made it no trek at all.

Just as she was finishing dressing, there was a knock on Lee's door. It was her uncle. He spoke to her long and earnestly, and concluded by telling her to say nothing to anyone: not to Barney, not to Coole, not to anyone. He needed to do some further checking. He simply wanted her to be aware of his suspicions, just in case . . .

The storm continued to scourge the East Coast through the night, but farther west, the weather was good.

Over Lake Tahoe, the night was clear but starless. Visibility was excellent, and the fog lights of the Jeep Cherokee easily picked out the inconspicuous sign that marked the turnoff for Tahoe Landing and the Lakeside Lodge, six miles from the Nevada border.

Kim, alone in the rented car, was keyed up and irritable. Departures from procedure made him uneasy. He wondered if he had been foolish to take precautions, but he had simply felt he must. With the precautions, worst case, he would be out a few thousand dollars. Without the precautions, worst case, he would probably be out his life.

On the seat beside him was a flat package, about eight inches long by three inches wide by a half-inch deep, sealed with wax and corded tape. He had picked it up shortly after lunch at Courier-Quick's office in the San Francisco financial district.

According to Oltington, it contained gemstones, several million dollars' worth, which needed urgently to be delivered to a cabin at a shuttered boating camp on Lake Tahoe. Kim knew the place. It was the same cabin in which Kim, cleaning up after Oltington, had come across the stout wooden Savile Row coat hanger that now adorned the hook in his office.

This was a one-time special favor for an important client, Oltington had told Kim.

Kim didn't like it. It was, he told Oltington, a radical departure from procedure. As for Kim's suspicion, amounting to certainty, that such a transfer must be connected to a narcotics deal, especially since Oltington had informed him that the recipients of the gems were Jamaican, Oltington swore there would be no actual drugs within a hundred miles of the cabin.

Kim didn't like it, but he agreed to do it.

He also took certain precautions that he felt no need to tell Oltington about.

There would be three of them waiting for him in the cabin, Kim was told.

Just three? What about backup?

According to Oltington, there would be only the three.

Kim didn't believe it. It wasn't that he didn't believe Oltington, who was probably telling all the truth he knew. But no backup?

It did not sound right, so Kim took precautions.

The Cherokee bumped down the track leading to the lodge, a track Kim knew to be exactly .7 miles long. At .4 miles by the Jeep's odometer, he stopped and dimmed his lights twice.

An answering pair of flashes came from the trees.

Kim left the engine running, climbed down, and walked into

the trees. A figure emerged to confront him. The man was wearing a wet suit and a scuba vest.

They spoke in low, rapid Korean. Kim followed the diver deeper into the woods to a small clearing. Another scuba-clad Korean awaited them. There were two other men in the clearing, both Jamaican, both soaked through, as if they had been dipped in the chill waters of the lake.

One was alive, the other obviously dead.

The live one was shivering uncontrollably, although whether out of fear or cold was difficult to tell. In any case, it was a question in which Kim had little interest.

The Jamaican's hands were bound with wire and a chamois windshield cloth had been stuffed in his mouth. The whites of his eyes gleamed like Ping-Pong balls.

Kim examined the dead one. It was clear from the condition of his clothes and the marks on his body that he had been subjected to interrogative techniques of extreme, advanced unpleasantness. Kim could imagine. There was precious little good feeling between his people and the blacks. Any blacks.

The man who had guided Kim into the woods went up to the surviving Jamaican and tucked a .9mm automatic under the prisoner's chin. In low, guttural tones, he adjured the man to be quiet, and jerked out the gag. The other Korean came over, carrying a portable transceiver.

In careful English, Kim rehearsed the Jamaican in his very brief lines. Then he held the transceiver close to the man's face and flicked it on. There was a rush of static, a babble of incoming patois, to which the Jamaican responded letter-perfectly. Kim flicked off the transceiver, the gag went back in. He grunted acknowledgment and turned back toward the path where he had left the car. The two other Koreans headed back toward the lake, their prisoner shuffling miserably between them.

Kim returned to the Jeep and continued down the driveway. His lights illuminated the darkened main lodge building; he passed it on the left and followed the drive to the last cabin.

He dimmed his lights three times; a light appeared in the cabin's front window and flashed three times, then steadied on the windshield, lighting up the Jeep's interior. Kim held up both hands, the small package in his right. After a few seconds, the light from the cabin blinked, then went out. A second later, the window was outlined by a pale yellowish tracing, a light behind the curtain.

Kim got out. He could hear a steady, strong lapping behind the cabin: big water out there in the dark. He kept his hands high and slightly in front, the parcel clearly visible in his left hand. It surprised him that the men inside the cabin hadn't cut him down by now. If those had been Colombians in there, he'd be lying with his blood soaking into the gravel. The men inside were overconfident, maybe a little bit high, too. Foolish, he thought. The business of death is death, no more, and should be done quickly.

He went slowly up to the door and knocked twice.

"Who that?" said a high voice just the other side of the door. Kim sensed himself being scrutinized through the peephole. He stood there, hands high.

"A messenger."

He thought he could smell marijuana. Ganja, the Jamaicans called it.

"Minute, then," said the voice. The lock was being worked.

Betting that the man on the other side would have shifted his attention away from the peephole, Kim moved his free hand slowly down and around to his back, to the .9mm Beretta automatic tucked in the waistband of his trousers.

The door came ajar. A grinning black face appeared in the opening and started to say something. Kim leapt forward, jamming the pistol into the man's mouth, and surged into the room, howling as loudly as he could. Propelling the Jamaican backward before him like a shield, he pulled the trigger twice. As he did, all his senses registered. Thick smell of marijuana. A table in the middle of the room, two men at it, one sitting, one standing, both armed. Just as he had been told.

With a great shove, he sent the reeling body of the man he had just killed crashing into the table. The impact and his howls had the collective effect of a stun grenade. For a fatal instant, the two men stood gaping, their weapons down. When they started to bring them to bear, he had them covered.

"No," Kim said. The barrel of his automatic weaved from one to the other, the gaze of its muzzle as steady as a cobra's eye.

"Put the guns down! On the table!"

"Hey, mon," said the smaller of the two, "no problem." A pistol and an Uzi were lowered carefully.

"Hey, mon, it's cool, huh! What you do that for?" An operatic gesture toward the body on the floor.

Kim said nothing. He moved closer and inspected the two men. They were an ill-matched pair.

"Take the glasses off," he said to the one standing. Off came a pair of expensive sunglasses. Without them, the face lost its character. The man's eyes were dope-dulled. A piece of shit, thought Kim, a useless piece of shit.

The seated man's face was bright and his expression alert. He continued to grin up at Kim. Wire-rimmed spectacles gave him an oddly intellectual look.

Kim made his decision quickly.

"You live," he said to the short one, "he doesn't," and he shot the taller man in the left eye just the way he learned in Vietnam: think nothing, feel nothing; point the weapon and pull the trigger.

The smaller man didn't move. He continued to grin even as his partner's body thudded to the floor. For just an instant his eyes went to the window.

"Don't get excited," Kim said, "they're not coming."

The grin went away.

"Hey, mon . . ."

Kim silenced him with a gesture of his pistol.

"I want you to take whoever sent you a message. Not just Kingston or wherever. All the way back up the chain. Pass the word."

He reached into his inside jacket pocket and pulled out a small, sealed envelope. Inside was a three-by-five index card. On the card were neatly typed two columns, each consisting of six alphanumeric clusters. The left-hand one seemed to be a code of some kind; the other column appeared to list sums of money. At the bottom was a brief message, like the rest of the contents meaningless unless the reader possessed the right context, and a telephone number.

"You wait an hour, then start walking. I'm leaving my car at the top of the driveway for you. You take it to Reno, drop it at the automatic check-in at the airport, and go back where you came from. You have thirty-six hours to get this where it should go. After that, people will be looking for you."

This was simply for effect, Kim knew. But a little theatrics never hurt. To send his message a second time would only drive his point home harder. By now, the initial transmission should be in the hands of its intended recipient.

It was.

In the Andes, the previous day had been tiring for the Don. His visitor from Palermo had been unyielding. Don Escobedo was tired when he settled himself before the monitors for the nightly run-through.

He tapped out a series of commands on the keyboard, and the screens lit up as usual. Then, as he was studying them, something odd and gravely unsettling occurred.

The familiar spread sheets blinked offscreen on all six monitors, and were replaced by boxes—approximately the size of a standard index card—displaying two columns of figures and alphanumerics, a two-sentence message, and a telephone number.

The Don studied the material intently. He windowed back a couple of data screens—this intrusion didn't seem to effect the proper functioning of his operating system—and compared the columns with certain other information. The match was exact.

He read and reread the message at the bottom of the box, grasping its meaning exactly. He leaned back wearily and ran a hand through his hair. He should have expected this. In the other man's position he would have done something similar himself.

The only question was: What should be done now?

It was a question he was pondering the next morning when he received an angry telephone call from Medellín. What was going on? The Kingston associates were in an uproar! This was supposed to have been a simple business, and yet three good men were gone, many children orphaned, and the entire Jamaica operation, essential to the smooth transshipment of product, disturbed. Then there was an envelope that had been given to the one survivor. The message it contained made no sense. Perhaps the Don could explain. It was being forwarded to him by special courier.

He made reassuring noises—business was not always predictable, surely Medellín if anyone understood *that*—and hung up. He was certain he already knew what the message was. Two days later, when he studied a much-fingered index card, his certainty was confirmed.

By then, he had concluded he had no practical options except to press forward. Matters had escalated. They must now be encouraged to run to their logical conclusion. After that, a new beginning could be made.

He picked up the card and activated the scrambler. Holding the card close to his eyes—it was shocking how nearsighted he was becoming!—he dialed the number at the bottom. While the call was patched through, he tore the card into tiny pieces and spilled them into an ashtray. With one of the cedar straws he used to light his cigars, he torched the tiny bits of paper while he waited for a phone to begin ringing several thousand miles away in an unassuming office building not far from Candlestick Park.

NINETEEN

▼

In the United States, the period from Thanksgiving through Christmas to Twelfth Night is a time of national mental stress. The suicide rate climbs; purveyors of alcohol and other psyche-deadening drugs do their best business of the year. Unlike primitive cultures, whose great annual festivals are springtime celebrations of rebirth and renewal, postindustrial society chooses a bleak season for its great rite and emphasizes penance and depletion, guilt and spending. Unction is sought through expenditure; the flashy wrappings swaddling the gifts of the season seem a metaphor for layer upon layer of contrition.

So say critics of Christmas the American way. But the angst and aggro claimed for the season had never afflicted Oltington. He loved Christmas! Loved the whole production: the sumptuary behavior, the lavish decorations festooning Embassy Row, the relentless round of parties, the heaps of tiny perfectly wrapped parcels given and received. He had enjoyed a solid Episcopalian boyhood steeped in the Dickens myth of fat geese on the table, and portly men dancing reels with foolish, beribboned ladies; he kept his Christmas accordingly.

It was not just the festivities, however. What August was for most people, the weeks on either side of Christmas were for Oltington: a time to relax and recharge. This was a time when initiatives were postponed, the pace of governing slackened, councils stood down, princes and potentates stayed home. In other words: the most restful of Oltington's seasons.

Ordinarily.

But not this year.

This year, with Christmas only weeks away and Washington gleaming with tinsel and good cheer, Oltington's spirits were heavy. He was beside himself with angst and aggro. He was scared.

To begin with, Kim had disappeared.

Well, perhaps the man hadn't exactly *disappeared*, but he had certainly removed himself from touch, and at a most inconvenient time.

It was something Kim had never done before. He had left a message on Oltington's V-mail drop that he was obliged to go to Seoul on family business, but would be back in a week. That had been ten days ago.

Normally, Oltington wouldn't have been unduly worried. When away from the office, Kim left his JEDI monitors in telemetric call-forwarding mode. The client continued to be serviced. Not that there was much going on just now. From the JEDI material passing through the Vice President's office, activity in the areas that interested Oltington was clearly moving at half-speed. But the JEDI PBXs and access code-strings for the coming year were due to be issued on Tuesday. Usually Oltington abstracted them before they were cached in the Vice President's personal computer and passed them on to Kim. Once they were in Number Two's data base, it was a bit of a bother to dig them out. And if Kim didn't make it back by Tuesday, his computers would be flying blind.

Family business in Seoul?

Kim had never mentioned relatives in Korea. As far as Oltington—or JEDI—knew, Kim didn't have any meaningful connections left in Korea, which Oltington had confirmed that very morning, when the boss had gone across the street with Di Maglio to bring Number One back to earth on a new economic initiative that had Silicon Valley talking secession.

Oltington had slipped into the Vice President's office, accessed JEDI's federal personnel records, and punched up Kim's dossier. The file showed neither parent living; a second cousin in Los Angeles. Another in Florida. No one in Korea. Either the NSC-CIA team assigned to vet SAG contractors had done a careless job on Kim's background or Kim was lying to Oltington. The first was unlikely; the latter made no sense.

On top of the Kim problem, there was the Master's call, which had caused Oltington's bowels to jump into his throat and the wassail *glogg* at last night's St. Lucia fete at the Swedish Embassy to taste like wormwood.

The old man had wasted no time on seasonal pleasantries. His tone was sour, chastising, rebukeful. Oltington knew that voice, but the last time he'd heard it was when his caper in Kerala got burned. That had been a long time ago. What had he done now?

"I want your help, Russell. I need very much to speak with Mona. I suspect you may know why. I cannot locate her. Have you heard from her recently? Where is she?"

In other words: I expect an answer, I expect it to be truthful, and I expect it now.

He tried to keep his reply even-voiced. It wasn't easy.

"My goodness, Master, but it's been ages—years—since I last heard from Mona. Didn't she go and live among the Bedouin? No, wait: I seem to recall hearing that she's signed on with a French Bank. Is it Credit Lyonnais?"

"Oh, Russell," sighed the old voice at the other end, "you *are* so tiresome when you're being disingenuous. Where is she?"

"No, it's not the Lyonnais. Sorry about that. It's CP she went with; you know, the thinking man's BCCI. I believe they're in Avignon. They should be able to help you find her. I must say, Master, you sound very out of sorts. What's our little glamour girl done?"

"Among other things, she tried to have me killed. But surely you knew that, Russell?"

"She did *what*?"

Oltington's surprise was absolutely genuine. Mona had done *what*? "You must be joking!" he added.

"Oh, I'm not joking," Henry Carew said. "In Scotland. Six weeks ago. Me and my niece Lee. You remember her, I'm sure, Russell; the handsome young woman at my Georgetown lunches? Surely you run into each other in Washington; I should imagine your social tangents overlap a good deal."

"Oh, I know who she is, of course," said Oltington lightly. "She's hard to miss. But, alas, I'm on the red carpet circuit and she's mostly over on the Hill being the crusading journalist . . ."

Oltington's mind was racing. Mona had tried to have the Master killed? Had she gone stark, staring mad? An insect like Leo Gorton was one thing, but the Master!

"Well, Russell, as you won't tell me what I need to know," the old man said with a derisive snort, "let me leave a message with you just in case you run into Mona. Would you tell her I wish to speak with her about two people of her acquaintance."

Keep the game going, Oltington told himself.

"If I run into Mona, Master, I'll be happy to. Who are they?"

There was a moment's silence. The Master was evidently considering something, then he said, "You know, Russell, come to think of it, I believe one of these people is an acquaintance of yours. A man named Peter Kim, a computer expert. I seem to recall you mentioning his name at one of our Thursday lunches at the Cosmos? That would have been back when you were at the SEC."

Steady now. "I can't say the name rings a bell. Who's the other?"

"A deceased civil servant called Clarence Greaves."

" 'Greaves'? How do you spell that?" Oltington's throat felt choked. Was his voice squeaking?

"G-r-e-a-v-e-s. Christian name Clarence."

"Got it." Then he said, gratuitously, "It means nothing to me," and wished he hadn't.

There was a pause at the other end, then the old man said, "No, I shouldn't think it would."

Another pause, then: "You know, Russell, it's really been too long since we saw each other. I'm dying to catch up with you, especially now that you're but a heartbeat away from the very center of the known universe. We could have a really good gossip. I could come down next week. College'll be out of term. Just name the time and place."

Oltington demurred. He could face down the Master on the telephone, but face-to-face? He doubted it. He pleaded the press of duty, the season, a visiting aunt. Perhaps after the first of the year.

When he hung up, Oltington poured himself a drink, then another, then a third and a fourth, hoping the alcohol might help him remember if he really had mentioned Kim to the old man. No, he decided, it was completely unlikely. At the time he met Kim, it was true he was still lunching every other Thursday with Henry Carew at the Cosmos, but it wasn't until three years later, when JEDI had been initiated, that Oltington had thought of Kim as the man to exploit the program's dark side and looked him up. By then, the old man had settled in New Haven and was supervising the building of his college.

In other words, the Master was jerking his chain.

Why had he mentioned Kim? Or Greaves? How did he know about Greaves? What connections had he made?

These were questions Oltington drank himself sodden trying to answer. When he dragged himself to bed, he was almost insensible and no closer to a solution. He needed to talk to Mona, that he did know. She had obviously done something stupid, whatever was going on was her fault!

Just as Greaves was Kim's fault! The killing of the RTC man had been a monumental error of judgment. Anyway, Mona didn't know anything about Greaves.

So why did the Master seem to think she did? She knew about Kim. Oltington himself kept her briefed, although there was no direct contact. Kim was handled by Oltington exclusively. But Greaves? No way!

Unless someone had told her, and who could that be, if it wasn't Kim? Oltington's mind reeled. This was all too confusing.

And where was Kim, anyway? Who did the fellow think he was, going off just like that! It wasn't as if the Korean was indispensable. There were plenty of first-class computer people around. Come to think of it, there were plenty of Koreans around. Dimly, it occurred to Oltington that he could substitute someone for Kim and have no one but himself be the wiser. He clutched his pillow and closed his eyes. In a minute, he was snoring.

When he awoke the next morning, it was eight o'clock and he was due to meet the boss at State at eight-thirty. He felt like gypsies were encamped in his mouth, cooking disgusting food and scattering garbage. He rushed through his toilet, brushing his teeth twice with his private decoction of baking soda, Listerine, and Alka-Seltzer. A frigid shower brought him halfway back to human status, a triple espresso from the corner takeout a bit further; by the time the staff car dropped him in Foggy Bottom, he was at least able to pretend interest in the arrangements for his boss's state visit to Burkina Faso.

When he got home at the end of the day, he had barely collapsed in his chair, unable to face even thinking about changing for that evening's brutal round, when the phone rang.

It was Mona.

What an amazing coincidence for her to call right on top of the Master, he thought when he heard her voice, but he was too tired, too pressed, too full of other questions to think much about that.

She was coming to Washington, arriving at Dulles Friday afternoon for a meeting the next morning—something to do with legal formalities connected with a client's real estate holdings. She would love to see Russell. Could he make time, and, if convenient, at his weekend cottage, which was convenient to Dulles? Her meeting was at the airport hotel.

Russell knew how boring airport hotels were, she said. Perhaps he knew of a country inn where she could be put up and they could dine? Someplace intimate and charming where they could walk in the countryside, where she could get some fresh air?

"Don't be silly, you can stay in my guest room. We can have dinner here."

What a nice idea. She would be passing through St. Moritz en route to Dulles. She'd bring a pound of Glattfelter's best caviar. It would be her contribution to the evening.

And, oh yes, she had a gift for Russell. A token of appreciation from the client, who was very pleased about the smoothness of the Gorton operation. The homosexual angle had been brilliant. Brilliant!

What a stroke of luck, he thought as he hung up. He could feel her out. Find out what she was up to. The rush of exhilaration blew his hangover away. Like an actor preparing, he began to go over his lines.

The week dragged endlessly. His anticipation was like quicksand. Every passing moment took forever. By Wednesday, all his arrangements were complete: the chef-owner of Washington's best French restaurant had been prevailed upon to prepare an elaborate heat-and-serve dinner for two, the flowers had been selected, the CDs chosen. He would decant the two bottles of 1966 Pétrus the Master had given him when he left the agency.

He left the office early Friday afternoon, the backseat of his car stacked with food-warmers and florists' boxes. He felt back in control, so much so that he even let his libido have an hour of harmless fantasy. When he got to the cottage, he was squirming with anticipation.

As the Gulfstream descended into the half-twilight, Mona Kurchinski analyzed her state of mind. Why was she so uneasy. Was it being involved in "wet work"? She hadn't been involved in anything like this since Aqaba in 1978. Could she handle it? She was certain she could.

Uneasiness had settled on her like fog on a sunny meadow. It was difficult to make things out clearly. Was she being paranoid? Were Bruno and Claude really being distant—or was it her imagination? Why didn't Don Escobedo get back to her? They had phones in Phnom Penh. People who usually jumped out of skins at the snap of her fingers seemed to be taking their time carrying out their tasks.

It's just normal strain, she concluded. What else could it be? So much had to be done; she would have been inhuman not to feel the tension. Nevertheless, when they landed and all the way in the limousine to Oltington's cottage, she couldn't help looking around to see if she was being shadowed.

Everything seemed in order. The material in the trunk was exactly as specified. She herself had everything she needed. On the seat next to her lay a flat parcel containing a superb state of one of Rembrandt's rare pornographic etchings.

It was three gifts she had for Oltington. She intended to disarm him with her generosity. One was the caviar, a five-pound tin. One was the Rembrandt. The third, like the etching, derived its value entirely from the human genius that inhabited it; its raw materials—an assortment of minerals and chemicals—had little market value of themselves.

Mona's third gift was herself.

She had wrapped it exquisitely: in a black silk St. Laurent evening chemise worn over thigh-high boots and nothing else, under a gift from grateful clients in Kazakhstan, an ankle-length cape of dark sable that matched her eyes.

The driver guided the Lincoln down the twisting lane flanked by storm-shorn maples and into the graveled-over clearing that served

Oltington as a driveway. The little house, huddled beneath the black mass of the forested hills, was alight and cheery. Mona told the driver to wait and got out of the car. A brisk, chill wind rattled the trees; she shivered inside the fur cape.

The Dutch door of the cottage opened, and Oltington dashed out and embraced her. His jolly figure was encased in a flamboyant check suit; at his throat was a paisley ascot, on his feet were pebble-grained brogans polished to a marine gleam. He looked the epitome of chic rusticity.

She threw her arms wide and went toward him, telling herself even as she called out his name: Just close your eyes and think of England.

But two hours later, it was Oltington's eyes that were closed. He lay back on the sofa, trousers pulled halfway down his plump thighs, Mona kneeling before him.

He couldn't believe this was happening. From the instant she had arrived Mona had seemed keyed up, in need of comforting, sexually electric, his for the taking. The vodka with the caviar—Stolich-naya Cristal viscous from a day in the freezer—had loosened her up. Her dark eyes took on a new glint. The Montrachet with the que-nelles softened her steely qualities. Usually all-business, she seemed relaxed, cozy. We will talk tomorrow, she told him, waving her glass about, her eyes vaguely unfocused by the powerful white wine. The Pétrus with the quail softened her further; the Château d'Yquem with the tart completed the job.

Seated next to her on the sofa after dinner, the balloon of Arma-gnac in his hand down to a few glycid amber drops, Rubinstein play-ing Chopin nocturnes on the CD, the fire dancing sinuously, its light playing over Mona's dreamy face, the universe empty except for the two of them, Oltington suddenly found himself in the situation of which had dreamt so long; the moment he had fantasized for so long was finally his.

He leaned toward Mona and kissed her.

The erotic combustion was instantaneous. It was as if in response she wanted to swallow him whole. Emboldened by the busy play of her hands at the back of his neck, he let his hand graze down her front, tentatively cup a worsted-sheathed breast, let a sly finger tantalize the hardening nipple beneath.

He wondered whether to be more bold.

She made up his mind for him.

"Here," she murmured, taking his hand.

With a movement so wanton that it almost undid him, she shot her legs akimbo, knees up, so that her chemise fell back, exposing pale thighs above the flared tops of her boots. She guided his hand to the dark, sweet, wet mystery at the heart of all being, pressed it against her, hand over his, intense and began moving against it, moaning slightly.

Hips easing back and forth, she kissed him lingeringly. He made as if to move his hand down.

"Wait," she whispered.

He felt rather than saw her get up and then kneel. He didn't dare open his eyes. He felt busy fingers at his belt, his fly, felt strong hands raise him slightly, he helping, sliding his trousers and his drawers down, felt her hand on him . . .

And then her mouth.

He had done great things in his time, but never before had Russel Oltington been at the epicenter of a miracle. It was as if he were hypnotized, reduced to a single pinpoint of unbearable excitement. He felt his whole existence shape itself to physical sensation, felt that sensation gather force like a wave and then start combing shoreward, faster and faster, pounding headlong the last, small, irreversible distance to completion.

Mona felt it too. Her left hand slowed its pumping, to hold him at this point.

With her right hand, she felt in the Hermés bag she had carefully laid on the floor and located the pistol, a small .25 caliber automatic of French manufacture, useless for anything except this kind of job. Head still bobbing, maintaining the desired level of intensity with her other hand, she withdrew the gun slowly from the purse just as Oltington began to come.

She pulled her head away. She continued to stroke him, keeping him shackled with excitation, raised her right hand, jammed the barrel against his left ear and pulled the trigger.

She hardly heard the report. Oltington's body jerked; whether in the first spasm of death or the last of excitement, she couldn't tell. Then he slumped, his mouth lagged open and he lay utterly still.

Mona stood up and shook her head, ridding it of alcohol fuzz. She looked down at her handiwork. For an instant, she felt a terrible pang of sadness. She had known him so long. He looked about fifteen years old; very peaceful except for a slow trickle of blood running down his forehead and across his jaw, staining the brilliant yellow and blue ascot.

She arranged her dress and got to work. From her shoulder bag, she took a pair of thin latex dishwashing gloves and put them on. From the sofa she took a small, cheap chintz pillow—no one would miss it—doubled it against a small cast iron skillet she found in the kitchen, no one would miss that either, wiped the automatic clean and put it in Oltington's left hand, then squeezed off one shot. She checked to make sure of the traces of powder on his gun hand and gathered up the ejected cartridge and flattened bullet from the second shot. That should take care of the forensic chaps, she thought.

She put the pillow and skillet back in the shoulder bag, along with the flattened bullet and empty cartridge. She examined herself. A gout of semen clung like a tiny pearl to the black fabric of her dress. She wiped it off with a tissue, threw that in the bag, then went to the door and flicked the outside light on, off, on, off, on. A moment later, the Lincoln pulled into the drive. The chauffeur took a leather legal case from the limousine's trunk, carried it over to Mona, and went back to the car.

In a closet, she found what she needed: an old, empty cloth duffel. Into this she transferred the contents of the legal case and put the duffel back on the shelf. The contents were a collection of child pornography: illustrated books, worn magazines and videotapes, some bearing crude, hand-lettered labels, others sophisticated commercial productions. There were also two much-handled manila envelopes of photographs and color print negatives that were clearly amateur work of recent vintage. Spontaneous, live-action stuff; the sort most highly sought after by connoisseurs of this type of material.

One particularly vile tape Mona set aside. She placed the tape in the VCR and pushed the play button. She did not linger for a sample.

From her bag, she now took a cellular phone to which a special jack had been wired and a tiny, professional-quality microcassette re- corder and connected them, then dialed the cottage's number. The phone on the table across the room rang four times, then Oltington's answering machine took over; at the beep, Mona activated the recorder. A gruff, angry male voice, an outraged father, hurled obscenities and threats of exposure at the message tape.

Mona disconnected the phone and satisfied herself that the mise-en-scène was as she intended it to be seen and interpreted. She stripped off the latex gloves, dumped them in her Hermés bag, picked up the legal briefcase, and went outside.

The car awaited across the little clearing. The driver came over and took the legal case. The Don is going to be extremely pleased, she thought.

She heard quick steps behind her and went for her bag, but fingers like steel claws seized her upper arms with a force that jerked a quick little howl of pain from her. The bag was yanked from her with violence that dislocated her shoulder; she cried out, but the wind was high and her faint scream melted into the night unheard. Through tear-stricken eyes, she saw the Lincoln pull away.

Her right arm was forced up behind her back in a hammerlock. She still hadn't gotten a glimpse of her assailant. Mewing like a hurt kitten, her elbow at an angle just shy of snapping, she was propelled around the corner of the cottage toward a shed which stood at the back of Oltington's tiny garden.

The shed was illuminated by a single forty-watt bulb dangling from a cord looped around a nail in the ceiling. A mildewed mattress had been thrown on the sod floor.

Mona was hurled onto the mattress. She pushed herself up to a sitting position, skirt rucked back, not thinking to cover herself, trying to get herself together.

When she saw her assailant's face, she knew who he must be. Slim built, flat featured, wire-tough straight black hair. Korean. In the bad light, his skin was almost khaki.

"What do you think you're doing, Kim?" she hissed. "Are you mad? Do you know who I work for?"

He said nothing. If I move he'll kill me, she thought, and remained stock-still.

He began to undress.

Damn you, Russell, she thought, and the thought almost made

her laugh. Damn you, damn you! You beat me, oh, you did, you did! Damn you, Russell! Then she began to weep, because she realized what had happened.

The man looking down was naked now, and stroking himself.

Still wordless, he put his hands on her shoulders, pushed her flat back; she felt herself penetrated by what felt like a bar of hot metal.

He began to move in and out of her with a terrifying self-control. No human should be allowed to fuck like that, she thought, feeling herself starting to go. She closed her eyes. Just lie back and think of England, she murmured, God will forgive you. Oh Jesus, she thought, and gave a little yelp of excitement. How odd of God to be more forgiving than the Don.

Kim took his time. It took the best part of a half-hour before he could no longer sustain the mental restraints he had learned long ago in the monastery at Kwong-Ji. When at last he came, Mona had experienced thirty-seven orgasms, the last dozen or so in bursts that left her weak and whimpering.

Kim withdrew slowly. He tore off a handful of her dress, wiped himself and considered the whimpering, disheveled creature groveling on the sordid mattress. It was hard to reconcile her with the elegant, self-possessed person of whom Oltington had so often spoken.

With no more expression than he would use to slay a fly, he reached down and grasped her auburn mane. He pulled her head up and with much the same type of blow that had killed Clarence Greaves, broke her neck.

When he left the shed, a van had replaced the Lincoln. He and the driver wrapped Mona's body in a plastic drop cloth and manhandled it into a packing case marked for Djakarta. Then they boarded the van and headed for Dulles, where the Gulfstream the Don had borrowed from his friend the Emir awaited.

Inside the house, the videotape ran out; the corpse of Russell Oltington stared unseeing at a screenful of meaningless snow.

TWENTY

▼

It all seems so clear, doesn't it?" Coole gloomily shoved the paper across the table. Lee didn't look down; she didn't need to—by now she was sick of the damn thing.

It was a photocopy of a large front-page clipping from *L'Aurore de Provence,* a weekly paper published in Avignon. The article was illustrated with three photographs. The largest, so grainy it was difficult to read, was a telescopic shot taken in bad light of a police launch working in the shadows of a bridge spanning the Rhone. This was identified as the Pont Daladier, which was not the famous bridge of the song, the Pont St. Benezet, whose ruins lay a few hundred yards upriver. On the boat's deck, three gendarmes were engaged in lowering an indecipherable shape from a girder. In the far background loomed a large complex of high walls and turrets: the Palace of the Popes. Only the most knowledgeable and sharp-eyed would have known to move down a quarter-inch, where it was possible to pick out a tiny sliver of the elegant cornice of the Banque Provençale de Credit et d'Investissement. The full facade of this fine eighteenth-century building was shown in a second, smaller photograph.

The text identified the shape the *flics* were lowering as a corpse: that of Mona Kurchinski, approximately forty, *financiere,* a permanent resident of the Hotel Europe in the Place de Crillon, and stated that Mme. Kurchinski served as a special consultant on Middle Eastern matters to the CP bank. A third photograph showed the deceased standing in a stylish porte cochere, flanked by two men whom Lee recognized as Claude and Bruno; all three were smiling. The caption stated that the photograph had been taken earlier in the year at the Cannes Film Festival; the text included the information that Banque Provençal was believed to have committed over a billion francs of its clients' money to international film production.

The lead was a pun—in extremely bad taste, Lee thought, supermarket journalism French-style—on the French children's song "Sur le pont d'Avignon." It read, *"Sous le pont d'Avignon, on y pend, On y pend!"*

Under the bridge at Avignon, there one hangs, there one hangs. The subhead wasn't much better: *"Mutilations horrifiques!"*

The account began "There was indeed dancing yesterday on the renowned bridge of Avignon, but this time it was at the end of a rope . . ." and went on to dwell on the similarities of Mme. Kurchinski's end with the mysterious death of the rogue Italo-Swiss banker Roberto Calvi, found hanging in 1988 beneath London's Blackfriars Bridge. As was customary in all such accounts these days, the writer dragged in references to the Gelli ring in Italy and BCCI. The article was rich in innuendo concerning CP, its clients, Mona's CIA background, and the fact that the deceased carried three passports: French, Swiss, and Lebanese.

Where the writer really let himself go was in dealing with the appalling mutilation to which the deceased had been subjected. Her nose had been surgically removed some hours after her death; her sexual organs had been cruelly abused. A possible Sicilian connection was conjectured; the Taormina *mafiosi* were known to leave the bodies of their victims with the genitals stuffed in the mouth.

But a nose? Obviously, the article suggested, there must be a relation to the cocaine trade, which after all, depended on the organ of smell.

By comparison, thought Lee, the stories about Oltington's suicide had been pretty low-key. The *Post* had run a graceful appreciation of the late Vice Presidential aide and popular District bachelor in its Style section. The "Moonie" *Washington Times* had hinted of a dark side of Oltington's life, of tendencies that exposed Oltington to disgrace and his boss to embarrassment; the *Times* article had provoked a flurry of heated letters, half eulogizing Oltington as the victim of a censorious society, the other half condemning him as symbolic of the pervasive corruption at the heart of American life.

"It just goes to show," said Barney, flicking the clipping back to Coole, "if something's worth doing at all, it's worth doing well. But her *nose*? Go figure!"

He started to guffaw, but the effort cost him pain, and he stopped in midlaugh and grabbed his drink.

It was two days before Christmas and the three of them were lunching at the Jockey Club in the Ritz-Carlton Hotel on Massachusetts Avenue.

We're a tidal pool of gloom in a sea of jollity, thought Lee, morosely stirring her white wine with a fingertip. I'm surprised the people next to us haven't asked to be moved to a new table.

Then it occurred to her that the two men at the adjoining table, talking in low, secretive voices, heads together, didn't look so all-fired happy either.

As it happened, she was right. One of the two men was the chief executive of a large Midwestern pharmaceutical company, the other his principal Beltway lobbyist.

The lobbyist was buying, since it had been at his instigation that his client had in the last two years directed some $3 million in corporate funds to a computer security firm in South San Francisco. The payments had been booked as "consulting fees," but both men knew that in fact the money had ended up in an offshore slush fund, which by now must be worth quite a lot, controlled by the late Russell Oltington. The question before the two men was: What the hell do we do now? They hadn't the ghost of an idea.

Neither had the three people at the next table with respect to *their* dilemma. Lee redirected her attention to her dining companions. They needed a plan of action, any plan. Well, maybe over the holidays, someone would think of something.

After lunch, Coole was headed for the shuttle back to Boston; the next day, Lee was off to Palm Beach for a dreaded family Christmas at her mother's. Barney would celebrate the holiday, probably his last, on Albemarle Street. It would be a couple of weeks before they saw each other again.

What a lousy way to end one year and begin the next!

"For want of a nail," said Coole glumly, refilling Lee's glass.

She knew exactly what he meant. They had everything except the clinching piece, but without that, they had nothing. They had all the elements of a story that could be bigger than Watergate, but they had no story. Everything they had was circumstantial.

"I should have seen it," Coole said, draining his own glass and refilling it in a single motion. "Kurchinski and Oltington. The Bobbsey Twins of the CIA's black banking division, their Master's pride and joy. Once Oltington saw the opportunity, it would be natural he'd bring Mona in."

"What do you think he was after? The money—like her?"

"I don't really know. We may never know. Oddly enough, Bernard, I rather doubt that it was the money that intrigued Mona. From what I know about her, she was one of those people who is hopelessly, helplessly addicted to action, whatever that action is at any given moment."

Barney nodded. He knew about action junkies. The press corps was full of them.

"But it would have been the money with Oltington, right? I mean, little boys must cost a bundle?"

"I wouldn't be too sure about that either. Not that what he was doing didn't require a great deal of money. But Henry Carew thinks these allegations of pedophilia are total hogwash, and I'm inclined to agree. Oltington may have led a rich secret life, but there is not a scintilla of evidence that it ever included sexual deviancy of any kind."

"So how come the guy was big on the dirty books and pictures? A guy told me what was on the tape in his VCR; I almost puked! Apparently he got himself off just before he pulled the trigger. Like those kids that hang themselves, maybe. You're saying all that crap adds up to a big, fat, stinking red herring?"

"It's possible. Think about it. Someone plants sensational evidence of sexual abnormality, knowing that the way the press is today, they can count on a frenzy of short-term sensation that will effectively exhaust any long-term, serious interest in the matter. I doubt we'll ever know. Lee's uncle tells me that Oltington was a classic case of still waters; that beneath the insouciant, self-trivializing public persona lurked rigid, passionate, right-wing sentiments and a very tough mind. I find that hard to believe, but I never knew the man, and so I'm unwilling to argue the point."

"Of course," Lee said, "that might explain why Oltington was so thick with the President's wife. I hear she's extremely conservative, practically a closet McCarthyite."

"Jesus, you mean while everyone thought Oltington and Mrs. Number One were giggling over who was doing whom in the Finnish Consulate, what they were really talking about was the overthrow of the Republic? Gimme a break!"

"Possibly not this republic," said Coole, "but there are others."

"So now we're talking Iran-Contra all over again?"

"Secret armies do cost money, Bernard. Serious money."

He let that thought sit for a second, then continued. "Whatever Oltington's motive, and whatever his exact scheme, we're safe in assuming it all hung on privileged access to JEDI. Oltington knew finance. He'd been on Wall Street and at the SEC. He knew how much profit certain kinds of inside information can produce for the Street, so he would have some idea of what it would be worth as well as what kind of information to keep a watch for. As a member of the Vice President's inner circle, he would have stood virtually at the bedside when JEDI was conceived and midwived. Of course, he would have known he would have to delegate day-to-day surveillance, and not to the customer, because he would want to keep his position proprietary. Hence Kim."

"What about the drug side?"

"I suspect that's where Mona pulled her oar. In addition to JEDI's oversight of global financial movements and markets, as in last July's foreign exchange caper, when CP ran counter to the stampede and scored a rumored two-hundred-million-dollar coup, the system offers real time reports on federal antinarcotics operations in progress as well as in the planning stage. To anyone interested in making an illegal dollar, whether from the sale of heroin or looting a thrift institution, JEDI is a resource of incomparable value. If what one hears about CP is one-tenth true, Mona would be in a position to peddle access to that resource to the best-regarded money managers in the universe of black finance. It would be, quite simply, the greatest inside-information coup in market history!"

"So where did Greaves—or Thunderbolt—fit into this trillion-dollar Super Mario?" asked Barney. "Billions is one thing, but here we're talking a few hundred grand, maybe a few mil. Chicken feed!"

"Precisely. Thunderbolt doesn't fit. My own surmise is that Thunderbolt may have concerned Oltington personally. To repeat myself, in finance every number has two significant properties, exists in two dimensions, if you will. The absolute and the relative. In absolute terms, a few million dollars is nothing compared to the size of the drug trade, say, but to the personal economy of a civil servant earning sixty-eight thousand dollars a year . . . you get my point?"

"You mean Oltington was skimming?"

"Possibly. Possibly he set up in business for himself, using Kim not only to monitor JEDI but also to intermediate additional funding sources Oltington may have set up. Since we identified Mr. Kim, the Granary has tapped into the records of a random sampling of forty Bay Area banks, looking for accounts in the name of Kim's firm. So far we've found thirty. All are active and show regular weekly cash withdrawals in a pattern that makes no sense in terms of the nature of Kim's business. Computer consulting is not cash intensive."

"Maybe the guy's a secret swinger. Or a Vegas nut?"

"I can assure that Mr. Kim is neither. In the event, to get back to Thunderbolt, I think we can assume that GoldWest—or the Bordrero Bay bank—may have been integral to a network through which perhaps billions in drug profits have been laundered. The CP-GoldWest connection suggests that Mona Kurchinski would have overseen this operation, along with Phoenix, which would have been another part."

"And Courier—which seems to be the link?"

"Possibly. We'll never know, will we? The important consideration is that if Oltington's private dealings utilized Mona's network, it is odds-on she knew about it; she may even have set up the machinery."

"The phony Thunderbolt may have been her idea, you mean?"

"Possibly. It smacks of too much cleverness and too little care."

"Okay—so now Greaves stumbles on Thunderbolt, Kim picks him up and tells Oltington, Oltington tells Mona, and she tells Oltington to have Kim take care of Greaves. Right?"

"With all due respect, Bernard—wrong. It makes no sense.

What Mona would have done in that case would simply be to shut the Oltington operation down or move it elsewhere. More likely the former, in my judgment."

"Which leaves Oltington with his thumb up his butt on sixty-eight K a year?"

"A bit pithily put, Bernard, but yes. And that would have been unacceptable."

"So the word never got further than Oltington, and *he* told Kim to deal with Greaves?"

Coole cocked an imaginary pistol and pointed it at Lee.

"Bull's-eye!"

"But Mona's all over this too! What about Loch Gryme?"

"That was all about Phoenix, don't forget."

"But why Kim, then? She must have had to borrow him. Why get Oltington involved? Why not another CP thug?"

"My guess is: because in that case CP would have to know. Mona, don't forget, functioned as the clearinghouse. Where this whole system was concerned, everything stopped with her, unless she chose otherwise. She chose not to turn Phoenix over to the CP strong-arm department because she didn't want anyone to know that something—namely us: you and me and Lenchin—had gone wrong at Phoenix."

"So suddenly everyone's covering up?"

"Correct."

"For each other?"

"Not really. I think of them as covering up in parallel, although unbeknownst to them, the tracks are actually converging. Then, somewhere, somehow, someone took a misstep and it collapsed."

"By which you mean whoever was at the top of the food chain, higher even than Mona, maybe one of the guys at CP, maybe some goombah in dirty pants sitting in Palermo, found out what was going on and decided to clear the decks?"

Coole nodded.

"Jesus," said Barney, "the poor fuckers! In a way you got to feel sorry for them. Here they set up a billion-dollar operation, running smooth as butter, with a nice little thing going on the side, and then a goddamn low-level GS stumbles in through the wrong door, like a drunk wandering into a ladies room, and Lee picks up a chickenshit local paper at a goddamn diner in East Jesus, California, and now they're all dead!"

"All except Kim," said Coole.

"Yeah! How come? What gives him immunity?"

"Mr. Kim is very resourceful. I suspect he knows a great deal about a great many things, and that he has communicated a general awareness of what he knows to your Mr. Goombah in Palermo or wherever. I think they may even have come to a working under-standing. It would certainly appear that Kim has replaced Oltington with a new client for whom he has already performed signal services of a noncomputer nature."

Coole explained. JEDI was fed daily information on all airline and reserved rail passenger movements, which it passed on to Inter-pol's antiterrorist data exchange in Frankfurt. The Granary had run a check on the files and found that, on the day preceding Oltington's death, a Peter Kim had traveled from San Francisco to Washington National via O'Hare on American, and—on the day after—had re-turned on Continental from Baltimore via D/FW.

JEDI also tracked general aviation activity. On the day of Olt-ington's death, a Gulfstream belonging to a minor Gulf States emir, a known client of CP, had arrived at Dulles. There had been one pas-senger, a woman, traveling on an Irish passport issued to Maura Con-cannon. The government of Eire had no record of such a passport having been issued. The plane had stayed overnight and departed the next day. No one at Dulles's general aviation terminal could recall seeing the woman reboard the aircraft, although a crate—roughly the size of a coffin, Lenchin's informant innocently told him—had been loaded in the Gulfstream's bay.

"Mona?"

"According to the French pathologist, she'd been dead at least seventy-two hours before her body was discovered. And her neck was broken, not from the vertical force produced by hanging, but by a sharp lateral blow."

"The same as Greaves? Kim, in other words?"

"It could be. And then there's this." He dug in a side pocket and pulled out a photocopy of another clipping.

"This was back in October. Somehow we missed it. By then we were looking in other directions."

The clipping was from the *Post* and described the discovery of a woman's body in the trunk of a vehicle abandoned in a remote long-term parking lot near Dulles International. Identification had been made from dental records. The woman had been an employee of the Justice Department.

Lee looked at Coole.

"Greaves's niece?"

He nodded. "The source, I suspect, of Greaves's JEDI pass codes."

"Did you have your troops go back and check the airline traffic that day?" asked Barney.

Coole shook his head. "What good could it possibly do?"

Barney waved a waiter down and ordered another double Dewar's. "So what do we do about Kim? Seems to me the only shot we got left is to get to him somehow."

"Which won't be easy. I sent Lenchin west to have a look around, see how Kim spends his day, what his routine is, whom he sees. Lenchin reports that he's being baby-sat, by four different teams of watchers. Three to a team in four different automobiles. All Hispanic, according to Lenchin. Real thugs."

"Matthew, Mark, Luke, and John, guard the bed that I lie on," said Barney, grabbing his drink off the waiter's tray.

"In a manner of speaking. Lenchin also reports that Kim's being watched over by his own people. His own car, for example, is never left unguarded; in the garage where he keeps it, it's always parked within a few feet of the attendant's booth. The attendants are, of course, Korean."

"So what are they hoping for, do you think? That he'll lead them to something?"

"My guess is that they're simply to ensure that he stays alive. According to Lenchin, Mr. Kim is the very picture of radiant self-confidence and prosperity."

Coole fell silent. On his mind, Lee knew, as on hers, as on Barney's, as on the minds of the people at the Granary, was the discouraging realization that they had hit the wall. It was over.

"I suppose," Coole said, "that we should weigh the possibility of turning over what we have to the authorities."

It was an alternative none of them wanted. So much time, ingenuity, and risk had been invested, several lives had been lost, several hundred thousand dollars of Carew money had been spent. There had to be a better way.

"Suppose we sleep on it 'til New Year's," said Barney, but he didn't sound like a man with an idea.

"Very well." Coole signaled for the check.

Outside, they bade each other good-bye. Lee and Coole jumped into taxis. Barney thought he'd stick around, have a couple of shooters with some guys he'd spotted at the bar.

He watched their taxis head off down Massachusetts Avenue and wondered whether he'd see them again. He was really feeling bad.

He turned back inside, his mind on mortality, and then an idea hit him. Instead of going back into the Jockey Club, he went to the pay telephone and placed a collect call to New Haven.

Three days later, the morning after Christmas, he took the Metroliner north. He spent that evening and the best part of the next day closeted with Henry Carew. The two men sat up most of the night. From time to time, raised voices pierced the stout door, causing the Filipino houseman and Baptiste to look at each other in alarm. A lot of drinking was done; the two even killed off a prized bottle of fifty-year-old Glenlivet that the Master had been presented by the rector of the University of St. Andrews.

The next day, Baptiste drove them north to the Granary, where they closeted themselves with Coole and, later, his man Lenchin. At the end of two days, Barney was chauffeured back to Boston by Lenchin and put on the southbound Metroliner. Before returning to the Granary, Lenchin stopped at a Cambridge computer store and spent $4,000 of the Master's money, paying cash.

It was three days after his return to Washington that Barney disembarked from a TWA DC-10 at San Francisco Airport. A Chevrolet Celebrity was reserved for him at Budget. Although in extreme discomfort, he drove north to the outskirts of Daly City and registered at a Holiday Inn hard by Route 101.

In his room, he placed a call to Lee in Palm Beach. He felt guilty doing so, but he lied about where he was, saying he had come out to the Mayo Clinic for some last-ditch tests and consultation and would be incommunicado for three days. He had told his wife the same story.

He thought Lee sounded tired. This had been a rough six months, and to have it peter out this way was a crusher. The weather in Palm Beach was sublime, she reported; in spite of everything, she thought she might stay another ten days. Barney told her to do it; he said he felt fine; just being here at Mayo made him feel better. He promised he wouldn't die anytime soon, that he'd see her after the first.

The fact was, he did feel fine—for the first time in months. Clear headed and optimistic.

After ringing off with Lee, he dialed a South San Francisco number. Kim answered on the second ring.

"This is Bernard Cagel, Mr. Kim. We've never really spoken although we have met once before, in Princeton, New Jersey, at the offices of a Mr. Leo Gorton. In his sauna, actually."

The voice at the other end was unruffled.

"Are you sure you have the right Kim," it said. "This is Data Security Consultants. I have never been in Princeton, New Jersey. I know no Mr. Gorton."

"I'm sure, Mr. Kim. You were also a close acquaintance of my late friend Clarence Greaves. I believe you also knew his niece? You were accompanied both times by your associate, Special Agent Arthur Chung."

This time there was a hitch before the reply came.

"I fear you really do have the wrong person, Mr. Cagel. Greaves? Chung? These are not names known to me."

Barney continued to load up the hook with all the worms in his baitbox.

"It was at Bordrero Bay Bank. North of here. In connection with your investment in Thunderbolt Video."

Again a hitch. The fish was studying the bait.

"No, I really think not, Mr. Cagel."

Barney changed to a harsh voice. Might as well give the sonofabitch a really big fat one to look at.

"Cut the shit, Kim! You want to see what I've got? Maybe not enough to nail you for murder one out here, or in Jersey, or DC, or Maryland, but sure as hell enough to cause you—and whoever you're working for—a shitload of inconvenience!"

Now there was silence on the other end. C'mon sweetheart,

take the hook, take it, Barney murmured! He gave the line a tweak. "At your convenience, Mr. Kim; you name the time, place, and other conditions."

More silence. He's thinking it over, thought Barney. He's nosing the bait.

And then Kim took it.

"Mr. Cagel, I know nothing of the things of which you speak, but I am a curious person, and you have engaged my curiosity. Am I correct in inferring that your interest is more than purely journalistic?"

Now Barney made the hook fast.

"You are. What I have is worth money and I need some. A lot. Right now. I'm a poor man, Kim, and as you may have guessed when you saw me in Princeton, a sick one. Really sick. In fact, I'm dying. If I was well, you'd be on your way to Leavenworth, but I'm not. My family is not provided for. You can do the providing, in fact I think you're really going to want to provide the bejesus out of this when you see what I've got."

Another momentary silence, then: "Perhaps we should meet."

It was agreed to rendezvous at seven the next morning in the parking circle of the Palace of the Legion of Honor in Golden Gate Park. The museum was closed for long-term repairs. It was unlikely anyone would be there that early on a Saturday morning.

Barney arrived a few minutes ahead of time. He parked where he could look out over the city, which lay under a furry blanket of low fog, although up where he was it was already clearing. It was an odd vista: only the uppermost stories of the Montgomery Street skyscrapers and the tops of the towers of the Golden Gate Bridge betrayed the humming city under the fog.

He felt primed and ready for action. He had slept soundly. On rising, he had called Washington and spoken to Claire and Little Barney. They were well, they missed him, they wanted him to hurry back. He told them he'd see them tomorrow night at the latest.

Precisely at seven, a silver BMW drove into the circle and stopped across from where Barney sat. A man got out and walked toward the Chevrolet. Barney rolled his window down and watched him approach. Even with his clothes on, he knew the guy.

Kim came up to the car, put both hands on the door edge, and studied Barney. For a couple of beats, he said nothing. Barney decided to make the first move.

"Nice to see you again, Mr. Kim," he said in a pleasant voice.

Kim didn't return the smile.

"May I ask where you kept your car last night, Mr. Cagel?"

"Outside my motel. Why?"

"Better we talk in my car, then."

He opened the car door, Barney took his shoulder bag from the passenger seat, and gingerly eased himself out.

"Let me," said Kim, reaching for the bag.

"Thanks," said Barney. "Got my Powerbook there. The stuff I want to show you's on the hard disk. You ever use one of these? This's the one-eighty-five, with the color screen. Fantastic!"

Kim smiled and allowed how he was a Mac fan himself.

They walked to the BMW. Barney looked around. If there were baby-sitters about, they must be up in the trees.

Kim opened the door on the passenger's side and handed Barney his bag. He got in and started the engine.

"To save time," Barney said as Kim backed away from the curb, "why'n't I show you this stuff while we're driving?"

"As you wish."

Barney pulled out the Powerbook and flipped open the cover.

"Well, Kim," he said, "here's looking at you!" and pressed the power switch.

Kim turned, saw Barney's smile, and in a horrible moment of realization, knew everything. He started to move but it was too late. There was a thunderous crack and in a microsecond the universe was born all over again in a frightful burst of noise and incandescence.

The Colombians parked down the hill heard the explosion. The earth rocked and there was a momentary whirlwind that tore leaves from the trees. A plume of smoke rose into the sky.

Farther down, Lenchin winced at the crash. He counted slowly; by thirty seconds, the pillar of smoke had reached what he estimated was eleven stories; there wouldn't be enough left of anyone within a hundred yards of the burst to fill a measuring cup.

He heard sirens break out down in the city. He U-turned smoothly and headed back toward downtown, stopping to use a pay phone when he judged it was safe. Behind him, the pillar of smoke mounted steadily in the clearing sky.

The smoke cleared by early afternoon. The story itself lasted not much longer. Only one occupant of the BMW could be positively identified: Bernard Cagel, founder-editor of a Washington journal. According to Cagel's associate and partner, Lee Boynton, he had been tracking a very hot story about the drug trade. Apparently he had gotten caught in a cross fire.

The BMW was ultimately traced to a San Rafael dealership whose records showed it as having been sold, for cash, to a Henry Kung. The latter proved to be none of the eighty-six Kungs listed in the San Francisco telephone book, and desultory police footwork in Little Korea failed to turn up any leads until six months after the explosion, when collection agents managed to break the locks on an office in South San Francisco whose lessee, a one-man corporation called Data Security Consultants, was six months behind on its rent.

They found a room filled with expensive, sophisticated computer equipment. The computer files were blank; the hard disks on all six machines appeared to have been crashed more or less simultaneously, presumably when Pacific Gas and Electric had turned off the electricity.

In the office's paper files, however, was found the bill of sale for the BMW, along with other documents variously addressed to a Mr. Kung, a Mr. Chung, and a Mr. Dong.

In Washington, where Barney Cagel was well known, the story had longer legs, but he was finally written off as another Danny Casolaro, a zealous reporter who went where he shouldn't have gone. His partner Lee Boynton tried to keep the story going; for a while, it was noised about that she was thinking of doing a book about the Cagel mystery. At the National Press Club there was talk of getting up a purse, a scholarship fund for Little Barney, but then people figured, hell, Lee Boynton was loaded, and surely she would take care of Claire and the kid, and the good intentions, like the story, wore down to mere wisps and then vanished into the ether.

Two months after Barney Cagel died, a memorial service was held for H. Russell Oltington in a secondary auditorium in the Rayburn Office Building. The venue had been chosen by the Vice President, exercising his prerogatives as president pro tem of the United

States Senate. Attendance was small, the service brief, an observance of the decent thing one does for a long-time acquaintance about whom delicate posthumous questions had been raised. The Norwegian Ambassador drew the short straw and delivered the eulogy. The First Lady sent regrets: She had hoped to attend, but her presence was required in Atlanta at a conference on birth control.

After the ceremony, when the last guest had shaken the Vice President's hand and departed, Number Two paused for a moment on the Rayburn Building's wide front steps to confer with Craxton and Di Maglio. It was a day worth savoring, and they lingered. In the distance, above the Washington Monument, sunlight dancing on the fuselage of an airliner making for National briefly captured their attention.

The plane was a USAir 727, originating in Des Moines with service to Washington National via the airline's Pittsburgh hub. Seat 24A was occupied by an impassive Korean man who had sat bolt upright the entire flight with two large square manila envelopes, neatly sealed with packing tape, on his lap. They bore labels addressed in handwriting that a graphologist would have identified as that of Peter Kim, deceased.

On disembarking, the passenger from 24A hailed a taxi, and after some linguistic confusion with the Somalian driver, was taken to a building on Seventeenth Street.

There, another small comedy of linguistic errors ensued.

Asked his business, the Korean gentleman held tightly to his two envelopes, and repeated over and over to the uniformed guard at the security desk, "Lobba woowah, lobba woowah."

The receptionist was a black woman not normally patient with people—especially Koreans, whom she regarded as the worst of ghetto exploiters. But it was a nice day, for once her feet didn't hurt, and so she was patient. Finally, she managed to persuade the man to let her see the labels on the envelopes.

"I see," she said, "these are for Mr. Robert Woodward."

She dialed a number. A moment later, she could be heard to say, "Yes, sir, no, sir. No, I think you're going to have to come down yourself, sir. I don't think he'll give these to anyone else but you, in person. You better come yourself, sir."

Woodward said he'd be right down.

TWENTY-ONE

▼

I was a morning right out of the Bordrero Bay tourist brochure. The sea wore a gentle slate-blue swell; spread low along the horizon like misshapen pillows ranged across the back of a sofa was a line of fat, unmoving cumulus clouds; the temperature had edged above seventy and the beach was full of people. Whale-watching boats had been chugging seaward practically since first light. From where she was sitting on the beach below Constancia's house, Lee could almost hear Bordrero Bay's merchants and publicans rubbing their hands. She closed her eyes and let the sunlight play over her. She was exhausted.

She had broken her book tour in San Francisco and come up here, needing a couple of days to recharge before facing the terrors of LA. So far the tour couldn't have gone better. Her publisher's chief of publicity had deemed her "about as promotable as God makes 'em, designed to spec for 'A.M. Pittsburgh'." She and Woodward were splitting the promotional load. He was handling the heavy, chin-scratching stuff, "MacNeil/Lehrer NewsHour," Brian Lamb on C-Span, and the like; Lee was out on the hustings doing "Cleveland Today" and "Buffalo Bill" and chatting up local book editors. They had divided the national breakfast shows and done Larry King together. It was hard work.

But it was paying off. There were 225,000 copies of *Black Money* in print and the publisher was going back for another 100,000 copies; in its third week, the book already stood at number three on the

Times's nonfiction best-seller list, was going to number two the following week, and the publisher thought it might make it to the top slot. The reviews had been sensational. *Black Money*'s revelations had cranked up the reviewers' moral outrage and infused their praise with a seductive zest.

It had all happened so quickly. It was hard to realize it was still two months short of two years since Lee had picked up that scruffy local paper in the Healdsburg Diner and read about the "sodomization" of Bordrero Bay. Only seventeen months since Barney'd gotten himself blown up and the nation found itself consumed by what "MacNeil-Lehrer" had christened "Kimgate."

It had turned out Coole had guessed correctly why persons unknown seemed so concerned with keeping Kim alive. For almost three years, he had set down a detailed record of his activities, which he sent to a friend in Iowa with instructions to deposit the material in a safe-deposit box. The friend was further instructed if Kim should go for ten days unheard from, the material should be turned over to Robert Woodward of *The Washington Post* and Watergate fame, or, if Woodward should be unavailable, to James Stewart of *The New Yorker,* who had laid Milken bare.

To the *Post*'s credit, it had put the national interest first. On the advice of her editors, the paper's publisher directed that the windfall be shared with the federal government. A meeting was arranged with the Attorney General; she closeted herself with President and a multiagency strike force was organized over the weekend at a top-secret meeting at Camp David. The Vice President was given the reins; it was the plum job of his distinguished career.

It was immediately apparent that other major jurisdictions of international finance would have to be brought in; the Federal Reserve saw to this. On Monday morning, 168 CP branches around the world were seized. Accounts totaling $6.85 billion in approximately three hundred other banking and investment institutions in the United States and offshore were also sequestered. FBI agents appeared at the headquarters of Nanny and Courier Services. Trading in the former's shares was suspended pending further announcements.

On Tuesday, the *Post* went with what it had and followed up with lead articles on the following two days.

When Lee read the first story, she felt faint with envy. But after the follow-up pieces appeared, she realized that the *Post* had only the bare bones. The paper was treating this like an exponentiated BCCI with a specific drug and money-laundering angle. A huge story, but not as huge as it could be. Lee had the material needed to give the story Watergate impact.

Kim had furnished a summary account, and pointed a finger in interesting directions, but it was clear that he had been highly selective; the *Post* knew only what he had given them. Lee inferred—accurately, as it turned out—what Kim had omitted from the material that had been given to Woodward. It was clear, for example, that Kim had edited out his own lethal activities. He had apparently disclosed nothing about Phoenix and, more surprisingly, about Thunderbolt. With respect to the latter, Coole suspected that Kim had seen to it that those funds had been diverted to a holding pen of his own choosing and would never be traced.

Nor had Kim identified Oltington by name.

Lee knew about Oltington, of course. Thanks to the Granary, Lee knew everything Kim did. Indeed, she knew more.

When Lenchin called from San Francisco, Coole's people were ready. Within minutes, Du Bose was inside Kim's computers; within an hour he had vacuumed them dry and then crashed their operating systems and wiped their directories clean. The raw material was given to Shirley, who turned it into gold.

Added to everything else, it gave Lee the whole picture: not just the data—what the Granary knew and Shirley had worked up—but the life and death side, the human interest. She had a terrific story to tell. An investigative account with the qualities of a Le Carré or Grisham thriller. She held trumps; the *Post* may have scooped her, but only with respect to a fraction of what was there.

It was all hers to use as she chose. She had paid for it. So had Barney. Coole saw no obligation to turn the material over to Uncle Sam. Kim had given the feds enough, he argued; let them fend for themselves. Finally, just to be on the safe side, Lee persuaded him to feed a few choice bits to *Le Monde* and *Forbes*.

It had been Coole's idea that Lee approach Bob Woodward with the idea of pooling what she had with the *Post*'s stuff, doing a second, major series of articles, and then turning the whole into a blockbuster book. Barney would have wanted that, he told her. She had no qualms about approaching Woodward; Barney had always said he was one of the good guys, and he proved to be. A deal was quickly struck; a publishing auction was set up on the basis of a no-names outline, and U.S. rights went for $6,000,000. Overseas, the advances were comparable. Lee divided her half-share between the Granary scholarship fund and a trust for the upbringing and education of Bernard Cagel, Jr.

It was the second series of reports, with Lee on a guest byline, that set off the earthquake whose aftershocks were still being felt a year later, now amplified by the book.

The first shocks had been of a sensational nature suited to the supermarket tabloids, revelations that played to the public's prurient, personality driven sense of events. The discovery that a vault leased to J. Russell Oltington, the Vice Presidential aide who controlled a multimillion-dollar slush fund, contained a collection of Rembrandt etchings that Christie's valued at over $10 million was good for nearly ten days of public chewing-over.

But the unquestioned star of the early going was Don Escobedo. CP's state connections were a major embarrassment to the French government. The Elysee Palace was deeply displeased; as a result, the interrogation of Bruno de Fried and Claude Vertreuil by the Department of Internal Intelligence had been intense, causing them to finger the Don, whom the media promptly dubbed "the George Soros of black money."

The Don's face became a staple on television. Robin Lynch, doing a special on "Life-styles of the Rich and Wicked," took a camera crew into the Andes foothills and filmed the *estancia*. By then it had been stripped of its choicest holdings. In Dublin, the Cardinal had said a special mass to celebrate the return of the Beit Vermeer to Irish soil, and the mayor of Boston had proclaimed a day of thanksgiving for the homecoming of the Gardner Museum picture.

Among the oddest of the Don's effects was a glass bell containing a human nose preserved in paraldehyde. The chief of Lima police coveted the curiosity but was finally prevailed to send it to Paris, where French forensic specialists matched it to Mona Kurchinski's exhumed corpse and returned her to potter's field intact.

The Don himself was not available for interviews. He had flown his splendid Andes coop minutes ahead of a joint Peruvian-U.S. strike force, and was rumored to have since been simultaneously seen in Kansas City, Karachi, and Kuala Lumpur. The authorities were not the only people looking for him. His former clients were on his trail with equal gusto and commitment of resources.

Inevitably, the scandal progressed from individuals to institutions. The size of the money involved began to sink home. To date, over $11 billion had been seized. The DEA was holding the biggest sale of forfeited or seized drug-related assets in history. People were used to coming across full-page newspaper advertisements offering drug dealers' automobiles, stereos, laboratory equipment. Now there appeared in the "tombstone" pages of *The Wall Street Journal,* the *Financial Times,* and the larger metropolitan dailies offerings, denominated in multiples of hundreds of millions, of substantial businesses.

Advised by Goldman, Sachs, the DEA had broken up "Nanny" and put her subsidiaries on the block—Energy City went to British Petroleum for $864 million, Tip 'n Take to a Chicago investment group for around half that amount. CP's domestic offices were picked up by U.S. Trust. The remnants of Phoenix went to a London vulture fund bidding virtually blind; six months later, the investment was written down to zero. Leo Gorton's lavish Princeton headquarters was sold for $3,500,000 to Syntex, which announced plans to convert it into a research center. Even Courier Services found a buyer: AMR, the holding company for American Airlines, which restaffed the firm with its own employees made redundant by deregulation. As AMR's salty chairman observed, "It seems that making money by hauling money is more profitable than making money by hauling people."

After a brief turf dispute with the RTC, the DEA was given the right to auction the remaining assets of GoldWest. Bordrero Bay Bank and the other units in its division were bought by Bank of Alaska.

Eventually, the full weight of public outrage made itself felt. The press, anxious to redeem itself for the somnolence of the 1980s, fed the flame. There were antimarket torchlight parades in London and New York and million-person vigils in Red and Tiananmen squares. The once-haughty "globalized financial system" was savagely attacked. Faced with terrifying alternatives, the money havens capitulated: first Lichtenstein, then Switzerland, followed by the Bahamas, Macau, the Channel Islands. Where money appeared conclusively drug-tainted, they opened their books of account.

Whether Wall Street could redeem itself was more problematic. Public uproar had been provoked to an extent that the S&L and junk bond scandals had signally failed to do. The public was confronted with the reality that "free market" meant the freedom to saturate the financial system with money earned in the filthiest form of human endeavor, that the "entrepreneurial capitalism" of the 1980s might have involved a large component of drug money, and that "deregulation" meant the freedom to multiply dirty money through a massive fraud of the deposit insurance structure, a fraud that the American taxpayers would be paying off well into the next century. Not since the age of the robber barons had Wall Street stood so low in public esteem. To many, it appeared that Marx might be given a second chance at the golden apple: with the enemy this time not labor-exploiting industrialists but financial technocrats barely out of knee pants with computerized souls.

The political reverberations were every bit as dramatic. The revelations about Oltington and JEDI claimed the Vice President as an early victim. Like a twist of tissue put to the match, his splendid career—twenty-odd years of committed, often ingenious public ser-vice—became ash.

Ordinarily, the existence of a multimillion-dollar slush fund ad-ministered from close to the apex of the Washington power pyramid would have produced a gaping public yawn. But this time the spark found tinder: the nation was utterly caught up in Kimgate, and the populace aflame with outrage. By comparison, Iran-Contra seemed chicken feed, morally and financially. Americans began asking them-selves: Are we living in Italy or what? In New York, a federal grand jury was empaneled; it was rumored that *Fortune* 500 CEOs were on the subpoena list for contributing to the Oltington fund.

The President moved to consolidate his new political strength. He replaced the Vice-President with the Chairman of the Federal Reserve Board. The First Lady went offcamera. No longer did she drop in on meetings of the Council of Economic Advisors. Free trade no longer seemed to interest her; she was now heavily involved in childhood literacy.

To dismantle JEDI was an early priority. The system had become a favorite target of the press, which overplayed the *"1984-*

Big Brother" angle to the point that *People* put George Orwell on the cover. On "60 Minutes," Mike Wallace depicted JEDI's capacities for oversight as an outright, totalitarian threat to the liberty of the citizen. JEDI had no place in American life, it was argued, not in the kind of democracy we intended ourselves to be. It represented the node of a cancer whose metastasis was guaranteed; it exemplified the philosophical threat posed by the relentless advance of efficiency-seeking technology, the danger inherent in government by technocrat. When "60 Minutes" revealed that a cadre of IRS agents had bartered JEDI-derived information to a leading credit card company in return for confidential asset and expenditure data, the reality was clear. JEDI would have to be terminated.

The President had the good sense to listen to knowledgeable advisors: the system was not without its virtues; indeed, as a resource for law enforcement, it was still incomparable, especially now that its data banks were filling up daily with private-sector information furnished by institutions anxious to be in step with the new morality. It was the bath water that was fouled, not the baby.

He therefore didn't simply press a button and crash the equivalent of three million disks. JEDI was dispersed and reapportioned among its constituencies. Responsibility for overseeing coordination was delegated to an interagency committee chaired by the new Vice President.

So, Lee thought, it was worth it. A significant sector of the international community of evil had been routed, a significant portion of its evil gains recaptured. Public morality had been reinvigorated.

But she couldn't stop thinking about Barney. How Coole and her uncle had sent him to his death.

Sure he was terminal, with only months left, maybe weeks, but what right had Coole and her uncle to take those from him! Without consulting her!

She was furious with Coole. What could he have been thinking of? Obviously, Kim's phone had been tapped, and when Barney had approached him, that had been the last straw and his car had been bombed. Coole had no right to put Barney in harm's way! In her anger, she overlooked the fact that Lenchin had said that Kim was being "double-baby-sat," covered by his own people.

She hadn't spoken to any of them since Barney's funeral. His remains—such as they were—had been buried, oddly, at her uncle's house in Rhode Island. It felt strange to sit here in the bright Pacific sunshine and think back to that gray, drizzly morning in the winter-bare garden at Little Meadow.

To bury Barney there had been her uncle's idea; as he put it, he would be in the adjacent pew when the time came. Claire didn't care; she didn't seem to want to have anything to do with any of it. She was getting out of Washington, taking Little Barn and going to live near her sister in St. Louis.

The old man, wanting as always to leave his stamp on events, had commissioned Barney's marker. It was a handsome bronze plaque that bore Barney's name and dates and a quotation from Pope: "Not Fortune's worshipper, nor Fashion's Fool, Not Lucre's Madman, nor Ambition's Tool." Lee had to admit that it fit.

After that, Lee had thrown herself into the book, seeing no one, committing herself entirely first to the collaborative writing, then the editing, and copy editing, and proofreading, and finally the whole exhausting business of publication and promotion.

Now, suddenly, she was beat. She flopped back flat on the sand. The steady sound of the waves made her sleepy.

"Hey! Lee! Yoo-hoo!"

Constancia was calling her from up on the bluff.

"This just came for you. Catch!"

A large envelope skittered onto the sand a few yards away.

Lee picked it up. A Federal Express from her uncle in New Haven.

Inside was another envelope, marked with the logo and address of a Holiday Inn in Daly City, California. It was addressed to her in Barney's scrawl.

She tore it open. It contained two closely scribbled pages and was dated the night before he died.

She read through it quickly, then twice again slowly:

> Hey kiddo!
> You know in the movies how young carrier pilots always write letters the night before they take off on what may be their last mission? Well, this is going to be mine, take it from me, and by the time you get this I fig-

ure the shit will have hit the fan, assuming Coole and I
and the old man have figured it right, and so I want you
to know how it was. I wanted you to get this earlier, but
as your uncle says, too many thoughts at once confuse
the youthful mind, so he and I figured: better let some
time go by and see what's what. And anyway who wants
to argue with him!

As Mr. Nixon and his buddy Henry the K. might say,
I wasn't exactly being candid with you when I told you I
was at Mayo's. I figured you might act badly if I said I was
about to have a *tête-à-tête* with our friend Kim with the
Dangerous Hands. The fact is, I've had an idea, a rrrreally
big idea, as Ed Sullivan might say, and I've sold it to Coole
and the old boy up in New Haven. I tried it out on them
when you went to PB. Sorry to have left you out of the
loop, kiddo, but I knew the reaction I wanted, and yours
wouldn't be it.

Anyway, your uncle and I sat up there in Little
Meadow, the sky just pissing rain, and drank a whole
bunch of whiskey and talked, and he bought the concept; it
appealed to his "Charge of the Light Brigade" philosophy;
Christ, he even quoted Macaulay at me, from "Horatius at
the Bridge": "And how can man die better than facing
fearful odds/For the ashes of his fathers and the temples of
his gods." Good stuff that, what, what?

So then we went up to Pride's Crossing, and gradually I brought Coole around to my point of view, of which
more anon.

By now you're maybe beginning to get the idea, so
let me cut it short. Honey, you and I go way back, so when
I say you've got no idea what feeling like shit is until you
feel the way I do, believe me. We were talking short time
anyway, and what's a couple of months more or less among
friends? Plus what father ever wanted his kid to see him
weighing ninety pounds and with tubes sticking out of his
asshole?

This way, I get to go out on top. Plus, I figure this

Kim's a cool customer—don't forgot I saw the sonofabitch ten minutes after he offed Gorton—and maybe all we get for my courtesy call is a "pleased to meet you, Mr. Cagel, nice to have made your acquaintance," and then where the shit are we? Nowhere! But I am the perfect candidate to make something happen, with the old guy with the sickle fingering my threads, and this is the point I sell to my two pals. As your uncle likes to say, it's the water above that drowns you, not the water below. Someone has to take the plunge.

Just don't let Lenchin spare the juice, I told them. That's all I want. Just load it up with enough gelignite or whatever to blow me clear to heaven and quickly! Actually, he tells me it's called C-4 and guaranteed to do the job.

I got to hand it to your uncle, the old SOB goes first-class all the way. He even sprang personally for a brand new Powerbook, the $4,500 top-of-the-line model as the machina ex deus, pardon my French, which seems like a lot of bread for a laptop that's only going to be switched on once. I'm looking at it right now, as I write this, and I tell you, my figures are flat itching to turn it on and see if it's as great as everyone says it is.

You can take it from there. I'm meeting Mr. "Tae Kwan Doo" tomorrow at a secluded rendezvous, and if everything goes according to plan, the rest, as they say, will be history. Or at least Kim and I will be.

My nose tells me there ought to be a book in here somewhere, and my deal with Coole is that you get to write it if you want. First dibs to the good guys. Maybe by the time you get this you've done it, in which case this'll make a hell of an appendix when you go into paperback. As for a lot of other stuff, well, I know you'll do the right thing. You always have.

So here's looking at you, keed. Which I suspect I'm probably doing as you read this. Me and Oltington and Gorton and the fabulous Mona and poor old Greaves and

God knows who else, and Kim, of course, because my suspicion is that up here all hatchets are buried and we just belly up to the celestial bar and watch the good guys and the bad guys go at it down below, the way you and I used to do at Clyde's when the 'Skins were playing, and buy each other drinks and slap each other on the back when someone made a great play!

Just one last thing. Don't take it out on Coole. This is your boy Barn's play all the way. Coole's basically a good guy. Not that he knows it. He's so tightassed he probably couldn't tell his mother he loved her, but if what I saw in Princeton is what you've been getting then love will surely find a way and meanwhile it has its compensations.

And now I'm going to say good night Mr. and Mrs. America and all the ships at sea. Your uncle laid a bottle of twenty-five-year old McAllan on me as a good-bye present, of which there's still a few inches left, and if Michelle Pfeiffer's kiss can't be the last thing I taste on my lips, there could be worse runners-up than one of Uncle's "wee drams!" So here's how.

XXXXXXXX

The letter was signed with a scrawled "B."

Lee read it through a fourth time, then stared out to sea. It would be appropriate to shed a tear, she thought, but somehow she couldn't. Barney hated weepers.

You sonofabitch, she thought, you selfish sonofabitch!

"Hey down there! Hello again!"

Constancia was back.

"Telephone for you!" the mayor called. "Guess who! It's Coole! He's calling from Aspen! Says something's come up that might interest you! Wants to talk to you! What do you want me to tell him?"

"Tell him I'm busy," Lee called back.

Tell him to go screw! Let him fry in hell!

The mayor's head vanished.

Then, without really knowing why, Lee screamed out, "No, hey, no, wait!"

A group of children playing nearby looked up, startled. A gull squawked and took off.

"No!" she shouted again, scrambling to her feet and making for the steps.

No, no, no, no, *no*! This was over: it was time to get on with whatever must come next. Everything had a season. Every season had an end.

"Tell him to hold on!" she shouted. "I'll be right there!"